# Perception & Illusion

# Perception & Illusion

## CATHERINE KULLMANN

Cover image: *Hearts are Trump,* George Goodwin Kilburne.
Photo: © Sotheby's / akg-images

*For Kurt, for over forty years of love, friendship, companionship, help and support in sickness and in health, in good times and in bad.*

# Matrimonial Maps

Matrimonial Maps charting the perils and pitfalls of the course of true love were popular in the late eighteenth and nineteenth centuries. I have taken the chapter headings for *Perception & Illusion* from the legend of a nineteenth century matrimonial map published in Ireland by lithographers Callaghan Bros. Cork and used here courtesy of the National Library of Ireland.

To view the map, please visit my website www.catherinekullmann.com

# Chapter One

*The Great Ocean of Love represents a period of life that all persons are supposed at some time or another to pass.*

*L*allie knew the instant she set foot in the house that her father was making one of his rare visits to Alwood. It was difficult to define what had changed. The house was quieter, almost unnaturally so and the atmosphere was charged with a peculiar tension.

"Excuse me, Miss Grey."

John, their only footman, noiselessly closed the door to the servants' quarters and carefully steadied a tray of decanters and glasses before carrying it to the library. He wore his best livery. Balancing the tray on one hand, he slowly turned the door knob so that it didn't squeak. Everyone knew that Mr Grey would not tolerate anything less than perfection and more than one servant had been turned off immediately for failing to meet his standards.

It was as if he needed to assert his position as head of the household, despite the fact that he was the most distant of husbands and fathers, Lallie reflected as she hurried to the schoolroom. Her stepmother was not inclined to stand on ceremony at home, but her father would expect his younger children to make a formal visit to the drawing-room before dinner.

Her half-brother James, who was entertaining his younger sisters with stories of his prowess at cricket during the recent summer half, stood awkwardly at her entrance. He had shot up since they had last seen him and was not yet comfortable in this new body.

"Lallie," he reddened at his new deep tone, "will you help me later with my neckcloth? You know how my father is."

She smiled warmly at him. "Of course I will. Beatrice and Eleanor, come with me now, if you please. Once you are ready, you may sit quietly in my room while I change my gown. I'll come to you then, James and we may all go down together."

Robert Grey was a slim gentleman of medium height, his clothes the epitome of restrained perfection. His curly fair hair was clipped close and brushed forward a la Caesar, a modish style that suggested a nimbus of laurel leaves crowning his high forehead. The head so embellished was habitually cocked a little to one side while the faint curve to his lips spoke of a jest that only he could appreciate.

"Good God," he said lightly, when his son followed his sisters into the drawing-room. "What have we here? A hobbledehoy?"

"Dear James has grown so much, hasn't he?" Mrs Grey said fondly, ignoring the boy's furious blush. "It won't be long before he's looking down on you, Robert. He takes after my father, of course."

Lallie bit the inside of her cheek to stop herself smiling at her father's petulant expression but something must have betrayed her inner amusement and his gaze swung to her.

"I trust you have been behaving yourself, miss."

He might have been addressing a recalcitrant ten-year-old instead of a lady of almost twenty-four and Lallie's chin went up. She met his eyes calmly. "I always do, sir."

He nodded dismissively and went to pour himself a glass of madeira. He sipped, then gestured to the pianoforte. "What have you prepared for our delight this evening, Eleanor?"

The girl blanched and glanced pleadingly at her elder sister.

"Come, I'll turn the pages for you." As they bent over the music, Lallie whispered, "You play very well and even if you make a mistake, he won't notice unless you stop. Remember how we practised keeping going?"

At Eleanor's nod, Lallie spread open a sonatina by Clementi and positioned herself so that she partially shielded the child from her father's gaze. She noticed that Mrs Grey was talking quietly to her husband on the opposite side of the room.

"He's not really paying attention," she hissed to her sister who sighed with relief and plunged into her music.

"Well done, brat," James exclaimed as soon as she had finished. By the time his mother had finished scolding him for his unseemly language and he had apologised to her and to Eleanor, their father had grown weary of domesticity and dismissed the schoolroom contingent. Lallie was obliged to remain and follow her parents into the dining-room. She could imagine the consternation caused in the kitchen by Mr Grey's unexpected arrival—while she and Mrs Grey usually sat down to a simple dinner of one course each evening, he would expect two courses with removes and a dessert.

Tonight he surveyed the table critically through his quizzing glass but, apart from complimenting his wife on the *Maintenon* cutlets, did not comment further on the meal, apparently content to satisfy her curiosity regarding the latest *on-dits*. He finally launched into a description of the Prince Regent giving Beau Brummel the cut direct.

"Brummel then dished himself completely," he continued with relish. "He looked at Alvanley and, as cool as you please, asked, 'Ah, Alvanley, who is your fat friend?' The Prince will never forgive him. He may be unable to prevent his wife roasting a wax effigy of him in front of her fire, but he will not tolerate such public insolence from one so far beneath him."

"Nor should he," Mrs Grey said. "I have little patience with these dandies who give themselves airs and set themselves up as the arbiters of all taste. They have ruined many a girl's chances by declaring her a quiz on her first appearance so that no-one will have anything to do with her. I even heard of one cub who cut his own father because his parent presented too rustic an appearance. You may imagine how wounded the old gentleman was."

"That's disgraceful!" Lallie exclaimed.

Her father waved away her protest. "It is the way of the fashionable world. One either sinks or swims. Of course you know nothing of that."

"That is hardly my fault, sir," she retorted, nettled. "If my grandmother had lived I would have made my come-out five years ago."

He narrowed his eyes at her. "To what avail, I wonder? Remember she had been completely cast off by her family. I once mentioned to her father that I had married the daughter of Lady Anna Staines. Martinborough looked down his nose and said, 'I wish you joy, sir, but I do not know either lady'. And the Marchioness was for many years Lady of the Bedchamber to Her Majesty, so it is most unlikely that either you or your grandmother would have been received at court or awarded vouchers for Almack's."

Silenced, Lallie was grateful that her stepmother rose as soon as Mr Grey had finished speaking.

"We shall leave you to your port."

"Go to bed, Lallie," Mrs Grey instructed once the door had closed behind them. "Good night."

"Good night, ma'am."

"They say that young Mr Neville is betrothed," Lallie told her maid as she prepared for bed.

"Oh, who to?" Nancy carefully drew the brush through Lallie's long, curling hair.

"A Miss Eaton. Her father is Sir William Eaton and she has seven and a half thousand pounds."

Nancy began to braid the dark hair for the night. "That will please his parents, especially his mother. He wouldn't have done for you, Miss Lallie. He's too much under his mother's thumb. What about the curate? Mrs Hersey would make a better mother-in-law."

"I doubt if he can afford to wed, especially a penniless girl. He must support his mother and two sisters."

Lallie liked the young clergyman, but was under no illusions about his circumstances and, if she were to be honest, did not feel that spark of attraction for him that she had felt for Lambert Neville. Still, her prospects were so bleak, she wasn't sure she could reject an honourable gentleman whom she liked and respected, even if she did not love him.

Nancy tied a small ribbon around the end of the thick plait to hold it in place. "Any man would be proud to have you as a wife."

Lallie looked fondly at her former nurse. As usual, she was dressed in a neat print dress in subdued shades, over which she wore a starched cotton apron and matching fichu that was pinned at her breast with a mourning brooch containing a lock of Lallie's grandmother's hair. To Nancy, this was the emblem of her sacred charge to care for Miss Lallie and she wore it as proudly as a soldier would a medal. Her fair hair was pulled severely back from her forehead into a tight bun which was covered by a lawn cap, but her face was still smooth and her blue eyes bright. She had looked like that as long as Lallie could remember.

"How old were you when I came to you?" she asked suddenly.

"Just sixteen, Miss Lallie. I'll never forget that day. The house was all at sixes and sevens, with you coming so sudden and your poor mother took so bad."

"And my father? Was he there?"

"He waited with your grandfather in the library. They called him in at the last. We had laid you in her arms, just for a moment, before the end, and she smiled faintly and was gone, poor lady. He looked down at her, said 'my poor Louisa, lost to me, lost to me', kissed her brow and left the room."

Funny, Nancy thought, she had almost forgotten Mr Grey coming into the nursery the next day and standing beside the cradle. He had smiled oddly and said, 'my daughter, o my ducats, o my daughter,' and departed. She had thought 'ducats' to be a pet name, like 'duckling' or 'ducky', but Mrs Staines, who had come in behind him, had looked most strange, angry even and she had never heard him use the word again.

"But I had Grandmamma and Grandpapa and you," Miss Lallie said. "You were younger then than I am now. Did you never want to get married, Nancy?"

"Not really, Miss Lallie. I had my offers, of course," she said proudly, "but none that would have tempted me to leave the Rectory. Will that be all, Miss?"

"Yes, thank you, Nancy. I'll sit and read for a while. Good night."

"Good night, my dear Miss Lallie." Nancy skimmed her hand over the younger woman's hair in a familiar caress. While in public she punctiliously denoted her young mistress's standing as the eldest daughter of the house by addressing her as Miss Grey, in private she made no secret of her devotion to the girl who had been hastily deposited in her arms as a new-born infant while more skilled attendants strove in vain to save her mother's life.

Lallie drew her shawl more closely around her shoulders and curled up in the big, threadbare armchair. It had long since been removed to the attics but Mrs Grey had raised no objection when her stepdaughter had asked if she might have it brought to her bedroom. Now the chair was Lallie's refuge. Here she could read or just let her thoughts drift. Her days were fully occupied; she spent the mornings in the schoolroom while the afternoons were devoted to whatever task Mrs Grey might care to allocate to her.

'We have no place for idle hands here,' she had said six years previously when Lallie had come to live at Alwood. 'Your sisters may now benefit from your expensive education and otherwise you will assist me in my household duties. There is always something to be done.'

But once the evening tea-tray had been removed Lallie was excused, especially on those occasions when her father graced them with his presence.

So the squire's heir was betrothed. She smiled ruefully, remembering how he had dazzled her at his coming of age ball. She had been in alt when he had twice requested her to stand up with him. Not only that, he had called the next day to invite her to drive out with him and his sister. But her stepmother could not spare her and not long afterwards he had departed for London to acquire some 'town bronze', as his father had put it. That had been the end of his interest in a provincial miss.

Lallie sighed. How different her life might have been if Grandmamma had not succumbed to that virulent attack of influenza. Her memories of those grim days were all confused. Her father had been sent for but by the time he arrived in Cornwall the funeral was over and he had insisted on leaving the next day, taking her with him. The journey to Sussex had seemed endless; her head had ached the whole time. She had no memory of arriving at Alwood, just what a relief it had been not to be jolted in the carriage. Then she had been very ill; by the time she had been allowed to leave her room, it was as if a curtain had descended, separating her from her previous life.

At least I have Nancy, Lallie thought. What would I have done if my father had not agreed to take her too? And she is so good to stay with me, even though she has to look after the others as well. She might have preferred to remain near her own family.

Downstairs, Robert Grey poured a glass of port for his wife, who had returned to the dining-room. "Otherwise, all is well here?" he asked casually.

"As well as can be. That is good news about young Neville, although his mother was just as opposed to a match between him and Lallie as we were."

"But that was some years ago."

"Lallie still harbours a certain tenderness for him, I think, although I warned her at the time that only a bride with a good fortune and of impeccable breeding would satisfy his mother and that she could not lay any claim to her grandmother's family; in fact to be disowned, as Mrs Staines was, was worse than having no connection. That taint is not, of course, attached to our children," she finished with a smug smile.

He raised his glass in appreciation. "How old is she now?"

"She'll be twenty-four next week."

"The devil she will!"

"Why, Robert, what is the matter?"

"Her trust comes to an end when she is twenty-five. The trustees will write to her directly then, seeking her instructions."

"Surely you will continue to handle her affairs?"

"She would have to agree. I found her rather pert this evening."

"She is certainly not as amenable to direction as she once was, especially since she became friendly with the Herseys. They have set up a little literary circle, as they call it, and it would have looked very odd if I had tried to forbid Lallie to join. Don't forget I have no true authority over her, should she choose to question it. Allowing her a little independence now may help us retain her income and her services. She is sincerely attached to the girls and has proved to be an excellent governess at no expense to us. Remember her trustees also pay her maid's wages. All in all, Lallie's presence contributes some one hundred and forty pounds per annum to this household. I should feel it if she were to leave us. Who knows what she may decide to do once she becomes aware that she is heiress to a little competence."

Her husband looked thoughtful but said no more.

The following Sunday, Lallie peeped discreetly as the party from Hazlehurst filed from the opposite pew. Miss Eaton was tall and slender, with guinea-gold curls spilling across her forehead from beneath a cunning jockey-style cap. It was trimmed with forget-me-nots to match the blue Cossack mantle draped so beautifully over a white muslin gown. She smiled beatifically at her betrothed before taking his arm to follow the squire and his lady down the aisle.

They were perfectly matched, Lallie thought glumly. How could she have expected him to remain interested in 'a dumpy little squab of a thing with coal-black hair and green eyes,' as her stepmother had put it when they were considering her new gown? 'In earlier times they would have thought you a witch,' she had said. 'And we must be careful you don't look like a pouter pigeon; you need long stays to contain you, child.' The result left Lallie feeling trussed and plumped like a chicken on the spit.

Outside the church she politely wished Mr Neville and his future wife every happiness.

"Thank you, Miss Grey. I'm sure we shall become great friends," Miss Eaton replied graciously. "Mrs Neville tells me there is a positive dearth of good society here. We know Mr Grey from town, of course, and I'm convinced you must have had your Season."

"It wasn't possible," Lallie answered and made way for the next well-wisher with no further explanation.

"Where is Lallie?" Mr Grey enquired as the Alwood party turned homewards.

"She has gone to the Herseys'," his youngest daughter Beatrice said importantly. "She is to remain there until Evensong."

He did not reply but later said to his wife, "Ursula, I am not happy with the Hersey connection for Lallie. It struck me today that he was rather taken by her."

"What of that?" she asked impatiently. "He probably reminds her of her grandfather. Wasn't he a rector?"

"All the worse. No, I am determined that if she is to marry, we should profit by the settlement for, as you rightly point out, we shall be the ones who lose if she leaves us. She has a nice little fortune and I am sure I can think of someone who would be prepared to share it if I put him in the way of it. There's Frederick Malvin, for example. He's practically at Point Nonplus—would have been long ago, if it weren't for that rich aunt of his. She is forever pulling him out of the River Tick."

"Malvin? Is he related to Lord Malvin?"

"His grandfather was brother to the first viscount so, while there is a connection, he cannot claim noble blood. It grates on him, I think, although he would never admit it."

"But he remains on terms with his cousins?"

"I think so. Why?"

"We—all of us including the children—have been invited by Lady Halworth—the wife of my uncle, the Admiral," she explained impatiently in response to his questioning look, "to visit their new estate in Berkshire this summer. It is not far from Malvin Abbey so if Mr Malvin could be there at the same time—"

"He and Lallie might conveniently meet." Mr Grey nodded approvingly. "I'll have a word with Malvin when I return to town while you may write to your aunt and accept. When does she expect us?"

"She said August or September; I am to let her know. I'll accept generally now and say I shall confirm the dates once I know what your plans are."

# Chapter Two

*The Amour, a branch of the Inclination River, is dangerous and in some parts not fordable. On the banks have been found the Slow Worm and the Scorpion; this renders it dangerous, although the scenery around is very romantic and inviting.*

A tender hand gently stroked Hugo's hair back from his forehead.

"It's getting light," her soft voice whispered. "You must go."

Still half asleep, he reached over and pulled her to him. "Not yet."

"You must," she insisted. "Hugo!"

Hugo Tamrisk reluctantly opened his eyes. "It's not even dawn, Sabina," he protested, trailing his hand over luscious curves.

She gripped his hand, stilling it. "The servants will be up betimes today."

He sat up at this. "What? Why?"

"I must return home."

Sabina's marriage had, of course, been a forbidden topic between them. She was an attractive, fashionable matron whose husband did not generally accompany her on her annual visit to town and who, it was rumoured, favoured a different gentleman each year. Certainly this year she had early on indicated that his attentions would be welcome. Their ensuing liaison was his first longer one and he had enjoyed the intimacy that went beyond the mere carnal, despite knowing that their affair must end with the Season.

He leaned over to kiss her. "I'll miss you," he said simply and was surprised to see tears in her eyes.

"I'll miss you too," she said.

He touched her cheek. "I wish I had known last night was the last time."

"I deliberately didn't tell you—I didn't want it overshadowed by the thought of our parting." She pressed her lips to his in a sweet kiss. "Good-bye, Hugo."

"Good-bye, Sabina." He opened his mouth to say more, but she stopped him with a finger on his lips.

"It is better like this," she whispered. "Get dressed and Smith will see you out."

Two days later Lord Malvin caught up with his brother-in-law outside the Houses of Parliament. "Thank goodness that's over for this session. Come back to the house for a bite to eat, Hugo. Clarissa has gone on ahead to the Abbey to ensure all is prepared for Arthur when he is well enough to travel and I'm sick of the clubs."

"Arthur continues to improve, then? I am glad to hear it."

Malvin sighed. "He says the wounds are not healing as well as they should. But he'll do better with us than in a military hospital."

"I am sure he will. You must have been proud to hear the comments about the splendid victories in the Peninsula, especially Vittoria."

"Yes, but at what cost? Wellington lost almost five thousand men."

"It will be worth it if we finally have Bonaparte on the run."

Malvin nodded. "This war has dragged on too long. After ten years, we all long for peace. It will be good to have Arthur home, even for such a reason. You must come and help us keep him amused."

"First I must see what's happening at Tamm, but let me know when you consider that he needs distraction."

A week later Hugo turned his matched bays into the grounds of Tamm Manor, raising his whip to acknowledge the lodge-keeper who had hurried to open the gates.

"Welcome home, sir."

"Thank you, Hay. Is all well with you and Mrs Hay?"

"Yes sir, thank you, sir."

Hugo nodded and continued glumly towards the house. It was a glorious summer's day; high above him a lark trilled against a blue sky but even its bright effervescence failed to lift his spirits.

'Welcome home,' Hay had said. A perfunctory, dutiful greeting, perhaps, but all the welcome he would get.

Tamm Manor might be the abode of his forefathers, but there was nothing inviting about the rectangular stone house which defied the elements to impose its solidity on the wild landscape, seeking neither the shelter of trees nor the adornment of flowers. Successive wives of Tamm had attempted to soften the surroundings of the house with neat parterres and formal gardens, but over time these had succumbed to lack of interest and attention, leaving a tracery of unkempt geometric patterns and an over-grown maze.

Entry to the house was by way of the great hall on the first floor, a cavernous space fully two stories in height. The favoured guest might be permitted to proceed from here to the saloon and from there, if particularly fortunate, to the withdrawing room, bedroom or even closet of my lord or my lady. For Tamm was built in the old style, with separate, three-chambered apartments for the master and mistress, other senior family members and important guests on the first and second floors, while less significant persons found accommodation on the floor above. The rustic and the attics were the preserve of the servants, except for the body-servants who each occupied a cubicle in his master's or her mistress's suite so as to be at their beck and call.

Hugo did not pull up at the flight of stone steps that rose from the rustic, ground level to the massive oak door but drove around to the stable yard. Time enough to see his father at dinner, he thought as he mounted the back stairs.

"Anything strange, Willis?" he asked his valet casually as he pulled off his boots.

"Nothing, sir. We still dine at four, I am told. His lordship's appetite has diminished, but Mrs Morton assures me that an adequate repast will be served."

Three-quarters of an hour later, Hugo crossed the hall to the saloon which separated his late mother's apartments from those where his father clung to the faded glories of his long reign. Lord Tamm was already installed in his great chair at the head of the dinner table and scowled from under beetling brows.

"It took you long enough to get here."

Hugo bowed, ignoring this greeting. "I trust I find you well, sir."

"Well enough," grunted his lordship, who would never admit to any infirmity or weakness. He waved Hugo to the chair on his right, then with, "Mr Stiles, if you please", invited his chaplain to say grace, accompanying this request with a gesture so graciously condescending that it invariably reminded his son of an imperious cardinal whom he had encountered in Rome ten years previously.

"*Per Jesum Dominum Nostrum,*" the chaplain finished.

"Amen." Hugo responded automatically while mentally reviewing the events of the past Season for a topic that might interest his father. Not politics. After a second apoplexy had rendered Lord Tamm too infirm to attend the House of Lords, he had barely waited for his son to reach his majority before ousting the incumbent of the parliamentary borough he controlled. But although Hugo had been duly elected to the House of Commons in the ensuing by-election, the Tamrisk voice heard in Parliament was no longer that of his lordship and Hugo had no desire to encourage a rant on his own whiggish tendencies or engage in a heated discussion with an increasingly feeble man of almost eighty.

The interment of the Dowager Duchess of Brunswick, mother of the Princess of Wales, at Windsor and the resulting discovery of the coffin of King Charles I roused Lord Tamm's interest. He looked at the portrait of the unfortunate monarch that hung over the carved stone fireplace beside one of his successor.

"Tamrisks were always king's men. My great-grandfather fought at His Majesty's side and later followed his son into exile."

Hugo nodded. "Going by Sir Henry Halford's description, our portrait is very like. He mentioned the pointed beard which was reddish-brown, in contrast to the beautiful dark brown of the hair."

Lord Tamm found this particularly gratifying. He eagerly accepted Hugo's offer to obtain a copy of Sir Henry's description of his examination of the royal corpse and later chuckled at the exposure of the so-called fasting woman of Tutbury who, when subjected to close scrutiny had been forced to recant her profession of living without food, admitting that she had 'occasionally taken sustenance for the last six years'.

"Apparently, the imposture was a lucrative one," Hugo remarked. "I am told that she invested four hundred pounds in funds last year."

"The more fools they who were taken in by her," Lord Tamm snorted.

The table talk the next day was not as amicable, his lordship revisiting his favourite theme—the urgent need for Hugo to marry and sire an heir.

"You owe it to your name, sir! And don't make my mistake and marry an untried chit who proves incapable of doing her duty. If you take my advice, you'll find a young widow who has already borne a son. It don't matter if she's poor—she'll be all the more grateful, especially if you do something for the boy. You needn't keep him about you—school and then the navy, that's the thing! She shouldn't be too old, mind, about twenty-four or twenty-five, so that she has many breeding years left to her!"

"I am not a stallion seeking a broodmare, sir," Hugo declared coldly. "If it comes to that, what proof do we have that it is the dam rather than the sire who determines the sex of the foal?"

"I never thought you so great a fool, boy! It is clearly a weakness in the female if she cannot tolerate the male essence! Henry the Eighth had the right of it—it should be grounds for divorce."

Perhaps marriage is not such a bad idea at that, Hugo found himself thinking some two hours later in the sanctuary of his own rooms. Oh, not to placate his father or simply to get an heir on some unfortunate woman although when he thought about it, he might like to have children of his own. No, he would marry for the comfort and companionship he had experienced with Sabina, for the intimacy of the shared jokes and midnight suppers after the House had risen, for the warm welcome to his wife's bed.

He had come to take his loneliness at Tamm for granted. He had been ten when his mother died, but had already been removed from her orbit to commence the instruction and training required of the heir to Tamm. He had been permitted to visit her withdrawing room for half an hour each evening but his sisters were also present and more often than not he had amused himself with her pet spaniel while feminine conversation flowed over his head.

It's too late to do anything about it this year, but next Season I'll make a point of seeking out eligible ladies. Or perhaps there might be someone at Clarissa's house party. It would serve her right if I found a bride under her nose, given how prone she is to proclaim that, 'Tamrisk men should no longer procreate but let the line die out'.

Grinning, he went to his writing desk and scribbled his acceptance of his sister's invitation.

# Chapter Three

*The Young are cautioned at the entrance to avoid the Whirlpool of Impetuosity, which has often proved a source of regret and frequently the ruin of many.*

"Lady Malvin called while you were out," Lady Halworth informed her husband.

"Did she? We are honoured indeed!"

She smiled sympathetically at the Admiral's sarcastic comment. Successive marriages to two officers of His Majesty's navy, one of whom had been knighted for his services to the crown, had left her in no doubt of her own worth.

"Doubly honoured, for she invites us to a *soirée* she is giving next week. We are all to go. She is giving a large house party and apparently relies on her neighbours to provide some distraction. There is to be music, and dancing after supper."

"Malvin is a very pleasant fellow as is his cousin Mr Frederick Malvin—I run into them frequently in town," Robert Grey remarked. "I regret I cannot say the same of his lady; she is Tamm's eldest daughter and they are a stiff-rumped lot."

"Well, we shall find out, no doubt." The Admiral beamed at the company assembled around his dinner table. "Now, what shall we do tomorrow?"

19

As she savoured an excellent dish of mushrooms that went well with collops of tender veal, Lallie wondered if she really wished to attend such a daunting evening as Lady Malvin's promised to be. She had not warmed to her ladyship that afternoon but then recollected that that lady's address of "Miss Err" did not suggest that she would take much notice of her.

Mrs Grey bustled into Lallie's bedchamber the following morning. "We must review your gowns in preparation for the Malvin *soirée*. You will not wish to appear too dowdy or provincial. Let me see. That white embroidered muslin might do. You have prettily rounded arms—if we puff the sleeves into a little cuff, that will draw attention to them, and perhaps we should lower the neckline a little. You are no longer a child, after all."

Lallie was amazed at this change in her stepmother's tune. Hitherto she had been much more inclined to deplore Lallie's deficiencies than to emphasize any attractions.

"Soft pink ribbons—no, green to match your eyes," Mrs Grey continued. "We shall thread some through your hair. You need new evening gloves as well. I'll speak to your father; perhaps we can arrange a little shopping trip to Newbury."

"Stand still, do, Miss Lallie or I'll never get this properly pinned," Nancy admonished her charge. "These short stays make the gown fit much better," she said approvingly.

"They are so much more comfortable—the long ones just squashed everything together," Lallie admitted.

"Too much, maybe," Nancy grunted. "I know Mrs Grey said to lower the neckline, but I think I'll add a little lace. If I thread some of the narrow ribbon through it and ruffle it, it'll be just the thing." She placed a last pin. "Don't dare twitch until I take this off, Miss Lallie!"

Safely back in her morning gown, Lallie couldn't resist opening a drawer to admire her new evening gloves. Made of the
finest white kid, they were fitted at the elbow but fell in modish
soft folds to the wrist. She had also purchased a dainty ivory fan
picked out in gold and exactly the same shade of Pomona green
as her new ribbons.

"I couldn't believe it when my father gave me such an
immense sum; only imagine—ten guineas! I was sure I would
never manage to spend it all. He said this would be my first
appearance in fashionable society and I must do him credit."

"I'm sure you'll look very pretty, Miss Lallie, and if you only
behave as Mrs Staines and your governess taught you, you'll do
very well. We'll wash your hair the day before," Nancy decided,
"I'll ask Cook for some egg-yolks to bring up the shine."

"Now there's a beauty," Captain Arthur Malvin commented
beneath his breath. "I've been too long among the senoritas,
Hugo; I've forgotten what a real English rose looks like. Just
look at those gilded curls and dewy lips! Is her skin as soft as it
looks, do you think?"

Hugo turned to see what lady had inspired these raptures
and froze.

"I wonder who she is," Arthur continued. "She's with the
Nugents, but I don't recall having seen her before."

Hugo had recovered his composure. "She is Lady Albright,"
he said curtly.

"Do you know her? Can you present me? If we walk that
way now, we may intercept her quite neatly."

Somewhat reluctantly, Hugo obeyed. He would have preferred to greet Sabina away from prying eyes and certainly not
while she was on the arm of an elderly gentleman whom he pre-
sumed to be her husband, but it would look strange if he ignored
Arthur's request.

Lady Albright smiled politely but did not offer her hand. "What a surprise to see you here, Mr Tamrisk."

"Lady Malvin is my sister," he explained.

"Ah, we are in like case then. We are staying with Lady Nugent, who is Albright's sister and Lady Malvin kindly included us in her invitation."

"May I present my nephew, Captain Arthur Malvin?"

Her eyes widened as she looked from one man to the other. "Nephew?"

Arthur bowed. "He is older than he looks," he confided solemnly.

She threw him a sparkling glance and Hugo suddenly couldn't bear to see her flirt with another man. She seemed to avoid his eye; her attention remained focussed on Arthur even as she leaned on her husband's arm with an air of fragility that was completely foreign to her. Why the act, he speculated sourly. They were soon joined by another couple and the Albrights moved on.

Sometime later, Arthur winced. "I'm going to take possession of that window seat—despite the cane, I can't stay on my feet much longer. I don't know why my mother insisted on inviting so many." He sank onto the cushions with a sigh of relief. "That's better. Go away, Hugo. If you find any more beauties, preferably ones who are not with their husbands, you know where to find me."

That must be what Lady Catherine de Burgh is like, Lallie thought as, having dutifully made her curtsey to her host and formidable hostess, she entered the great drawing-room where some fifty ladies and gentlemen were scattered, with more spilling out onto the terrace that separated it from the beautiful gardens she could spy below. The younger Halworths had joined a group of their contemporaries and Lallie was about to follow them when the Admiral offered her his arm.

"Come, my girl. That must be Malvin's younger son sitting over there looking glum. He was wounded at Vittoria, I understand, and sent home to recover. The sight of your pretty face will cheer him up much more than my weather-beaten phis."

"Pray don't get up, sir," Lallie begged the young man who, ignoring her plea, struggled to his feet to greet them with a charming smile.

"Captain Malvin, is it not? Sir Jeremiah Halworth, late of His Majesty's Navy at your service, sir. My niece, Miss Grey. Take your seat, man! No need to stand on ceremony—we fighting men must hold together."

"If Miss Grey were to be seated," the young officer suggested, "that would resolve the issue for us."

Lallie smilingly accepted the chair Sir Jeremiah set for her and listened spellbound as the two men launched on an exchange of reminiscences that undoubtedly would have caused raised eyebrows and a reprimand for being unsuited to a lady's drawing-room had either the Admiral's wife or Captain Malvin's mother overheard them. The captain, clearly cheered by this robust approach to his situation, did not hesitate to trump the guest's yarns and she could not but chuckle at their more outrageous escapades.

Soon others drifted nearer and she found herself at the centre of the group who listened enthralled as the captain concluded an elaborate anecdote involving a donkey, another officer and a *senorita* with a verve that provoked a burst of almost raucous laughter.

Judging by her reproving look, Lady Malvin was not as amused. She caught her daughter's eye and directed her to the pianoforte, then advised the company in sweetly iron tones that Miss Malvin would play some Haydn for them.

"Come and join me, Lallie."

Mrs Grey beckoned from the settee where she sat chatting to an older gentleman who stood and bowed gracefully despite his portly figure.

"Charmed to make your acquaintance, Miss Grey. Frederick Malvin at your service."

Lallie curtseyed politely. "Good evening, sir."

He gestured to the place he had vacated. "Please, Miss Grey."

As he spoke, Mrs Grey moved to the end of the settee. "There is room for three, sir."

"If you permit."

"Sit, Lallie," Mrs Grey ordered. "Miss Malvin is about to begin."

Lallie had no choice but to obey and Mr Malvin took his place beside her, sitting angled into the corner, one leg thrown over the other. He rested one arm on the back of the settee as if to give her more room but this made her feel uncomfortably close to him, almost as if his arm were around her shoulders. She inched nearer her stepmother, astonished that she did not object, but Mrs Grey seemed to find nothing amiss. Lallie remained perched on the edge of the seat, her back rigidly straight so as to avoid any possibility of coming into contact with her neighbour's person and prayed that the musical entertainment would soon be over. Unfortunately too many young ladies were eager to perform and she was forced to endure almost an hour in this strained position before her host unwittingly came to her rescue.

"What, are we only to have gloom and misery?" Lord Malvin exclaimed after the fourth lachrymose lament. "Come, Miss Grey, you will sing something livelier for us, will you not? You are not one to dwell upon doom and deserted females, I'll warrant, nor star-crossed lovers neither."

Lallie rose to her feet with alacrity.

"My lord, I vow you have no sensibility," Lady Malvin protested. "Pray pay no heed to him, Miss Grey and sing just what you please. Now, whom shall we ask to play for you?" She looked around the room. "Tamrisk?"

Lallie swallowed as a tall, austere man who had been standing behind the chair of an elegant blonde lady advanced on her. He was very dark, with strong cheekbones and deep eye sockets set above a beak of a nose and a determined chin, above which his lips were fixed in a straight line.

"Miss Grey, may I present my brother, Mr Tamrisk?" Lady Malvin said.

He inclined his head as Lallie curtseyed. "Have you made your choice, Miss Grey?"

"I have, but I am used to accompanying myself, Mr Tamrisk," she answered with a conciliating smile. "If you do not wish to play—"

"It will be my pleasure," he contradicted her, "Especially if you have found the charm to soothe my brother-in-law."

"I hope so. This was a favourite of my grandmother's. She always said that if girls were not so quick to accept Spanish coin, there would be a dearth of deserted maidens."

She leaned forward to place the music on its stand, catching an appealing scent of fresh linen overlain with a faint, aromatic spice as he moved closer.

His lips curved in a surprisingly attractive smile. "*Sigh no more, Ladies.* That should do the trick."

Despite his concentration on his music, Hugo was able to appreciate the pretty back presented to him by the singer and the vivacious features reflected in the gilt over-mantel mirror opposite her. She sang easily, her warm mezzo-soprano effortlessly filling the room as she adjured love-sick girls to '*sigh not so, but let them go*' with a raised eyebrow and a tilt to her lips that suggested there were far better fish in the sea. The wry inflexion in her tone was balanced by the smile in her voice so that the final '*hey, nonny,*

*nonny*' was received with warm applause which she acknowledged with a charming smile before looking back at him.

"Thank you, sir."

"It was my pleasure. You have a beautiful voice, Miss Grey."

"Thank you, my dear!" Lord Malvin came up to them beaming. "That has put us in the proper mood for supper."

Hugo very correctly offered his arm to his partner. "May I have the honour, Miss Grey?"

"Over here, Hugo!" Arthur waved from a large round table in the centre of the supper room.

Having seated Miss Grey, Hugo went to make a selection from the buffet for her. He was rewarded by an unaffected smile of thanks on his return and was impressed by the contrast to more fashionable young ladies who took every service as their due.

"Do you remain for long in these parts, Miss Grey?"

"I'm not sure, sir. Another week or so, I think."

"Where is your home?"

"In Sussex, near Battle."

"An unusual name. To which battle does it refer?"

"The Battle of Hastings. There are remains nearby of a most picturesque old abbey that was built by the Conqueror. The high altar, it is said, was on the spot where King Harold was slain."

"Was it indeed? It's odd how these events somehow belong more to a mythical time and place than to real localities. I took the opportunity afforded by the Peace of Amiens to visit the continent and found it quite strange to walk in the Coliseum, for example."

"How I envy you," she exclaimed, her emerald eyes shining. "I love to read of other countries but to be able to go there yourself must be beyond anything! What was your most memorable experience, sir?"

Hugo drank some champagne. "There were so many, Miss Grey, that it is hard to single one out, but what immediately springs to mind is hearing the *Miserere* sung in the Pope's chapel during Passion Week. Only picture it; it is very late in the evening, with the darkness intensified by the sombre appearance of the ladies who sit together, all dressed in deep mourning with black veils. The only light comes from the candles on the altar, their gleam faintly illuminating Michaelangelo's depiction of the *Last Judgement*. As you strain to see it in the flickering glow, you begin to imagine the figures are about to become alive. Suddenly sublime strains soar from the darkness, weaving a web of transcendent cadences that floats heavenwards—"

He broke off, embarrassed at having shared this very personal recollection on such an inappropriate occasion, but Miss Grey's eyes shone.

"I remember my grandfather, who was a clergyman, recalling the same experience. He said that it was as if the very angels begged for mercy on our behalf."

"That's it," he said and their eyes met in a moment of complete accord that was shattered by Arthur's younger brother Matthew saying jovially,

"Saw the Pope, did you, Uncle? Did you kiss his toe?"

Matthew did not wait for a reply, but turned his attention to the Admiral's son. "I say, Halworth, I hope your parent is not going to be as stingy with his game as old Fusty was."

"Old Fusty?"

"Foljambe—the previous owner of Longcroft Manor—died last year. He was confined to the house for at least a decade, but wouldn't hear of a fellow taking out a gun or a rod on his land. His people enforced it strictly too—or so they tell me," he added hastily.

"I am sure my step-father would be delighted to invite his neighbours for a day's sport," Mr Rowe, Lady Halworth's son from her first marriage, replied. His stern gaze capably conveyed the message that this statement was not to be understood as a carte blanche to make free of the Admiral's estate and preserves.

When the first strains of dance music were heard from within, the company rose as one. A Mr Pargeter, who had been sitting on Miss Grey's other side, immediately begged her to stand up with him. Hearing this, Hugo civilly thanked her for her company and, ignoring Miss Pargeter's expectant glance, contrived to quit the supper-room without having committed himself to any lady.

"I thought you would have been quicker off the mark, Hugo," Arthur reproached him. "Any of old Douro's officers would be ashamed to have had such a march stolen on them. Such a taking little thing, too, with those cat's eyes. Not one of your usual *ton* damsels," he concluded. Hugo, who had previously admired the slanted green eyes and provocative combination of a little turned-up nose perched above a plump upper lip, could only agree.

"Miss Grey? May I have the pleasure of dancing this next with you?"

Inwardly shrinking, Lallie forced herself to place her fingers on Mr Frederick Malvin's proffered arm. There was something calculating in the way he looked at her that she found disturbing but she could not refuse him without condemning herself to languishing as a wallflower for the rest of the evening. At least it was a dance where the gentlemen stood opposite the ladies rather than beside them and she did her best to avoid her partner's warm glances. He paced rather than danced the steps with an air of ineffable self-satisfaction as if she should feel honoured to be partnered by him and, when the figure required them to join hands, he did not hold hers lightly but pressed it with an emotive glance. His plump, kid-gloved fingers felt like warm slugs, she thought distastefully, and the way his gaze lingered on her exposed bosom made her glad that Nancy had added the additional ruffle.

Behind him, at the side of the ballroom, she noticed her stepmother nod and smile approvingly, although she couldn't imagine why. Perhaps Mrs Grey took Mr Malvin's invitation to Lallie as a compliment to herself. They were more of an age, after all.

"I swear, Arthur," Hugo declared "I have never met such an insipid bunch of girls as I did this past Season. And here they are no better. It's as if meekness has suddenly become the mode!"

Arthur laughed. "Look for someone with a little more fire to her; Miss Grey for example." He nodded towards the dancers.

Hugo frowned. "Isn't your father's cousin too old for her?"

"I should say so! Mamma was not pleased when he turned up unannounced, but she felt she could hardly refuse to put him up." He grinned. "Some say he's not quite the thing, but so far he has contrived to remain on the right side of the line and my father would prefer not to have an open breach."

The dance ended and the two men watched as Frederick offered Miss Grey his arm.

Arthur gripped his cane. "I'm off to request Miss Grey to sit out the next dance with me. There's a cosy alcove where we may remain in view of the company, but it's too small for a third to come and spoil sport."

"An excellent idea. I'll come with you and solicit her hand for the following one."

"But no lingering, Hugo," Arthur warned him.

"You have an unfair advantage with these *têtes-à-têtes*," Hugo complained. "When dancing there are others in the set and one must pay attention to the figures."

"You may take yourself off, Uncle," Captain Malvin ordered as soon as Lallie had acceded to Mr Tamrisk's request.

Mr Tamrisk shook his head. "The youth of today have no respect for their elders," he sighed. "Until later, Miss Grey."

Lallie looked after him as he sauntered away. "He is your uncle? I thought you were of an age."

"We are, more or less. We are really more like cousins, but I enjoy teasing him about it." The captain inhaled sharply.

Poor man, he must be in pain, Lallie thought and gently slipped her hand under his arm to provide some support. She stopped for a moment to admire a vase and only moved on when she felt the tension in him ease. She sat down as soon as they reached the seat he had selected and he sighed as he took his place beside her.

"It must seem strange, coming from such a war-torn country as Spain to the peace of England," she remarked.

"It was the stillness that struck me first," he said. "An army on the move is never quiet, you know, not even when they have camped for the night. There is always some sort of alarums and excursions and the command to stand to your arms may echo at any time." He grinned. "Frequently it may be due to a donkey having escaped from its tether to maraud through the camp in search of what it may devour. Nothing is safe from them, I assure you, Miss Grey."

"Do you miss it?"

"At times," he admitted. "You are with your comrades and there is a great sense of a combined endeavour. But whether I miss it or not, as long as Boney has not been defeated, it is my duty to return to my regiment as soon as I am fit."

That will take some time, Lallie thought compassionately, considering his thin, almost gaunt features and the shadow of pain that was never far from his eyes. He shifted uneasily in his chair.

"Were you in town for the Season, Miss Grey?"

"No, Captain. I am used to lead a quiet life in the country. In fact this visit to the Admiral is the most excitement we have had in a long time."

"How do you occupy yourselves in the country, then?"

"I teach my sisters, and then we read and make music, or play games together. And we visit one another—our little society is not large, but we contrive to keep ourselves amused."

He laughed. "It's the same with us, especially when we are in winter quarters. There are all manner of balls and entertainments and some rough-and-ready hunting as well. The Melton men would quite look down on it, I assure you." He looked around his mother's ballroom. "You forget what peace is like," he said quietly, almost to himself.


When the Boulanger was announced, Mr Tamrisk came to claim his partner.

"Our dance, I believe, Miss Grey."

"Indeed, sir," Lallie replied. She turned to her companion. "Please do not get up, Captain. I have enjoyed our talk."

The captain stood despite her gentle command. "As did I, Miss Grey. Thank you."

She smiled at him and took Hugo's arm to walk onto the dance floor. She chuckled involuntarily and he looked down enquiringly.

"Something amuses you, Miss Grey?"

"Oh, it is just a silly little thought." She waved it away.

"Now I am even more curious," he murmured.

"Pray do not misunderstand me, sir, but I was wondering why it is assumed that the minute a lady is in a gentleman's company, particularly in a ballroom, she is unable to walk without his support."

"Do you prefer to stand on your own feet?"

"Generally yes."

They took their places in the set. She had left her hand resting on his arm and he said softly, "I am glad you do not intend to put your theories into practice, Miss Grey. It might be assumed that you stand up with me under duress."

"Of course, not sir. I have observed you to be a most proficient dancer. Any lady must be glad of such a partner." She spoke solemnly, but her eyes laughed and his attractive smile flickered again. The music started and they joined hands with the others to form a circle that skipped first in one direction and then in another.

The first couple moved into the figure, the gentleman dancing alternately with his partner and each of the other ladies until they returned to their own place and the circle formed again. Now it was time for Hugo and Lallie to advance. She danced lightly, even joyously, her hand reaching for his each time to dance around him before releasing him to the next lady. When each couple had danced the figure, the set circled again before opening to form a line. There were several sets and everyone joined hands to dance in a twisting, spiral follow-my-leader fashion around the ballroom. It was odd, Lallie thought, how the feel of Mr Tamrisk's right hand clasping her left was more meaningful than that of the gentleman on her right.

The music came to an end and the dancers stopped, gasping for breath.

"That was worse than a long set of Sir Roger," Hugo said. "Would you like something to drink, Miss Grey?"

"Thank you, sir."

With an arched brow and a quizzical look, he ostentatiously offered her his arm and she took it, laughing.

"Where is your home, Mr Tamrisk?" Miss Grey asked as she sipped her lemonade.

"I divide my time between London and our seat in Devonshire."

"Which do you prefer?"

Hugo was floored by this artless question. He did not wish to confess the loneliness of Tamm and temporized, saying, "It is hard to say. On an oppressive day in town I long for the bracing air of the moors or the sea and on a wet winter's day at Tamm I miss the diversions of town."

"Tamm is where you grew up, isn't it? I think our childhood home always has a special place in our heart."

If one is fortunate, he thought but only said, "Yes" and then, ashamed of this curtness, added, "Yours was a happy childhood, Miss Grey?"

"Oh yes." She finished her lemonade. "We should go back."

"A most successful evening, Clarissa," Lord Malvin complimented his wife after the last guests had retired.

"Where's Frederick?" Arthur enquired lazily.

"Disappeared in a huff," his father answered shortly. "He took umbrage when I told him I wouldn't permit high stakes in my house. Piquet for a guinea a point! It was one thing when he was playing with Grey—they're two of a kind, but I saw him eyeing young Pargeter as if he were a pigeon ripe for the plucking."

"It wasn't only Pargeter he was eyeing," Arthur said disapprovingly. "I saw him dance with little Miss Grey. She's far too young for him."

"She didn't dance only with him," Matthew pointed out. "She danced with Hugo and me among others and sat out with you." He yawned. "I'm for bed."

"I'll go up with you." Arthur struggled to his feet and linked his arm with his brother's as they left the room.

"Frederick wasn't the only one taken by Miss Grey," Lord Malvin said indulgently after the door had closed behind his sons.

"It's not a connection I would wish for Arthur," his wife answered. "She has very little to offer, has she not?"

"I think she would make a fine wife for any man," Malvin replied. "There's no nonsense about her; she is pretty-behaved and thoughtful, too. Without her and the Admiral, Arthur might still be sitting at that window in a brown study."

"That is very true," Clarissa conceded. "We must be grateful to her for that. Poor boy, he is still in a lot of pain."

"But is on the mend," her husband said stoutly. He bent and kissed her cheek. "Now my dear, do you go to bed. I fear you will be worn out tomorrow." He went to the door with her, saying on his return, "You'll take a nightcap with me, Hugo?"

"Thank you, Tony. I deserve it after fending off that batch of damsels and attendant mothers."

"There'll be no escaping them until you take yourself off the marriage market."

And why not with Miss Grey? Hugo thought. It would annoy his sister if he were to pay court to her. And she was a pretty little thing—a cosy armful, in fact.

# Chapter Four

*The Mountains of Deceit are infested with vast numbers of Tigers and Tiger Cats, serpents of various kinds have been caught here after much toil and labour.*

Hugo was greatly entertained by Clarissa's chagrin at the Admiral's acquisition of the manor pew with his purchase of Longcroft Manor.

"One had to accept the precedence of the Foljambes, for they had been here forever," she declared as they left for church on Sunday morning, "but they are now extinct and there can be no doubt that we are the principal family in the district. Who are the Halworths, after all?"

"Now, Mamma, there should be no distinctions in church; does scripture not teach us that we are all one in Jesus Christ?"

Clarissa frowned at her son. "Don't be blasphemous, Matthew. Remember your catechism. We are to do our duty in that state of life unto which it has pleased God to cause us and if He has seen fit to place us in an exalted state, we must uphold it. I should have thought the bishop would have instructed the churchwardens to transfer the Foljambe pew to us, but he apparently neglected to do so and on the first Sunday the Admiral was conducted to it in great style. And Malvin refuses to intervene."

"I'm not surprised," Hugo remarked. "It would be rather undignified, would it not? Much better to ignore it."

She glared at him. "Stop smirking, Hugo. The manor pew at Tamm is yours by right and you also have a private chapel."

"With chaplain," Arthur added. "What will you do when you come to your title? Do you propose to retain him?"

Matthew hooted with laughter. "I can just see you bidding him say grace before you dine *à deux*." The exaggerated wave of his hand that accompanied this remark had even his mother smiling.

"You may curb your imagination," Hugo retorted. "Stiles is a useful companion to Tamm, I suppose, but I never could abide him. He's an arrant lickspittle and his unctuous ways are even less appealing now when he tries to ingratiate himself with me. Besides, I have no fond memories of him as a tutor; he was dull, prosy and too inclined to use the rod."

"He hates women," Clarissa said unexpectedly. "'Let the woman learn in silence with all subjection'," was his favourite verse.

Hugo raised an eyebrow. "You were not an apt pupil then."

She reddened. "Poor Mamma couldn't stand him either. He had a way of praying at her, she was used to say, implying that she was not pleasing to God because she had not borne a son."

Lord Malvin smiled at her. "Only a weak man would want a silent or submissive wife."

She smiled back, her flush deepening.

"Lallie! I can't find my handkerchief."

The sniff which punctuated this hissed appeal was perfectly audible to Hugo who had been directed to the side bench in the Malvin pew and so sat at right angles to the one in front. From this vantage point he was able to watch, amused and impressed, as Miss Grey dealt competently with the small crisis. Appeased, the little girl edged nearer, slipped her hand into that of Miss Grey, and heaved a resigned sigh as the sermon continued. Miss Grey looked down at her with a soft smile, touching her finger to her lips in silent admonition.

Frederick Malvin had inserted himself on Miss Grey's other side. He had joined the Greys on arriving at the church and insisted she take his arm. Hugo's brows twitched together. In another man, this could have been construed as a declaration of intent, but Malvin had never been inclined to dangle after well-bred women. He was known to have rougher appetites which he satisfied in the more curious brothels.

Lallie shifted uneasily, trying to move away from the plump thigh that pressed against hers. Mr Malvin exuded a nauseating stale odour that reminded her of the library carpet the morning after a decanter of brandy had been spilled. Her queasiness grew when he leaned nearer to share her hymnbook, his unpleasant breath hot on her cheek as he sang off-key in her ear. She swallowed, trying to take shallow breaths, then clenched her stomachic muscles and stared fixedly ahead as she mouthed the responses and the words of the hymns.

At last the vicar pronounced the blessing. When her bugbear left the pew, she hung back, ostensibly to retie the bow on Beatrice's bonnet, but he lingered until she could tarry no longer.

"Beatrice, you will walk with me," Mrs Grey commanded.

The child went to her mother's side and Lallie had no choice but to go too. As she stepped into the aisle, Mr Malvin seized her hand and tucked it into his crooked elbow.

"Allow me, Miss Grey."

As before, he did not wait for her consent to this perfunctory request, but towed her down the aisle, his arm trapping her so close to his side that her skirts brushed his leg as they walked.

She could feel her face grow hot. We must present a very off appearance, she thought. Thank goodness we're not at home, where everyone would see. As it was, when they reached the bottom of the aisle, she saw Ruth Halworth look askance and nudge her brother knowingly.

If Mr Malvin noticed this byplay, he did not comment on it, declaring as they descended the church steps, "You are a devoted sister, Miss Grey, but it is a pity to see you *waste your sweetness on the desert air,* as the poet has it. I have told your father he is a rogue to have kept you from town so long, but he swears you have no desire to leave your loved ones."

Lallie didn't know how to reply. In the end, she said simply, "I am indeed much attached to my sisters, sir."

His free hand covered hers where it rested on his arm. "But not to the exclusion of all others, I trust, Miss Grey?" He smiled toothily as he spoke.

She tugged at her hand, looking around in frantic hope that someone, anyone might break up this unwanted *tête-à-tête.* Finally, in desperation, she begged, "Pray release me, sir."

His grip tightened, crushing her fingers. "Now, my dear, there is no need to be so coy."

"Cousin, we are ready to depart. You will not wish to keep her ladyship waiting, I know."

To Lallie's intense mortification, Lord Malvin himself had come to detach his relative who set her free with an unctuous, "Until we meet again, Miss Grey".

"My lord, sir."

She contented herself with a brief farewell curtsey addressed to both gentlemen, fervently hoping that his lordship did not think she had clung to his cousin or encouraged his attentions.

"All goes splendidly," Mr Grey said to this wife that evening. "My friend Malvin is quite enamoured of the chit. He and I leave for Truro in the morning to complete the settlements—he will give me his vowels for my cut, it is the simplest way to manage that side of things—and then he'll go on to London to arrange for a special licence. We'll meet him there on our way home and they can be married in town. But mind, not a word to the girl! Indulge her a little while I am away and she'll be all the more eager to do our bidding."

Mrs Grey stared at him. "So quickly? I'm not sure that it is wise to rush matters, husband. Lallie is biddable, it is true, but if you go too fast she may balk. Why not have him follow us to Sussex and court her there?"

"He insists it must be done at once. Besides, in London she will have no-one to turn to, unlike at home where she is well-liked and the curate half in love with her. Enough, madam," Mr Grey held up his hand sternly when his wife started to speak again. "My mind is made up. I shall be most displeased if you disobey me in this."

While Lallie thought nothing of her father's departure, she was overjoyed that Mr Frederick Malvin was not among the parties from Malvin Abbey that visited Longcroft Manor two days later, the gentlemen to shoot and fish, and the ladies, who drove over afterwards with Captain Malvin, to chat and stroll through the gardens.

"Shall we challenge these two young ladies to a game of billiards, Captain?" The Admiral gestured to his daughter Ruth and Miss Malvin.

"That would be ungentlemanly, I fear," Captain Malvin replied. "Perhaps Miss Halworth would do me the honour of partnering me?"

This left Miss Malvin with the Admiral, but she accepted the challenge cheerfully.

"What about you, Lallie?" Ruth asked. "Will you come with us and ensure fair play?"

"I thought I might take the children on a nature-walk and then to play hide-and-seek in the old orchard. What do you think, girls? Tony?"

"If it is not too much for you, Miss Grey," Lady Malvin's daughter-in-law said over the loud agreement to this suggestion.

"Of course not, I'll enjoy it too," Lallie assured her.

"Caught you!" seven-year old Tony Malvin exclaimed gleefully, pouncing on Lallie as she attempted to dart from tree to tree. She squealed in alarm, but yielded to her captor and obediently covered her eyes to commence her warning count as the others scattered to hide again. She had not yet reached twenty when she heard the boy cry, "Papa, Uncle Hugo! We're having such a jolly time," and opened her eyes to see him run towards a small group of gentlemen who stood at the entrance to the orchard.

"Oh, is it so late?" she gasped, uneasily conscious of the hair that threatened to tumble down her back and the ripped flounce she had hastily pinned. Her troops were similarly dishevelled. "Come, children, we'll slip up the back stairs and get you tidy before your Mammas catch sight of you."

"Did you have any luck, Ned?" she asked her cousin-in-law as they began to stroll towards the house.

"Not too bad. Several brace of partridge, one of pheasant and a couple of hares."

"And who is this fine fellow?" She held out her hand to the St John Newfoundlander that came forward to sniff inquisitively at her fingers.

"May I introduce Horace, Miss Grey?" Mr Tamrisk said with a grin. "An old friend."

"A very elegant one," she said, scratching behind the dog's ears. "See how his snowy white shirt front gleams against his black coat. Even Mr Brummell would approve."

Hugo was touched by the sight of the happy children clustered around Miss Grey. Tony, the only boy, had not been excluded. And if she had been charming in her ball-room finery, she was even more tempting in her present unkempt state. Herrick had the right of it with his sweet disorder, he thought appreciatively as she tidied her hair, her raised arms causing her breasts to push roundly against her spencer.

The little company parted at the house. Miss Grey whisked the children away while Mr Rowe led the gentlemen first to the gun-room and later to the lawn. Here comfortable chairs had been set for the older generation as well as for Captain Malvin, whom Lady Halworth firmly directed to one beside the rug where Miss Grey, delectable in a fresh primrose gown trimmed with green ribbons the colour of her eyes, and her cousin Miss Halworth lolled gracefully. Hugo calmly appropriated a couple of cushions and sat on the grass near them.

"Feeling your age again, Uncle?" Arthur asked solicitously. "Do lean against my chair if you're too tired."

Hugo ignored this sally. It was a perfect September afternoon, the sun bright but not so warm that one must seek out the shade, although the ladies wore wide-brimmed hats to protect their complexions. The leaves displayed the first tints of autumn and a mere hint of crispness in the air gave notice that such days must now be savoured all the more.

Lady Halworth has a proper appreciation of men's appetites, he thought approvingly as the platters of sandwiches, pies and cakes were passed from group to group. No kickshaws and an excellent ale as well. A deliciously savoury smell filled the air when footmen appeared with trays of little skewers of crisp meat seasoned with herbs.

"If I close my eyes, I am back at a bivouac in the Peninsula, roasting our meat over a fire," Arthur remarked. "It wasn't always as tasty as this, though; at times we were grateful to get a haunch of goat or a tough old hen."

"These are called shish kebab," Miss Halworth said. "Mamma discovered them in Turkey and decided they were just the thing for a party. There they are larger, of course, but she had these small skewers made especially for such occasions as this."

"I love a pick-nick. I don't know why, but everything seems to taste better in the open air," Miss Grey remarked.

She nibbled a cube of meat with obvious relish, something the jaded *ton* maidens would never do. Hugo much preferred Miss Grey's honest appetite. Would she savour other delights as frankly? Even as the thought crossed his mind, she looked up and caught his eye.

She didn't bridle or look away with a maidenly blush, but calmly met his gaze and asked, "Don't you agree, Mr Tamrisk?"

"Yes and no, Miss Grey. Nothing seems to taste as good as the ham sandwich you have carried with you all morning on the moors unless it is the hearty dinner served on your return home."

She cocked an eyebrow. "So one's bread tastes better if earned in the sweat of one's face?"

"I suppose that depends on whether one enjoys one's labours," Arthur said. "In general I enjoy mine, despite occasional particular deprivations such as the hunk of stale bread eaten in the pouring rain. What about you, Miss Grey, does your bread taste sweet?"

"Whether it does or not is immaterial, Captain," she replied quietly. "Eve's lot remains the more bitter of the two."

Miss Halworth flushed and beckoned to a passing footman. "You must try the curd puffs," she exclaimed. "Cook prides herself upon them."

Hugo obediently helped himself and the conversation drifted into shallower waters. But back at the Abbey, Miss Grey's comment niggled at him to such an extent that he found himself compelled to consult the big bible in the library.

'*Unto the woman he said, I will greatly multiply thy sorrow and thy conception; in sorrow thou shalt bring forth children; and thy desire shall be to thy husband, and he shall rule over thee.*'

Which of the three pronouncements had occasioned her remark? And why?

# Chapter Five

*The River of Respect disembogues into the Gulf of Sincerity.*

Lady Nugent surveyed the guests gathered on the terrace of Nugent Castle. "Before we start, would anyone like to climb the old tower? The view from the top is magnificent; it is so clear today that we should be able to see the white horse at Uffington."

Lady Albright, who had risen with the others, suddenly swayed.

"My lady?" Hugo steadied her with a hand under her elbow. She was paler than usual and still had that air of fragility.

She shook her head. "It's nothing. I stood up too fast, I think. It is very close today."

"Stay here and rest in the shade, my dear," Lady Nugent advised her sister-in-law. "You may view the tower any day you are here."

"Well, Miss Grey," Hugo enquired as he fell into step beside her, "Are you in need of masculine support this morning or do you prefer to walk unaided?"

Her cheerful smile immediately raised his spirits. "I confess I do, sir, if you will not take offence."

"On the contrary, ma'am," he said promptly. "I have no taste for clinging vines."

She laughed. "It never occurred to me that gentlemen must also find it irksome."

"Especially when the damsel in question believes in tripping it over-daintily and takes four steps to one of your normal ones."

"Where are your manners, Tamrisk?" interrupted Lady Malvin who had come up behind them. "You have neglected to offer Miss Grey your arm."

Hugo compressed his lips but said nothing. How could he reply without exposing his companion to the sharper edge of his sister's tongue? But, to his touched amusement, Miss Grey took up the cudgels on his behalf, remarking pleasantly,

"I must applaud Mr Tamrisk, who accepts that a lady's ability to walk unaided does not vanish mysteriously as soon as his arm becomes available."

"I so agree with Miss Grey," Arabella cried. "I don't know how often I have been irritated by having to take the arm of some dreary gentleman."

"Now, how am I to take that?" Hugo demanded.

Miss Grey flushed and began to stammer, "I-i-indeed, I did not mean it so."

"I would not call you dreary, Uncle Hugo," Arabella said handsomely.

"Nor would Miss Grey, I trust." He raised his brows challengingly and was pleased to see a little twinkle in the eyes that met his.

"Certainly not, although my judgement must of course be based on our short acquaintance."

Arthur gave a crack of laughter. "Very true, Miss Grey, and if your opinion of my uncle wanes as your knowledge of him waxes, pray don't hesitate to come and walk beside me."

"That proves that my cousin is right," Miss Halworth interjected.

"I'm sure she is, but why?" Arthur enquired.

"If she wishes to escape from an escort, it is much easier to do so without making a scene if she has not taken his arm. Some men are not always gentlemanly, if you take my meaning."

"A girl should never find herself in the company of a gentleman unless her mother or chaperon deems him a suitable acquaintance," Lady Malvin pronounced firmly.

"That is all very well, provided all Mammas are as careful of their daughters as you are," Arabella said fondly.

"It's a tricky spiral stair," Lord Nugent said as he opened the door to the turret. "I shall go up first and open the door to the roof so that we have light, then I'll come down to lead you up, with a lady following each gentleman so that she is always between two of us. That will be safest."

Lallie found the curving climb quite easy, provided she stayed near the wall where the stone steps were widest and held her skirts carefully away from her feet with her right hand. She took a deep breath as she stepped onto the roof. The air seemed fresher and the sun brighter up here. She had never been so high in her life. She walked over to the parapet, which came up to her shoulders and peered over but could not see very much.

"Here, Lallie," Ruth gestured to her. "If you stand on this stone, you will have a much better view."

She hopped down, assisted by Matthew Malvin, and Lallie stepped up. Now the parapet seemed much lower and she could look down to the ground far below where the captain sat with his mother. A gust of wind tugged at her bonnet and she anchored it with her hand. Looking down made her feel slightly queasy, even light headed, and she closed her eyes against the sensation.

Two firm hands at her waist steadied her in an impersonal clasp. "Just take a deep breath, Miss Grey," Mr Tamrisk's kind voice said in her ear. "You'll feel much more the thing directly."

She did as instructed and then cautiously opened her eyes. "It is being so high," she explained.

"I know. It takes some people that way. You'll find it better if you look into the distance rather than down. Can you see the horse over there on the hillside to your right?"

She turned gingerly. "Oh! I had not thought it would be so big. Isn't it wonderful? What beautiful lines, what a proud arc to its neck! And so white against the grass. It looks as if it's running."

"I've always thought so."

Evidently noticing that she had recovered from her momentary weakness, he released her but remained by her side.

"What sort of people were they, to create such a being," she wondered as they looked across the downs to White Horse Hill.

"We'll never know, but it's another of those things that reach across time to connect us to the past."

"If they were able to imagine and design such a thing, they both knew and appreciated beauty, and had time to indulge it."

"They were able to divert their labours from securing their existence, you mean?"

"Yes. Or perhaps it had religious significance."

"Or they wanted to demonstrate to their neighbours how wealthy and strong they were," Hugo suggested. "I think we are leaving, Miss Grey."

As Lord Nugent shepherded his flock back down the stairs, Lallie looked at her rescuer. She appreciated that he had neither teased her nor loudly proclaimed to the group that independent Miss Grey had needed a man's supporting hand.

"Thank you for your assistance, Mr Tamrisk."

"It was my pleasure, Miss Grey," he answered simply.

Lady Nugent was a keen archer who had twice won the captain's medal and been acclaimed Lady Patroness of the Royal British

Bowmen for the year, with the privilege of sporting white feathers in her hat. She deeply regretted the cessation of meetings for the duration of the war with France and made up for it by inviting her neighbours to private competitions. Now, a statuesque and commanding figure in her dark green dress trimmed with yellow at the shoulders and hem, she ruthlessly segregated the novices and sent them with her son and daughter to be instructed in the noble art of the bow, well out of the way of the more accomplished toxophilites who were to compete against one another.

"Each lady will draw a gentleman as her partner and after each round the two couples scoring lowest will be eliminated with the distances increasing by ten yards for the next round until only two couples remain, who shall shoot for the grand prize. We shall commence with distances of thirty yards for ladies and fifty for gentlemen."

Hugo watched the ladies cluster round their hostess. "Six or seven rounds, would you say, Tony?"

"At the least," his brother-in-law agreed.

"We are to be partners, Mr Tamrisk." Lady Albright, who appeared to have recovered from her earlier indisposition, came up to them waving a slip of paper, followed by Mrs Rowe who claimed Lord Malvin.

"Try this bow, Miss Grey." Miss Nugent said. "It was mine when I was younger—I think you will find it more to your liking. Even a couple of inches make a difference, you will see."

Lallie looked up at the willowy brunette. "Thank you. This does feel more comfortable somehow."

"Now, stand sideways to the target. Stretch out your left arm holding the bow and with your right hand pull the arrow and the string back until the index finger is near the corner of your mouth and the elbow is behind the arrow. Make sure that your shoulders are in a line and sight along the arrow so that you are aiming for the target." Miss Nugent adjusted Lallie's stance as she spoke. "Draw your shoulder-blades together and quickly release the arrow, pulling your hand back to the side of your ear as you do so." She clapped her hands as the arrow flew straight towards the target. "Well done, Miss Grey!"

Lallie held her breath, willing her arrow to strike home but it fell short.

"Try again," Miss Nugent commanded. "Once you have the knack, it is just a question of practice."

Having shot ten more arrows, four of which at least reached the target, even if nowhere near its centre, Lallie was more than ready to relinquish her place to Ruth. Her back and shoulder muscles ached, but it was exhilarating exercise.

On the other side of the glade, the competition had grown more intense and she wandered nearer to have a closer look. Captain Malvin was shooting now, from a chair, she saw. It was good that he was able to participate. As she watched his arrow flew to the centre of the butt.

"In the gold again," someone cried over the ripple of applause.

Mr Tamrisk and Lady Albright, who apparently had been eliminated, sat on a bench in the shade of a large oak. They looked comfortable together, more like old friends than recent acquaintances, Lallie thought, and turned back to the others.

"Are you well, Sabina?" Hugo asked quietly.

"Very well, Hugo. Why do you ask?"

He shrugged. "You seem frailer than you were in the summer, somehow. The heat never affected you in town."

She looked down at her hands and he fought the urge to stroke her neck just below the fair curls that had escaped from her bonnet.

"Sabina?"

She glanced up. "It is still a secret, Hugo, but I'm with child." She smiled softly, tears shimmering in her eyes. "Albright is overjoyed. We have been married for over six years now."

And his first marriage had been childless. Hugo swallowed the obvious question, the one a gentleman could never ask. Instead, he said, "I am very happy for you both."

"Thank you."

He glanced around. Everyone's attention was focussed on the butts where the competition had reached the final rounds. "Sabina?" he said quietly and then, when she looked up at him, "You know you may call on me should you ever be in need of assistance."

She touched his hand discreetly. "I know, Hugo. Thank you."

But it wasn't as simple as that, Hugo thought, when she moved away from him. He couldn't rid himself of the suspicion that she was carrying his child, a child he could never acknowledge and would very likely only meet for the first time when he or she was admitted to adult society. Another man would claim paternity of his son or daughter. He shook his head. He had vowed to be a better father to his children than Tamm had been to him. What a way to begin! Dismayed and confused, he skirted behind the archers and onlookers, making for the trees beyond the clearing. A walk would help to clear his head.

"Well done, Miss Grey!"

Distracted by the cries and applause, Hugo veered to the right where a loose circle of onlookers watched Miss Grey and his nephew Matthew play battledore and shuttlecock. Although in his top boots Matthew must have stood eight inches taller than she, she made up for this deficit by an amazing lightness and agility, revealing delicate ankles as she stretched in full flight to return the feathered cork with astonishing precision. Her face glowed with pleasure.

"Five hundred!" someone called.

Matthew grinned and she responded with an open, joyous smile. They continued to bat the shuttle backwards and forwards until, at seven hundred and eighty-eight, a little gust of wind took it too high for Miss Grey to reach. She shrugged and laughed as applause broke out while Matthew wiped his brow theatrically before thanking her for an excellent bout.

"I must thank you, Mr Malvin. It's the highest score I have ever achieved. To be honest, I was torn between wishing the shuttle would fall and hoping we could keep going longer."

"You're very adept," remarked Hugo who had joined them.

She shrugged. "It was all the rage at home this summer. We seemed to play it constantly. Next year it will be something else."

"It's strange how these crazes come and go," he agreed.

"What an interesting day this has been," Miss Grey said as they walked back towards the castle.

Hugo looked down at her, pleased with his success in detaching her from the main group. They were not too far behind the others for it to be improper, but distant enough to permit a private conversation. "Why is that?"

"Oh, so many new experiences. Climbing the tower, for example. I have never been so high and even it if felt a little strange at first, it was wonderful to be able to see so far. And then the archery. I have never before drawn a bow. I must see if we can set up an archery society at home. It would be something different and I particularly like that ladies may participate just as well as gentlemen. Too often we are excluded or relegated to admiring the gentlemen's prowess."

He smiled. "'*He for God only, she for God in him*'?"

She burst out laughing. "Are we back to Adam and Eve?"

"We seem to be. It appears you have revolutionary tendencies, Miss Grey."

"I suppose I do," she confessed cheerfully.

More of Milton's lines ran through Hugo's mind. Would she yield *'with coy submission, modest pride, And sweet reluctant amorous delay'*? Probably at first, he thought, but then she would very likely seek a more equal footing. Look at her enjoyment of the game with Matthew, which was all down to the rhythm of give and take. She was intelligent, open-minded, which was important, and not missish. He wanted to know more about her.

"Have you any brothers, Miss Grey?"

"Just one, James. He is away at school."

"So you are the eldest?"

"Yes."

"I don't recall seeing you in town."

"I haven't had a Season," she answered quietly, "at least not in London. We have our own parties and assemblies at home, of course."

"A riot of dissipation, I have no doubt."

Her lips twitched at his dry remark. "Alas no, not even during our month in Hastings last year. There they pride themselves on offering innocent recreational delight."

This was said with a mischievous little twinkle that enchanted him. "Did you indulge in sea-bathing?"

"Not precisely indulged," she said candidly. "It was prescribed for my sister who had suffered a series of debilitating colds over the winter and I accompanied her. I might have enjoyed it if I could have gradually entered the water at my own pace, but the dippers plunge one under without mercy and poor Eleanor became hysterical and clung to me. It was all I could do to calm her. I thought we would never return to dry land or be warm again."

She needed very little encouragement to talk about the children. She acted as their governess, he was astounded to hear, and gained great satisfaction from their progress and achievements.

"You're a very good sister," he remarked as they reached the castle.

Her face softened into a tender smile. "I love them."

She said it so simply, as if it were the most normal thing in the world. Perhaps it was—in a world that was unknown to him. What must it be like to bask in that unquestioning love, to know yourself so cherished?

Hugo sighed, Miss Nugent called to them and, too soon, their private interlude had ended.

Lallie was dreaming. It was as if she were captured in a spinning top, tossed here and there, never sure where she was. Now she was Miss Lallie, cherished granddaughter of Mrs Staines, celebrating her seventeenth birthday.

"I've written to your other grandparents, dearest, and we are agreed that we shall bring you out next Season. Lady Grey does not feel there should be any problem and I am determined to play my part."

Everything blurred. When it cleared, she was Miss Grey, a new-comer to Alwood who was neither overly indulged nor in possession of any particular advantages and returned to the schoolroom, this time as instructress.

The top twirled again and suddenly Miss Grey was someone to be treated with all the respect and courtesy due to a young lady, receiving the polite attentions of no fewer than three handsome, aristocratic men. In her dream they revolved past her; Captain Malvin, Mr Matthew Malvin and Mr Tamrisk. When she woke, it was Mr Tamrisk who remained with her. He was nothing like as forbidding as he had first seemed. She had enjoyed talking to him; he had seemed genuinely interested in her stories of the children and had apparently not been shocked by her remark about Eve's lot, although Ruth Halworth had scolded her when they were on their own, describing it as unladylike. Mr Tamrisk had been kind to her on the top of the tower. She had felt safe with him.

Miss Malvin had mentioned that he was only to spend one more day at Malvin Abbey, so she would not see him again. Lallie's heart felt—not precisely sore but a little tender at the thought. If she were young and foolish, she might have been tempted to day-dream a little or see more in his attentions than was meant. But she was too sensible to build castles in the air, she told herself, as she got out of bed. She need not wear a new gown today—there was nothing planned and one of last year's would do.

"I'll just tell Mamma we are going out."

Ruth opened the parlour door, stopping so abruptly on the threshold that Lallie had to swerve to avoid treading on her heels.

"I beg your pardon, Mamma. I did not realise you had callers. Good afternoon, Mr Tamrisk, Captain Malvin."

"I came to take my leave of you," Mr Tamrisk said, after the flurry of greetings, "but I see you are about to go out."

"Not anywhere in particular—just to stroll around the lake to the rotunda," Ruth said. "We can go later."

"Perhaps we might accompany you?" Captain Malvin suggested before she could take a seat.

"That's an excellent idea," Lady Halworth urged them. "It is a very pleasant walk."

They separated quite naturally into two couples, Lallie and Mr Tamrisk going ahead while Ruth followed with the captain. Lallie's head was in a whirl. It had been such a shock. She almost wished he had not come—she had reconciled herself to never seeing him again. Her heart had given a betraying little jump when he rose from his chair and she had felt her lips curve into a welcoming smile.

"Do you return to Devonshire tomorrow, Mr Tamrisk?"

"Not directly, no. I must spend a few days in town first."

They paused to watch a kestrel hover above them.

"I love to see them hang in the air like that," Lallie remarked. "It's as if they are defying nature."

The bird stooped suddenly and rose again, something small dangling from its claws. She made a face. It was too beautiful a day to be confronted with death.

Mr Tamrisk seemed to realise what she was thinking. "It's all part of the cycle of life," he said quietly. "Without death, we would have no balance."

"That is true," she acknowledged, "just sometimes it comes too soon."

"All the more reason to appreciate life," he reflected as they walked on. "What do you appreciate, Miss Grey?"

She stared at him. What a strange question. She had never thought of it before. "All manner of small things," she answered slowly, "my music, a new book, the satisfaction when one of my sisters masters something new; they are so pleased and I am pleased for them; the beauties of nature. What of you, sir?"

He was silent for some moments and then smiled ruefully. "I should ask your pardon for posing such a personal question, but you have served me with my own again. I find myself in complete agreement with you, Miss Grey."

She shook her head. "That is not fair, sir. By agreeing with me you avoid revealing anything of yourself. And I doubt that you instruct your sisters."

"I wouldn't dare." His broad smile made him look as young as Mr Matthew.

She chuckled. "I was trying to picture you testing Lady Malvin's knowledge of the multiplication tables."

"Heaven forfend!" He threw up his hands in mock horror but then said more seriously, "What you meant was the pleasure of achievement. You find it in your teaching; I find it in my work in Parliament. I am the member for Tamm," he explained in response to her questioning look. "Much of the work is tedious and mundane but there are times—the Slave Trade Act is a good example—when one can proud of what is accomplished."

"You may well be, sir," she answered, feeling how small her world was compared with his. "Do you continue to work with Mr Wilberforce?"

"In some matters, yes. I do not agree with him on everything. What music do you prefer, Miss Grey?"

"I prefer Mozart's sonatas to Haydn's and I enjoy singing Mr Moore's Irish melodies. They have a charming simplicity and are quite different to our English airs."

"That is true. It is thrilling to hear him perform them, and I use the term deliberately. He intones a sort of musical recitation to a seemingly extemporary accompaniment, combining words and music into a unique whole."

"Like a bard of old? How I would love to hear him," Lallie exclaimed. "What other music appeals to you, sir?"

"Do you know Herr van Beethoven's sonatas for the pianoforte? No? They are quite out of the common way—it is as if the music comes from deep within his soul. And I also admire many of Handel's arias, especially those where the voice and a solo instrument entwine in subtle repetition. My brother-in-law and I frequently perform them together."

Lallie would have liked to hear more, but they had reached the little rotunda and the conversation became general. While the Captain and Ruth discussed the amenities of the neighbourhood, she was inwardly planning to procure some of Herr van Beethoven's music. Learning it, she would recall today's walk. Once, her eyes met Mr Tamrisk's. He smiled gently at her and she smiled softly in return.

"Lallie! Watch me!"

Mrs Rowe approached the Rotunda, accompanied by a flock of little girls. Beatrice ran ahead, proudly bowling her hoop. So she has finally got the knack of it, Lallie thought as she went down to meet her. They would all go back together, no doubt. With a wistful sigh, she bent to admire Beatrice's prowess.

Having made his farewells to Lady Halworth, Mr Tamrisk turned to Mrs Grey. "I hope I may call when I am next in Sussex, ma'am. I should like to further my acquaintanceship with your family."

*'Further my acquaintanceship with your family'.* The words reverberated in Lallie's head. Had he really said them or had she imagined them? But no, there was a general—not precisely a gasp, more a holding of breath and her stepmother was struggling to conceal her surprise. Surely she would not be so discourteous as to refuse her permission?

Mrs Grey's gaze drifted towards Lallie who looked back impassively. It seemed like an age but it was probably only moments before the older woman said calmly, "Of course, sir, if you wish."

"Thank you, ma'am."

Then he was bowing over Lallie's hand. "Thank you for your charming company, Miss Grey. I look forward to our next meeting."

Torn between embarrassment and incredulous delight, Lallie could only murmur, "I too, sir."

Mr Tamrisk's warm smile glinted briefly before he moved on and she had to face Captain Malvin.

Once their callers had left the parlour, Lallie went quietly to a window from where she could watch unobtrusively as they drove away. The silence behind her grew—there was no hope for it; she must face her family.

"You've made a conquest, Lallie," Ruth said gleefully. "I thought Mr Tamrisk had displayed a distinct partiality for you, yesterday as well."

Lallie blushed vividly. She could not deny that Mr Tamrisk's attentions seemed particularly addressed to her but it was all so strange and she was unwilling to enter into any conversation about him.

Mrs Grey came to her rescue. "Time enough to be thinking of that if he does call," she said briskly. "It is as likely that he was seeking some diversion while he was in the country and was just doing the pretty now. I would not get my hopes up too much if I were you, Lallie. As Tamm's heir he would be a great catch, especially for a girl like you."

This was not said unkindly but still served to dampen Lallie's spirits.


"That sounded dangerously like a declaration," Arthur commented as his uncle's bays trotted down the avenue. "If you're not careful, you'll find yourself fronting the altar one of these days."

"Perhaps I will," Hugo replied calmly. "It's time I married. If Tamm had had his way, I would be married with hopeful sons these many years."

"Does the old man not realise that his nagging has had the opposite effect?" Arthur asked curiously.

"Never. I can only be grateful that his health confines him to Tamm and so he cannot pester me when I am away from there."

"I haven't seen him for years. Has his temper improved at all?"

Hugo shrugged. "Not a whit. However if you feel like a change, you'll be more than welcome to come and stay."

"But if you're going to Sussex," Arthur asked slyly, "who will be there to entertain me? You need not think to fob me off with the chaplain!"

# Chapter Six

*The Islands Demon, Calypso, Luxury and Indolence are remarkably unhealthy and dangerous. The ruins of a temple dedicated to Bacchus are still visible; also the animal called the Basilisk is said to have been found there.*

Lallie laid down her napkin and rose from the table.

"Come, girls. It's time you were in bed. Beatrice is almost asleep."

"Take them to Nancy and return here," Mr Grey ordered. "I have something to tell you."

Lallie suppressed a yawn as she led her sisters from the room. She was out of sorts after seven hours in a jolting carriage, but was not hopeful of a good night's sleep amid the noise and bustle of the *Bull and Mouth* where three galleried tiers of rooms surrounded the busy yard. She felt slightly apprehensive. What might her father wish to say directly to her and not convey through Mrs Grey?

When she returned to the snug private parlour, the remains of their meal had been cleared away, the twin copper lamps over the side-table lit and the fire made up. Her father was pouring himself a glass of wine while her stepmother sat in front of a tea-tray. She handed Lallie a cup wordlessly.

Mr Grey held his glass to the light as if to admire the rich colour and then sipped it thoughtfully. "I am pleased to inform you, Lallie, that I have received a most flattering offer for your hand."

"For my hand?" she repeated, bewildered. Whatever she had expected, it was not this.

"In marriage," he clarified brusquely, casting his eyes heavenwards as if to complain about her obtuseness. "It is from a gentleman with whom I am well acquainted and who has convinced me of his esteem for you. I have no hesitation in entrusting you, my first-born, to him." He favoured her with a benevolent smile and appeared to await her grateful appreciation of these sentiments.

Lallie stared at him, baffled. She knew very few eligible gentlemen and was not in expectation of an imminent proposal from any of them. There was Mr Hersey, of course, but her father could hardly claim to be 'well-acquainted' with him and why would he need to advise her of such an offer in London? As far as she knew, he had only recently met Captain Malvin and Mr Matthew Malvin. Mr Tamrisk, who had left Berkshire the same day Mr Grey had returned, had signified his intention of calling on them in Sussex; also it was unlikely he had had any opportunity for private conversation with her father. Mr Halworth was too young and had never shown any particular interest in her.

"I am sure you have guessed that I speak of Mr Frederick Malvin," her father continued smoothly.

Frederick Malvin? The very thought made her skin crawl. Aghast, she blurted out, "You must be joking, sir." She swallowed, sickened by the memory of plump, grasping fingers and a stale odour.

"I would never joke about such a matter," he responded loftily. "Do you think you are incapable of attracting such a gentleman? You are too modest, my dear. I assure you my friend Malvin is very taken by you. A charming girl was how he described you to me, a most alluring, unplucked rose. I was very happy to agree to his suit."

This was beyond everything! "You may have agreed, sir, but I have not!"

"As your father, I may speak for you," he returned calmly, "and I have spoken."

"Not on my behalf, sir."

He drew himself up, but before he could say anymore, Mrs Grey intervened. "It is a very advantageous match, Lallie. Remember you will be twenty-five next year. Surely you do not wish to dwindle into an old maid. It's not as though you have any better prospects."

"If I do not, whose fault is that, ma'am?" Lallie rejoined coldly. "It is not too late for me to have a Season."

Mr Grey curled his lip. "At twenty-four, almost twenty-five? Why, you are almost an ape-leader. What a figure of fun you would cut among the girls making their come-out."

"If I am so ineligible, I am more surprised at Mr Malvin's offer," Lallie retorted. "I did not want for partners at Lady Malvin's soirée."

Her step-mother sighed. "It is dangerous to mistake polite-ness for genuine interest, child. At a small private affair such as Lady Malvin's, a good hostess will ensure that there are no wallflowers. Did you not notice that it was chiefly members of her family who asked you to dance? The Season is different."

"Enough!" Mr Grey snapped.

Lallie rose to her feet. "I am sorry to have to disoblige you, sir, but I cannot accept Mr Frederick Malvin's suit. I should be grateful if you would convey my regrets as well as my thanks for his obliging offer."

"You will do as you are told, girl."

Mrs Grey frowned at her husband and addressed her step-daughter. "Don't be foolish, my dear. You will much prefer to have your own establishment, after all, and your own children too. You are so good with Eleanor and Beatrice that I am persuaded you must welcome the prospect of being a mother."

Lallie shuddered convulsively. "Not if *he* is to be the father. I, I find him extremely distasteful, ma'am," she whispered desperately.

"Pah! Maidenly modesty!" Mr Grey dismissed her protest. "These fears are very natural, I suppose, but it were better not to dwell on them. Once you are a married woman you will see things differently." He straightened to his full height and fixed his eyes on his daughter. "You will marry just as soon as Mr Malvin has obtained a licence; tomorrow, or at latest on Monday."

"I will not."

His eyes narrowed at her defiance. "You will do as you are told, girl! Do not dare to set yourself up against me. You will not like the consequences, I assure you."

There was a cruel note to his voice, a more cutting tone than ever she had heard before. Her knees shook and her heart pounded in her breast, but she managed to speak firmly, even boldly. "I assure you that I shall never marry Mr Malvin. My consent is needed and I will refuse it, even at the altar."

He loomed menacingly over her. "And then? Do not think to return to this family if you refuse such an opportunity. By your own action you will have cut yourself off from us. You will leave this inn with nothing but the clothes you have with you, to earn your bread as best you might. Mark my words, you would regret your disobedience within a se'nnight, but by then it would be too late. You would be one of those unfortunate women, reduced to selling over and over again what was once sought honourably in marriage."

He licked his lips. A hectic flush stained his cheeks and he bared his teeth, raising his hand so that despite herself Lallie shrank from the coming blow.

Mrs Grey came up behind her in a precipitous rustle of skirts and jerked her away.

"Husband, I am sure that on reflection Lallie will recognise her error and apologise to you in the morning for her intransigence."

She didn't wait for a response to her conciliatory words but snapped at her stepdaughter, "Go to your room at once!" She tugged Lallie to the door and thrust her out onto the wooden gallery. "Lock your door," she hissed. "Put your trunk up against it."

Lallie shakily made her way past the chamber where her sisters slept with Mrs Grey's maid in attendance to the one she shared with Nancy who opened at once to her sharp knock. She pushed in past her.

"Quick, lock it." She began to drag the trunk away from the wall. "Put this against it."

"Whatever is the matter, Miss Lallie?" Nancy asked as she came to help her.

"You'll never believe it, Nancy," Lallie choked on a sob. "My father has decreed I marry Mr Frederick Malvin tomorrow or on Monday at latest."

"Frederick Malvin?"

"He's the one who forced himself on my notice at church last Sunday. You remember?"

"The greasy bald-pate?" Nancy, who had sat in the gallery of the church with the other servants, asked contemptuously.

"I refused the offer, said I would continue to do so, even at the altar and Mr Grey—Mr Grey replied that he would cast me out from the family if I refused such an opportunity."

"The scurvy scoundrel, to even threaten such a thing. But he wouldn't do it, Miss Lallie."

"I don't know, Nancy." Lallie shivered. "I've never seen him in such a rage. He is usually so coolly collected, but now!"

"You never crossed him before," Nancy pointed out. "'Tis easy enough to be pleasant when you always get your own way. A proper little roost cock on his dunghill, he is."

"I think he would have struck me if Mrs Grey hadn't pushed me out of the room." Lallie shivered again. "I don't envy her having to face him."

When Mrs Grey came into Lallie's room early the next morning, she bore the same signs of a sleepless night that Lallie had seen on her own and Nancy's faces. Her face was drawn and pale and she didn't move with her usual briskness. Her brow was furrowed and her eyes heavy and shadowed as if she had the headache.

"Well? Have you come to your senses?" she demanded sharply.

"If by that you mean will I agree to marry Mr Malvin, no," Lallie answered bluntly.

"Think very carefully before you give your final refusal, Lallie. Your father is determined that the match will go ahead as he agreed. You would be well-advised not to risk his wrath. He does not often lose his temper, but when he does—," she broke off, shivering.

"I'm sorry, ma'am," Lallie said desperately, "but I think I would rather marry any other man in the world."

"Don't be stupid, child. There are many worse than Mr Malvin," Mrs Grey said dryly. "Think about that, my dear. You will have time enough to reflect. You are to remain in your room until your father returns. He has instructed that you are to receive no food until you have sought his forgiveness for your obduracy."

"How petty!" Lallie exclaimed. "Does he think to starve me into submission?"

"A little hunger sharpens the mind," Mrs Grey said thinly. "Here!" She tossed a reticule onto the bed. "You need a new one—I noticed your old one was badly frayed. I'll leave you to your reflections, Lallie. I trust you will make the right choice."

"How very odd," Lallie said when the door had closed behind her stepmother, adding contemptuously, "Does she think that a new reticule will suffice to change my mind?"

"Look, Miss Lallie," Nancy said in hushed tones. She had up-ended the reticule and now held out a diamond and pearl brooch.

"That's Mrs Grey's! It's her favourite—it was her mother's."

"There's twenty guineas here too, and a letter."

Lallie unfolded two sheets of paper with shaking hands. "This says that she makes me a present of the brooch and the money, and the other is a character for Miss L L Staines, who has been governess to her children for five years. She highly recommends her to any future employer."

"You are to stay in your room until Mr Grey returns," Nancy said slowly. "That means,"

"He is not here now," Lallie finished.

The two women looked at each other.

"She is telling me to leave while I can," Lallie concluded. "She knows he will not relent."

"She must feel she can safely give you the brooch because it was not a gift from him," Nancy said, more respect in her voice than she had ever accorded Mrs Grey. "And twenty guineas as well."

"It will make it easier to get away. I have about five pounds and my grandmother's pearls as well as some trinkets."

"I have seven pounds, twelve shillings," Nancy revealed. "That's over thirty pounds—a good beginning."

"You'll need your money for yourself, Nancy," Lallie protested. "I'll give you an excellent character and I am sure you will have no problem finding another position. Nobody is going to employ a governess who has her own maid."

She felt her heart break as she pointed this out. To lose Nancy would be the worst of all.

"If it comes to that, we'll see. But for now I'm going with you," Nancy said placidly. "The first thing is to get you away from London. What about your other grandparents, the Greys? Would it be safe to go to them?"

"I haven't heard from them since I came to live at Alwood, but surely I would have been told if they had died? I don't think they would turn me away. My father has an older brother as well, but I've never met him."

"It sounds as if there was a falling-out between Mr Grey and his parents," Nancy remarked shrewdly. "If so, it's all the better—he won't think to look for you there. Where do they live?"

"In Hampshire, near Basingstoke."

Lallie didn't know whether she was on her head or her heels. It was barely twelve hours since her father issued his ultimatum. How could her life have changed so quickly? And all because of his spite at being thwarted, she thought. He can never have loved me or even cared a little about me.

"As well there as anywhere," Nancy resolved. "We must sort through our belongings; see what we can take with us. The big trunk is too heavy. Then I'll find out about the Basingstoke coach. And I'll fetch some breakfast. No need to heed his wishes."

Three-quarters of an hour later, Nancy softly closed the door to their room and followed her young mistress as she crept silently along the wooden gallery, staying close to the wall so that they were less likely to be seen from below. A hackney coach waited in the yard at the foot of the stairs. They scrambled in, placing their luggage on the rear-facing seat, the jarvey whipped up his horse and they were gone.

# Chapter Seven

*The Rivers in this part of the country are, Inclination River, with its branch Amour; also the Rivers of Benevolence, Respect and Esteem.*

Arriving at the *Bull and Mouth* in a post chaise followed by their own carriage conveying their daughters, maids and valet, the Greys had been met by the landlady, stately in an imposing black silk gown, who had civilly enquired if they would be pleased to alight. On hearing that they required three rooms as well as a private parlour and accommodation for their male servants, a bevy of maids assisted by a flock of porters had been assigned to see to their every comfort.

Two females deposited at the entrance to the *Belle Sauvage* by a hackney coach and burdened by a small trunk, a servant's box and several bandboxes were, Lallie discovered, at best obstacles to be avoided and at worst the subject of uncouth, not to say vulgar, attention. Clutching her bandboxes, she pressed close to Nancy who, shouldering the small trunk she had taken from the girls' room and grasping her wooden box in her other hand, forged her way across the yard to the ticket office.

Lallie was grateful for the illusion of protection afforded by the light veil Nancy had insisted on tacking to her bonnet. Her pearls were well-concealed under her clothing, as were her other trinkets and Mrs Grey's brooch. A horn blared and she shrank back to permit the departure of a laden coach and six. Lallie looked at the passengers clinging to the top and squeezed into the basket and called, "Inside seats only, Nancy; for both of us."

A groom walking a tandem-harnessed glossy pair to a private chariot barked, "Out of the way there, miss!"

Obediently she stepped aside. As the little caravan passed, the hind horse lifted its docked tail and deposited a steaming mound at her feet. She backed away clutching her skirts, only to be admonished to watch where she was going by a rough voice behind her, while at the same time a stable boy armed with shovel and wheelbarrow pushed his way past to remove the malodorous heap. On the far side of the yard, a smart gentleman, tiger up behind, drew his curricle to a halt and a merry young family climbed into their carriage. Her heart ached. Would she ever see her sisters again? She had hurried her goodnights last night, not knowing it would be the last farewell.

"Miss Lallie?" Nancy touched her arm and she turned back. "It don't leave 'til four, but he thinks there is one that leaves *The Swan* at noon. Wouldn't that be better? If we're to wait here, we'll have to take a private parlour. Being so near, it would be one of the first places he would look, so we can't stay in the coffee room."

"Would we be safe, even in a private parlour?" Lallie asked miserably. "He would only have to say he was my father and they would show him up with a smile."

"Pray excuse me."

They both jumped at the sound of the cultivated male voice, but did not otherwise respond.

"Forgive me, I did not mean to alarm you," the gentleman behind them added contritely.

Nancy turned her head slightly. "Sir?" she asked in forbidding tones.

"Is there any way I can be of service to your mistress?"

Afraid she had conjured up his kind voice, Lallie stole a glance from beneath the brim of her bonnet. Tears stung the back of her throat when she saw Mr Tamrisk standing before her, hat in hand. She longed to throw herself into his arms, arms she was sure would open to receive her, but managed to reply steadily, "Thank you, sir, but we are in no need of assistance."

"Are you sure?" he asked gently. "This is no place for you, my dear. Will you at least let me escort you to the coffee room where you may wait while I purchase your tickets?"

Lallie shook her head. "Thank you sir, but it is not necessary. We shall manage very well. However, I should be most obliged if you would forget you had seen us here."

His concerned smile vanished. "What's this? Surely not an elopement? Permit me to tell you, ma'am, that it is a poor lover who requires his inamorata to make her own arrangements."

"It is nothing of the sort," Lallie hissed, blushing furiously at this acerbic remark.

"The opposite, more like," Nancy said grimly.

Mr Tamrisk raised his brows incredulously. "Are you running away?"

"Sssh!" Lallie looked around nervously before answering curtly, "I am an adult woman and may go where I please."

He took her hand. "If you are in trouble, I beg you will permit me to help you. I assure you of my utmost discretion."

Lallie fought the temptation to cling to him. She could see nothing but genuine concern in his dark eyes. Perhaps it would help to talk things over with someone else. "We cannot stay here," she began haltingly. "The risk is too great."

"Then allow me to take you to my home. There we can talk undisturbed."

It was very improper, but they would be safe with him, she knew. "Very well, sir."

"My curricle is just over there." He bent to pick up the trunk.

She looked at him, appalled. "But it's an open carriage."

He didn't argue. "I'll find a hack."

What the devil was going on? Delayed by a hack that had pulled up at the *Belle Sauvage*, Hugo had been stunned to recognize its passengers as Miss Grey and a maid and even more shocked to see both women burdened with luggage. He watched the maid count out a few coins before they disappeared beneath the stone arch. Determined to find out what was happening, he had waited impatiently until a large coach had departed before he could turn his pair into the yard, on tenterhooks until he caught sight of her again. Thank God she had agreed to come with him. Now she sat opposite him, her eyes closed. She had put back her veil and her exhausted pallor suggested she had not slept.

At Tamarisk House, he jumped out and flipped a guinea to the Jehu.

"You weren't here," he said briefly and the man raised his whip in acknowledgement before climbing down from the box to unload the luggage.

"Send Phipps to me in the library," Hugo instructed his butler and continued to the book-lined room where he settled Miss Grey in an armchair beside the fire.

"Sit down, Nancy," he said over his shoulder.

"Thank you, sir." The maid retreated to a chair by the wall where she sat primly upright.

He smiled comfortingly at his guest. "My housekeeper will show you to a bedroom. Ring once you have refreshed yourself and she will bring you to my mother's parlour. You may rest there while we talk."

"Thank you, sir. You are very kind."

When the two women had been led upstairs, Hugo rang for the butler. He needed a clear head. "Bring me some coffee—and we have had no visitors this morning. I am not at home to anyone until I say otherwise."

He went to sit in the chair Miss Grey had just vacated. It smelt of her, he thought sentimentally, a unique mixture of flowers and lemon-peel. He turned his head against the high back, luxuriously drawing in the fresh fragrance. How pleasant it was to know she was in his home. But what had brought her here? What could have impelled her to leave her family so intemperately? The opposite of an elopement, Nancy had said. If she wasn't running away with some rogue, it looked damn likely that she was running from one. Where were her parents in all this? Two days previously, she had been safe in Berkshire. There had been no hint of another man then, let alone a betrothal. What could have happened so quickly? Why was she afraid of being discovered?

He brooded over his coffee until the housekeeper returned.

"The young lady is in the parlour now, sir. I've brought her some chocolate."

Now he would get some answers.


That chaise-longue had been his mother's favourite place in the house. He had never seen her there; she had been dead for years before he had set foot in the London house, but those who knew her told him how she had loved to lie there looking down into the garden. When he had had the house redecorated on coming to London, he had refused to change this room. It pleased him somehow to see Miss Grey in her place.

At his entrance, she put her cup down on the table beside her and said, "Thank you, sir. I feel much more the thing. I am not usually such a poor honey, I assure you."

"I never thought you were, Miss Grey," he replied swiftly, pulling up a chair to sit beside her. "You have clearly had a severe shock. Will you tell me about it?"

"Your father can't have been serious," Hugo objected when Miss Grey had come to the end of her tale. "People say these things in anger, but they don't really mean them, do they? I'm sure he came to his senses over night."

"I hoped he would too, but when my stepmother came in this morning, she was adamant he would not relent."

"I had not realised that Mrs Grey was your stepmother," he said, surprised.

"My mother died when I was born. I was brought up by her parents, and my dear Nancy, of course." She smiled fondly at the maid who again sat by the wall near the door. "My grandparents are both dead now—when Grandmamma died six years ago, I came to live with my father. Well, really with Mrs Grey and the children," she amended. "My father spends most of his time in London, or at any rate not at home."

That threw a different light on things, Hugo realised. If Grey was a distant parent and his wife had had his adult daughter foisted on her, he might choose to accept any offer that took the girl off their hands.

"You think to appeal to his parents?"

She nodded. "I have not heard from them since I moved to Sussex, but I hope they will give me temporary shelter at least, while I consider how to go on."

"It was the brooch, sir, that decided us," Nancy said from across the room. She came over and unpinned something from the inside of Miss Grey's spencer.

"A handsome piece," Hugo acknowledged, turning it so that the pearls and diamonds gleamed in the autumn sun.

"Mrs Grey would never have given it to me if she had not considered the circumstances truly dire. It belonged to her mother."

He glanced up. "She gave it to you just recently?"

"This morning, with twenty guineas and a character I might use if I wished to seek employment as a governess."

"What did she say when she gave you this gift?"

"Nothing. She just said that I needed a new reticule and threw one onto my bed. Everything was in it."

"What she said and what she did were at odds with one another, sir," Nancy put in. "If he asks her, she may repeat word for word what she said to Miss Lallie and it will seem as if she was trying to convince her to do his bidding. But she let us know that he had left the inn and after she had tossed down the reticule, she said, 'I trust you'll make the right choice'. A nod is as good as a wink, as they say."

"She did what she could," Miss Grey commented.

"So it would seem," Hugo agreed.

Miss Grey looked at the clock. It was past noon. "The coach leaves at four. Mr Tamrisk, would you be so obliging as to send someone to purchase two inside seats for us? I don't wish to leave it too late in case they are sold out. And he must be discreet, in case anyone is enquiring about us."

Hugo drew a breath. Now for it!

"Miss Grey, I cannot like the idea of your travelling by public coach, even with Nancy by your side. I should be happy to put my carriage at your disposal, but what if your grandparents are from home or unable or even unwilling to come to your aid? It is some years since you have heard from them and they are not young. Would you permit me to escort you to them?"

She sat up at this, her eyes wide. "It is most kind of you, sir, but I could not so impose on you."

"It would be no imposition, I assure you, and it would spare me some sleepless nights worrying about you." Did she blush a little at this? Heartened, he continued, "I would also be able to be of further assistance, should it become necessary. Sir Howard lives near Basingstoke, you said? We could be there by evening."

The most beautiful smile shaped her lips. "Mr Tamrisk, I should be forever grateful to you."

He shook his head. "You honour me with your trust, Miss Grey."

Mr Tamrisk's elegant travelling chariot accommodated two passengers with additional provision for two servants in the rumble behind. At first it felt strange to Lallie to be shut in a closed carriage with a gentleman but with her precipitous flight she had already shown her disregard for the conventions of polite society and she could hardly expect Mr Tamrisk to perch beside his valet while she and Nancy travelled in comfort within. This hurdle taken, she resolved to strike a sisterly note with him.

"What a handsome carriage! I especially like the colours— maroon, silver and that dusty pink that reminds me of a damask rose in my grandmother's garden."

"We call it tamarisk, Miss Grey. They are the colours of our livery."

"Tamarisk. Is that where your name comes from?"

"Yes. According to family lore, Geoffroi de Tamm, who accompanied the Lionheart on crusade, plucked a sprig of tamarisk and attached it to his surcoat before riding into battle. Afterwards he was known as Geoffroi du Thamarisque."

"How romantic!" she exclaimed. "And you are descended from him?"

"Yes. Since then the title has descended in an unbroken line from father to son."

"You must be very proud of such a lineage."

He shrugged. "To be frank, Miss Grey, to be heir to such a tradition is as much a burden as a source of pride. It is the be-all and end-all of my father's existence and if he had his way, it would be mine as well."

"You wish to be your own man?"

"Yes. While it's important to cherish and learn from the past, we must also value the present and look to the future. Once the war is over, and it cannot be long now, there is much to be done. Take the franchise—it must be extended and reformed." He smiled ruefully. "Now there is an example of where my father and I don't agree. As far as he is concerned, the Magna Carta went quite far enough and there is no need for a House of Commons. But let us talk of happier things. This travelling chariot is an old friend who has been to Naples and back with me," he said whimsically.

"Tell me about your travels," she said. "I recall your mention of the Coliseum. Were there other places that reached across time to you—Pompeii, for example?"

"Yes, but not Pompeii. I found it sad, tragic, fascinating—but dead; a husk of its former self. There is no sense of the present there, no continuum. Rome still lives."

"Perhaps I could obtain a position with some foreign family. I believe English governesses are greatly in demand in Germany, or at least they were before Napoleon made travel so difficult."

"Both in Germany and Austria I heard great praise of an order of nuns known as the English Ladies who have founded schools for girls there. But I suppose Protestants are unable to join them." This sober statement was belied by the teasing glint in his eye.

"I don't think I would like to be a nun but I like the idea of a sisterhood. One would not be so alone. A governess is something betwixt and between in a household, not family but not quite a servant either. I hadn't thought of seeking a position in a school." She smiled at him. "Thanks to you and Mrs Grey, sir, I have the opportunity to consider my situation more calmly. Last night

I could hardly think for dread of the day ahead. But I am free of them now, Mr Grey and Mr Malvin, I mean. I was afraid he would bring him to press his suit. He is very persistent—if Lord Malvin had not rescued me after church last Sunday—I was so mortified and I think he liked it that I was ill-at-ease."

Her shoulders had drooped and she spoke disjointedly, almost muttering to herself. Hugo resisted the temptation to take her hand. He must not impose on her in any way while she was under his protection. Her slight hesitation before she climbed into his carriage had not escaped his notice, but he had thought it best to ignore it and behave as if she were, say, his niece Arabella. He turned his head away to give her a chance to compose herself.

He had had to bite his tongue when she prattled on about the merits of teaching over governessing. 'Sisterhood', for heaven's sake. But now was not the time to press his suit although his mind was made up—he had known that from the moment he approached her at the inn.

She had fallen silent, those enchanting eyes were closed. The blare from the yard of tin as they turned into the *Bush* at Staines made her jump and gaze bewildered at her surroundings.

"We must change horses here," Hugo said soothingly, leaning across her to lower the blinds. "May I have them bring you something—some lemonade, perhaps?"

"Nothing, thank you, sir." She fumbled at the brim of her bonnet and drew down her veil.

"We won't stop for very long. Excuse me while I instruct the groom about the horses."

When Hugo returned to the carriage he handed Miss Grey a small glass. "It is ratafia—it will help you feel more the thing,"

She smiled her thanks and sipped obediently at the red-brown liquid.

"Are you warm enough, Miss Grey?"

"A little cold, perhaps," she acknowledged.

He removed a soft rug from a compartment and spread it over her lap. "We'll stop to dine about four. Your grandparents probably keep country hours."

"You are so thoughtful, Mr Tamrisk! They will very likely be thrown into a dither by our arrival. I don't wish to discommode them unduly." She finished the cordial and he passed the glass back through the window to a waiting servant.

"Let them go!" he called to the groom who immediately released the horses' heads. The postilions rose in their stirrups and soon they had clattered out of the yard and were rolling along the turnpike.

"Try and rest for the next stage or so, Miss Grey," Hugo suggested. "I'll wager you didn't sleep very well last night."

"No," she admitted.

"You might be more comfortable without your bonnet," he recommended cautiously. "The brim seems to be in your way."

"It is," she agreed, untying the ribbons. She lifted the hat from her head, then, sighing, leant back against the squabs and tugged the rug up to her chin before slipping her hands beneath it like a tired child.

"Good night, Miss Grey."

She murmured an almost inaudible response, turned her head into the corner of the seat and within a few minutes he could tell by her deeper, more even breathing that she slept. The tension that had gripped him since he first caught sight of her that morning eased and he stretched out his legs, curiously content that she had accepted his help, trusted him to protect her.

The carriage lurched into a turn and was suddenly flooded by sunlight that, dimmed by the linen blinds, washed the interior with a golden glow. It was like a benediction, he thought. Lulled by the steady pace set by the postilions, he let his mind drift. How often had he travelled this road, on to Salisbury, Exeter and from there to Tamm? He couldn't say, but knew that he had rarely had company on the tedious journey. A painful hope seized him. *If she accepts me, I'll never be alone again.*

"Miss Grey?"

Lallie felt a gentle touch on her shoulder.

"Miss Grey, we shall soon reach the *White Hart* at Blackwater."

A gentleman's voice. She was in a carriage; the four o'clock coach from the *Belle Sauvage*? But where was Nancy?

"Miss Grey." The voice was more insistent and somehow familiar. Mr Tamrisk's, she suddenly recognised. She was in his private chariot. She felt her cheeks grow hot. How could she have slept in his company? He had urged her to rest, she remembered.

"Miss Grey!"

Lallie blinked and opened her eyes. He sat beside her, half turned towards her, his stern features softened by an unusually warm smile.

"You are awake," he said briskly. "We shall dine here—they keep a very good table." He bent and picked up her bonnet from the floor. "You will wish to don this, I think."

She sat up with a gasp, her hands flying instinctively to her hair. She caught it up, fishing for loose hairpins and jamming them in. It would hold. Goodness knew what she looked like, but the bonnet would hide it. It was only after she had tied the ribbons in their usual jaunty bow that she ventured to meet her companion's eyes.

"You look charming," he said. "I am always impressed by the way females can put themselves to rights so quickly and without a mirror. I have even seen my niece re-tie her sash behind her back."

"We start practising very young," she told him with a smile. "If you can re-tie a ribbon or a sash, you might save yourself a scolding for being untidy."

He laughed. "Was your Nancy such a stern nurse?"

"Not at all. She used other methods, saying 'only babies can't tie bows, Miss Lallie', and of course I was determined to show her that I was not a baby."

The carriage came to a halt. Mr Tamrisk's valet opened the door while beside him Nancy waited.

The landlady was all smiles and curtsies. "Mr Tamrisk, sir, how pleasant to see you again. Do you care to dine, sir?"

"We do, Mrs Crump. A private parlour, if you please, but first show my cousin and her maid to a separate room."

She curtseyed again. "Certainly, sir. This way, ma'am. I'll have warm water sent up directly."

She led them up a flight of stairs to an airy bedchamber with pretty blue-sprigged white curtains and, more importantly, a close-stool behind a screen.

Lallie quickly removed her gloves and pelisse and went to avail herself of this convenience.

"Why did he say I was his cousin?" she asked Nancy afterwards as she washed her hands and face at the basin. The cool water revived her a little.

"I suppose he wanted to make clear you're not his bit of muslin," Nancy replied dryly.

"Oh! I hadn't thought of that. I suppose this is all very improper, but it doesn't feel so. He is so very gentleman-like, isn't he?"

Nancy nodded. "It was lucky for us that he spied us this morning."

"And was kind enough to come to our aid. We might only be leaving London now."

"Or scrambling for a bite to eat in some coffee-room with the coachmen and all the riff-raff." Nancy handed Lallie a towel. "Come and sit down, so that I can tidy your hair. It looks as if you've been pulled through a bush backwards."

"How much further have we to go, Mr Tamrisk?" Lallie enquired. The creamy watercress soup had eased the knot in her stomach and she had allowed him to serve her some trout stewed with fresh mushrooms.

He looked up from his plate of mutton-pie. "It is fifteen miles to Basing, so say an hour and a half to two hours to reach there. According to *Cary's Itinerary*, your grandfather's seat is about a mile south-west of it. We should be there between six and seven o'clock, all going well."

"You are going to a great deal of trouble on my behalf, not to mention the considerable expense you are incurring," she said hesitantly. Before she could say any more he held up his hand.

"Miss Grey, we have not fallen out up to now but if you offer to reimburse me, I fear we shall. I am honoured to be permitted to stand your friend."

"Yes, but—"

He cut across her protest. "Would you not help a friend if you could?"

"Yes, of course I would. But you must at least permit me to thank you, sir."

"Only once." The severe look that accompanied this grudging consent made her chuckle.

"Very well, Mr Tamrisk, I shall wait to express my heartfelt gratitude until I bid you farewell."

"You're cheating," he challenged her.

"Certainly not," she retorted indignantly. "I merely acknowledged your condition that I may only thank you once, otherwise I would have said—" Her eyes brimmed with amusement and he laughed as he interrupted, saying,

"Miss Grey, I see you are a quibbling casuist. But be warned; I am not to be fooled and I shall exact a forfeit for each transgression."

# Chapter Eight

*That part of the country in the immediate vicinity of the Lake of Affection is truly charming; the climate serene and mild.*

Lallie swallowed convulsively as the carriage turned into the approach to Sir Howard Grey's home. "I hope they will receive me."

"I am sure they will," Mr Tamrisk said comfortingly.

They rounded a bend to see a long house some two stories in height, made of a faded pink brick that seemed to bask in the fading rays of the sun. Candle-light gleamed through leaded window panes and as they approached, the front door swung open invitingly. A butler flanked by two footmen descended the shallow flight of steps.

"We are welcome, it seems," Mr Tamrisk remarked.

Willis jumped down before the horses came to a halt. He murmured something to the butler who at once sent one footman indoors and waved the second to the carriage door before coming forward himself to bow as Mr Tamrisk alighted and handed Lallie down.

"Welcome sir, welcome, Miss Grey. If you would be pleased to come with me?"

He led them into an oak-panelled hall where Lallie had eyes only for the frail lady wearing a lace cap and a pretty shawl thrown over her stooped shoulders, who stood beside a white-haired gentleman leaning on a cane.

"Miss Grey and Mr Tamrisk," the butler announced.

The lady hurried forward. "Is it indeed you, Lalage? Oh, my dearest girl, to see you again after all these years!"

She held out her arms and Lallie walked into them, carefully closing her own arms around her grandmother who felt as slight as a little bird. She tried to speak but couldn't. Her eyes were misted and her throat full of tears. She gulped and tried again. "Grandmother, I hope you will forgive this intrusion."

The old man snorted and limped forward to embrace her. "Intrusion? Nonsense! You must know you are always welcome here. But why are we standing in the hall? Come into the parlour."

"Just come up to my room first, my dear, and remove your outer garments," Lady Grey amended this invitation. "They'll have rooms ready for you in a trice, but you will like to tidy yourself, I'm sure."

Gently but firmly, she tugged Lallie towards the stairs, pausing only to look back and say, "Of course you will spend the night with us, will you not, Mr Tamrisk?"

"The night? You must remain until Monday, sir. You will not wish to travel on the Sabbath-day," Sir Howard instructed his guest. "Elcott here will see to the carriage and your luggage."

"I should be very happy to, Sir Howard but pray excuse me while I have a word with the post-boys," Hugo said hastily. He had forgotten that tomorrow was Sunday. How gratifying to have unimpeachable grounds to remain with the Greys for at least two nights.

"Of course, of course. Then you must take a glass of wine with me while the ladies are primping. I took the opportunity of the peace ten years ago to replenish my cellars and have an excellent Chambertin that is now at its peak."

"So you're Tamm's son," Sir Howard said when they were ensconced in a cosy parlour. "How does his lordship? I haven't seen him these many years. He and I came up to Oxford together; not that we were cronies, you understand. He was too conscious of his importance as the future twenty-fifth Baron to associate with anyone below the noblemen-commoners."

"In that respect he has hardly changed, sir," Hugo said wryly. "His health has declined sadly in recent years and he rarely leaves his rooms."

"I hope I am spared that fate. Better a quick, clean end than a lingering one, but that decision is in the hands of Providence." Sir Howard shook his head at the unhappy thought, but then perked up and raised his glass. "Your good health, Mr Tamrisk."

"And yours, sir." Hugo savoured first the rich aroma and then the complex flavours. "A fine wine indeed," he said respectfully.

Sir Howard drank again. "A bottle tastes better when you share it with a *connoisseur*. My lady takes a glass to oblige me, for I detest drinking alone, but is not the same."

"I am happy to be of service, Sir Howard. You may call on me at any time."

The old man returned Hugo's companionable smile. It was only after he had poured the second glass that he remarked, "I hope you did not find today's travel too arduous. Did you set out from London?"

"Yes sir, shortly after one o'clock. We stopped to dine at the *White Hart* in Blackwater and came on here."

"Tell me, Mr Tamrisk, how did you come to accompany my granddaughter?"

Sir Howard spoke mildly, but a steely glint in his eye revealed that this was no idle question.

"I had the pleasure of making Miss Grey's acquaintance some two weeks ago when she and her family were staying with Mrs Grey's uncle, Admiral Sir Jeremiah Halworth in Berkshire and all were invited by my sister, Lady Malvin to a soirée at Malvin Abbey."

Sir Howard frowned for a moment. "Halworth? Oh yes, Ursula's mother's brother."

Better to make my intentions clear from the beginning, Hugo thought, and continued smoothly. "We met subsequently at various entertainments in the neighbourhood and I came to hold Miss Grey in the highest esteem. As a result, before leaving Malvin Abbey, I asked Mrs Grey if I might call on her family when next in Sussex. Mr Grey had already left Berkshire by then, but Mrs Grey gave her permission."

Sir Howard nodded approvingly. "All very proper."

Hugo looked him in the eye. "You may imagine my concern, Sir Howard when, about half-past nine this morning, I saw Miss Grey and her maid alight from a hack and disappear into the yard of one of the largest and busiest posting inns in London. They were on foot and carried their luggage."

The old man frowned. "What the devil were they about?"

"My thoughts exactly, sir. I immediately turned into the yard. They were waiting at the booking office and I went to see if I might be of assistance. It became clear that Miss Grey was both distressed and fearful of discovery. When I promised her my assistance and assured her of my discretion, she agreed to come to my home where we could talk privately."

"What did she tell you?"

"In a nutshell, her father sought to compel her to marry one of his intimates on pain of being cast out onto the world should she refuse. But I think you had better hear the full story from her own lips. She thought to seek refuge with you but could not be sure you would receive her as she had not heard from you since she went to live with her father's family."

"My wife wrote to her in Sussex, but she never replied," Sir Howard said remorsefully. "We should have persevered."

Hugo continued his explanations. "As you may imagine, I was not happy with the idea of her travelling by public coach. I considered putting my carriage at her disposal, but was not prepared to risk her finding you from home and the house shut up. In the end, I thought it best to accompany her."

"I am greatly in your debt, Mr Tamrisk. When I think of what might have happened—" Sir Howard broke off, shaking his head. "That reprobate of a son of mine! He will have nothing to do with us since I refused to pay his gambling debts."

"He must have come about, sir, for he lives quite expensively—and chiefly apart from his family, by what I have observed."

The door opened to admit the ladies and the gentlemen rose.

"Come and sit here, my dear," Lady Grey patted the sofa beside her. "Here is Elcott with the tea-tray." She waited until the butler had left the room before saying, "Sir Howard, Lalage has been telling me a little of her story, but I said you would wish to hear the whole." She handed her granddaughter a cup and saucer. "Now, my dear, have your tea and begin when you are ready."

Lallie sipped her tea resignedly. Would this day never end? Grandmother had not seemed to understand that a daughter might not accept her father's choice of husband although she had frowned at Mr Grey's threat to turn her out.

From across the room, Mr Tamrisk caught her eye and smiled encouragingly. I have one friend, she thought. Reassured, she took a deep breath and began.

Her grandfather interrupted her after a few minutes. "Who is this Frederick Malvin?"

"He is an acquaintance of my father's—they are about the same age, I think. He was staying with Lord and Lady Malvin, but I do not know the relationship."

"He is second cousin to Lord Malvin," Mr Tamrisk intervened. "His grandfather was brother to the first viscount. He's a man about town who tends to live by his wits and is more tolerated than welcomed by my brother-in-law. His recent appearance at Malvin Abbey was unexpected and undesired."

Lallie was just about to resume her narrative when Mr Tamrisk spoke again.

"If I may speak candidly, Lord Malvin does not consider his cousin a suitable *parti* for a young lady. He disapproved strongly of his interest in Miss Grey, going so far as to call him from her side last Sunday when my sister realised that his overly assiduous attentions were making Miss Grey most uncomfortable."

Despite Lallie's embarrassment at this plain-speaking, she was also grateful as it supported her decision to refuse the proposed match. Seeing her grandmother nod understandingly, she could not help smiling at Mr Tamrisk as he continued.

"I don't know if my brother-in-law subsequently spoke to his cousin, but he left Berkshire the next day."

"As did my father," Lallie realised. "Their plot must have been hatched by then. Mr Grey said Mr Malvin was very taken by me." She made a face. "Apparently he considers me 'a most alluring, unplucked rose'."

"The saucy rascal," her grandfather snarled while Mr Tamrisk bristled like an angry dog.

Lady Grey patted her hand consolingly. "It's over now. Go on with your story, my dear. What happened when you rejected Mr Malvin's suit?"

"It wasn't a suit, was it, ma'am? They never intended to give me a choice."

"And so I decided to accept Mr Tamrisk's kind offer to convey me here," Lallie finished.

"We are eternally grateful to you, Mr Tamrisk," Lady Grey declared, "and only sorry that it should have been necessary, although we are of course delighted to have dear Lalage with us," she concluded her rather muddled sentence. "Your home is with us now, of course, Lalage, but we can discuss everything else tomorrow. You must be weary after such a night and day. But you are safe now."

"I pressed it last night, Miss Lallie," Nancy said the next morning as she held out Lallie's pelisse. "There's no ironing done here on the Lord's Day, I was told, nor any other work that is not absolutely necessary. It's only since her ladyship turned seventy that they drive to church. Everyone else walks."

This was confirmed by Lady Grey when they met in the hall. "You and Mr Tamrisk will accompany us in the carriage now but once you have met your uncle and his family, you will have their company as far as the heir's house, and from there you may simply walk through the park."

Lallie was puzzled. "The heir's house?"

"The Grey men tend to be hot-tempered and some three generations ago the then Lady Grey decided that the only way to keep the peace was for the heir and his family to live separately, so she had a handsome new house built across the park. It also serves as a dower house."

They were met at the church by a robust, ruddy-faced man of about fifty, his thin, discontented-looking wife and their three children who came forward at once to greet their grandparents.

"Such a surprise for you, my dears," Lady Grey said. "Here is your cousin Lalage come to stay with us. Lalage, meet your Uncle and Aunt Grey and Howard, Maria and David."

Mr Grey's eyes narrowed. "You must be Louisa's daughter. You have her eyes." He looked wistful. "And to think that you are older now than she was when she perished. How cruel life can be!"

"There is no need to be so mawkish about something that occurred, what, twenty-five years ago?" his wife interjected. "I understand Miss Grey never knew her mother and so cannot mourn her."

Taken aback both by the lady's lack of sensibility and her dagger-looks, Lallie answered quietly, "It is true I cannot mourn her as one whom I knew and loved dearly, but the lack of a mother must always be felt, despite the best endeavours of others to replace her."

"Time to go in," Sir Howard announced and offered his arm to his wife.

The others lined up behind them in what seemed to be a customary ritual. Lallie and Mr Tamrisk fell in after the children, the servants coming last and remaining at the back of the church.

As she took her place in the Grey pew, Lallie could hardly believe that it was just a week since Mr Frederick Malvin had so embarrassed her in Longcroft church. How could her life have changed so utterly in so short a time? And yet, the week that had begun and ended catastrophically, had also been filled with new delights. There had been the visit of the Malvins and Mr Tamrisk to Longcroft Manor, then Lady Nugent's fête and finally the day Mr Tamrisk called to take his leave. I never thought I would see him again so soon, and in such circumstances. What must he think of the Greys now?

The walk back to the heir's house was equally regimented; the only light relief afforded by the children who could not restrain their curiosity about their new cousin. They were even more intrigued to learn that she had a brother and two sisters who were much nearer to them in age and demanded to know why they never came to visit. As Lallie had no answer to this pertinent question, she was relieved when the inquisition was cut short by a sharp admonishment from their mother to stop plaguing their cousin with questions.

"You will come and see us, won't you?" the children begged when the little group separated. Her new aunt supported this request, but so coolly that it was more an expression of forced courtesy than a desire to see her again.

"What do you say to strolling up to that gazebo, Miss Grey?" Mr Tamrisk indicated an airy, structure that crowned a low rise some three-quarters of a mile away. "I need to shake out the fidgets after all our sitting yesterday."

"Oh, so do I!"

They set off at a brisk pace, arms swinging. The air was wonderfully invigorating, with a fresh tang that spoke of the final turning away from summer, no matter how seductively the sun might yet shine. The gazebo was little more than a round floor and roof separated by eight slender pillars. Two curved seats had been fitted on either side, leaving openings front and back that served as entrances. Sloping fields and slanting lanes led the eye to a succession of rolling hills clad in faded greens, russets and browns. Here the church steeple pierced the sky, there a snug farm snoozed beside a band of trees in Sunday idleness and beyond, in the distance, the meandering silver band of a stream gleamed in front of a bank of willows.

Now was her chance. They may not be undisturbed again before he left. Lallie clasped her hands at her waist to steady herself. "Mr Tamrisk?"

Her companion, who stood at the opposite side of the gazebo admiring the pastoral scene, swung around at once. "Yes, Miss Grey?"

"I want to thank you now for your help yesterday. When you leave tomorrow we shall hardly be private, and I must express my deep appreciation of all you did for me. I don't know what good angel caused you to be at the *Belle Sauvage* at just that moment or inspired you to come to my aid, but I am so grateful to you."

"It was nothing, Miss Grey. I am happy that I could assist you."

"It was a very great thing, sir," she countered gravely. "Your concern for me meant that I could make the journey free of worry and anxiety. In addition, your support yesterday evening convinced my grandmother that my apprehension about Mr Malvin was justified. At first she simply couldn't grasp why I would not obey my father. 'He will know what is best for you,' she said, although why she should be so sure of that when it is ten years and more since she has seen him, I don't know."

"She didn't think, I suppose. Old people are inclined to cling to the watchwords of the past. Are you happy to remain here?"

"Yes. It will not be very different to my previous life, I suppose, at least as long as my grandparents still live. I am used to country life and I am sure I can make myself useful."

"I'm sure you will. You are capable of anything, I think." He took a step towards her. "Miss Grey, I had already come to hold you in the highest esteem, but I must tell you that the grace and courage with which you confronted an appalling situation have made me admire you all the more."

A smile trembled on her lips. She had been afraid his opinion of her would be diminished by the events of the previous days.

"I didn't feel very brave, Mr Tamrisk, I assure you," she said ruefully. "It was a question of 'needs must'. And I had Nancy, who insisted on coming with me although I am sure she could easily obtain a new position."

"She is a stalwart auxiliary," he agreed, coming closer. He seemed very serious, his features as intent as she had ever seen them.

"It is only a few days since I sought your stepmother's permission to call when next I visited Sussex." He smiled faintly. "I must confess that I had every intention of doing so before returning to Tamm. But fate has intervened and, who knows, perhaps the good angel who led me to you yesterday had another, ulterior motive. I hope so. Lalage, my dear Lallie, will you marry me?"

She felt the blood drain from her cheeks. Her heart quivered in her breast and she stumbled back, plumping down on the wooden seat to stare dumbly at him.

In two strides he was beside her. "Forgive me, I didn't mean to distress you."

She shook her head. "It was just—I hadn't expected—you caught me unawares." She shook her head again, annoyed at these stammers. A mysterious lightness lifted her spirits and she smiled joyously. "You didn't distress me, sir, on the contrary. You honour me with your offer."

He dropped to one knee, his face lit by a hopeful smile and held out his hands. "Lallie, will you be my wife and Mistress of Tamm; the mother, God willing, of my children?"

"With all my heart, sir." She placed her hands in his.

"Hugo," he said, "My name is Hugo."

"Then, with all my heart, Hugo."

He stood, pulling her to her feet, then released her hands so he could take her into his arms. She smiled up at him and he feathered gentle kisses across her cheek and the corner of her mouth, before his lips tenderly met hers. As their pressure increased, she responded instinctively, her mouth moving against his. He gathered her closer to him and his tongue—his tongue!—moved along the seam of her lips and probed between them, demanding entrance.

Lallie gasped and pulled away. He didn't seem to take offence, but smiled down at her and touched her cheek, murmuring something that sounded like 'not here' and 'too fast'.

"We should go down to the house and tell your grandparents before anyone mentions that they have seen us silhouetted against the sky."

Lallie blushed. "What would my grandmother say?"

He grinned and kissed her again, quickly. "Your grandfather would probably call for his horsewhip."

For once, she was happy to link arms with a gentleman. Without noticing, they fell into step, adopting a languid rhythm that had their shoulders and thighs brushing as they went. Not two, but one, Lallie thought. Mr—no, Hugo—must have felt it too, for he tightened his arm to bring her closer to his side and with his free hand covered hers resting on his arm. Strange how something that had been so repulsive when Mr Malvin did it now felt so right.

"We must make plans," he said eagerly. "Would you object to marrying sooner rather than later? You would then be completely protected from your father. Also, Parliament is to meet on the fourth of November and I should like to present you to my own father before the new session starts."

Lallie was flattered by this haste. Perhaps he was moving a little fast, but he had many responsibilities. She felt a little prickle of excitement. It would be her duty to support him. She would be Mrs Tamrisk, wife of an MP, and the future Lady Tamm. Whole new worlds suddenly opened up before her. This was what Grandmamma had hoped for me, she thought. And what would I do in the meantime if I insist on a delay?

"In the circumstances, a long betrothal might be impractical," she conceded. "What do you suggest?"

"I must obtain a special licence in any event as the chapel at Tamm Manor is not a parish church and it is usual for us to marry there." He laughed. "I'm told that my parents' wedding was the first after the passing of Hardwicke's marriage act and if the then chaplain had not thought of procuring a licence, it could have led to later difficulties regarding the validity of the marriage. My father still gets so irate at the thought of having to seek Cantuar's permission to marry beneath his own roof that he is at risk of suffering another apoplexy. Like your grandmother, he has not moved with the times, although she is apparently willing to listen to another opinion."

Her prospective father-in-law did not sound like the most pleasant of gentlemen, Lallie thought but she simply remarked practically, "Mr Malvin also wished to procure a special licence. Will they not think it odd if you apply for another one for the same bride?"

He looked startled. "Heaven alone knows! As soon as I reach London, I'll go directly to Doctors' Commons. Perhaps it would be a wise precaution for you to give me a letter in which you confirm your intention to marry me and none other."

"I'll write it this afternoon," she agreed. "Hugo, what if my father comes to hear of your request?"

"I see no reason why he should—as you rightly pointed out yesterday, you are of age and may make your own decisions. But if he does and seeks to make difficulties, rest assured that I shall deal with him."

He spoke grimly and she said hesitantly, "I am sorry to cause you so much trouble."

He stopped and turned to face her. "Firstly, if there is trouble, it will not be of your making and secondly, I should welcome the opportunity to furnish Mr Grey with my opinion of him. I shall not seek him out, however, as long as he leaves you in peace. He has thrown away whatever entitlement he may have had to your regard and respect and, as far as I am concerned, he may read the notices of our marriage along with everyone else."

"That is probably for the best," she answered, relieved. "I should like to write to Mrs Grey and return her brooch but I suppose it is wiser to wait until we are married."

"It will be easy to send a messenger from London once we have removed there in November."

"It must be done discreetly." she added anxiously. "Is there someone you can trust to make sure Mr Grey is not at home before he approaches her?"

He nodded. "I'll send Hobbs, my head groom. He is most reliable."

# Chapter Nine

*The Settlement Isles lie to the east of the Great Ocean before the Bay of Delight.*

On Tuesday afternoon Hugo followed Sir Howard into Lady Grey's parlour where, having greeted his hostess, he pressed a kiss on Lallie's cheek and sank onto the settee beside her.

"Fortune favours the bold," he said lightly and laid a roll of parchment in her lap.

She spread it open at once to display an impressive document embellished with a large seal. "This permits," she tilted it to catch the light, "'the Honourable Hugo Geoffrey Tamrisk a Bachelor and Miss Lalage Louisa Grey a Spinster daughter of Robert Samuel Grey Esq' to marry 'at any time and in any church or chapel or other meet and convenient place'. Did you encounter any difficulties in obtaining it, sir?"

"No, none. I am acquainted with Sir John Nicholls, the Master of the Faculties, from Parliament. Although we do not always agree politically, he made no bones about approving my request, especially as there was the precedent of my parents' marriage. He also informed me that Mr Malvin's application had been rejected on the grounds that a simple licence would permit the marriage without the calling of banns in the church of the parish where either of the parties resided."

Lallie sighed with relief.

"Well done, my boy," Sir Howard said. "How do you propose to proceed?"

'My boy'? Hugo was tempted to ask where was the child. He was a Member of Parliament, for God's sake, not some young cub just down from Oxford. But then he noticed the old man's kind smile. He means it affectionately, he realised, as if you were a son or nephew. He doesn't seek to denigrate your efforts or put you down.

"Mr Tamrisk?" Lady Grey prompted him.

"Proceed?" he repeated blankly. "Why, take Lallie to Tamm and marry her, of course."

There was another pause. Beside him Lallie had caught her breath and now was biting her lip as if trying not to laugh, her eyes dancing with amusement.

"I'm afraid my grandmother has been making plans while you were away," she said apologetically.

"Our granddaughter cannot arrive at her new home in a harum-scarum fashion," Lady Grey informed him. "This is a marriage, not an elopement. I can imagine what Lord Tamm would have to say if you were to present to him a bride who arrived without a proper escort and with not much more than the clothes she stood up in."

Hugo closed his eyes briefly at the horrific vision conjured up by this trenchant statement and yielded gratefully to a higher authority. "You are quite right, ma'am."

"In addition, you will wish to ensure that all is prepared for your wife," Lady Grey continued.

His heart sank. If they had to wait for the necessary refurbishments, it would be at least six months before they could wed. "Perhaps Lallie would prefer to decide for herself what changes she wishes to make," he suggested hopefully.

His betrothed looked a little apprehensive but nodded firmly. "That would be best, I think."

He smiled gratefully at her. "When can you be ready, Lallie?"

"We thought I could wait to purchase most of my bride-clothes until we are in town in November, but Grandmother has kindly commissioned her mantua-maker to make some gowns for me now so that I won't disgrace you when I arrive. She will bring them on Monday and do the final fittings here."

"My elder son and his wife will accompany Lallie to Tamm Manor," Sir Howard announced decisively. "He will act in my stead, give the bride away and also agree the settlements."

"Of course, sir. I had hoped to discuss them with you before I leave," Hugo said.

Lallie looked from one to the other. "Settlements?"

"To make financial arrangements for you and your children," her grandfather explained. "You must have pin-money. In addition, Mr Tamrisk must make provision for you, should you be left a widow, and for your younger children who will not be covered by any entail. It is vital that it be done before you are married, for once you are wed all your property becomes your husband's."

"But I don't have any property," Lallie objected.

"That can't be right," Lady Grey contradicted her. "When your parents were married, the settlements provided that your mother's fortune would pass to her children in the event of her death. It wasn't very much, two thousand pounds, I think, but as you were her only child, it must all have come to you. And I imagine you were Lady Anna's heiress as well. Do you recall the name of her man of business?"

"Mr Lambe, in Truro," Lallie replied. "But he never said anything about money when Grandmamma died."

"It was probably held in trust for you as you were still a minor."

"You must write and request him to call on you at Tamm Manor," Hugo declared, more than puzzled by this turn of events and silently thinking that Mr Robert Grey had probably appropriated whatever monies were due to his daughter when she came of age. No need to hint at that, he said to himself, we'll find out in due course. And why was her other grandmother suddenly referred to as Lady Anna?

"You may leave it all in your uncle's hands," Sir Howard told his granddaughter.

She shook her head. "I am sorry, Grandfather, but I am of age and, with all due respect to my uncle, would prefer to be informed about my affairs."

"I am sure Mr Grey will be willing to advise you if necessary," Hugo said diplomatically. "Do you think you would be ready to leave this day week? That would allow for three days comfortable travel and I'll arrange for Mr Lambe to call on the Saturday following."

"What about your sisters?" Lallie asked, as she and Hugo strolled in the garden before dinner. "Do you propose to invite them to the wedding?"

"I hadn't thought about it. Should I?"

"I think so. I have already met Lady Malvin and their presence would make it all seem more normal somehow."

"I suppose it would. Arthur could be my best man and it would give me the opportunity to have a word with my brother-in-law about his cousin's machinations."

"We don't know to what extent they were his machinations," Lallie pointed out fairly. "Perhaps my father told him I was agreeable to the match."

"Hmm. Why then press for an immediate wedding? There's something smoky there, I'm convinced of it."

"Look!" Lallie stooped to inspect a cluster of late-blossoming roses. "It's the autumn damask, the same pink as in your livery." She inhaled deeply. "I had forgotten how beautiful they smell."

He bent and broke off three, stripped them of their thorns and handed them to her with an ornate bow and a lurking smile. "Will you wear my colours, fair lady?"

She responded with a matching curtsey. "I should be honoured, good sir." She opened the top buttons of her pelisse and slotted the flowers through a button-hole. "Are there some at Tamm?"

"I'm not sure."

"Then I shall ask my grandmother for some cuttings to take with me."

She wore her pelisse over her dinner gown and Hugo's eyes were drawn to the little hollow at the base of her throat that was now revealed. He felt in his pocket and handed her a jeweller's box.

"For me?"

"To mark our betrothal."

"Thank you, Hugo." She opened it carefully and stared at the exquisite cross made out of five faceted peridots. It hung from an intricately wrought gold chain. "Oh, what beautiful gems!"

"They match your eyes."

His compliment made her look deliciously flustered and she rose on her toes to press a shy kiss on his cheek. "Thank you," she said again and then turned her back to him. "Will you put it on for me?"

He carefully slipped it round her neck beneath the collar of the pelisse. She bowed her head to give him access and when he had fastened the clasp, he could not resist brushing her delicate nape with his lips. She shivered and looked back at him, wide-eyed.

"Let me see," he commanded.

She spread open the high collar to display the cross glowing against her creamy skin while the petals of the dusty pink roses brushed it below.

Hugo swallowed. "It suits you," he said huskily

"I cannot wait to see it. You are very kind to think of me."

"It is my pleasure and my privilege."

He had answered almost mechanically as he fought the temptation to peel her out of the close-fitting garment. You must go slowly, he admonished himself; she is so innocent, not like Sabina who was well-versed in the ways of love-making. He wrenched his thoughts away from this involuntary comparison which somehow seemed disloyal to both women and deliberately changed the subject.

"I'll travel by post-chaise to Tamm and leave the chariot here for you and Nancy. My groom Hobbs will ride beside it and see to your comfort at the inns along the way. If you require anything, you need only mention it to him." He smiled at her. "Your grandmother is quite right; I must ensure that your apartments are ready for you, or at least as ready as I can make them. You will see that there is much to be done."

By leaving at daybreak on Thursday and making another short night of it, Hugo was able to reach Tamm Manor by Friday afternoon. He hurried through the hall, saying as he went, "My compliments to his lordship and if he will give me half an hour's grace, I shall join him for dinner," and took the stairs two at a time. He had stripped off his clothes by the time Willis arrived with hot water and sat impatiently to be shaved.

"Not a word to anyone about Miss Grey until I have told my father," he warned the valet. "I must wait until we are rid of Stiles."

Lord Tamm grunted a brusque greeting and demanded to know what his son had been doing since he saw him last. Hugo was able to divert him with anecdotes of his visit to Malvin Abbey until the meal was over when, instead of leaving with the chaplain so that his father could be returned to his withdrawing room in private, he said, "Will you take another glass of port with me, sir? I have some welcome news for you."

The old man brightened at once. "Never tell me you have chosen a bride!" he exclaimed.

Hugo laughed. "That's just what I have done."

He nudged his father's glass nearer to his hand and raised his own. "Pray drink with me to Miss Lalage Grey."

"Grey? Gray?" Lord Tamm muttered after he had complied with this request. "There are so many of them. To which family does she belong?"

"I believe you are acquainted with her grandfather, Sir Howard Grey," Hugo answered calmly.

"Of Hampshire?"

Hugo nodded. "Her father is his younger son."

"Hmm. It is not a great match, but tolerable, I suppose. Who was her mother?"

"Louisa Staines, daughter of Lady Anna Martyn and William Staines."

"Martyn? A daughter of Martinborough, you mean?"

"Yes. The present Marquis is Lady Anna's brother."

His father frowned. "Was she the chit who ran off with her brother's tutor? Old Martinborough cut her off completely, I remember. No one ever heard of her again."

"Yes."

Lord Tamm slapped his good hand onto the table. "And you think to bring her granddaughter into this family? I might have known you'd make a botch of it, Tamrisk!"

Hugo stiffened. "Lady Anna was a devoted wife and more mother than grandmother to Miss Grey, whose own mother died at her birth. I expect you to speak of her with respect and to welcome Miss Grey as my bride and the new mistress of this house. I am adamant in this, sir."

"There is no need to mount your high horse," his lordship snapped. "What of the Martinboroughs? Do they recognise the girl?"

"I doubt it as they ignored all Lady Anna's pleas for reconciliation. In any event, Miss Grey has no intention of thrusting herself upon their notice."

"Proud, is she? Humph! She may be as aloof as she likes elsewhere as long as you're master in your own home! When is the wedding to be?"

"In about ten days' time," Hugo answered, relieved to have successfully negotiated these shoals. "I do not wish to wait until Christmas and am anxious to present Miss Grey to you before I return to town for the opening of Parliament," he continued smoothly. "She will arrive here next Friday, escorted by Sir Howard's heir, who will act on his father's behalf. I have written to my sisters and hope that they and their families will be here to meet her."

"You have it all in hand, I see," his father said. "Very well. My felicitations, Tamrisk," he added curtly. "Ring for the footmen; I wish to retire."

Lady Grey's comment about the need to prepare for his bride rang dismally in Hugo's ears as he left the saloon. He was only too well aware of the manor's shortcomings. It was sadly old-fashioned, his father having steadfastly responded to his wife's suggestions of redecoration and modernisation with, 'we'll see when you have given me an heir, my Lady'. By the time she had succeeded in meeting this demand, his mother had been too worn down to consider any undertaking other than having new hangings and carpets made for her own apartments and even these, now almost thirty years old, could not at the time of purchase have been considered to be in the first stare.

"Morton, I wish to see Carey, Mrs Morton and you in the library immediately."

Within five minutes there was a tap at the door and the three filed in, clearly curious about the reason for this unprecedented summons.

Hugo smiled reassuringly. "I wish to inform you that Tamm will soon have a new mistress. Miss Lalage Grey has consented to be my wife."

After a short pause and exchange of glances. Carey, the steward, cleared his throat. "On behalf of the staff may I extend our congratulations, sir and our warmest good wishes on this auspicious occasion."

The housekeeper and butler joined in with a chorus of, "Wish you happy, sir."

"Thank you. Miss Grey will arrive here next Friday and the wedding will take place at the beginning of the following week. I hope that my sisters and their families will attend."

Mrs Morton's beaming smile faded. Her horrified look was mirrored on her husband's face.

"Next week, sir?" she repeated faintly.

"I am relying on all of you to ensure that everything is ready to receive Miss Grey," Hugo told them, shamelessly transferring the burden.

"I'll do my very best, sir," the housekeeper said, "but I must have extra help."

The butler bowed. "As will I, sir."

"I'm sure everyone on the estate will be proud to help with the preparations for Mr Tamrisk's bride," Carey said. "I'll ride out first thing and pass the word."

Mrs Morton squared her shoulders. "Just send them to me, Mr Carey. In the meantime Morton and I will put our heads together."

Hugo smiled at her. "I knew you wouldn't let me down."

"Of course we won't, Mr Tamrisk, sir," she promised him. "But I'm warning you, things'll be uncomfortable over the coming days. There'll be no avoiding it."

She departed to marshal her forces for an arduous campaign of beating and shaking of carpets and hangings, dusting, mopping and waxing of floors and panels, burnishing of metals and polishing of windows so that the house gleamed as never before. Under her vigilant eye, every piece of porcelain and glassware was removed, washed and replaced while her husband reviewed the contents of the cellars and ensured the silver was buffed to a mirror-like shine. The walled garden and glasshouses would have been pillaged to supply countless vases had the gardener not made a passionate appeal to Hugo, complaining that no flowers would be left for the bride and, in addition, his domain would be barren when the new mistress came to inspect it. Grumbling, Mrs Morton agreed to restrain her decorative impulses.

To Hugo's surprise, this was the only discordant note. He kept out of the way as much as possible, riding out in the mornings with Jenkinson, his land agent, and was touched by the sincere good wishes expressed by everyone he met, one old dame blatantly prophesying, "We'll be ringing the bells for an heir next year, sir."

"We must do something for the tenants," Hugo said as they rode back, "but not next week. It will be too much for the staff, and also for Miss Grey, I think."

"I must make the most of these days with you, my dear," Lady Grey announced two days before Lallie was to leave for Devon. "At least you will be passing this way quite frequently on your way to and from town. I hope that your husband will often agree to break the journey here. We thoroughly approve of the match, Lalage. He has behaved impeccably throughout and did the right thing without any prompting at all, although your grandfather was prepared to speak to him."

Lallie looked up from the fine lawn chemise she was hemming. "The right thing?"

"In making you an offer," Lady Grey said. "Imagine if it were to become known that you had spent the better part of Saturday alone with him. I don't know which was more improper—to be in his house or in his private carriage."

"But no one knew, and when we stopped to dine, he said I was his cousin," Lallie protested.

"Which only shows that he was aware of the niceties of the situation," her grandmother said triumphantly. "You are most fortunate and I trust you will be a good wife to him."

Lallie didn't know why this admonition dampened her spirits; it wasn't as if she intended to be a bad wife, after all.

"I've been thinking a lot about my mother these past few days," she said. "Will you tell me about her and my father? How did they meet? Grandmamma never really talked about it—perhaps I was still too young, but now I want to know more."

"That is only natural," Lady Grey said. "Let me see, now. Your grandfather and I had taken a house in Bath that summer, for we had both suffered grievously from *la grippe* in the early part of the year and were still sadly pulled down. Peter and Robert decided to join us, for Bath was much more fashionable then than it is today. It was Mr King who introduced us to Mr and Mrs Staines and their daughter in the Lower Assembly Rooms one evening." She smiled wryly. "In fact it was your uncle who first took an interest in Miss Staines, to our great pleasure, for he was already five and twenty and it was time he thought of marriage. But then—I have never known whether it was to spite his brother or if he genuinely fell in love—Robert began to court her. He can be most charming as you probably know, my dear, and soon out-romeo'd Romeo. Peter stepped back once he realised that her interest was fixed on Robert, who within two months had sought and won her hand.

"She never behaved in any way that was not completely proper," Lady Grey assured Louisa's daughter. "She was a very prettily-behaved girl, who had been sheltered all her life, for she was not very strong. In fact it was on her behalf that the family had come to Bath. We were happy to give our approval, for we thought the responsibility of a wife and family would steady Robert, who was free of the burden of duty the heir bears, and inclined to lead a fashionable life.

"Well, my love, you know how sadly it turned out. They went to Italy on their wedding journey and by the time they returned, dear Louisa was *enceinte* and in quite a poor way. So much so, in fact, that instead of setting up house on their own in London, as they had originally intended, she went to stay with her parents so that her mother might care for her until the baby came. When matters reached their tragic end, it was decided you should remain with the Staines."

Lallie listened in silence to this melancholy tale. "Thank you, ma'am." She hesitated, then continued, "Now that I am to be married, I was especially anxious to know the circumstances of my mother's passing."

"I do not know the details, but I can certainly tell you that she did not enjoy good health, even before she was married." Lady Grey leaned closer to Lallie to confide, "She was used to suffer terribly each month—you understand me, my dear. It was hoped that this would improve once she was married and had borne a child, but it was not to be." She scrutinised her granddaughter. "I should not refine too much on your mother's end. You seem to be in much better health, Lalage and do not suffer in the way she did, do you?"

"No, or no more than seems usual."

"It is a woman's lot, I am afraid," her grandmother agreed. She moved to sit beside Lallie on the settee. "I think, my dear, it is time I spoke to you of the duties of a wife."

When the Malvins arrived on Wednesday, Hugo swallowed his pride and sought Clarissa's advice on making his bride's apartments more attractive.

"I see what you mean," she remarked as she looked around the rooms set aside for the heir's wife. "These have probably not been redecorated since our grandmother's day. I like the tulip design on those armchairs—the pink and green is quite cheerful against the cream. But otherwise, the whole effect is very dark. And it is so bare. Miss Grey is young, after all."

"She will be free to make any changes she likes but that will take time."

"Of course, it will be different when she has her own things here—books, her music, little ornaments—trifles like that," she explained impatiently in response to his enquiring look.

He shook his head. "She'll have very little."

"What do you mean?" she asked sharply.

"Where's Tony? I might as well explain to both of you at once, especially as it concerns him too."

Lord Malvin strolled in from the saloon. "Did I hear my name? I must say, Hugo, the place has never looked so well."

"Mrs Morton has worked wonders," Hugo agreed. "Sit down. I must talk to you about your cousin."


"I tell you this in confidence, of course, but also because I wish you to be prepared for any remarks Frederick Malvin may make to you," Hugo concluded. "I don't propose to do anything unless he forces my hand—as Lallie points out, we don't know how complicit he was in the whole thing—but I should like to be confident of your support if necessary."

"You have it," Lord Malvin declared. "If he wishes to remain on terms with me, he'll behave himself."

"About Lallie's apartments, Hugo; have you looked in Mamma's rooms?" Clarissa asked. "She will have brought her favourite things down when she moved there. There should be some little tables and pretty things to put on them; some books too, although nothing will be new."

"I'll look through my own shelves," he said at once. Why hadn't he thought of this himself?

"Welcome, Miss Grey, welcome sir, madam." The inn-keeper bowed obsequiously. "We are indeed honoured. All has been prepared as Mr Tamrisk stipulated."

"Hobbs said that a private parlour has been reserved each evening and a dinner ordered," Nancy said as she helped Lallie remove her carriage dress. "The landlady will bring up the bill of fare in a moment and you are to say if you wish to make any changes. And I am to request anything I think might add to your comfort."

"Such consideration." Lallie was touched. Hugo had gone to so much trouble on her behalf.

Despite this thoughtfulness, the arduous journey left her weary to her bones. It was hard to fall asleep in a strange bed and, unable to shake off the rocking motion of the carriage, she slept fitfully, her rest disturbed by the stamping of horses and the rattle of coaches, the sound of the post horn and the ostlers' cries of "horses on". When they arrived at the next inn the following evening, Nancy ordered her to remain in her bedchamber rather than joining her uncle and his family for dinner.

"I'll have them send up a tray, Miss Lallie. But first you'll have a bath. You'll want to look your best tomorrow, when you arrive at your new home."

Lallie sank thankfully into an armchair. "I own I would like some time to myself tonight. My bones had been shaken up so thoroughly that I imagine an anatomist would be puzzled to identify my skeleton as that of a woman and not some strange being."

Nancy gave a final whisk to the mixture in the little saucepan and poured it into a pretty blue and white posset cup. "Now, Miss Lallie, you enjoy that and then into bed with you."

"Thank you, Nancy."

Lallie inhaled the aroma of warm cream and eggs beaten together with sweet sack and sprinkled with nutmeg. Nancy always made it for her when she was unwell or to ease her monthly cramps. She frowned, remembering the shock of her first flow.

'You're a young lady now, my love, able to bear a child,' Grandmamma had explained. This was even more frightening but she had soon become accustomed to the changes in her body. Now she would have to let her husband know when she was indisposed, or so Lady Grey had said when she told her what her marital duties would be. If the menses did not come one month, it would be the first sign that she was with child. But for that to happen, she had to come together with her husband.

'It will be a little unpleasant at first, but that will soon pass if your husband is considerate, as I am sure Mr Tamrisk will be,' Lady Grey had said. 'But remember, Lallie, while you must permit him whatever liberties he wishes to take, it does not do to get too fond or too ardent, for what might delight a gentleman in his mistress could disgust him in his wife.' At Lallie's surprised look she had said a little awkwardly, 'there's no point in closing one's eyes to these matters, my dear. It is well known that among the highest levels of society, and you are marrying into them after all, marriages are made more for family convenience than for pleasure, which gentlemen tend to seek elsewhere.'

It seemed strange to think that another person would have such rights over her body. She had said this to Nancy, who had answered robustly, ''Tis only what's natural, Miss Lallie and if there is no pleasure in it, why are so many girls ruined or go to the altar with a big belly? That's what I want to know.'

But ladies weren't ruined. Maybe it was different for them, as Grandmother had implied.

Shortly before two o'clock the next day they drew up at the *Globe* for the final change of horses. A tall gentleman in a caped greatcoat was at the chariot door even before the team was unharnessed. Lallie's heart leaped when she saw him. Now it would be 'all right', as the coachmen said. Hugo didn't release her hand when she stepped down from the carriage, but stood smiling at her before he bent and ducked his head beneath the brim of her bonnet to kiss her cheek.

"Welcome, my dear Lallie. I thought you might like to travel the last stretch in the curricle."

"That would be wonderful. You cannot imagine how tired I am of being shut in," she said honestly.

"It is a tedious journey, is it not? I hope Hobbs has looked after you."

"Oh yes, he was most attentive and it was all so well organised. Thank you."

"I'll just go and explain to your uncle and then we may be off."

He lifted her to her seat, carefully tucking a rug around her. A maid came running with two hot bricks wrapped in flannel and Hugo stooped to place them under Lallie's feet. She felt his hand on her ankle for a moment. It was strange to view his dark head from above; she could see the trimmed hair below his hat neatly outlining the base of his skull and suddenly remembered how he had kissed her neck when he had fastened the chain of the peridot cross. She shivered and he looked up, concerned.

"Are you cold?"

"No, not at all."

# Chapter Ten

*The chief Rivers are Envy and Spleen; the former is well known for the bitterness of its water—the latter falls into the Lake of Contempt.*

Hugo inwardly wished all the interested onlookers to the devil as he gathered up the reins and led the way out of the yard. She was here at last. He smiled happily at her, the previous, chaotic week forgotten.

"It's about another hour. We go inland, now. Tamm lies between Dartmoor and the sea."

"Which do you prefer?"

"I love the freedom of the moor. And you?"

"The sea," she confessed. "I could watch the play of light and water all day."

"Do you paint?"

"Not well enough to capture a scene to my satisfaction, but I can never give up the attempt."

He glanced down at her. "You must give our moors and rivers a chance. I'll hope to convert you next week when we go to my shooting box near Ashburton. It won't be much of a wedding journey, but at least we'll be private. One can have too much of one's family."

She laughed. "I take it your sisters came."

"All of them and their husbands and their children."

"My uncle and aunt have brought their children as well, and their governess."

Hugo looked over his shoulder at the cavalcade of carriages following them. "I'm told there hasn't been such excitement at Tamm since my parents' marriage more than fifty years ago."

He dropped his hands and the horses moved into a fast trot. For Lallie, who had never travelled in a curricle before, it was both exciting and alarming to bowl along, perched precariously over the two large wheels, with the wind rushing past her face. She tied the bow of her bonnet more firmly and prayed that she would not be covered in dust by the time they arrived. But soon they left the turnpike for country lanes and Hugo had to reduce his speed.

"What strange, reddish-orange beasts," Lallie remarked.

"They're our own south Devon breed—one of our three Cs: cattle, cider and cream."

The interest in their procession increased, with little clusters of people waiting at gates or crossroads to bow and curtsey as they passed.

"They are eager to see you," Hugo explained.

Lallie had not imagined there would be so much interest in her arrival. "I hope I don't disappoint them."

He patted her hand. "Impossible! I've lost count of the number of people who have said, ''Tis 'oigh toime Tamm 'ad a mistress, zur'."

She smiled at his rustic burr and waved to the children while he called greetings to the adults.

Soon they turned past a bowing gatekeeper and his family to drive through the park. They rounded another bend and there the house stood foursquare, arms akimbo as if to say 'who dares challenge me?'

Lallie hardly had time to consider it before they pulled up. A soberly clad man descended the steps, followed by footmen in the maroon, silver and tamarisk livery that Hugo had described only two weeks previously.

"Welcome to your new home, Lallie," he murmured as he lifted her down from the curricle. "I hope you will be happy here."

She smiled up at him. "Thank you, Hugo. I'm sure I will."

He urged her up the stone steps into a vast, dark hall where a formal welcoming party waited. Lallie passed down the line, exchanging bows and curtsies as well as dutifully brushing cheeks with her sisters-in-law to be.

"May I show you to your bedchamber, Miss Grey?" Lady Malvin enquired as soon as Mr and Mrs Grey had also run this gauntlet. "You will wish to refresh yourself before Hugo presents you to his father."

"Thank you, ma'am. You are very kind."

Lallie followed Lady Malvin up two flights of the stairs to a large bedchamber redolent with beeswax and lavender. Her ladyship glanced around disapprovingly at the dark furniture and heavy hangings. "I hope you will not be too uncomfortable. Everything is so old-fashioned here."

Unsure how to reply—to agree would be to insult Hugo's home and to demur would be to contradict his sister, Lallie chose to admire the bowl of Guernsey lilies on a table in front of the window. "What a wonderful, flame-like colour!"

She turned with relief when a small side door opened to admit Nancy followed by footmen bearing the imperials from the top of the chariot.

"Is this your maid?" Lady Malvin enquired.

"Yes. Allow me to present Nancy Anderson, who was first my dear nurse and has been a loving support to me all my life. This is Lady Malvin, Nancy, who is Mr Tamrisk's eldest sister."

Nancy returned her ladyship's curious gaze, curtseying gravely. "My lady."

"Tell the footmen if you need anything, Miss Grey. Tamrisk will come to escort you to Lord Tamm's apartments in half an hour."

"Half an hour!" Nancy exclaimed when she had shut the door behind her ladyship. "We'd best make haste then, Miss Lallie. It's just as well I pressed the green and white stripe last night. It's at the top of the trunk and should not be creased. Better make yourself comfortable, first."

When Lallie returned from behind the screen Nancy had poured warm water into the bowl. "You've time for a cat's lick and a promise, that's all, and then sit here so I can tidy your hair."

Lallie hastily removed her gown and went to the wash-stand. It felt good to wash the dust from her face, knowing she had reached her journey's end.

Nancy deftly brushed out the black curls, threaded a green ribbon through them and pinned them on the top of her charge's head.

"You'll do for now. Here's the other petticoat. That one is too heavy for this gown."

Once the petticoats were changed, she helped Lallie into her gown, fastening the internal strips of fabric that supported her bosom and closing the front of the bodice over them before she tied the tapes that shaped the skirt. She had just buttoned the bib-front when Hugo tapped on the door.

Lallie shook her skirts into place and took the peridot cross out of its little case while Nancy went to admit him. "She's just ready sir." She quickly fastened the gold chain. "Best take a shawl, Miss Lallie."

"A good idea," he commented, taking it from her to drape it around Lallie's shoulders. "The house is not very warm."

He guided her down the stairs to a large room at the end of the hall. "My father's apartments are through here," he said and extended his hand as formally as if they were about to dance the minuet.

This was not very home-like, Lallie thought as she rested her bare hand on his. Without gloves, it felt very intimate.

"Ready?" His fingers turned for a moment to grip hers reassuringly.

For a moment she let her fingers cling to his then she put her shoulders back, lifted her head and smiled. "Yes."

Footmen sprang to open the doors to a dim inner chamber where panelled walls were hung with old-fashioned portraits framed with gilt that glinted dully in the fire-light. It was impossible to determine the precise colour of the curtains—something muddy that might once have been green or reddish-brown, Lallie thought, or perhaps even the Tamrisk pink. The room smelled stale as if it had not been properly aired for decades. A few uncomfortable looking chairs were set against the walls but evidently no-one had been invited to sit and their assembled relatives stood awkwardly in a wide semi-circle.

They moved apart to permit the betrothed couple to approach the old man enthroned in a high-backed chair beside the fire. His right hand gripped the carved arm while his left rested on the furred lap robe that concealed his lower limbs. His sharp nose seemed too large for his pale, thin face and a droop to his features reminded Lallie that Hugo's father had suffered two apoplectic fits. Clad in an opulent banyan of grey-blue velvet, with costly lace at his throat and wrists and wearing an ornate velvet negligé cap embroidered in russet and gold, he suggested nothing more than a faded oriental potentate among the remnants of his court.

Hugo led her forward and bowed. "Sir, I have the honour to present my betrothed, Miss Grey."

Lallie curtseyed more deeply than usual and rose gracefully. "Miss Grey, welcome."

"Thank you, my lord."

Lord Tamm inclined his head slightly and clicked his fingers. A footman hurriedly opened a pair of scissor spectacles and placed it in his raised hand. With its aid, he scrutinised his future daughter-in-law.

"Hmph! You appear to have good, child-bearing hips at any rate. Now that Tamrisk has finally agreed to do his duty and marry, it is to be hoped that we see an heir within the twelvemonth."

Lallie felt her face grow hot. Was this crudeness what she had to expect in her new home?

"My lord!" Lady Malvin protested.

"My lord!" Her father mimicked her. "We must trust that Hugo's bride has a better sense of her duty than your fool of a mother had."

Lady Malvin paled. Her husband immediately moved closer to her while Lallie wished the ground would open and swallow her.

Hugo's face might have been hewn from marble. "I will thank you to moderate your language, sir."

Lord Tamm flushed with temper but he caught his son's stern eye and said no more.

He's like a child, Lallie thought; he has spoken without thinking and knows he has overstepped the mark. But what a thing to say! And in public! She glanced hesitantly at Hugo. He smiled apologetically at her but addressed Mrs Grey.

"I trust you did not find the journey too wearing, ma'am."

"Not at all, Mr Tamrisk."

"Your man Hobbs was an excellent *cicerone*," Lallie's uncle, who had ridden a considerable amount of the way, offered.

"He knows the road well," Hugo agreed.

When a discussion of the sights between Hampshire and Tamm became more general, Hugo murmured to Lallie, "Come and look at the portraits. This is the best of them."

He led her away from the others to a striking portrait of a middle-aged man astride a fine bay horse. The rider stared confidently into the room, one hand on his hip and the other firmly on the reins.

"It's by Rembrandt," Hugo said. "I don't know where he found the funds to pay for it, for he had joined the King in exile, but it is the one thing the then Lord Tamm brought back to England at the restoration."

"It's magnificent," Lallie said. "He has a look of you, I think."

"Sharp-nosed and beetle-browed?" Hugo asked, grinning.

She smiled back, "If you insist, but I was thinking as much of the set of his head on his shoulders."

He laughed and moved on to the depiction of a gentleman whose forbidding countenance was framed by the curls of a full-bottomed wig. "My grandfather; I never knew him," he explained briefly.

Behind them Lord Malvin and Mr Grey had picked up the burden of conversation and soon Lallie felt recovered enough to re-join the group. When Lord Tamm enquired stiffly about the health of her grandparents, she was able to make a civil reply and after some twenty minutes of stilted conversation, his lordship dismissed his visitors, "except for you, Tamrisk."

"I'll walk out with Miss Grey first and return in a moment, sir," Hugo answered.

At the door to the hall, he kissed Lallie's cheek. "I don't know how long this will take, but the others will look after you and I'll see you before dinner."

She looked up at him. He seemed harassed. "Don't worry about me, Hugo," she said impulsively. "I'll do excellently, I'm sure."

His expression lightened. "I do not doubt it."

Lady Malvin led the company to a large, rectangular room above the one that linked the apartments of the Lord and his Lady.

Here, the old-fashioned chairs and sofas were placed in congenial groups and more portraits peered down from the walls.

"Please sit, Miss Grey," Lady Malvin invited, indicating the chair beside her. She gestured towards the heavy oak doors set in each of the side walls. "These are the apartments of the heir and his wife; they mirror those below. You will remove here when you return from your wedding journey, but my sister, Mrs Forbes, and her husband occupy Mrs Tamrisk's apartments at present. It would not be fitting for you to be just across the saloon from Tamrisk before you are wed."

Lallie was surprised by such a separation of husband and wife. 'Your husband will come to you,' her grandmother had said, but she hadn't understood that it could have been meant so literally—and over such a distance, not discreetly from adjacent rooms or just across a landing. It made it all so—so deliberate, even purposeful, like a stallion being brought to a mare. She frowned, struck by a sudden image of Lord Tamm, flanked by a candelabrum-bearing footman, pacing in state across the rooms that separated his and his wife's bedchambers. Would Hugo come to her like that? And would everyone know when he did?

"Are you cold, my dear Lallie? I may call you that, for we are to be sisters, are we not?"

She blinked and looked at Lady Malvin.

"And I am Clarissa," her ladyship continued. "Remember you may call on Hugo's sisters for advice or assistance at any time."

"Yes, indeed," Hugo's younger sister chimed in. "I am Amabel and this is Henrietta," she gestured towards the youngest, a lady in her mid-thirties. Her husband was Mr Forbes, Lallie recalled.

"Will you take a glass of madeira, Miss Grey?" Captain Malvin enquired, "or do you prefer orange wine?"

"Please call me Lallie—and I should like some orange wine." She badly felt the need of a restorative. Her aunt caught her eye and smiled sympathetically.

"Where are the children?" Lallie asked.

"They're in the old nursery with the others," Henrietta said. "You will meet Amabel's and mine tomorrow."

Lord Malvin grinned. "And young Tony. He insisted on coming to the wedding—said it had been so jolly playing with Miss Lallie at Larchwood."

"We dine at six o'clock today," Lady Malvin informed the Greys. "Usually Tamm keeps earlier hours, but we were not sure when you would arrive. We meet here at a quarter to the hour and then join him in the dining-room."

As Lallie discovered later, this required a ceremonious descent, two by two, from the upper saloon to the lower one, each couple, on entering the room, making a formal reverence to his lordship, who was already installed at the head of the table. To her great relief, she was not placed beside him at dinner, but sat at Hugo's right at the opposite end.

Overawed by the occasion and uneasily aware of a strange tension that thrummed beneath the polite dinner-table conversation, she responded briefly to his initial overtures but by the time she had finished her soup and enjoyed the breast of pheasant he had carved for her and served with celery stewed in cream, she was feeling more at ease.

"Will you take wine with me?" he asked.

"With pleasure, sir," she replied quietly and he signalled to the footman to fill their glasses. In silence they raised them, bowed to one another and drank.

"I feel I should apologise for such a wretched welcome." Hugo glanced up the table to where his father sat glowering, making little or no effort to respond to his neighbours' attempts at conversation. "Believe me, Lallie, I cannot sufficiently express my pleasure in seeing you here in my home, to know that it will soon be your home too." He looked deeply into her eyes as he said this, causing her to blush and give him the first real smile since his father's crass remarks. "You may find it strange at first, but I'm sure you will soon make your own of it."

"How long has it been without a mistress?" she asked curiously. There was certainly little evidence of the presence of a lady of the house in the rooms she had seen.

"It will be twenty years in December. I lost my mother not long after my tenth birthday."

"Did one of your sisters not take her place?"

"Clarissa had married several years previously and Henrietta, who is four years older than I, went to live with her. Amabel married Bynge three months later." He spoke calmly, but his expression was curiously blank.

Lallie looked at him appalled. "One might say you lost them all at once."

"Yes." His fingers tightened on the stem of his glass and she gently touched his hand in silent sympathy. "So you see there is much to be done here. But not yet."

"Of course not, Tamrisk," Lady Malvin interrupted from his other side. "Your bride must first be introduced to society."

"We shall be in town for the opening of Parliament," Hugo informed her.

Clarissa spoke briskly to Lallie, across her brother. "Excellent. I shall accompany Malvin in November so you will not want for company. Hugo mentioned that you wish to visit the *modistes*. I shall be delighted to introduce you."

"And I," Henrietta volunteered cheerfully.

The table was now cleared and the second course brought in. Lallie toyed with some crisply fried fillets of sole in a lemon sauce as Clarissa returned to the fray.

"You must be presented on your marriage. It will have to be the Birthday drawing-room, I suppose."

Hugo's fork rang on his plate. "The first drawing-room after we return in spring will be soon enough. I see no reason to make a special journey to town just to attend an earlier one, should the Queen decide to hold it."

"Is that a plate of white peach tarts I see?" Captain Malvin interrupted. "Send them down here. You must try them, Lallie; they're a speciality of Tamm."

The pale tarts, filled with an exquisite peach preserve, were indeed delicious.

"I believe it's due to the peaches," Hugo told Lallie when she commented on them. "There is an old tree trained in a sunny corner of the garden. The fruit is not very good to eat, but Mrs Morton makes this preserve each summer. Would you like another?"

She laughed and shook her head.

Clarissa caught her eye and rose. "We shall leave you gentlemen to your port. They won't be long," she told Lallie as they mounted the stairs. "My father takes a glass still, but that is all. Once he has finished it, Hugo will bring the others back up here so that Tamm can retire. He cannot walk more than a few steps and does not wish to be observed shuffling, as he puts it. His valet and footman will help him to his room once all are gone."

When the gentlemen joined the ladies, Mr Forbes went directly to an old harpsichord and was soon tracing a maze of variations on an intricate theme. They seemed to lead the mind inwards, inviting it to follow along the winding paths and distance itself from the cares of the day. As she listened, Lallie felt her entire body ease and relax so that her head fell forward and her eyes closed involuntarily. Embarrassed, she bolted upright, but only Hugo seemed to have noticed her lapse.

"Why don't you retire, Lallie," he murmured. "Everyone will understand."

"Are you sure your sisters won't mind?"

"Why should they? Come, I'll escort you to your room."

Lady Malvin looked up in surprise when he lit a branch of candles.

"I trust you are not deserting us so early, Tamrisk? Surely you can spend one evening with your bride?"

Lallie was astonished at her exasperated, almost acerbic tone.

"I beg your pardon, Clarissa, but Lallie is exhausted. I wish to see her to her room, but shall of course return to enjoy your delightful company."

The cutting politeness of Hugo's reply was worse than any insult, or so it seemed to his betrothed, who had never before seen him look so arrogant, but none of the others seemed to make anything of it. She felt awkward at being the cause of this exchange, but could not think how she might retrieve the situation. Hugo remained standing, the candelabrum in his hand and, with an inchoate thought that she should support him, she rose to her feet saying, "I beg you will excuse me, Clarissa."

"Of course, my dear. I wish you a very good night."

Lallie could barely keep her eyes open as he accompanied her along the gallery and up the stairs. She fought against the inclination, but had to yawn. "Oh, pray excuse me!"

He laughed. "My poor dear! You'll feel much more the thing tomorrow. I hope you will sleep for as long as you wish. We do not meet for breakfast here; everyone remains in their apartments. Tell Nancy to send a footman for your tray when you are ready."

At her door, he set the candles down on a table then turned and put his hands on her shoulders.

"Good night, my sweet. Pleasant dreams."

Lallie felt something soften within her at the old-fashioned endearment. "Good night, Hugo."

He kissed her lightly and opened the door.

Having closed the door on his bride, Hugo remained for a moment on the landing, anticipating the night when her bedroom would no longer be forbidden to him. Just a few days more! With a wry grin, he headed back to the salon. If only I don't strangle Clarissa in the meantime!

# Chapter Eleven

*In passing that part of the ocean near the Settlement Isles, a skilful pilot will be required as the winds blow hard, and frequently contrary.*

"I thought you would be older," Lallie exclaimed when Lady Anna's man of business, a neatly dressed, pleasant-faced man in his mid-thirties, was shown into the library.

"You are thinking of my father, Miss Grey. Alas, he is no longer with us."

Hugo pulled out a chair for Lallie at the table in the middle of the room and waved the solicitor to another. "Pray be seated, Mr Lambe. My solicitor and Miss Grey's uncle are also in attendance, but we prefer to speak privately first."

"Thank you." Mr Lambe folded his hands on the table in front of him. "I must tell you frankly, Miss Grey, that I was most surprised to receive your letter advising me of your intention to marry Mr Tamrisk, as it is not yet a month since your father and a Mr Frederick Malvin sought me out to draw up the settlements for your marriage to Mr Malvin."

"Did you do so?" Hugo asked sharply.

"I saw no reason not to, sir. Mr Grey assured me that he was acting on his daughter's behalf as her fortune is in trust until her twenty-fifth birthday and that she was agreeable to the match."

"Fortune?" Lallie repeated.

"Yes, left in trust to you by your grandmother, Lady Anna Staines."

"But Grandmamma didn't have a fortune. She had been cast off by her family and the Staineses were not overly wealthy."

"She inherited it from Mrs Caldwell, a great-aunt on her mother's side who had herself been forced into a distasteful marriage when very young."

"I had no idea," Lallie said weakly. "It was only when my other grandmother, Lady Grey, mentioned my mother's marriage settlement that I wondered whether I might have any sort of portion. My father and stepmother have always given me to understand that I was more or less penniless and a charge on them."

"Penniless? Nonsense!" Mr Lambe snapped, incensed. "Your grandmother made more than ample provision for you. It is in trust until you are twenty-five and the income has been paid quarterly to your father since you went to live with his family."

"So he knew of it?"

"Of course he knew of it! You cannot mean—did he never mention it to you, Miss Grey?"

"Never." Lallie could say no more.

"God bless my soul!" Mr Lambe was visibly distressed. "At the time, he was most insistent that you make a clean break of it, and perhaps it was better if you did not hanker after your previous life, but I cannot think it good for you to have had practically nothing to remember your grandparents by or to have been deprived of the consolation of knowing that they had provided for you so munificently. It verges on the fraudulent, indeed it does, and to think I was his unwitting accomplice! If you were not married by your twenty-fifth birthday, I would have written to you directly to seek your instructions, for the trust ends then and you become mistress to a considerable fortune."

"Considerable?" Lallie repeated faintly.

"Yes, Miss Grey." The solicitor steepled his fingers and leaned back in his chair. "Simply put, you have sixty-five thousand pounds in funds, as well as a house which is let at present and produces a rent of two hundred and eighty pounds per annum."

Lallie was thunderstruck. After long moments, she stole a look at Hugo who sat unmoving, a look of horror on his face.

"Miss Grey?"

At Mr Lambe's gentle prompt, she shook her head.

"When I think that they let me believe that I was destitute; dependent on them and must contribute as best I could towards my expenses. They had intended to employ a governess for Eleanor—she was almost five when I came to them and Mrs Grey was carrying Beatrice. But they said I should instruct her—after all I had been expensively educated and so could do my bit.

"I didn't mind helping," she told her listeners earnestly, "and I love my sisters dearly—it was wonderful to have them after being an only child, but Grandmamma had spoken of bringing me to London for a Season when I was eighteen. I did mention it to Mrs Grey, but she said it was no longer possible."

"Iniquitous!" Mr Lambe exclaimed. "Of course the trustees would have released funds for such a purpose."

Lallie laughed bitterly. "I didn't realise I was the silly goose who laid the golden eggs."

"My poor dear, don't say that." Hugo knelt to put his arms around her. "Their behaviour is to their great discredit, not to yours."

A sob escaped her and she turned her face into his shoulder. "Of course I would have helped if they had asked me; I would have been so glad to share," she whispered. "I was happy to be there, I thought they loved me. It's the deceit I cannot bear."

"I know." He stroked her hair as she clung to him.

After a few minutes, she fished in her reticule for a handkerchief and blew her nose. "You mentioned a house, Mr Lambe. Did you mean Larkhaven?"

"Yes, Miss Grey."

"Oh! It was our home, Grandmamma's and mine," she told Hugo with a watery smile. "We had to leave the rectory when Grandpapa died. Larkhaven is such a comfortable house, sunny and airy in the summer and so cosy in the winter. The gardens are beautiful. I thought it was gone. I asked Mrs Grey once and she only said 'someone else lives there now'."

After a pause, she asked hopefully, "Mr Lambe, might some of our furniture and other belongings still be there?"

"They are all there, Miss Grey. The house is let furnished, but your and Lady Anna's personal effects are stored in a locked attic. You may recall that Mr Grey would only permit us to send one trunk to Sussex."

"And my harp?"

He smiled kindly at her. "I beg you will not think it presumptuous, but my father had it removed to his home, which is now mine. He thought that it could not be good to store such a fine instrument in an unheated attic. It is quite safe, I assure you."

"That was so thoughtful of him. He always loved to hear me play when he called to see Grandmamma. I must be very rusty now," she added wistfully.

Hugo released her and got to his feet. He had lost his usual air of calm competence and looked questioningly from her to Mr Lambe and back again. "I confess I don't know what to say. Lady Grey mentioned that Miss Grey's mother's portion of two thousand pounds should come to her, but, frankly, I half-expected to hear that Mr Grey had managed to get his hands on it. The settlements now become a much more serious matter."

Lallie studied his expression hoping for a hint of what troubled him but before she could say anything Mr Lambe remarked sympathetically, "I see it is a shock to you, sir."

"I had no idea," Hugo's voice trailed away but then he said more definitely, "I should like to discuss this privately with Miss Grey. Mr Lambe, you will excuse us."

"Of course, Mr Tamrisk. If you permit, I shall take a stroll in the grounds."

"Mr Lambe," Lallie said urgently as the solicitor went to the door, "Please don't mention this to anyone else—my uncle for example. He will have to know, of course, but I should prefer that we first decide what is to be done."

Hugo stared into the fire. What the devil was he to do now?

"Is something wrong, Hugo?"

He could only shake his head.

"Hugo?"

"You're a great heiress, Lallie," he said heavily. "You might have your choice of husbands."

"Of fortune-hunters, certainly."

Was that how she now saw him? "I feel as if I've wronged you by rushing you into marriage." He couldn't look at her, couldn't bear to see her agree.

"You could only have wronged me if you had somehow known about the money," she said behind him. "Even Mr Lambe noticed how shocked you were. Your offer and my answer were honest. There was nothing false on either side, was there?"

He met her gaze in the over-mantel mirror. "No, but your circumstances have changed now. If you had been aware of them, would you have decided differently?"

"Do you wish to withdraw your offer? I shall not hold you to it, I promise you, but the least you can do is look me in the face while you cry off."

He spun around angrily. "Of course I don't wish to," he ground out, "but I will not tie you to our betrothal if you wish to be released from it."

Stalemate, he thought, when she dropped her eyes and walked towards the window. Her shoulders were slumped and her arms folded under her breasts. She stood there for a moment, pondering, then swivelled back to confront him. Now her head was up, her shoulders back and her arms spread wide in exasperation. Her eyes flashed green fire.

"I don't understand you, Hugo. You proposed to me when I had no money, you still wished to marry me when you thought I might have a little money and now, when it emerges that I have a lot of money, you think I should wed any other man but you."

Her voice changed, became cool and impersonal and she tossed her head dismissively. "Perhaps, Mr Tamrisk, you would condescend to tell me where you draw the line? What do you consider to be a permissible fortune for your bride? If you have such strict requirements, you really should give advance warning to any lady to whom you consider making an offer. Or perhaps you could simply insert a notice in the Gazette." A wicked smile curved her lips. "Yes, and require any interested ladies to furnish your man of business with a certified statement of their means."

Hugo had to laugh despite himself. "You little devil! What an absurd notion! When you put it like that I admit I seem very foolish." He grew more solemn. "Lallie, are you sure you won't regret this? Perhaps we should postpone the wedding and give you time to think. I'm sure one of my sisters would act as chaperon or invite you to stay with her if you don't wish to return to the Greys."

Her lips twitched. "Regret not handing my inheritance to a different man? Hugo, how many gentlemen would be made uneasy by this news or condescend to have this conversation with me? Or, if it comes to that, discuss the settlements with me instead of telling me to leave it to my uncle and Mr Lambe? I know I can trust you."

His scruples dissipating in the glow of her faith in him, Hugo yielded and opened his arms to her. He waited for what seemed an eternity but it was in fact only a few seconds until she walked into them. As they closed about her, he heard her whisper, "I feel safe with you."

That was the avowal he craved. She needed him! His brow rested against hers for a moment and then he kissed her. This was no gentle kiss but a claiming; his tongue plunging into her mouth. She did not push him away but clung to him, her lips opening, her tongue stroking his until he gasped and broke away.

"Enough, Miss Grey. We have work to do!"

"Hugo, what are we to tell your sisters?"

"Why must we tell them anything? It's our business, not theirs."

"Yes, but none of us expected the discussions to last so long. And you saw how discomfited my uncle was by the whole thing. If he had had his way, I would have been returned post-haste to my grandfather. It's fortunate that he has no real authority in the matter, but he might let something slip, perhaps to Lord Malvin, if only to vent his spleen at being ignored."

Hugo thought for a moment. "My father will have to know, for his signature will be required too. You've seen that he can't be relied upon to keep his tongue between his teeth. It's probably best if we tell the others ourselves."

"Could we tell them in confidence? I have no wish to enter society as a great heiress."

"And I would prefer to avoid the label of fortune-hunter," he said wryly.

"Hugo! You know it is completely untrue."

"Truth has never stood in the way of slander, especially among the *ton*. You'll discover that for yourself."

"All the more reason not to feed its appetite," she pointed out severely. "It's just as unflattering to me, as if you would only marry me because of my money. If we want to tell them before dinner, we must hurry and change. When will you speak to his lordship?"

"I'll go in to him now. Shall I call for you in half an hour?"

Hugo dismissed the footmen and closed the doors of the upper saloon then joined Lallie on the sofa.

"We apologise for inconveniencing you but our discussions took longer than we had expected and after due consideration, we have decided to share the reason for this with you."

Lallie had to repress a smile at his listeners' expressions of intense interest but they were all too well-bred to give voice to their curiosity.

"Lallie is most anxious that word of this should not escape to the outside world," Hugo warned them, "but you should know that she is the beneficiary of a very considerable trust left to her by her maternal grandmother." He ignored the chorus of gasps that greeted his statement and continued, "It was of course necessary to ensure that the settlements were not to her detriment, but I owe it to her to tell you that they also considerably benefit this, her new family."

Lallie blushed. "I think we have agreed a fair balance," she said softly.

"So you are an heiress. How exciting!" cried Arabella. "What a pity you are getting married on Tuesday. Just think of the Season you might have had!"

Lallie shrank against Hugo's side.

"That is precisely the sort of vulgar comment we wish to prevent," he said repressively.

"Indeed." Clarissa said. "I am surprised at you, Arabella."

The girl flushed. "I beg your pardon, Lallie. I won't say a word, I promise you."

"Thank you for trusting us with this information," Lord Malvin said and the others murmured in agreement. He smiled at Lallie. "I see it is too soon to congratulate you on your good fortune."

"I haven't come to terms with it yet," she admitted.

"You really had no idea?" Amabel asked sympathetically. "It must have been a shock."

"For Hugo as well," Lallie said with a sidelong smile.

"I suppose he assumed his most noble demeanour and wanted nothing to do with it," Matthew said with a grin.

"He has no choice," Henrietta pointed out. "It is the law that is at fault. Why should a woman's property automatically become her husband's when they marry?"

"Anything else is unthinkable. A man must be master in his own house. Man and wife are one flesh, commanded by the husband," Mr Grey declared. "Think of Saint Paul."

My poor aunt, Lallie thought, noticing that lady bite her lip as if to stop herself replying. It's no wonder she always looks so disgruntled.

Hugo looked at his sisters. Amabel appeared to be amused, but Henrietta seemed ready to launch into combat while Clarissa's expression suggested there was a bad smell beneath her nose.

"When it comes to matrimony, I am more in favour of a parliamentary system than an absolute monarchy," he said lightly.

"I am relieved to hear it." Lallie smiled at him and turned to Mrs Grey. "I'm sorry we neglected you so much today, Aunt. How did you occupy your time?"

# Chapter Twelve

*The Cape of Good Hope is a fine point of land, whence on a clear and calm day the Island of Perseverance may be distinguished.*

"You'll need this. The chapel's cold, Miss Lallie."

Nancy folded a turnover Norwich shawl and draped it over her mistress's shoulders so that that the exotic floral border formed two deep decorative triangles.

Lallie turned to admire the effect in her mirror. "It's just the thing."

"Will you wear a bonnet?"

"I don't think so; it's not as though we'll be leaving the house."

"What about the wedding?" Nancy asked practically. "You have such a pretty bonnet and Lady Grey's lace veil."

"Perhaps we can attach the veil to a ribbon or a hair ornament."

The chapel, which opened from the hall, was an oblong space running to the side wall of the house which was pierced by two slender windows. A plain wooden cross hung between them and below it stood a simple communion table. A chair and massive lectern stood to one side, the latter on a low dais so that the reader would be elevated above his congregation. There was no altar rail, but below where one would have been, two high-backed armchairs were set against the wall on either side, at right angles to the table. Below these, opening from a centre aisle, were four pairs of pews and then four of plain benches.

It was an austere room, made sombre by the wainscoting that lined the walls to a height of some four feet and matched the age-darkened oak of the furniture. A round pewter candelabrum hung from the ceiling over the communion table and matching sconces were attached to the walls. There were no flowers or other ornaments.

Such a joyless place, Lallie thought as she accompanied Hugo to the front of the room. What a pity she couldn't be married in Grandpapa's old church of St Mary's. Several hundred years of prayer had sanctified the walls which bore mute evidence to the generations of parishioners who had found spiritual succour there. She would have had friends and neighbours to wish her joy as the bells pealed above her and Hugo's heads. And she could have busied herself with the preparations for her wedding day.

She would have paused at the first pew, but Hugo led her to the two chairs on the left, facing his father who was already installed opposite. She supposed she must become accustomed to such prominent positions now.

The chaplain entered to read the service for the seventeenth Sunday after Trinity. Lallie noticed that he shortened the gospel, omitting the parable, but she supposed the reminder that, '*he who exalteth himself shall be abased; and he that humbleth himself, shall be exalted,*' might not be to his taste or that of his noble patron. Her grandfather had always taken that parable of the wedding-guest to heart.

"What a beautiful morning," Henrietta said when they emerged from the chill, gloomy chapel into the bright sunlight that flooded the hall. "Shall we walk over to the old churchyard? I should like to visit Mamma's grave."

"An excellent idea," her husband said. "We'll take the children; they want to see the stronghold, as they call it."

Leaving the children to their explorations of the ruined castle whose crumbling stone walls stood stark and black against the sky, Hugo and Henrietta continued on to the little Norman church that was the last resting place of the Tamrisks. With nave and vaults long since full, a small walled churchyard now held the tombs and headstones that related the fortunes of the family in more recent centuries and bore witness to an ancient lineage descending from father to son in unbroken succession.

In a sunny corner shaded by a beech tree, the most recent Lady Tamm lay together with three little daughters who had died at birth or in infancy. While Henrietta laid a posy of purple Michaelmas daisies and golden chrysanthemums over her mother's heart, Hugo considered bleakly the inscription that charted these much too short lives. Involuntarily he found himself praying that he and Lallie would be spared such a fate and resolved to be a better husband than his father had been in such heart-rending circumstances. If put to the test, he and his wife would mourn together, sharing their sorrow as they would their joy at the gift of a child.

"What troubles you, Hugo?"

"The realisation that I am about to give hostages to fortune," he admitted. "What if something were to happen to Lallie or a child?"

Henrietta put a gentle hand on his arm. "We must all live with that question if, as Dr Donne puts it, we are *'involved with mankind'*. Sometimes I think it's the tithe exacted by love. And yet, to turn one's back on love, on life for fear of possible pain and loss—that to me would be too great a price to pay for what would be a cowardly sort of peace of mind."

"And they say women are the weaker sex!" he exclaimed. "From a purely physical perspective, I suppose they are."

His sister laughed. "In terms of brute force, you mean. When it comes to what they can endure—wait until your wife has given birth before you presume to make such comparisons."

He flinched and looked over to where his bride-to-be stood with her aunt. As if she felt his gaze, she looked up and smiled at him and he crossed past the graves to her, feeling as if he went from death to life.

"Is this church still in use?" Lallie enquired.

"Of course. It is the parish church," Hugo told her.

"Then why doesn't the family attend it?"

"I don't really know. We never have."

"I remember going occasionally with Mamma when she was well enough, but in later years it was too much for her," Clarissa put in. "Tamm never came; he always preferred to have Mr Stiles read the service at the manor."

Lallie opened her mouth as if to speak, but then said nothing.

"You appear puzzled, Lallie," Hugo encouraged her.

"I don't wish to criticise but my other grandfather, the Rector, always said it was important that the principal landowners attend their parish church. It gives a good example and helps maintain the connection between them and their people." She regarded him seriously. "You said people were saying it was time Tamm had a mistress again. Perhaps that is part of what they meant. This is the real family church. All the Tamrisks are buried here. I would much rather walk over here, Hugo, than sit in that barren chapel."

He smiled at her. "I can see you're going to be an excellent Lady of Tamm. It's too late to make any changes before the wedding, but we could call on the vicar before we go to town."

"I'd like that."

Matthew Malvin strolled over. "Mamma and the others wish to go back to the house. Arabella and I are taking the children down to the stream. What about you two?"

"Lallie?"

"Let us go, too. Perhaps my aunt will entrust my cousins to us."

Once they had left the churchyard and were safely among the trees, the children abandoned all Sunday decorum and ran whooping along the path, veering off every few minutes to gather beech nuts or acorns, to admire some toadstools or to balance along a fallen tree-trunk. Despite young Miss Bynge's reminder that it was past Michaelmas and very likely the devil had spat on them, they stopped to pluck the last blackberries before reaching the little stream.

"Why do you want that bark, Cousin Lallie?" Howard Grey demanded.

Lallie looked at the piece in her hand and laughed. "Habit, I suppose. It is perfect for a boat. I used make them with my brother and sisters."

The other children came nearer. "Do they really float?"

"If you're careful."

"Show us, please."

Hugo let Amabel's daughters tow him away while Matthew went to help Henrietta's son and daughter look for more bark, twigs and leaves. Roderick Malvin and Howard Grey, perhaps more used to rural pastimes, were happy to forage for themselves as well as for Howard's brother and sister, while young Tony Malvin insisted on accompanying Miss Lallie.

Hugo spread his coat on a fallen log.

"Your seat, ma'am."

Lallie spread her handkerchief on her lap. "I'm sure one of you gentlemen has a penknife in his pocket."

"Take mine, Cousin," Howard said eagerly as they clustered around her.

With the tip of the knife she deftly bored a tiny hole in the curved inner surface of a piece of bark, fitted a twig into it so that it stood upright and carefully threaded a leaf on to it so that it was suspended like a sail.

"It looks like a real boat," David said, awed. "Will it really sail?"

"Yes, if you are careful putting it into the water."

Roderick immediately produced his own knife. "Let me try!"

"And me!"

"And me!"

Despite the occasional bickering over whose boat was better and the odd cry of anguish or despair when a leaf tore or a twig snapped, Hugo couldn't remember when he had enjoyed a morning at Tamm more. He might have been in paradise, sitting beside Lallie, the warmth of the sun on his back, its dappled light flickering with the movement of the leaves and the ripples in the water, her unique scent mingling with the aromas of fallen leaves and the freshness of the purling stream.

On his other side, David leaned against him, a warm, comfortable weight. Under his breath, the child droned, '*I saw three ships come sailing in, come sailing in*' as he moved his boat to and fro over waves only he could see.

"Finished," Howard announced.

"Can we race them?" Roderick asked.

"If we put them in the water here, we could run and see which is first under the bridge and out on the other side," Clara Forbes suggested.

"Just be careful," Lallie said. "We'll all be in the suds if someone falls in. Hugo, will you help David, please."

"I can do it myself!"

"I'm sure you can. You must bend down and float it very gently on to the water." Hugo hovered anxiously, ready to grab the child if he toppled over. But he managed his task and the small vessel was soon caught by the current and bobbed out into the stream.

"Now we must hurry," he said, swinging David up and striding with him towards the little bridge.

"Mr Tamrisk has seven-league boots," the child crowed gleefully as they overtook his brother and sister.

"What? I am an ogre?" Hugo growled playfully and sniffed loudly at David's neck. "*Fee, fi, fo, foy, I smell the blood of an English boy.*"

David shook his head. "It's *fo fum* and *English man*," he said reprovingly. "You must eat Mr Matthew, not me." But then they reached the bridge and he was fully occupied in tracing the progress of the little flotilla.

"Mine has just gone under the bridge," Clara cried and dashed to lean over the parapet on the other side.

By the time the last boat had been given up for lost, it was time to hurry back to the manor. This was what Tamm should be like, Hugo thought, as he carried David the last stretch while Matthew performed the same service for Anne Bynge; full of laughing children and simple pleasures. He looked at Lallie who walked between Howard and Roderick, listening intently to whatever they were telling her. Pray God, one day, they will be our sons with her—or our daughters. I don't really care which.

Hugo was charmed to find his betrothed the sole occupant of the saloon on his entrance before dinner. He hastened to take her hand and drop a swift kiss on her mouth. "How delightful to have a few moments to ourselves," he murmured just as Amabel and Tom came in. It was equally satisfying to acknowledge the polite 'good-evenings' with Lallie at his side. So this is what it is like to be one of a couple, no longer solitary. We'll be doing this for the rest of our lives, host and hostess at Tamm.

The sensation remained with him throughout dinner and, afterwards, when he and Lallie joined in the music-making, he was assailed by a lightness of heart so intense that he found himself pressing his heels to the floor so that he would not seize her and dance her around the room.

When the ladies announced their intention to retire, he readily agreed to Captain Malvin's suggestion of a hand of cards.

"Go on down to the library, Arthur. I'll take Lallie upstairs and join you then."

# Chapter Thirteen

*After landing at Bride's Bay, the Temple of Hymen attracts the attention of the traveller.*

Lallie stretched languorously in the big bed. It had been a perfect day. The hours she had spent with Hugo and the children had seemed a foretaste of her married life. Just one more day and she would be his wife. Soon, she hoped, they would have their own children.

She drowsily reviewed her preparations for her wedding. Her gown and shoes were ready and Nancy had carefully stitched the veil to a bandeau decorated with silk flowers. She would wear her grandmother's locket which held portraits of her mother and her grandfather. That way all three would be with her. Suddenly she was wide awake. The chain of the locket had broken after dinner and she had put it into her reticule for safekeeping. She climbed out of bed, lit a spill at the fire and touched it to a candle. She would put the locket on the dressing-table, where she would see it in the morning and remember to tell Nancy to have it repaired.

Or maybe she should ask Hugo herself. She must have it for Tuesday. The reticule wasn't on the dressing-table. Lallie lit more candles and hastily opened the drawers. Nothing! Perhaps Nancy had put it away with the matching gown. No. It must still be in the saloon. She would slip down quickly and retrieve it. No one would notice. The gentlemen were in the library and the ladies had gone to bed.

Candle in hand, she sped along the dark passage and hurried down the stairs to the saloon. The door to Henrietta's withdrawing room was ajar and she could hear her talking to her sisters.

"I vow the children are in love with her. All they can talk of is Miss Lallie and her bark boats."

Smiling, Lallie snatched up her reticule and turned to quit the room.

"Poor child. I hope she knows what she is doing. The Tamrisk men are all alike." Lady Malvin's voice was full of concern.

Henrietta sighed. "Tamm hasn't changed at all. Look what he said to her that first day, and before us all, too. If Charles's father had said something of the sort to me I would have sunk into the ground."

"Hugo put a stop to it," Amabel pointed out fairly.

"But he is looking for a dutiful wife. You know what he said last May—it made the rounds of the *ton*. When he married, he would wed a quiet country mouse with nary a squeak to her. She would know her place and leave his to him."

"For her sake I hope she provides him with an heir or, better, two as quickly as possible and does not have to endure what Mamma did." Clarissa's voice broke on a half-sob. "I shall never forget the scoldings and tirades when you two were born or when she miscarried. Tamm only allowed her a scant month to recover before resuming his tri-weekly demands. He was like clockwork—Mondays, Wednesdays and Fridays and she would get paler and more silent as the evening wore on. And of course we mustn't forget his vituperative abuse each month when it became apparent that she had once again failed in her duty."

"'Tis a wonder you ever married, Clarissa, with that example before your eyes," Amabel said softly.

"It was the fact that Anthony was so loving towards both Julian and Mattie that attracted me to him; that and the way he spoke so fondly of their dead mother. He was very kind to Mamma and me, too. We were not used to that in a man."

There was an affectionate smile in Clarissa's voice but Amabel sounded sad. "No, but then I found Thomas and you took Henrietta to Malvin once Mamma died."

"For which I shall be forever grateful," Henrietta stated. "Tamm would have made me responsible for the household and ignored me otherwise."

"I think he planned to marry again as soon as possible," Amabel said, "but then he had the first apoplectic seizure. It took him some time to recover from it and Thomas warned him he could have more."

Henrietta spoke again. "I wonder what Lady Albright will think of Hugo marrying so suddenly. They were extremely close last Season."

"Were they? I had neither the time nor the inclination to pay attention to Hugo's doings. I hope he has the sense to make a clean break with her, although now that I come to think of it, they seemed quite intimate at Lady Nugent's last month." Clarissa yawned. "I suppose we should retire."

The sound of movement in the inner chamber broke Lallie's numbed daze and she fled as if the furies were at her heels. As voices suggested that the ladies were in the saloon, she reached the top of the stairs and rushed to gain the safety of her bedroom where, huddled into a chair, her knees drawn up beneath her shawl, she tried to piece together what she had heard.

She set aside the sufferings of poor Lady Tamm. She couldn't imagine Hugo treating her with such disrespect. But what of the rest? He had said he wanted a quiet country mouse with nary a squeak to her, who would know her place and leave his to him. What did he mean? He wanted a mistress for Tamm, certainly; he had made that very clear, and someone to bear his children. But he took it for granted she would accompany him to London. Proximity would be necessary if he was to get her with child, of course, and he had his responsibilities as Member of Parliament. I'll have to wait and see, she thought sensibly. He didn't mind my suggestion that we attend the parish church in future and made no bones about discussing the settlements with me.

Lallie sat up, reassured, and then fell back again. Lady Albright: compared to her, she was certainly a country mouse. She had seen for herself how friendly Hugo was with the lady. Was this what her grandmother had hinted at when she said gentlemen tended to seek their pleasure outside marriage? She had warned Lallie not too become too attached, to remember that she would be Hugo's wife, not his mistress? Not that Lady Grey was aware of the connection with Lady Albright, or at least Lallie didn't think she was, but she had also remarked on how pleased she and Sir Howard were that Hugo had decided 'to do the right thing'. Clearly they had felt he was obliged to make Lallie an offer.

Had he thought so too? Even before we met at the *Belle Sauvage* he had asked permission to call on us in Sussex, Lallie told herself. But was that because he thought he had found his country mouse? Did he offer to release me when he found out about my fortune because he was afraid that a wealthy heiress would refuse to act the submissive wife? He has never said he loved me or asked if I love him. A wistful smile trembled on her lips as the answer to the unput question rose unbidden from her heart. I do of course, but does he want my love?

She pressed her lips together. Very likely he does, but only as long as it doesn't inconvenience him. He certainly won't welcome it if I hang out of his sleeve or demand more of his time and attention than he is willing to give. It's too late to cry off now. All I can do is take my cue from him—and find my own sphere, make my place there. I think he'll always be kind and, God willing, there will be children who will love me.

"You have the headache?" Nancy said the next morning. "Well, it's not to be wondered at, after all the travel and excitement. Better today, than tomorrow."

"I didn't sleep very well," Lallie admitted.

"Why don't you rest this morning? There's nothing you must do, is there?"

"No, but you must make my excuses to Lady Malvin. Oh, and the chain on my locket broke. I need it repaired before Tuesday."

Nancy peered at the little trinket. "That should be easy to fix. I'll get you settled first and then take it to Mr Carey."

"Miss Lallie? The housekeeper has sent to ask if you would like a nuncheon, a baked egg, perhaps, and Mr Tamrisk wonders if he might be permitted to enquire how you go on."

Lallie sat up, feeling greatly refreshed. "Help me dress quickly, Nancy."

"Will you see him here? If I stay in the room there can be no objection and you'll not be disturbed. I'll sit over there, well away from you."

Lallie laughed. "Why not? All they can do is make me marry him. And a baked egg would be lovely."

"Slip into this morning gown and I'll have your hair pinned up in a trice."

A concerned Hugo arrived together with her tray. "How are you feeling, Lallie? Is your headache improved?"

"Much improved, thank you."

"Would you like to take a turn outside with me when you've eaten? Have you seen the walled gardens?

She hesitated before replying, "I should really prefer not to meet anyone else, sir."

He nodded understandingly. "The house is full of relatives, I know! But why so formal?" he added with a teasing smile. "If you called me Hugo, I could suggest we slip down the back stairs."

She had to chuckle at that. "If you please, Hugo."

They were able to make their escape unnoticed and soon were strolling in the mild sunshine. She refused his proffered arm and kept herself a little apart from him with pretexts of identifying the shrubs and flowers or looking for an elusive bird singing high above them.

"Lallie, please don't let my father discommode you," Hugo said abruptly. "He is old and difficult, but I promise that I will make sure he is civil to you. I've already warned him not to repeat remarks of the type he made the other evening."

"But will he agree?"

"He will."

He did not elaborate but she was left in no doubt that he meant what he said.

"Do you ride?" he asked.

"Yes and no. I haven't ridden since I went to live in Sussex, but before that I had a sweet little mare. I wonder what happened to her. Is Mr Lambe still here? I could ask him."

"I don't think there is anything suitable for a lady in the stables," Hugo said thoughtfully, "but if not I'll look in to Tattersall's when we are in town. I prefer to ride when I visit the tenants and sometimes you might like to accompany me."

There was a clear indication of his expectations. "Of course. I'll include a new habit in my bride-clothes."

"You're a beautiful bride." Nancy hugged her nursling carefully so as not to disturb her finery. "I wish you happy with all my heart, my dearest Miss Lallie."

Lallie choked back a sob and returned the embrace fiercely. "I'm so glad you're here, Nancy."

"I'll always be there for you," Nancy vowed. There was a tap on the door and she quickly blotted a few tears, then twitched and shook Lallie's skirts back into the correct folds before admitting Lallie's uncle.

As she walked down the stairs, Lallie saw that the wedding guests were clustered in the hall below, not waiting in the chapel for the bride to arrive, as would be customary. Lord Tamm sat to one side of the open chapel door while at the other was set a small table on which lay a wreath of flowers. Hugo waited in the centre, sternly handsome in a coat of darkest blue superfine, pale kerseymere waistcoat and knee breeches, his immaculately tied cravat rivalling his silk stockings in snowy whiteness. His intent gaze was fixed on her.

When she and Mr Grey crossed the floor to the chapel door, the others moved to form a semi-circle behind them and the chaplain stepped forward.

"Who giveth this woman to be married to the Heir of Tamm?"

Lallie was puzzled. Surely that came later in the ceremony, not outside the chapel? And what an odd way to refer to Hugo. But her uncle had already answered, "I do".

"In accordance with ancient custom," the chaplain continued pompously, "kneel and bow your head"—did she imagine that he accorded a special emphasis to these instructions?—"to receive the bridal chaplet bestowed upon you by your bridegroom—rosemary, for fidelity and gillyflowers, white for purity and red for love, symbols of the vows you will presently make to your new lord."

He gestured grandly and a footman placed a red velvet cushion, richly decorated with gold cord and tassels, on the floor in front of her.

Lallie stared at it. Did Hugo seriously expect her to kneel at his feet? She longed to refuse, but her courage failed at the thought of making a scene in front of their assembled families. But she would not bow her head. She gracefully sank to the ground, her head proudly held high in a silent challenge to her husband-to-be. *You must prove that you are worthy of my reverence.*

Aromatic scents surrounded her as Hugo lifted the wreath and set it gently on her head. He immediately offered his hand but she would not let him raise her, standing as lithely as she had knelt. She held his gaze for a moment and then slowly extended her right hand. He took it lightly and bent low to kiss it. It was a real kiss, his lips warm against her chilled skin and in a moment she felt them again on her cheek.

"My sweet Lallie," he murmured in her ear, "You look ravishing—you take my breath away."

She smiled coolly. "Thank you, Hugo."

He transferred her hand to his left one and nodded to the chaplain. "Mr Stiles, you may proceed."

The rest of the service was in accordance with the Prayer Book. Lallie's hand was steady when she placed it in Hugo's and her voice did not quaver when she made her vows. Hugo spoke his clearly and sincerely. The ring slipped easily onto her finger. During the remainder of the ceremony, her eyes returned constantly to the little gold band. Such a simple and yet such a potent symbol of her changed identity—no longer Lallie Grey but the Honourable Mrs Tamrisk. Inside I'm still Lallie, she told herself stubbornly.

"My felicitations, Tamrisk, Mrs Tamrisk," Lord Tamm said stiffly after they had signed their names on the vellum folio that recorded the marriages of generations of Tamrisks. She stooped to accept his lordship's dry peck on her cheek before turning with Hugo to receive the good wishes of their guests.

Lallie sat back in her corner of the carriage, relieved that Hugo had decreed they would depart immediately after the wedding breakfast. She stole a glance at him from under the brim of her bonnet. It was hard to read his expression. Strange to think that he would come to her bed tonight. At least I won't have to spend my wedding night amid a houseful of interested relatives and servants, she comforted herself.

The lodge keeper and his family were lined up at the gate, waiting to wish them Godspeed. Father, mother and two little girls bowed and curtseyed, the elder child clutching a small posy of flowers.

"We must stop, Hugo."

"Congratulations and good fortune to you and your bride, Mr Tamrisk, sir," the keeper called heartily, while his wife gave the girl a little push.

"Go on," she whispered.

The child came forward and thrust amethyst-hued autumn crocus bound in glossy dark green leaves into Lallie's hand. "For you, mum," she whispered.

"And?" her mother prompted.

"We wish you joy on your wedding day."

Lallie smiled at the children. "They're beautiful. Thank you—what's your name, my dear?"

"Becky, and this is Susan."

"Thank you, Becky and Susan, and Mr and Mrs Hay." She smiled at the parents. "It's very kind of you indeed.

"That was very thoughtful," she said as they drove on. "It's so pretty"

She had left the chaplet behind without a thought, but would keep these flowers and press them. Her head was beginning to ache and she untied the ribbons of her bonnet and lifted it from her head so that she could lean back properly, then stole a sideways glance at her husband's harsh profile. Almost as if he felt her gaze, he turned his head, his eyes gleaming.

"There is one important ceremony I have omitted," he said huskily. "I haven't yet kissed my bride."

He slid along the leather bench and took her in his arms. He lifted her chin gently and waited until her eyelids rose and her eyes met his.

"Mrs Tamrisk," he said and brushed her mouth with his lips.

Then he kissed her again, more deeply this time, his tongue sweeping in to tangle with hers. Lallie felt a tingle run through her body directly to the private place between her legs and she gasped. Her lips throbbed. He raised his head and smiled down at her.

A sudden gust of wind spattered rain against the glass, rocking the carriage. Hugo spread a rug over Lallie's lap but, unlike on the journey to Hampshire, he opened it to cover his knees as well before clasping her firmly to his side.

"That's better," he murmured against her hair.

It was certainly much warmer and, supported by her husband, Lallie did not have to brace herself as the carriage was buffeted by the wind.

"The lodge is quite snug compared with the manor," he said. "Mrs Bragge will have good fires lighting and a country dinner waiting for us."

"It sounds cosy. Do you go there often?"

"Several times a year. I generally invite some friends in the autumn, but between the Malvins' invitation and the early opening of Parliament, it wasn't feasible this year. As it is, we'll only have a week or so now."

The large cottage with the thatched roof was indeed a snug retreat. Downstairs, a comfortable parlour served both as gun-room and library, the walls lined with book-cases as well as a locked compartment where Hugo immediately stowed his Mantons. He hoped to fit in some shooting, Lallie thought, a conclusion that was bolstered by the arrival of his dogs Horace and Virgil. They seemed to know the house and after conducting a tail-wagging inspection of the ground floor, settled down in front of the parlour fire.

"Do you mind them?" Hugo asked. "I can tell Hobbs or Bragge to take them."

"Not in the least," she answered robustly, "as long as they stay out of my bedchamber, that is. They are clearly used to being here."

"They are my long-time companions," he admitted.

"Mrs Bragge is that flustered at having a lady staying," Nancy reported as she brushed Lallie's hair. "She's put me into the smallest bedroom; there's just one big room in the attic for the men-servants. 'I'm so relieved you're here, Miss Anderson' she said to me, 'you'll be able to tell me what to do for the mistress. We're so honoured that Mr Tamrisk brought her here; we want to have everything just so for her.'"

"She seems a pleasant woman," Lallie said.

"Yes, and willing," Nancy agreed. "Her two daughters are good girls, she said, not that there would ever be any of that sort of goings-on here. Gentlemen chasing the maids or bringing their lightskirts with them," she explained in response to Lallie's puzzled look.

"Oh! I never thought of that. I wouldn't have expected it of Mr Tamrisk," Lallie said.

"Nor would I. He seems a very nice gentleman, from all I've heard. You've a fine husband there, Miss Lallie." She pulled Lallie's hair back over her shoulders. "We won't plait it. I'll tie it back with this cherry ribbon—it matches the ones on your night-dress."

Too restless to get into bed and wait for her husband, as her grandmother had directed, Lallie looked around the room.

Mrs Bragge had clearly made every effort to transform it into a bridal chamber. A scented nosegay filled a little vase on the console table that stood below a gilt-framed mirror to serve as a dressing table. Cream draperies sprigged with pink flowers billowed at the bed; the pink echoed in the curtains at the windows and the watered silk panels of the mahogany screen that concealed the washstand with its set of pretty bedroom ware. Little ornaments scattered about the room suggested that the housekeeper had used some of her own treasures to alleviate the air of casual, masculine comfort that permeated the rooms downstairs. Touched, Lallie went to the mantelpiece to inspect them more closely.

The door open behind her and she whirled around, skirts flying.

"Mind the fire!" Hugo leapt across the room and tugged her away from the hearth.

"I was quite safe!"

"Perhaps, but you didn't look safe. I have no wish to explain to the world that my bride chose to immolate herself on her wedding night, like a Hindoo widow."

"I can see that that might be awkward," she agreed solemnly.

He grinned. "Clarissa would never let me forget it."

"And just imagine the difficulties you might have in finding another bride. Even the most match-making of mammas must disapprove."

"I am quite happy with the one I have," he murmured, framing her face with his hands and bending to kiss her, his lips soft on hers. "Will you come to bed, Lallie?"

She nodded, suddenly speechless.

He smiled understandingly. "There is no need to be afraid— it is the most natural thing in the world."

"That's what Nancy said," Lallie disclosed with a blush.

"I knew her to be a sensible woman," Hugo commented, urging her towards the bed. She felt his hands on her shoulders.

"We can do without this pretty dressing-gown, I think," he murmured and drew it down her arms until it slipped off. He tossed it onto a chair while Lallie hastily climbed into bed.

"Scoot over," he said, letting his banyan fall to the floor. He was wearing a night shirt, but as soon as he was in bed, he pulled it over his head and dropped it beside the banyan.

Lallie felt her cheeks grow hot. She didn't know where to look. At least the bed clothes covered his lap, but who would have guessed that a man's chest was so hard and well-defined, or that it was covered with hair?

Hugo settled against the pillows and put his arm around her shoulders, drawing her to lie against him as she had in the carriage.

"We'll just get comfortable," he murmured, his voice deeper than usual. His fingers stroked gently down her neck to her shoulder, soothing her and she slipped further down the bed and rested her head on his shoulder. He was so warm, and she could feel his heart thrumming beneath her.

He continued to pet her softly. He turned slightly and gently placed his free hand on her breast, caressing her with soft, feathery strokes that soon were somehow unsatisfying.

"Lallie?"

When she looked up, he kissed her deeply while at the same time he eased down the neckline of her nightgown. He found the ribbon and deftly untied the bow, spreading the sides apart so that her breasts were bare. His fingers brushed over her nipples which had peaked in the cooler air, then he began to trail kisses down her neck and onto her breast, his hair skimming over her newly sensitive skin. It was strangely pleasing to have him there and Lallie was tempted to hold him to her, but it was not about what she wanted, she remembered. When his questing mouth found her nipple, she squeaked and felt rather than heard his answering soft chuckle.

Now his hands were gathering her nightgown and bundling it up to her waist. His roving hands dipped lower, between her legs. She stiffened against his touch and he shushed her gently. "Don't be afraid," he said again, stroking slowly while pressing a little so that she found herself opening to him, permitting his fingers to slip inside her. He moved them gently and then more vigorously. It was strange but not unpleasant.

"Lallie," he said tenderly, "this may hurt a little, but only this first time."

"I know."

"Then, may I come into you?"

"Yes, Hugo."

He rolled over to lie between her legs, facing her and supported on his forearms. She felt something rounder, firmer nudging at her entrance. He flexed his hips and pushed in a little. It felt hard and stretched her uncomfortably.

"Don't fight against me," he murmured. "If you let me in, I will fit."

She giggled nervously—had he been reading her mind?

He bent and took her mouth in a hard kiss that quite distracted her then surged deeply into her. She jerked against the sharp sting and he stopped moving at once, softening his kiss and nipping and sipping at her mouth until she responded.

If I just move, yes like that, she thought, it should be more comfortable. She wriggled again. That's better.

Hugo had been holding himself still against her, but he now began to move again, pressing in and withdrawing in a rhythm that built in intensity until he groaned and his hips moved in short, sharp thrusts. He groaned again, shuddered and was still. He had spent his seed, she realised. It was done. A little sigh escaped her.

He eased carefully from her body and rolled to his side, his arms holding her to him. He was gasping. She lay quietly in his arms until he breathed more evenly and then pulled away a little. She felt hot and sticky.

He turned his head and kissed her. "Thank you, Lallie, my dear wife."

"We're really married now," she said.

"I hope you've no regrets, Mrs Tamrisk."

She could hear the smile in his voice. "None, Mr Tamrisk. Do you?"

"How can you ask, after you gave yourself to me so sweetly?" He stroked her hair gently and they lay in contented silence for some minutes.

Lallie sat up and pulled her nightdress to rights. "Hugo, can you hand me my dressing-gown, please?"

"Why?" he asked sleepily.

"I must wash," she told him, embarrassed. Grandmother had said she would bleed the first time.

He reached over to the chair and handed the garment to her.

"Thank you."

She put her arms through the sleeves, grateful that the skirts would conceal her lower body as she left the bed. Safely behind the screen, she washed quickly and donned the fresh nightgown Nancy had left for her. When she returned to the bed, Hugo had already fallen asleep. She blew out the candles and, somewhat hesitantly, lay down again beside him. Now she was a woman, a wife, soon she might be a mother. For the rest of her life, she was bound to him. He had been considerate, she thought sleepily. It hadn't been as bad as she had feared. And the worst was over, if Grandmother was to be believed. She turned on her side, facing the edge of the bed and stretched carefully so as not to touch him. There was no more to be done and no more to fear. She had her place in life now. 'Mrs Tamrisk', she murmured to herself, as her eyes closed.

"It's your turn to choose," Hugo said the following evening.

Lallie laughed, closed her eyes, and plucked a book from the book-case. "*The Sermons of Dr Jonathan Swift*. How did that come here?"

"I have no idea. It must have escaped from some vicarage. You may select another," Hugo announced loftily and took the leather-bound volume from her hand.

She snatched it back, shaking her head. "You must play fair, Hugo! We agreed that we would each select a book blindly and read to the other from it for at least ten minutes. If I didn't quibble at Mr Egan you must endure the good doctor's discourses." She flicked through the book. "*On Sleeping in Church*," she announced.

"An excellent subject; I shall apply myself to it instanter," Hugo stretched out his legs, folded his arms and closed his eyes. "Pray proceed!"

As he listened to his wife's warm voice, he resolved to take the first opportunity to review the bookshelves and remove anything that might not be suitable for a lady. Over the years, various guests had left a motley collection of volumes behind them and while Egan's *Sketches of Ancient and Modern Pugilism* might be tedious for feminine ears, at least there was nothing harmful in them.

He had been determined not to spend his wedding night at the manor—he would have felt the presence of his father and sisters too strongly; his lordship encouraging and his sisters very likely deploring his prowess. He was equally bent on spending it under his own roof, which ruled out Tamarisk House in London as they would have had to spend four nights on the road before reaching it. The shooting box had seemed ideal, but he had been so concerned with the preparations at the manor that he had given little or no thought to what would be required apart from giving Mrs Bragge carte blanche to prepare everything for his bride. He must remember to express his appreciation to her.

When Lallie had finished reading and it was his turn to select a book, he made sure he found Robinson Crusoe and, on learning that she had never read it, suggested they make that their evening entertainment over the next days. Tomorrow they would drive to Ashburton to purchase watercolours and paper for Lallie and she had insisted he should take a gun out the next day. He had not expected married life to be so agreeable, Hugo thought contentedly as he prepared for bed.

# Chapter Fourteen

*The Floating Isles of Flattery lie near to Coquet Island. This island is large and well-populated, but the soil is unfavourable to cultivation. Parrots and Cockatoos are found here in great abundance.*

Hugo flicked through the little bundle of post. "Take this to Mrs Tamrisk."

The butler bowed, replaced the letter on his salver and paced down the side of the long table to where Lallie sat opposite her husband. She glanced at it and set it aside to read later. If at first she had been apprehensive about returning to Tamarisk House, her fears had been allayed by the respectful, warm welcome of the butler and housekeeper. Appealed to regarding the hour at which she wished breakfast to be served, she had pondered briefly and said firmly, 'ten o'clock'.

It was now shortly before eleven and she picked up her letter and rose. Hugo glanced up. "What are your plans for today, Lallie?"

"I must talk to Nancy and the housekeeper and would like to look around the house. And you?"

"I'll drop into Brooks's later, but must read this first—it's a report I have been waiting for. I'll be in the library if you need me."

An hour later, having explored the house thoroughly, Lallie returned to the downstairs parlour, a stylish room that gave onto the garden via a terrace and a small flight of stone steps. She had been particularly taken by the sofa set beneath a temple-like baldaquin and felt quite exotic sitting there behind a small round table that held her books and papers. The room was furnished in an unusual shade of blue-green that reminded her of a duck's egg; gilding on the baldaquin and over-mantle mirror gave an impression of opulence, as did the Axminster carpet in the same shades.

Feeling delightfully in charge of her own home, she sent for her housekeeper who contrived to guide her new mistress in the selection of dishes and menus without the slightest hint that she might not be overly familiar with the ways of the *haut ton*.

"If I might suggest, madam, that you dine at seven o'clock any evening you are not expecting company? That will give you ample time to go on to other entertainments."

Lallie didn't betray by the flicker of an eyelid her surprise at such a late dinner hour. "That will be perfect, Mrs Phipps. We'll leave breakfast at ten o'clock for the present."

"Lady Malvin, madam."

Lallie jumped up from the sofa and went forward, hands outstretched. "My dear Clarissa, how good of you to call so soon."

"I hope it's not inconvenient, but there is much to be done." Clarissa brushed cheeks with her sister-in-law and sat down.

"Tell Mr Tamrisk that her ladyship has called," Lallie instructed the butler.

"Oh, is he here? I had thought he would be at his club." Clarissa looked around critically. "I don't know this room. It's quite pretty, although the Pompeian style is now outmoded. But it could have been worse, I suppose, given that Tamrisk men have so little taste. You're looking well, Lallie. I trust Tamrisk is not neglecting you—or being overly assiduous in his attentions," she added as an afterthought.

"He is all consideration," Lallie murmured, grateful that Hugo's arrival put an end to this inquisition.

"Good day, Clarissa," Hugo dutifully kissed the air above the tilted cheek. "How are Malvin and all the family?"

"Very well, I thank you. Now," she announced briskly. "I have arranged a dinner for you on Saturday. It is quite select, fifteen couples apart from the family, and will give Lallie an excellent introduction to the *ton*." She smiled at Lallie. "It is chiefly those who rule the country who are in town now, of course. This presents you with the ideal opportunity to establish yourself within *le vrai beau monde*. Once there, you will be excellently placed to enjoy the Season next year when the world and his wife come to London. As a bride, you should wear your wedding-gown, but without the chemisette. I presume you had short sleeves made as well."

"Yes, Nancy will change them. She is very skilled with her needle but not convinced of her ability to dress hair. Where could she learn the latest styles?"

Clarissa subjected her to a long scrutiny. "I see what she means. We can arrange for *Monsieur Denis* to call and cut your hair—together with some modish ornaments, that it all that is needed—and give Nancy a few hints."

Hugo, who was lounging in his chair, shot up at this. "Cut her hair? Lallie doesn't need to cut her hair—it's beautiful the way it is."

"Just like a man," Clarissa said, exasperated. "You must leave these things to us women, Hugo."

Secretly flattered, Lallie said appeasingly, "If you don't wish me to, I won't."

He waved a dismissive hand. "Far be it from me to intrude upon such feminine territory."

And where does that leave me, Lallie asked herself later.

In the end, wishful to present a modish appearance, she agreed to a judicious trimming of her locks. They still reached below her shoulders, if no longer to her waist, while a few inspired snips created a fringe that curled prettily at her forehead and temples. Both mistress and maid were satisfied with the result and as for Hugo—he didn't seem to notice.

"Very elegant," Hugo pronounced, coming into Lallie's bedroom prior to their departure to Clarissa's dinner. His eyes gleamed as he surveyed her.

"Is that indeed your wedding gown? I would not have thought it." His gaze lingered approvingly on the deep *décolleté* where his peridot cross just reached the top of the valley between her breasts. Smiling, he handed her a jeweller's box.

"To mark your first appearance as Mrs Tamrisk."

Lallie carefully opened the leather case and gasped at the pair of exquisite peridot bracelets and matching ear-drops. "Hugo! You are too generous."

He shook his head. "It's no more than you deserve," he replied, fastening first one bracelet, then the other around her wrists. They gleamed and glittered against the pale ivory of long kid gloves that wrinkled in fashionable, soft folds about her arms, seductively suggestive of stockings that might slither down at any moment

Eyes sparkling to match his gift, she attached the ear-drops and went to admire the effect in her mirror. "They are so beautiful, Hugo. Thank you."

With a shy smile, she came to press a kiss on his lips.

She's getting used to me, he thought as he pulled her into his arms.

"Don't crush my gown," she admonished him, but her smile deepened and she reached up to kiss him again. A clock chimed. "We must be going. Clarissa will never forgive us if we're late, especially when the dinner is in our honour."

"In your honour," he corrected as he released her. "Is this your shawl?"

"Not like that," she protested when he draped it around her shoulders and rearranged it so that it was caught stylishly at her elbows and fell loosely behind her in a graceful arc.

"That won't keep you warm," he grumbled.

Nancy agreed with him. "The master is right, Miss Lallie. Wear your cloak and carry the shawl. If you're to arrive early, you'll have plenty of time to put yourself to rights before the other guests come."

"Am I now to have two of you fussing about me?" Lallie complained, but she made no further protest when Hugo wrapped her in the cloak.

He ushered her out to the waiting carriage. It was the first time he had looked forward to one of his sister's entertainments. Tonight was very special. It was their first appearance as a married couple and he would have the privilege of introducing his bride to the *ton*. She had gained in poise since that first evening at Malvin Abbey and seemed quite comfortable at the prospect. In fact, she looked enchanting tonight; a figure of cream and gold and ivory brought to life by the tints of her rosy mouth, her black curls and the lambent green of her eyes and jewels.

"Did you enjoy your first encounter with *le vrai beau monde?*" Hugo enquired lazily as they drove home.

"I did. They're not very different to any other group of people, are they? It was very kind of Clarissa to go to so much trouble."

"Yes." He removed his gloves and began to play idly with one of her bracelets, running it up her arm until it stuck fast and then releasing it to slide down to her wrist.

"You're tickling," she protested.

162

"Am I?" His fingers wandered up to the patch of bare skin between her glove and her sleeve. "Are you ticklish here? And here?" He eased a finger under the narrow cuff.

She tugged his hand away, trying not to smile. "Stop it, Hugo."

He caught both her hands and held them on the seat. "You are my captive," he declared and bent to press a kiss between her breasts. "I've wanted to do that all night."

The carriage rocked to a halt. Hugo straightened up and quickly kissed her mouth before the footman could open the door. "Send Nancy away," he murmured in her ear as they mounted the stairs, "I'll tend to you tonight."

Lallie's heart fluttered strangely as they entered her room. Nancy was on her way to the door almost before she could announce she wouldn't need her any more that night.

As soon as the door closed, Hugo untied the ribbons that held Lallie's cloak together at her throat. He lifted it from her shoulders and tossed it aside before removing the ear-bobs and cross. He then moved behind her to unlace her gown. She stood passively as he drew it down from her shoulders, his lips moving down her spine so that she shivered beneath his kisses. She looked quite wanton, she thought, studying her reflection in the cheval-glass, especially when one noticed the intent male figure behind her. Her dress was eased past her hips to puddle on the carpet and then her stays were whisked away.

Hugo raised his head. Burning, dark eyes met hers in the mirror. "Madam?" He offered his hand to assist her step out of the circle of fabric, leaving her to stand, blushing, in chemise, stockings, slippers, gloves and bracelets.

"Take down your hair," he ordered huskily.

As if in a trance, Lallie obeyed, removing the combs and pins and shaking her head to let her locks tumble about her shoulders.

She ran her gloved hands through them to put them into some sort of order and Hugo's eyes narrowed.

"Pull it forward, over your breasts," he commanded. She obeyed and suddenly found herself lifted and carried to the bed where he laid her carefully against the pillows.

"Don't move," he ordered, toeing off his evening pumps. Lallie obeyed, her gaze riveted on the muscular body revealed as he stripped hastily before following her down onto the bed. "Don't move," he said again, and resumed his explorations with a slow, intense concentration that left her spellbound.

She seemed to have strayed into another world, a world of sensation lavished upon her by her husband as he slowly removed her remaining garments. His caresses led her inexorably into the unanticipated depths of a winding labyrinth, only to be seized at its centre by a breathless rapture. Caught in the ecstatic moment, she was barely conscious of Hugo stiffening above her until, with a long groan, he collapsed onto her breast.

"My God," he said after some minutes, and then, "I'm sorry, I'm too heavy for you." He lifted himself from her to lie beside her, pulling up the bedclothes to cover them.

"My God, Lallie," he said again and turned to kiss her gently.

"Mmmmm?" she responded, too bemused to speak.

He laughed softly. "Nothing, go to sleep," he murmured, and drew her securely to him.

London in November was grey and damp, wrapped in smoky fog that reeked of the ordure generated by hundreds of thousands of people and horses. The streets were filthy and Lallie was grateful for the pains taken by the purveyors of goods to the nobility and gentry to ensure the cleanliness of the side pavements in front of their premises. Ably abetted by Clarissa, whose notion of the wardrobe befitting Mrs Tamrisk's station was generous in the extreme, she spent hours visiting the most fashionable modistes as well as milliners, plumieres, and shoemakers. Then there were the fascinating little shops that sold dainty trifles such as fans, reticules and gloves. Frequently these excursions were linked with the invitation to join Clarissa on her morning calls or, on a rare fine day, to accompany her on an afternoon promenade in the park. Other days she spent with Henrietta.

You are fortunate Hugo's sisters are so supportive, Lallie reminded herself one wet afternoon. Just imagine if you had been left to your own devices, especially in this dreary weather. She had set herself the task of organising her personal accounts and was attempting to record her purchases as well as the gowns she had commissioned from *Madame Hortense* but her thoughts constantly drifted to Hugo. Most mornings he left the house after breakfast and she did not see him again until the evening— perhaps for dinner if Parliament wasn't sitting late. If they were invited elsewhere, he sometimes accompanied her, other times he looked in at some rout or supper-party in time to escort her home.

You are more than a month married now and the honeymoon is over, she told herself firmly. You must make your own life, Lallie. Her husband no longer came to her bed every night, but still frequently enough that she could not complain of being neglected although she had not again experienced the magic of that night after Clarissa's dinner. She knew now what he wanted of her—'don't move', he had said, not once but twice—and she made herself lie passively beneath him although at times she longed to clasp him to her. She had even survived the embarrassment of letting him know she was 'indisposed' when her courses came and, what was even more difficult, informing him that they were over. She hadn't known what to say and, in the end, had mentioned airily at breakfast that she was now 'quite well' again. He had taken the hint and come to her that night.

She bent again over her accounts book. This was a lot easier when I had little or no funds, she sighed and then had the grace to laugh at herself. It's really only *Madame Hortense;* I think I know what I have ordered from her, but we never discussed price. Clarissa appears to think it is vulgar even to consider it, but I need to know where I am. It would be dreadful if I started running up debts. How should I explain it to Hugo?

If *Madame Hortense* was surprised to find Mrs Tamrisk at her door at nine o'clock the next morning, she did not show it but ushered the lady to a seat.

"I wish to talk to you undisturbed, *Madame*," Lallie said bluntly. "I require, if you please, a detailed account of my purchases from you."

The modiste gave a knowing little smile. "There is no need to be concerned, *Madame*. We will send the bill to your husband—*monsieur* will surely not deny his bride."

"You will send the bill to me," Lallie replied crisply. She felt like laughing aloud at the change in the modiste's expression.

"*Madame* intends to manage her own affairs?"

At Lallie's surprised, 'of course', Hortense dropped her air of tacit feminine complicity and became all business.

"If that is indeed the case, and *Madame* proposes to settle her accounts promptly," a raised eyebrow accompanied this remark and Lallie nodded in confirmation, "she will find my charges most reasonable. But only for you, *Madame*—I must charge more when it may be months if not years before I am paid. Some ladies are always several quarters in arrears."

"Then why do you continue to make for them?" Lallie asked curiously.

The modiste shrugged. "It is the way of the *beau monde*; one must comply if one wishes to have their custom. Where they lead, others follow."

"I prefer to be beforehand with the world," Lallie said, smiling.

"It prevents the headache," *Madame* Hortense agreed.

"We must hurry," Lallie said as they left the shop, "I don't want to be late for breakfast."

As she and Nancy crossed to their carriage, a group of gentlemen who had spilled out from Gentleman Jackson's salon halted to let them pass. One of them bowed extravagantly. It was Frederick Malvin and Lallie turned her head away sharply.

"Phew! You must have offended the lady, Malvin," she heard one of his companions remark behind her. "Who is she?"

"A nobody—a little country mouse with ideas above her station," was the sneering reply.

Lallie sank back against the squabs. She was shaking.

"The impudence!" Nancy said fiercely. "He isn't fit to touch your hand, Miss Lallie. You must tell the master. He'll deal with him."

"I can't," Lallie said. "I should have to repeat what he said, Nancy. Don't ask it of me."

"Couldn't you just say you saw him?"

"Perhaps. I'll do it at breakfast if the opportunity presents itself."

But by the time they reached Tamarisk House, Hugo had left.

# Chapter Fifteen

*The grand source of the Rivers Envy and Spleen is thought to issue from the Mountains of Malice.*

"What news?" Ursula Grey asked without turning away from the mirror where she was admiring the look of a flattering new cap.

Her husband laid the November issue of *The Gentlemen's Magazine* in front of her and pointed to the rubric *Births and Marriages of Eminent Persons*.

"*At Tamm Manor, by special licence, the Hon. Hugo Tamrisk M.P. to Lalage Grey, eldest daughter of Robt. G. esq.,*" he read aloud. "The little jade must have gone directly to him. How did she know where to find him? Tell me that, Ursula."

"I'm sure I don't know, Robert. I'm glad to know she is safe, however," Mrs Grey declared, not disclosing that she had already received a brief note from her stepdaughter advising her of the marriage and returning her brooch and twenty pounds with sincere thanks. "He did seem greatly taken by her in September. I hope he will be good to her."

"And well he might be," Mr Grey snarled. "He pocketed at least sixty-five thousand quid on his wedding day."

Her jaw dropped. "What do you mean?"

"Nothing, nothing at all. He's a very wealthy man, that's all."

"Robert!" It was seldom that Ursula's voice took that steely tone, but when it did her husband knew there was nothing for it but to listen and comply. "How much was Lallie's fortune?" She rose and moved in front of him to block any attempt at escape.

"I just told you," he answered sullenly.

"You gave me eighty pounds each year for her expenses and another twenty for her pin-money. How much were you getting?" She did some rapid calculations. "Two to three thousand?"

"It was really Louisa's inheritance and should have come to me in the first place," he retorted self-righteously, then drew himself up to his full height, smirked at his wife and made to quit the room.

"We're not finished, Robert!"

"Kindly do not take that tone with me, Ursula. It is not seemly and you know I detest shrews."

If Mr Grey's lofty rebuke was an attempt to remove to higher ground, it did not succeed.

"I suppose we should be grateful that Lallie is unlikely to sue for recovery of your ill-gotten gains," his wife said icily. "It is time you faced up to your responsibilities and, for once in your life, thought of someone other than yourself. Through Lallie's marriage our children will have access to the topmost level of the *ton*. If she chooses to assist in bringing out the girls, there's no knowing how high they might look, and as for James—there is so much she or her new relatives might do for him, provided you don't spoil matters. A careless ne'er-do-well as a father will not serve to recommend any of them. What sort of example are you to your son? James will be fourteen this year and I certainly don't want him to follow in your footsteps."

He bridled at this, but she continued ruthlessly.

"You are no longer a boy, Robert or even a young man. Before you know it, you'll be one of those aging gamesters who hover on the fringes of the clubs hoping to find a pigeon ripe for plucking. Have you not noticed that your cronies are getting either younger or more disreputable as the decent men among your contemporaries withdraw to a more settled way of life? It is time you changed your ways. You must try to make up with your daughter and accustom yourself to behaving in a manner more appropriate to your circumstances."

"Make up? How?"

"By apologising for the misunderstanding when the opportunity presents itself. You will know how to do it—you always did have a smooth tongue. The important thing is that it is all glossed over; the last thing we want is for her to refuse to acknowledge us."

"That would be fatal," he agreed. "I understand they are in town. Perhaps it would be best if I called at Tamarisk House to see her privately."

She nodded. "An excellent notion! In addition, I shall write and congratulate her on her marriage. The girls will send her little notes as well. She is very attached to them and it will do no harm to remind her of her sisters."


The solicitor peered over his steel eyeglasses at his new client. "You cannot enforce the contract, sir. It is illegal to force a woman into marriage, even if the lady in question had not already wed another."

"But I have been injured by her," Frederick Malvin declared. "I have borrowed against my legitimate expectations and since that damned notice appeared, the cent-per-cents are hounding me. Her father signed the settlements, damn it."

"In that case you could sue him for breach of contract, providing the lady is a minor, that is."

"She is not," the other said shortly. "She is almost twenty-five."

The solicitor shook his head. "Then your only recourse under the law is to sue her for breach of promise of marriage. I take it you have evidence to support your case, apart from the settlement document, that is. Letters between you, little gifts exchanged, witnesses to your courtship and betrothal."

"It was all arranged between me and her father," Mr Malvin said sulkily. "I applied for a special licence," he offered.

"That would be no help, unless the lady had signed the application or signified in some way that she was agreeable to the match."

"I had her father's word for it! He went to see her trustee with me."

"Did you in fact make her an offer of marriage, either written or oral?"

"Directly? No."

"And indirectly?"

"I danced with her and sat beside her at church. Her parents approved. It was all agreed between us."

"Between her parents and you, you mean. Did she ever give you cause to believe she would welcome your suit?"

"She gave me no reason to assume she would not."

The solicitor frowned. "That is not enough, sir. If you will take my advice, you will let the matter go. I cannot imagine any jury finding in your favour if you were to go to court and you would only make a laughing-stock of yourself into the bargain. The next time you contemplate marriage," he added blandly, "I suggest you secure the lady's consent before raising the wind on your expectations."

"Damn your eyes! You may save your advice for those who want it, sirrah!"

Mr Malvin clapped his hat on his head and stormed out of the office. He would have his revenge. For a start, he would see what he could get out of Grey. Maybe the threat of an action would bring him somewhere. And that daughter of his, daring to cut him! He would make her sorry.

"There is no need to send the usual fee note," the solicitor told his clerk as the door slammed behind his visitor. "He won't pay and I would as soon have nothing more to do with him. Should he call again, I am unavailable."

Hugo looked at his wife. She had dismissed the servants, so presumably she wished to discuss something with him. How had it come to this, that the only time she could be sure of doing so was at breakfast? It was his sisters' fault of course. They had swooped down and taken possession of her and, once again, excluded him.

He sipped his coffee and waited for Lallie to break the silence between them. When the door clicked shut, she said, "My father called yesterday."

His hand jumped. He carefully replaced the cup on the saucer and wiped his fingers. "He had the temerity to come here? When?"

"About five o'clock."

"Did you receive him?"

She nodded. "I thought it best. I am bound to encounter him somewhere and it was better that our first meeting was in private. I had Nancy join me."

Hugo raised an eyebrow. "What did he say to that?"

"He gave me one of his cool smiles and said, 'I see you now have a lady-in-waiting'. When I replied that I had not felt very comfortable the last time I had been in his company, he at once became more conciliatory. He had thought he was acting in my best interest and he wished to apologise for any misunderstanding that might have arisen between us, in particular for any words of his that might have caused me to leave the protection of my family. He hoped they would not lead to a permanent breach between us and said that my sisters missed me sorely."

Her voice broke on the last words and Hugo went to kneel beside her chair.

"I miss them too," she whispered.

He covered her hand with his, furious at Mr Grey who had known exactly where to place the dart.

172

"How did you respond?"

Her hand twisted and clung to his. "I didn't know what to say, Hugo. I do love the girls and James, and I can't forget how Mrs Grey enabled me to escape. By cutting him off, I would cut them off too, would I not?"

"It is likely he would forbid any contact," he agreed.

"On the other hand, I didn't want him to think he merely had to apologise and all would be forgiven and forgotten. And while he says he regrets his actions now, I'm not sure that he does. I remain convinced that he meant everything at the time. To say there was a misunderstanding implies that I was as much if not more to blame in reacting as I did and I refuse to accept that."

"Nor should you."

"So I said that while I would be prepared to put what had happened behind us, it was difficult to mend a shattered trust and I would prefer the connection between us to remain coolly civil for the time being. However, if Mrs Grey and the children wished to write to me, I would welcome their letters and would reply."

She looked anxiously at him. "What do you think, Hugo? Did I do the right thing?"

"I think you dealt with it perfectly, Lallie." He sat back on his heels and smiled at her.

"I also asked him not to call again. It will be enough to meet him in public, I think."

"I agree."

So she had been at home yesterday afternoon. It was on the tip of his tongue to ask her if she wished to do something, anything with him later on today when the doorbell pealed.

Lallie's hand slipped from his. She jumped up. "That will be Clarissa."

Hugo got to his feet and went to finish his cold coffee.

# Chapter Sixteen

*The Island of Perseverance, on the opposite side, is good if the travellers be on a right course: further lies the Island of Obstinacy.*

Preparations for Christmas at Tamm were much more sedate than at Alwood Hall. On Christmas Eve the ashen faggot, which here replaced the Yule log, would be lit in the hall with the household in attendance but there would be no other festivities.

"What of the tenants and the villagers?" Lallie asked Hugo. "Is something done for them, especially the poor among them?"

"Carey and Jenkinson, my land agent, see to all that, but we are not involved."

"You perhaps not, but I should certainly be. It's late I know, but I'll talk to them and the vicar as well."

On Christmas Eve the hall was perfunctorily decorated with greenery. Once it was dark, the doors to the saloon were opened to display Lord Tamm seated in his great chair, attended by his son, daughter-in-law and the most senior members of his household. The indoor and outdoor servants waiting in the hall made their reverences before a footman opened the great oak door to admit four men bearing a great faggot of long green ash-sticks bound tightly together with nine bands of ash. They carried it ceremoniously into the hall and rolled it to the hearth where it was secured by two chains that apparently were fitted there just for this purpose.

Hugo stepped forward to light the bed of tinder on which it was placed—Lallie learnt later that this was the remains of the previous year's faggot—and the company watched anxiously as the first flames licked along the outside of this year's offering. Once they flickered and caught, jugs of sparkling cider were passed from hand to hand, spilling into tankards and beakers and layering the scent of tart apples over that of the new fire.

"What are the girls watching so intently?" Lallie asked Mrs Morton, nodding towards a group of maids who stood gig-gling and pointing beside the hearth.

"They each pick out one of the bands that bind the faggot, ma'am, and believe that the one whose band breaks first will be the next to marry."

Hugo reappeared accompanied by the head groom and the head gardener who bowed to their old master.

"Some more servants will come up now," he said to his wife. "Carey and Stiles will manage it; let us go into the hall."

They moved from group to group chatting with the staff while the steward brought forward a select few to talk to his lordship; in general those who had been in the family's employ-ment for many years. A flare and a sharp crack heralded the breaking of the first band, causing cries of "Becky, 'tis Becky", to the blushes of the girl and the bashful grin of one of the grooms as more cider was brought in celebration.

This was the only hint of spontaneity in proceedings which Lallie found constrained and dreary compared with the ceremony and merriment that would have accompanied such an evening at Alwood or Larkhaven. There were no words of appreciation from the master to his servants; no reciprocal expressions of gratitude from the servants to their master, no Christmas wishes conveyed and no toasts drunk. The servants seemed uneasy to be above stairs. They were on their best behaviour and Hugo's and her perambulation through the hall resembled more a royal progress than the friendly intermingling of family and staff that would acknowledge all present as one household.

"Does anyone play the fiddle or a tin whistle?" she asked in desperation after yet another chorus of 'yes, ma'ams'. "We could have some dancing."

After some shuffling and giggling, a footman and a maid (cousins, someone whispered to her) vanished and returned with their instruments.

"Can you play 'Gathering Peascods'?"

"Yes, ma'am."

"Come and dance," Lallie ordered her husband.

He touched his forehead, grinning. "Yes, ma'am!"

They walked into the centre of the hall where Lallie beckoned encouragingly to the staring servants. "Come! Join us!"

After a startled moment, the young groom seized Becky and tugged her onto the impromptu dance floor. The infectious rhythm did the rest. Soon ten couples bowed and curtseyed before launching into the lively dance. By the time they finished with a grand chain, the ice was well and truly broken. The non-dancers had moved to the side of the room and the almost painfully low hum of stilted conversation was transformed into a boisterous, more natural sound as they made themselves heard over the music and the clapping and rhythmical tapping of feet.

"You're a good girl and a good wife," Lord Tamm said when Lallie joined him after four dances. He was nodding in time to the music. "It used to be like this long ago, you know. I don't know where the joy went."

He reached over to take her hand, gazing wistfully at the dancers and causing Lallie's tender heart to ache a little. She could think of nothing to say—by all accounts he was largely to blame for the lack of joy at Tamm, but she left her hand in his and they sat companionably watching the merry throng.

"It reminds me of my boyhood, before my grandmother died," Lord Tamm said. "She was used to lead the dancing too, but it stopped then. My mother did not approve."

"You did not think to revive it later?"

He patted her hand. "My wife was never the contented bride that you are, my dear. She did her duty, but no more. It would never have occurred to her that the servants might wish to dance or that she might dance with them. This," he gestured, "the faggot, was old-fashioned superstition to hear her talk.

"It was a match made by our fathers. Hers had taken the wrong side in '45 and although he escaped the worst sanction, he was left with very little so he could not dower her properly, but he owned a small parcel of land that marches with our western border. My father was wishful to have it and I was happy to go along with the match. You will have seen her portrait—you know how beautiful she was, but to her it was all duty." His voice hardened. "When I realised that, I was determined that if duty was all she offered, she would fulfil that duty to the last jot. And so she did, even if it took her over twenty years to present me with my heir."

Lallie frowned distastefully at the odd note of gratification in his tone, almost as if he had taken pleasure in compelling his wife's submission. She withdrew her hand from under his and went to dance with Hobbs.

Golden flames signalled the simultaneous breaking of another two bands, leading to a pause for the distribution of yet more cider.

"Just as well. I must catch my breath. The master has me run off my feet," Mrs Morton said to Lallie. She chuckled and patted her bosom before fanning herself with her hand. "'Tis good to see the old revels return to Tamm."

"What made you think of dancing?" Hugo asked as they shared a late supper in her apartments.

"Why, it's usual at such celebrations, isn't it," Lallie replied, astonished. "There is almost always someone able to play and people like it; it puts them at ease. Didn't you approve?"

"Of course I did. It made the evening much more enjoyable. In other years I think the servants felt so uncomfortable that they could hardly wait to be dismissed."

"We'll do more next year," she promised, "especially if we can be here earlier. Arriving on the twenty–second is really too late." She raised her glass. "Merry Christmas, Hugo."

He touched his glass to hers. "May it be the first of many together."

She handed him a soft package. "It's just a token," she said shyly. "A little Christmas gift I made myself."

Hugo unfolded the wrapping to find six linen handkerchiefs that were finely hemmed and exquisitely embroidered, white on white, with a monogram of "HT" bracketed by sprigs of tamarisk.

He stared at them silently for so long that she started to fidget. At last he looked up and smiled almost painfully at her.

"Thank you, my dear. It is the first time anyone has made me a gift with her own hands. They are almost too beautiful to use, but I know I shall not be able to resist having such evidence of your thoughtfulness with me."

Lallie was amazed. He had three older sisters and even Arabella was eighteen. Every lady was proficient in some form of needlework. Surely over the years at least one of them would have made something for a brother or uncle? But then he came round the table to thank her with a long kiss and all thought of his sisters was put to flight.

Once Christmas was over, Lallie could turn her attention to the trunks Mr Lambe had sent from Larkhaven and, to her pleased surprise, the carrier had also delivered a box from Alwood containing her personal belongings.

*I have omitted your old gowns,* Mrs Grey had written, *as they are not suitable for your new station in life. The ladies of the literary circle send their felicitations and beg you will accept the volumes of Pride and Prejudice as a memento of the happy hours you spent together. I hope too, dear Mrs Tamrisk, that you will accept the enclosed fan as a token of my affection and esteem.*

The fan, one that Lallie had always admired, was clearly a peace offering. She smiled wistfully at the little sampler Beatrice had embroidered and the water-colour of their village Eleanor had painted. I must have them framed, she thought, and I shall have a gown made to match the subtle shades of the fan.

"Are you going to open the trunks? May I help?" Hugo asked eagerly.

He was like an excited child, watching as she carefully turned the keys in the locks, throwing up the lids of the trunks and boxes as soon as they were opened, and then went more slowly from one to the other to examine the contents.

"Grandmamma's lavender water!" Eyes closed, she savoured the scent. "Here is Grandpapa's balsam—he used it after shaving for his skin was greatly prone to irritation. There were marigolds in it, I know. I must see if the receipt is there, for your father's cheeks are inclined to be dry and sore. Oh and here are Grandmamma's silver brushes and combs and her lace caps—she always prided herself on her pretty caps—and her fans. And here, Grandpapa's diaries. Grandmamma kept them by her bed and was used to read in them each night before going to sleep. 'It's like a goodnight kiss,' she said to me once."

Tears filled Lallie's eyes. "Why did no one ever tell me this was still there? There would have been room for it at Alwood, you know."

Hugo hugged her consolingly. "You have it now."

Here at Tamm, he sought her company more often than he had in town. Of course, there was less for him to do, she supposed. When he came to her bed he remained longer and there was something comfortably intimate about falling asleep, his arm around her and his cheek on her hair.

"I hear Albright is dead," Lord Tamm announced.

Hugo dabbed his lips with his napkin and said calmly, "Is that so, sir? I had not seen any notice."

"On Twelfth Night, I am told. And without an heir. He was sadly disappointed in his first wife and this second one doesn't seem to have done any better."

Hugo stared blindly at his plate. He had heard nothing of Sabina since Lady Nugent's archery fête. Had she lost the child or was her condition generally not known? He became dimly aware of Lallie's voice.

"I am sorry to hear it. He seemed a very pleasant man. I only met him twice, but found him most amiable."

"Were you introduced to his wife as well?" Lord Tamm demanded.

"Yes."

"Then pray write to her and convey my condolences with your own."

Seated at her escritoire, Lallie reviewed the little conversation. She was forced to admire her husband's composure. No one could have guessed from his impassive features that his father had just requested his wife to write to his mistress. But Lord Tamm presumably knew nothing of the connection and she could not admit to being aware of it. Before he had withdrawn to the library, Hugo had curtly issued his own instructions.

"When you write to Lady Albright, pray add my condolences to yours and his lordship's. And, as you are writing at my father's request, I think it would be more appropriate for him to frank the letter."

Very neatly done, sir, she said to herself, drawing a sheet of paper towards her. Members of both Houses of Parliament were entitled to frank letters and she usually took hers to Hugo, but presumably he wished to avoid scrawling his name across a letter to his paramour, especially one written by his wife. He had also subtly suggested the tone her letter should take. She supposed she should applaud the delicacy of his sentiments but, as she bent to her task, his consideration for the other woman stung her heart.

Grateful for any diversion, Lallie flicked idly through the pages of *The Ladies' Universal Register*. The mail had been delayed by the fog and heavy snow that had confined her to the house for much of January. Even though the paths in the walled garden had been cleared, the soles of her half-boots were too thin to walk for long on the frozen ground. At Mrs Morton's suggestion, she had borrowed pattens from one of the maids, but had felt so unsteady that she had had to cling to Hugo's arm, much to his amusement.

She would have a pair of calfskin boots made in London, she decided, akin to gentlemen's boots. She could wear them walking or with her riding habit. Hobbs had already suggested he look out for a sturdy Dartmoor pony for her before the next winter as it would be a sin to risk the pretty mare Hugo had bought her in such conditions.

She skimmed a description of the Frost Fair held on the frozen Thames. Hugo hoped to return to town by the first of March. Would they still travel if the weather remained so cold? She would be glad to get away from Tamm. Yawning, she turned the page.

*Tonnish Topics and Society Secrets.* There would hardly be much of interest at this time of the year, but it was amusing trying to decipher the innuendos. Grandmamma wouldn't have approved; she would have called the insinuations malicious and uncharitable, Lallie thought as she glanced down the columns. Suddenly she sat bolt upright, the journal crumpled between her clutching hands.

*Did T—Risk Hymen's bonds too soon? Does he regret his rush to the altar now that his Bright star shines free of all constraints? Perhaps not. Having already shown his disdain for another's nuptial vows, will it not be All one to him if he betrays his own?*

It's impossible! She must be mistaken. She took a steadying breath and read the offending passage again. It did seem quite apt, she thought dismally, but surely she was wrong in identifying Hugo and Lady Albright? She didn't know which suggestion was worse; that he might regret his marriage now that his mistress was free or that he would happily resume their liaison. Not for the first time, she regretted the impulse that had sent her in search of her locket. Perhaps it would have been better if she hadn't overheard Hugo's sisters talking about their brother. No; better to be forewarned, she thought sadly, especially if such comments were general. It would be dreadful to be taken unawares.

In the library Hugo frowned over a letter from his closest friend.

*Old Norris is more unbearable than ever. He was Albright's heir, as he never tired of reminding us, but it now appears that Lady A is in an interesting condition, with the child due in April. He only discovered this when he came to the funeral and, I hear, was so unpleasant that she has forbidden him the house until the question of the succession is decided. I hope her husband made proper provision for her, poor lady, for N. will not be kind to her should she bear a daughter. He is already hinting that his 'poor cousin' may have been subject to the 'worst possible deception'. Not that these hints could bring him any benefit for, as you know, in law the husband must always be the father; 'Pater est quem nuptiae demonstrant'.*

*As far as I am concerned, it is simply a case of 'sour grapes' on his part. While it is generally better to ignore these things, I took the opportunity of saying so the other evening when the subject came up at Brooks's. Luckily, N. has never been popular while the lady is well liked and those present agreed with me. Forgive me for being the bearer of bad news, but I thought you should know.*

*Yours, as ever, Gervase.*

Hugo tossed the letter into the library fire. What a coil. Poor Sabina. Norris had a reputation for being spiteful, so people would be less inclined to believe him, but the story was clearly making the rounds. What if it reached Lallie's ears? What could he say to her?

Moodily, he poured himself another glass of brandy. He felt a certain obligation to Sabina. Was there some way he could assure her of his support without making matters worse? He shrugged. He could do nothing from here. Once they were in town, he would take some discreet soundings.

"Leave it, Hugo," Gervase Naughton advised his friend. He dropped a log onto the flames, dusted off his hands and lifted the jug. "More ale?"

"Thank you." Hugo drank deeply. "It just doesn't seem right, Ger."

Mr Naughton propped his feet on the brass fireplace fender. "There's nothing you can do," he pointed out. "Not only is she in deep mourning, she expects to be brought to bed within the next weeks. She won't leave the house and you certainly can't journey into the country to call on her without putting the cat among the pigeons. The odds are there's a rabble of female relatives there to support her."

"I suppose you're right," Hugo conceded reluctantly.

"You know I am. If you play these games, you must abide by the rules, the chiefest of which is discretion. And, if it comes to that, there was no whisper of Albright denying paternity, was there? According to my uncle, he was delighted at the news."

"Then why didn't Norris know earlier?"

"He, Albright, I mean, couldn't stand him. My uncle only knew because they met at the opening of Parliament. Albright didn't remain in town afterwards but went home directly."

"She told me he was very pleased," Hugo remembered.

"There you are! All Norris can hope for is that the child is a girl. My sister says that would be her preference if she were in her ladyship's position. Much simpler than being the dowager mother of an infant peer, especially with a resentful heir presumptive."

"I never looked at it that way, but there is some truth in what she says," Hugo acknowledged. "However, I think Lady Albright would prefer to give her husband his heir, even posthumously."

"You don't think he encouraged her, do you?" Gervase demanded, startled. "You're not unlike him, you know. He was white at the end but when he was younger, his colouring and physique must have resembled yours."

Hugo shrugged. "God alone knows. Pour me some brandy, there's a good chap, and tell me what you think of the news from France. Are we going to pull it off at last?"

Hugo walked slowly home from Gervase's Albany set, deep in thought. Could Sabina really have duped him? Were stud services all she had required of him? He couldn't believe it. With her, for the first time in his life, he had experienced intimacy not only of the body but also of the spirit. There had been tears in her eyes that last morning. No matter how mixed her motives might have been, he couldn't believe her pleasure in his company had been feigned. And he had enjoyed their liaison, he remembered ruefully; it was her loss that had made him for the first time consider matrimony.

"Watch out, sir!"

Hugo stepped back out of the way of the heavy dray laden with barrels and nodded an acknowledgment of the carter's warning.

"I hope you are not planning to make my daughter a widow as quickly as you made her a wife, Tamrisk," a light voice said behind him.

He looked over his shoulder. There, his right leg crossed nonchalantly in front of the left in Mr Wilson's fifth position for dancing, immaculate from the precise tilt of his hat to his clinging pantaloons, stood Mr Grey, the epitome of the older Bond Street lounger.

Hugo looked down his nose. "Your daughter, Grey, is no longer your concern. You would do well to remember that. Good day to you."

Content to see the mocking smile wither on his challenger's lips, Hugo nodded briefly and strode on. His father-in-law's dart had stung. Had he indeed wed Lallie too quickly? At the time he had felt driven both to make her safe and to make her his. And she had certainly resisted vehemently when he had offered to free her from their engagement. She didn't seem to regret their marriage; she had found her feet quickly enough, both at Tamm and here in town, where she was surrounded whenever she went into society. She had made friends with his family— she spent more time with them than she did with him—she always seemed to be out with Clarissa or Henrietta or Arabella. Almack's first ball was next week. It would be even worse from then on.

Lallie yielded sweetly to him in bed, it was true, but, in the depths of his heart, he must admit that she did not respond as ardently as he would like and always at the end there was that little sigh, as if she was glad that he had finished. So what have you to complain about, he asked himself savagely. That your wife is not as fond as you would wish? You can hardly tell her you wish she were less inanimate. And what good would it do you? Do you want her to fake a response like a whore?

One of the disadvantages of fashionable life, Lallie thought as she dressed for Almack's, was that she did not have the opportunity properly to enjoy a new gown. Where previously she might have had one or at most two new costumes each Season, and would have worked with Ursula and Nancy to refurbish her old ones, now she seemed to wear something new every day. Tonight's ball gown was her favourite. Its short puffed sleeves and underskirt were of the palest raspberry satin, with an overskirt of fine white gauze. The low-cut bodice was of a deeper raspberry with a provocative little trim of white lace that flirted with her breasts, while little tassels at the high waistline and hem would swing gently when she danced. Matching ribbons were twined through her hair and the most delicate pink satin slippers encased her feet. Her grandmother's pearls gleamed softly against her skin.

Hugo was waiting in the hall. "Exquisite as always," he said.

"You are most elegant yourself, sir," she returned, admiring the impeccable pale silk knee breeches and waistcoat, beautifully set off by a dark blue coat and a snowy cravat that managed to combine elegance and comfort.

"So this is Tamrisk's bride," Lady Jersey said with a condescending smile, while Lady Cowper said more warmly, "Welcome, Mrs Tamrisk."

"There you are at last," Lady Malvin exclaimed when they entered the ballroom. "Really, Hugo, could you not have come earlier? It is almost time for the dancing to begin. You will lead Lallie out, of course."

"Of course," he agreed.

This was the first London ball Lallie had attended and she was astounded by the number of people who came to speak to her or to seek an introduction. She had not expected to be besieged—she was neither an incomparable nor an heiress newly arrived on the marriage market—and was grateful for Hugo's solid presence by her side. Finally the dancing started and he led her onto the floor.

"I must congratulate you on your success," he drawled as they waited to commence the figure.

"I'm sure it's just that it is my first appearance," she answered sensibly.

The following evening, the talk was all of the fall of Paris.

"After so long," one mother said with a deep sigh. "It's like a miracle. I wonder how soon they'll be home."

"Presumably some troops must remain until we can be sure the country is pacified and a treaty has been signed," a gentleman put in.

"By Jove, yes. Think of the complexity of unravelling all that Boney has wrought," Lord Malvin commented.

"Everyone who was defeated by him will wish to have their boundaries restored to the *status quo ante* and all the victors will seek to be rewarded for their pains," Hugo remarked. "You may be sure that in some cases might will prevail over right. Europe will never be the same again."

"It must be an immense undertaking, stopping an army in its tracks like that," Gervase Naughton reflected.

"Especially when the army is so well-organised," Captain Malvin observed wryly to general laughter.

"Does it seem strange to be talking about the end of the war here in London?" Lallie asked him. "You must be glad it's finally over, but I expect you would prefer to be with your comrades in arms. You have been through so much together and it must be hard for you not to have been able to participate in the final victory."

"I do feel somewhat out of step, I suppose. I would never belittle the torments of worry and grief that soldiers' families suffer, but the experience there is so different to here. I can't but think of all that has happened in the six years we were in the Peninsula, of those who survived and the ones we left there. And I ask myself what will become of my men. Will they simply be disbanded to fend for themselves? I hope it will not be long until I am passed fit for light duties and able to re-join them."

"Have you seen this," Gervase asked Hugo as they headed towards Brooks's. He handed him a pamphlet entitled A *Sportsman in Town*. "It's the usual *ton* tittle-tattle, but couched in male rather than female terms. Look at the second page, halfway down the first column."

*It was neck and neck in the Albright Stakes, but we hear that the former holder has gained the day by a grand spurt at the finish. We trust the challenger will now concede gracefully and desist from further unsportsmanlike behaviour.*

"It's a boy, then," Hugo said numbly.

"It would appear so, but it could be purely speculative. Norris won't be pleased, especially if he gets wind of that rebuke."

# Chapter Seventeen

*The most elevated Mountains are those of Malice. The Lynx is said to have been seen here.*

"Ware boarders," Henrietta said softly as the group of chattering peafowl approached. They were members of a particular set; unsuccessful *débutantes* who were spiteful towards those whom they perceived to be their rivals in the matrimonial stakes, and younger gentlemen whose flimsy sense of superiority expressed itself in a so-called wit that amused itself at the expense of others. While the 'poaching' of Mr Tamrisk was a particular affront to the females of this group, for it was not to be borne that a country unknown had carried off such a prize, the males had seized upon his declared intention to wed a country mouse as an instrument with which to torment his bride.

Lallie could not have said when it became apparent that their attention was not kindly meant. Gradually she came to realise that repeated references to mice or squeaks or the use of phrases such as 'parson's mousetrap' or 'when the cat's away' were not inadvertent and that the participants in this game, of which she was supposed to be the oblivious butt, kept score through meaningful glances, titters and raised fans. Thanks to the support of the Malvins and the Fordes, who ensured that she was never left to face the clique alone, she was able to bear it stoically, refusing to give them the satisfaction of any overt reaction to their teasing.

Hugo, who rarely remained with her once they had been joined by either of his sisters, did not seem to have noticed anything untoward and she could not bring herself to mention it to him as this would entail her acknowledgement of his slighting remark; a mortification she had no wish to add to her present misery.

"May I present Mr Jasper Norris, Mrs Tamrisk?"

Lallie nodded coolly to the young dandy bowing before her, an exercise made more difficult by the immense starched neckcloth and high collar that forced his chin up and his head back into an unnatural position.

"Your obedient, ma'am," he drawled, taking up a central position in the semi-circle that formed about her. He had all the look of the self-considered wit determined to loose a carefully honed *bon mot*. Within five minutes he seized his opportunity.

"Speak up, pray, Fortune," he exhorted one of his cronies. "He mutters like a mouse in the cheese, does he not, Mrs Tamrisk?"

His sycophants tittered admiringly but Lallie ignored him, turning to speak to Charles Forbes.

Riled by this slight, Mr Norris quoted testily, "'*Good my mouse of virtue, answer me*'," at the same time slanting a look towards his companions as if to applaud his own cleverness.

One of the bystanders muttered under his breath, "Thirty—love."

Lallie had had enough. "I am neither a mouse nor yours, sir," she said icily. "If you wish to play the clown, I recommend you seek more appreciative company, for I do not find you in any way diverting but rather a dead bore."

"Well-said, Mrs Tamrisk," Lady Needham, who had been standing nearby, exclaimed. She raised her lorgnette to inspect Mr Norris disapprovingly. "As for you, sir, I suggest you take yourself off until you have learnt how to behave."

Crimson-faced and visibly deflated by this public rebuke, Mr Norris withdrew, deserted by his hangers-on who had already slunk out of her ladyship's range.

"It's high time you put a stop to that nonsense," Lady Needham commended Lallie. She was a small, elderly lady, whose faded beauty was revived by a smile of great charm. A turban of silver and amethyst silk sat just so on hair whose original red had faded to a soft gold. "I am glad to see you have a backbone, child," she added.

"I thought if I ignored them, they would go away," Lallie explained.

"It is unusual for that sort of craze to continue as long as it did," Lady Needham conceded. "Well, you have put your tormentors to rout. Come and meet my god-grandson, as he claims to be. I can recommend him as a dancing partner." She gestured to a tall, fair-haired man who obligingly swerved towards them.

"Ma'am?"

"May I present Mr Fitzmaurice as a suitable dancing partner, Mrs Tamrisk?" Lady Needham enquired, a twinkle in her eye.

Lallie smiled at him as he straightened from his bow. "Mr Fitzmaurice."

"May I have the honour, Mrs Tamrisk?" he requested. "It is wiser to obey her in the first instance," he added with a side-long glance at her ladyship.

"And see that you remember it," the older woman retorted.

"She is my mother's godmother," Mr Fitzmaurice explained to Lallie as they walked onto the dance floor. "We all go in terror of her."

Was that Lallie's voice in the hall? Hugo could scarcely keep abreast of her activities. Now that the Season was in full swing, she was rarely at home, darting in and out only to change her attire, or so it seemed to him. It was not only his sisters who kept her from him; she had acquired her own court of admirers who found dancing attendance on a young wife preferable to falling prey to a match-making mamma. In addition she had been inducted into the group of young matrons who swarmed around the Duchess of Gracechurch. His wife one of 'Flora's Fillies'? It was not to be borne.

And yet he could not keep away from the drawing-rooms and ballrooms where she shone. He refused to play the jealous husband glowering impotently from the side of the room but too often found himself striding towards her to claim the next dance, his glare banishing any other pretenders—like a dog with his hackles up, ready to growl at all comers, he thought disgustedly.

Lallie put her head around the open library door. "Hugo?"

He rose politely, teeth bared in a parody of a smile.

"Good afternoon, my dear. What an unexpected pleasure."

She turned scarlet at his sarcastic tone. "I beg your pardon for disturbing you."

Ashamed, Hugo fought for self-control. "I'm sorry, Lallie. Come and sit down. Is there something I can do for you?"

She advanced further into the room but didn't accept his invitation to sit.

"Not precisely for me, but for my grandmother. She writes that the bonesetter insists Sir Howard's arm remain immobilised for another two weeks and he is becoming more and more cantankerous. He cannot write; even reading is difficult, she says, as he cannot hold the book open, and of course riding is out of the question. She asks if I would come and help her divert him. Should you have any objection? You need not accompany me; I know you have many commitments and I daresay you would find it extremely tedious. I probably will too," she added candidly, "but they were very good to me last year and I should like to help if I can. I'll be back for Clarissa's ball."

"Of course you must go," Hugo said. He wouldn't have minded getting away from town, but apparently she preferred to be on her own. "Hobbs will go with you, of course, and a footman."

"Thank you!" She smiled gratefully at him. "I'll leave in the morning. I'll just pen notes crying off my engagements. I won't go to Almack's tonight either. I must let Clarissa know—I was to dine there first." She hurried out of the room.

As soon as the door closed behind her, Hugo sank into the nearest chair, dropping his head into his hands. How could he have been so churlish? It was no wonder she was so pleased to leave him.

Where had he gone wrong? If only he could go back and do, do what? There was no one moment that he could identify as having changed things between them. It was almost impossible to put his finger on what precisely had altered. He supposed, when it came to it, they had not so much grown apart as failed to come together. Or had he simply expected too much from her?

He couldn't bear to let her leave like that. He looked around the room for inspiration, picked up the latest issue of *The Gentleman's Magazine* and headed for her boudoir. She sat at her writing-desk in the window, her back to the door, head bent as she scribbled industriously. It was in these private moments that the distance between them seemed greatest. And yet, she never refused him. She was—dutiful, he thought sadly. And there was a glitter to her smile that had not been there before.

She sealed her letter and looked up. "Hugo?"

He proffered the magazine. "I thought you might like to take this to Sir Howard."

"That is most thoughtful. Thank you." She rose and went to the bell-pull while Hugo stood awkwardly, unsure what to do next.

"John should go first to Malvin House," she instructed the butler when she handed him the little stack of notes, "and tell Mrs Phipps I shall be in to dinner."

"I shall dine at home too, Phipps," Hugo said impulsively as the man reached the door.

"Very good, sir."

Hugo's spontaneous decision seemed to have nonplussed his wife. She contemplated him silently, then said, "I must talk to Nancy and Mrs Phipps. If you have time, would you speak to Hobbs for me, please?"

It was so long since they had dined *à deux* that Hugo was unsure where to join Lallie before their meal. She would hardly wait for him in the immense drawing-room. In the end he went to her bedroom where she sat at her dressing-table, just about to clasp a string of pearls about her neck.

"Let me," he said.

Lallie didn't protest but sat impassively while he fiddled with the clasp. She shivered when he laid the necklace against her skin and gave an embarrassed laugh. "Pearls are always cold."

He finished the little task and lifted his hands from her neck. "You look delightful."

For a fleeting moment her eyes met his in the looking-glass. "Thank you. It's a beautiful evening. Shall we stroll a little in the garden?"

The last time they had strolled together before dinner had been at her grandparents, he remembered with a pang. He had fastened a clasp for her then too and kissed her nape. And given her flowers. Had these little attentions meant anything to her?

Did she miss them? It was too early in the year for roses, but he broke off a small spray of Persian lilac and handed it to her.

Again that disconcerted glance but this time she smiled. "Thank you, Hugo."

She held it to her nose and inhaled luxuriously. "It has a wonderful scent," she commented, waving the blossoms gently to and fro as they meandered along paths bordered by neatly clipped low box hedges, the gravel crunching softly beneath their feet.

"Shall we sit for a minute?" he suggested when they reached a white bench set in a leafy arbour.

"Why not? The evening sun always feels like a blessing."

Hugo glanced down at her. She had raised her face to the sky, her eyes were closed and her dark lashes curled against her cheek.

Sitting beside her, he felt the tension that rode him constantly these days slacken its grip. An unexpected blessing, indeed. High above them, a blackbird fluted a twilight challenge and Hugo pursed his lips to whistle a light-hearted riposte.

"I didn't know you could do that," Lallie said, impressed, when the little contest ended.

He laughed. "It's not a particularly useful talent, I suppose."

"Perhaps not, but it gives pleasure and harms none." She got to her feet. "Shall we go in? I told Phipps we would eat in the breakfast parlour."

The new breakfast parlour was the one change Lallie had made to Tamarisk House, finding herself unwilling to face the morning gloom of the small dining-room, 'small' in that the table seated at most eighteen. She must have sun at breakfast. The new parlour was a corner room with windows to the south and east and was bright at any time of the day. Even now it was airy and inviting.

"This is a splendid idea," Hugo said as he seated her at the round table. "Is that the first asparagus I see? Excellent!" He took his place opposite her. "Will you take soup?"

Lallie let him serve her. Earlier in the library, he had regarded her almost disdainfully and his tone had cut her to the quick. But he had apologised quickly and since then was all compliments, smiles and flowers. He had even changed his plans in order to dine at home with her. I never know where I am with him, she thought.

"I told Hobbs to bring the carriage around at ten o'clock in the morning," Hugo informed her. "Is that convenient for you?"

"Yes, perfectly, thank you."

"Is there anything else I may do for you?"

"No, thank you. Nancy has it all in hand."

They sipped their soup in strained silence. Once the tureen was removed and a plump sea trout in lobster sauce set in its place, Lallie dismissed the servants. What must they think of the stilted conversation between their master and mistress?

"I shall be glad to be out of town for a while." The heartfelt admission had escaped her lips before she could censor it.

Hugo raised an eyebrow. "Tired of the Season already, my dear? Do you not relish your success?"

"Success?" she repeated wryly.

"Why yes. You are to be seen everywhere and never want for company or dancing partners if it comes to that."

"And that is what you call success?"

"Do you not?"

"I shall be happy to have made some lasting friends, but as for the rest! How many do you think will seek me out next year when someone else will have replaced Tamrisk's bride as the latest object of curiosity and interest? If I come to town again, that is."

"Would you prefer to remain at Tamm?"

There was a cool edge to his voice and Lallie felt herself flush. "Not prefer, but—it may be necessary."

His expression softened. "Lallie! Do you mean to tell me—?"

She grew hot under his intense scrutiny. "No, no, but circumstances may change. I was just thinking aloud."

"I see." His smile faded and he leaned back in his chair. "Arthur has another medical board next week—the final one, he hopes."

"He is anxious to re-join his regiment. He says that if it were not for the fact that they had Boney on the run, they would have sent him back months ago even though the wound would not heal properly. I'll miss him—he has become a sort of brother to me, at least since he stopped addressing me as 'aunt'."

Hugo helped himself to a meringue of young rhubarb. "How did you make him do that?"

"I said that I would be more than happy to take on the role and would begin by selecting a suitable bride for him. What did he think of Miss Finlay, for example? I would be delighted to make him known to her."

He grinned appreciatively at her smug smile. "You little devil! What did he say?"

"He laughed and said that on reflection he had enough aunts and would I have him as a brother? I was perfectly happy to do so, for I only have the one and he is ten years younger."

She would like to have some family of her own, Lallie thought wistfully. Although Hugo's relatives had been most kind, she would not feel comfortable in confiding in them. I wish there was some older lady I could talk to, there's the Duchess and Mrs Rembleton, of course, but I don't know them well enough.

"I'll leave you to your port," she said when the meal ended.

"No, don't," he said, rising with her. "Shall we try that duo for harp and pianoforte? We haven't played together for some time."

"The Dussek? I'd like that. I've been practising it recently but it's not the same on your own."

"No."

Hugo played middle C and waited while his wife ran her fingers over the strings in a ripple of sound, alternatively plucking and tightening them until her instrument was tuned to her satisfaction. She was so graceful, he thought, admiring the subtle curves of her arms and neck. She bit her lip, intent on her task and he wanted to kiss the little hurt away.

At last she looked over to him. Hands poised over the keys, he nodded and they plunged into the melody, now sharing the theme, now passing it back and forth between them, taking turns to shine and to support the other. He must concentrate on his music, but from time to time he stole a glance at the fingers flying up and down the harp-strings. They played well together—it was as if they breathed in unison. A brief pause and they began the slow, singing second movement. Why could they not find this harmony in their daily lives? The simple melody spun its magic but there was no time to dwell on their failings—the music pressed on, taking them with it to the final flurry and a last chord. Their hands stilled and their smiling eyes met in exhilaration and fulfilment.

"Oh, I enjoyed that, Hugo!" Lallie set the harp upright and stretched.

He beamed at her. "So did I. Have you another one? We could learn our parts while you are away."

She peeped up at him from beneath her lashes.

"What is it?" he asked curiously. Lallie never flirted with him.

"Charles Forbes has transcribed the orchestra part of Mozart's concerto for flute and harp for the pianoforte. He is looking for someone to learn it, then he and I could take the solo parts, he says."

"Good God! Do you have the music here?"

"Just the part for harp. But you could send to Charles for it. We don't need to attempt the whole at once, perhaps just try the first movement."

Had she deliberately set out to coax him? He didn't know, but it felt right, somehow. Hugo laughed. "Very well. I'll call on him in the morning."

He drew up another chair to the piano. "Come and play the Mozart sonata for four hands before we go."

"I'm very rusty," she said dubiously, "but I'll try."

This was even better. They attacked the music shoulder to shoulder, their hands scampering together along the keyboard, their bodies subtly swaying to the rhythm of the music, laughing when their fingers became entangled or stuttered to a stop.

"We have it now, Hugo," Lallie exclaimed at the end, her eyes shining. "Let's play it again, straight through."

Her rosy lips were temptingly near and he planted a quick kiss on them before leafing back to the first page of the score.

The new ease between them continued even after they left the music room and later, much later, when she sighed in his arms, for the first time Hugo wondered if it was a sigh of completion rather than resignation.

# Chapter Eighteen

*The Gulf of Despair is famous for the vast quantities of fish called Skate; that of Scandal is convenient for ships trading to this part. The Fort of Old Maids lies between these Gulfs.*

Mildly triumphant, Hugo played his Queen of spades to defeat the Jack and take the game and the rubber of whist.

"Well finessed, sir," an onlooker exclaimed, "a pretty tenace, upon my word."

"Tamrisk is known for his finesse," Mr Norris sneered from where he leaned against the mantelpiece.

Hugo and Gervase exchanged glances but said nothing. Norris clearly still resented the loss of his cousin's title and estates.

"Another rubber?" one of their opponents suggested, but Gervase shook his head.

"Only look how he contrived to deceive my poor cousin while at the same time wooing the country mouse!" Norris raised a pinch of snuff to his nose and sneezed loudly. "Why he is a veritable master at playing the reverse."

Hugo stood abruptly and prowled across the room towards his sniggering antagonist who backed away until some kind soul pulled him aside to save his coat-tails from the flames.

Hugo stopped and eyed Mr Norris disdainfully, oblivious to the hush that fell on the room. "You will hear from me, sir."

The flare of a guttering candle lit Norris's paling countenance. He bowed abruptly. "I am at your service, sir!"

The silence broke as suddenly as it had fallen. Hugo ignored
the babble and returned to the card table to settle up and make
his farewells.

"It couldn't be avoided, I suppose," Gervase remarked as he and
Hugo strolled along Jermyn Street.

"No. It's the first time he has had the temerity to say something in my hearing and to drag Lallie into as well was unpar-
donable." Hugo grinned suddenly. "It's fortunate she is visiting
her grandparents—I should be able to get it all out of the way
before she returns."

"What will you do?"

"I'll write to him requesting satisfaction. He may apologise
or meet me." They had reached Albany. "I'll leave you here for
now, old man. Come to breakfast?"

"Of course."

Hugo laughed. "I never asked you, did I? You will act for
me, won't you?"

"Of course," Gervase said again.

A weak, grey light straggled in through the open curtains, sig-
nalling the break of day. He would sleep no longer. He was
in Lallie's room. To sleep in her bed had somehow made her
absence more bearable, although the first night he had had to get
up and search her dressing table for her perfume. A few drops on
the pillow case, although not as complex as her unique, elusive
scent, had made him feel less lonely. Another time he would
remember to tell the housekeeper not to change the sheets after
she left. But hopefully there wouldn't be too many 'other times'.

Without her, the house was empty; vacant in a different way
to when he knew she was simply in and out between her many

errands and engagements. He hadn't realised how accustomed he had become to hearing her step on the stair or her voice in the hall, the rustle of her skirts or the cascade of notes from her harp tumbling through the house. Sometimes, if he dozed in her bed, she fell asleep and rolled to rest confidingly against him. Then he would turn carefully to clasp her to him, but never so tightly that she might not escape if she wished. For always, when he woke again, she had separated from him.

Did she miss him, Hugo wondered. Did her bed seem empty too? He hoped so, especially after that last night together. He had practised his brother-in-law's pianoforte arrangement assiduously—it provided some sort of connection with her. When she returned, he would suggest that they set aside one evening each week to dine quietly together and to make music.

But what if this morning's meeting went awry? She would be angry with him. Would she feel he had wantonly abandoned her? That might be true, but he didn't see how he could permit Norris to extend his slurs to her. She was innocent in all of this and he greatly resented the implication that he had paid court to her while dallying with Sabina. As God was his judge, that was not true.

Tormented by the thought that this lie might be repeated to Lallie as fact, he rose, shrugged into a banyan and padded into his own room. Seated at the writing table, he drew a sheet of paper towards him.

*My dearest Lallie,*

   *I pray you will never receive this letter or even know of its existence. If all goes awry this morning and I do not return to you, please believe me that since that first evening at Clarissa's I have had eyes for no woman but you. My liaison with a certain lady—I will not insult you by writing her name in a letter to you—was over weeks before I met you and there has been no other woman since.*

*I am desolated at the thought of leaving you and in such a way, but honour requires me to defend a vile slur that I wooed you while cuckolding another. I swear to you, Lallie, it is not true. You were never second-best. My heart beats only for you, my soul longs only for you and will continue to do so even if I must cross* that bourn from whence no traveller returns.

*You will be angry that I have left you and I beg your forgiveness. You may mourn me, but please do not mourn too long. That you are happy is the devout wish and fondest hope of your servant and husband,*

*Hugo Tamrisk*

Hugo folded the letter and sealed it, then touched his lips to the cooling wax. My dearest, he thought, and went to dress—buckskins and boots, shirt and waistcoat, a simply knotted cravat and a coat that permitted easy movement of his arms and shoulders.

By the time the plain town carriage drew up at Battersea Fields, the insipid dawn light had grown stronger although a covering of cloud hid the sun.

"All the better," Gervase commented. "No-one runs the risk of being blinded."

Hugo handed him the letter. "This is for Lallie. And here is her grandparents' direction. If things go wrong, please go there yourself to break the news. And—Gervase, tell her I was so very sorry to leave her in such circumstances."

"Trust me. But it won't be necessary," Gervase said confidently. "You're as good a shot as any I've seen. Ready?"

Hugo nodded and depressed the door handle. Once on the ground, he took the case of duelling pistols from his second.

"I'll take them now," Gervase said once he had jumped down. "You wait here while I go and confer."

Hugo turned his head at a sudden burst of birdsong, scrutinising the hedgerow until he found the red-breasted robin perched on an arch of bramble, singing his heart out. "You must defend your territory too," he said softly to the little bird. "May the day go well for us both."

He looked around at the dull greens and browns of the field. Strange to think this might be his last sight on earth. Was this what Arthur felt when he waited for battle to commence? He shrugged out of his great-coat and laid it to one side. He must put all thoughts of Lallie aside now—concentrate on the task ahead.

Gervase came up to him. "We're ready. Fifteen paces and you fire at the drop of the handkerchief. Here."

Hugo accepted the loaded pistol with his left hand, holding it midway around the barrel, the muzzle pointing backwards. The metal was cold against his bare hand as he strode to his assigned mark where he took up his position, his body turned sideways to minimise the surface offered to his opponent's bullet. Opposite him, Norris mirrored his stance.

"Make ready!"

Hugo carefully transferred the pistol to his right hand, bringing it round into the firing position with the muzzle down and the barrel away from him. It would be mortifying to fire too soon. Gervase now stood to one side, half-way between him and Norris.

A taut hush fell on the little clearing. Even the robin was silent now. Gervase raised a white handkerchief high in the air. Hugo tried to breathe evenly as he focussed his attention on the vital signal.

It fluttered towards the ground.

Now!

He raised the muzzle of his pistol, sighted carefully, took a steadying breath and fired. Two shots cracked and echoed. The world stopped in a puff of smoke.

An eternity later, the acrid smell of gunpowder stinging his nostrils, Hugo let his arm fall to his side. He took a deep breath. He was unharmed and Norris was still on his feet, thank heavens, although he had clapped his left hand to his right shoulder. He spoke quietly to his second who very soon advanced purposefully on Gervase. Hugo strained to hear.

"Our friends have exchanged shots and my principal has received a slight injury. Having given your principal the usual satisfaction, he does not hesitate to offer an unreserved apology for the intemperate words which your principal felt to be a slur on his honour and that of the ladies concerned."

Gervase replied just as gravely. "The point of honour being settled and your principal's apology deemed to be suitable reparation, I see no reason why our two principals should not shake hands and be friends."

The two men bowed to each other.

"Is your principal well enough to meet in the middle?" Gervase enquired less formally.

"Yes It is just a scratch—the ball went through the sleeve and scraped the skin; nothing more."

"I had not thought he would behave so decently," Hugo commented as, the final ceremonies completed, he and Gervase drove back to Tamarisk House.

"I suppose it's not be wondered that the loss of a peerage knocked him so off-balance," Gervase said fairly. "From something his second said, that remark about his unsportsmanlike behaviour cut him to the quick and he saw this as an opportunity to show the stuff he was made of." He fished in his pocket. "Your letter. I'm glad I won't have to deliver it."

"Thank you. So am I." Hugo could hardly wait to throw it in the fire.

She was here! Hugo hurried out into the hall. "Welcome home, Lallie."

"Thank you, Hugo." Lallie raised her face for his kiss. "I'm glad to be back." She lifted off her bonnet and handed it to Nancy with her pelisse before stripping off her gloves.

"Bring tea-things to my boudoir, Phipps, and I'm not at home to callers. I need a day's respite before returning to the fray," she added to Hugo who strolled with her to the back of the house.

"How is Sir Howard?" Hugo asked as she blended the tea-leaves in the glass bowl of the teapoy.

"If he had his way, he would have the whole household dancing attendance on him. He cannot endure the slightest discomfort or boredom; if he's alone for more than five minutes he contrives some excuse to ring the bell, even if it's only to pull down the blind by another half inch. Most of their servants are quite elderly, you know, and they were all exhausted. In the end, Grandmother set a chair outside his door and had them take turns, an hour at a time. She, of course, was expected to sit with him all the time as no one else could provide him with rational conversation or read to him."

"What about your uncle and aunt?"

"The children have the measles," Lallie said resignedly.

"So how did you handle Sir Howard?"

She smiled at him triumphantly. "I had him teach me to play chess. Any form of cards was out of the question, but he could manage chess quite well with his left hand."

"Very clever," he said admiringly.

"I've always wanted to learn. Grandpapa had started to teach me, but he died when I was ten and Grandmamma didn't know how to play."

"Did Sir Howard prove to be a good teacher?"

"He was better at showing than explaining," she said frankly. "I found a copy of Mr Hoyle's Rules and Observations and that helped."

"If you are interested in continuing, I could teach you," he offered.

"Would you, Hugo? I'd like that." She poured Hugo's tea, added sugar and handed it to him.

"Thank you," he said. "No one makes it quite like you do."

"But what of you? Did anything of interest happen here?"

He shifted uneasily. "The talk is all of France," he said evasively. "Napoleon has arrived in Elba." He put down his cup and slid nearer to her on the sofa. "I missed you," he said simply.

He was rewarded with a glowing smile. He framed her face with his hands and bent to kiss her tenderly. The house suddenly felt right again.

*The age of chivalry is not dead. Only last week, we hear,* Battersea Fields *saw the meeting between a* preux chevalier *and one who had slighted the honour not of the* chevalier's *new bride but rather of his former* Dulcinea. *A verray, parfit, gentil knyght indeed, but we would expect no less from the descendant of a gallant crusader, the companion of the* Lionheart *himself. Both parties acquitted themselves honourably and, the usual satisfaction being given, we are happy to report that a reconciliation was effected.*

Really, their allusions were becoming more and more obscure, quite gothick in fact. Lallie dropped *The Ladies' Universal Register* to the floor. She was resting before dressing for Clarissa's ball. Hugo would escort her there. She sighed happily. He had been most attentive since she returned. Perhaps this would be the month she conceived. Despite his reassurances, she would prefer to be with child before they returned to Tamm.

Her first priority then must be the nursery, she thought as her eyes closed, her lips curving as she imagined a little girl pulling at her skirts to help her stand, a little boy proudly practising his pothooks and hangers.

Where the devil had Lallie learnt to waltz? One shoulder propped against the wall of his sister's ballroom, Hugo watched with a disenchanted eye as his wife twirled gracefully around the floor with Luke Fitzmaurice, bending and turning, their arms raised to permit now one, now the other to pass under. He knew the waltz was all the rage but, damn it, could she not have told him she was taking lessons? They could have learnt together if it came to that. As the dance progressed he became more irate, especially when the couple danced side to side, both facing away but with flirtatious backwards glances. Now Fitzmaurice turned her so that they both stepped forward, her back to his torso. Hugo clenched his teeth at the sight.

The music stopped. He saw his wife curtsey to her partner, lay her hand on his arm and begin to stroll with him. He fought to get a grip on his temper—better not to approach her now—but he could not help following her progress through the crowd, her yellow satin gown glowing and shimmering among the girls' white muslins like a daffodil among lilies, until his view was obscured by two stout gentlemen who had stopped to chat. After some minutes he saw her again. She was still with Fitzmaurice, whose fair hair gleamed in the candle-light as he bent down to murmur something in her ear. Her fan was held flirtatiously before her face. Unable to watch any longer, Hugo turned away.

"Tell me, is it true?" The corpulent gentleman blocked all traffic as he paused to address his friend. "Did Tamrisk really call Norris out?"

Lallie caught her breath.

"So I am told. It was high time Norris was reined in," the other gentleman said. "Even if Tamrisk did deposit a cuckoo in Albright's nest."

"Norris was the only one to suggest it. It was decent if foolhardy of Tamrisk to stand up for the lady, especially when he's not long married to another."

Lallie's head swam. She clutched Mr Fitzmaurice's arm desperately. Don't let me faint, she prayed. If I do, they'll turn round and see me.

Mr Fitzmaurice put his hand over hers, steadying her. He subtly turned them away from the scandal-mongers and bent to murmur, "Hide your face with your fan; make it look as if we're flirting."

She fluttered the fan obediently, grateful for the waft of cooler air, and stole a glance at him over its edge.

"Excellent," he commended her, with a seductive look. "If we give a display of *'nods and becks and wreathed smiles'*, no-one will guess what we are really talking about."

Lallie mustered all her self-control to smile coquettishly at him. "I didn't misunderstand, did I, Mr Fitzmaurice?"

He shook his head slightly. "No, Mrs Tamrisk."

The two gentlemen walked away and Mr Fitzmaurice urged Lallie to move on.

"Surely it can't be true?" she asked with a little trill of laughter.

He took two glasses of champagne from the tray of a passing footman and handed her one. Raising his, he looked deeply into her eyes. "I admire your courage," he murmured. "I can't answer for the particulars, but it seems fairly certain that an encounter took place."

"I see," she said numbly and sipped her champagne. It tasted bitter.

"Come and stand at the window," he suggested. "The air is fresher." He put his arm behind her as if to urge her forward.

"It's fortunate the window is open," Lallie murmured, look-ing up at the thin, crescent moon.

"Why is that?"

"It's unlucky to see the new moon through glass," she replied mechanically and then laughed at herself. "What a stupid thing to worry about. When I think—I was visiting my grandparents last week," she whispered. "I had no idea—he could have been killed and I would have known nothing."

"These little affairs rarely come to that nowadays," Mr Fitzmaurice said robustly. He leaned towards her. "You have had a shock, I know, but believe me, Mrs Tamrisk; it is not as bad as it sounds."

She drank again. It tasted no better and she put the glass down onto the window-sill. "You've been very kind, Mr Fitzmaurice. I must remember that trick with the false flirtation. It is very clever."

"I am delighted to have been of service," he said gallantly, but his smile now was friendly rather than inviting.

"People are going in to supper. I think I shall have a head-ache and go home."

"Another convenient trick?"

"Provided one uses it sparingly."

Twenty minutes later, Lallie had reached the sanctuary of her bedchamber. She let Nancy undress her and help her into a dressing-gown but refused any further attentions. "I just felt a little queasy. It was so hot—I don't know how many candles were burning—and so many people. I'll sit here for a little. Good night."

She couldn't escape the horrendous images that filled her mind. He might have been killed and I would have known nothing about it. Someone would have come to find me at Grandfather's house. She began to shake as she envisaged the scene. Would the messenger have been left in the hall or, worse, ushered into the library where I was sitting with Grandfather? I would look up, surprised. He would look pale and serious and then he would say—with profuse apologies and regrets, of course, as if that would make any difference—Hugo would still be dead.

A sob escaped her as she pictured her dreadful journey, first to London and then accompanying his corpse back to Tamm and the dismal scenes at its end. A whole family devastated; one of the longest lines in the land broken. And for what? The dubious honour of a faithless woman! For her, I was to be widowed! Honour to whom honour is due, she thought bitterly. He was the challenger, they said. How could he even consider it? Even the slightest wound can prove fatal once infection sets in.

Why was it necessary for him to leap so to her defence? Is it because her child is also his? She must have known the risk she ran in breaking her marriage vows, especially before she presented her husband with a son. And, if it comes to that, why was he intimate with a married woman in the first place? How would he like to find a cuckoo in his nest? Not that I plan to indulge in tit for tat, but it would serve him right if I did.

Unable to remain seated, she got up to pace back and forth, back and forth. Did I only imagine he has been particularly affectionate since I came home? Perhaps he feels guilty. He told me he missed me that first afternoon. The hypocrite! I daresay he misses her more. Does he think of the child that might be his and wonder why I don't conceive?

Lallie's eyes burned. He's not worth your tears, she told herself and went to pour a glass of orangeade. She sipped the sweet drink slowly, letting it soothe her aching throat.

She was afraid to go to bed. What if he came to her tonight?

"There you are, Hugo! I was looking for you."

Was his sister's voice even cooler than usual? Hugo shrugged away the thought and asked politely, "What may I do for you, Clarissa."

"For me? Nothing. I just want to tell you that poor Lallie has gone home with the headache. She said she would send the carriage back for you."

"When was this?" he asked sharply.

"About two hours ago—just before supper."

"I shall make my own farewells, then. Thank you for a pleasant evening, Clarissa; an undoubted success, as always."

"Yes, it was a sad crush," she said complacently.

It's no wonder Lallie had the headache, Hugo thought as the carriage rattled homewards. He wouldn't confront her about the waltz tonight—no, confront was the wrong word. He would mention it casually, at breakfast perhaps. Or would he? What would she think?

If he had his way, he would forbid her to dance it with any gentleman but himself. It was too intimate, the way the lady must respond instinctively to her partner's lead and she had no choice but to dance the figures he selected for as long as he wished, sometimes in quite a close embrace. Other dances were communal with agreed figures but the waltz was very different. You might have twenty couples on the floor, each dancing a different variation or sequence of steps. And there was no interaction with the other dancers; a couple were in the most intimate proximity for the duration of the dance.

Resolved to see about waltz lessons first thing in the morning—or perhaps she would show him the steps; that would be better—he went to enquire how she was. He found her seated at a low table. She had set out the chess-men and seemed to be experimenting with different combinations of moves.

"You must be feeling better," he said, relieved. "Clarissa only recently told me that you were unwell, otherwise I would have come sooner."

"It is of no consequence," she answered, without taking her eyes from the chessboard.

"What are you working on? May I help?" he asked, advancing towards the board.

"No, thank you." She raised her head then to look at him. It was a strange, assessing look, almost as if he were a stranger. It made him uneasy.

"Hugo, is it true that you called Mr Norris out last week while I was in Hampshire?"

"Is that what Fitzmaurice told you?" he countered defensively.

She smiled thinly "No. Nobody tells me anything," a pause, "but it doesn't stop them talking. Did you challenge Mr Norris?"

"Yes," he admitted stiffly.

"Because of something he said about Lady Albright?"

"Lallie!"

She didn't say anymore, but fixed him with a steady gaze until he yielded.

"Yes." It was the truth if not the whole truth.

Her fingers tightened on the piece she was holding. After a long silence, she enquired, "Are you the father of her child?"

He raised an eyebrow. "Surely a lady should ignore such gossip."

"The whole world is talking of it, but I should not?" she asked sarcastically. "If you tell me it is not so, I will believe you."

He couldn't lie to her. "I don't know. She has never given me reason to think so, but it is not beyond the bounds of possibility."

Another silence. "I appreciate your candour," she said at last, her gaze turning back to the chessboard.

Was that all she had to say? What sort of a woman was she, that such a confession did not move her? She must be made of ice. Clearly, it was all one to her what he did or whether he lived or died.

The silence grew until he could bear it no longer. "'I appreciate your candour'," he mimicked savagely. "Are you so lacking in sensibility that that is all you can find to say?"

Her head came up. Thank God, he thought, but too soon. She met his gaze calmly, too calmly.

"Would you find it more flattering if I ranted and raved, wept my eyes out over the danger you have suffered and stormed heaven to spare you—retrospectively of course?"

He winced inwardly as she recited this hyperbolic catalogue with as little passion as if it were a tradesman's account. The hint of a mirthless smile on her lips flicked him on the raw. He took two steps towards her. "Lallie!"

She ignored him and continued, "Or should I merely vent my spleen in a curtain lecture?"

"If you wish."

That at least would be natural and, oddly, would show him that she cared. Then he could apologise and they would put it behind them.

"Tell me, Hugo," she asked coldly, "would any of these actions turn back time and render the duel unfought or undo any injury you or your opponent might have suffered?"

Despite himself, he answered, "No."

"Then I must beg to be excused. Good night." She turned back to the chess-board, a marble queen.

Dismissed, by God, as if he were beneath her notice! He had been judged and found wanting. Somehow he managed to get himself out of the room without taking her by the shoulders and shaking some genuine feeling into her or falling on his knees in front of her and suing for mercy.

Lallie waited until the door had closed behind her husband before rising stiffly. She made her way to the bed as if in a trance and stared tearlessly at the underside of the baldaquin above her until a sob broke free and, at last, she began to weep.

# Chapter Nineteen

*The Straits of Neveralter separate this country from the Great Barbarian Desert. Immense Mountains or Rocks of Ice renders this straight impassable.*

Somehow they managed to resume their life together. It was like darning the heel of a stocking, Lallie thought tiredly; you had to strengthen the frayed and worn edge before you could commence weaving across the gaping hole. And you must set your stitches slowly and carefully to avoid putting too much strain on the surrounding fabric or creating rough places that would quickly raise blisters on tender flesh. Their thread was the common courtesies of daily life, their needles the slight routines that had developed between them in their six months of marriage.

Hugo's look had pierced her when she came into the breakfast parlour the morning after that fatal conversation, but he had said nothing more than his usual, "Good morning, Lallie". She had replied as civilly and he had returned to *The Morning Chronicle* while she picked up the latest number of *La Belle Assemblée*.

It was fortunate that the final defeat of the French obliterated all other topics as England was swept into an ecstasy of rejoicing and celebrations. The Tamrisk/Norris duel was quickly forgotten as families looked forward to welcoming sons and husbands home from Spain and France, many of whom they had not seen for five years and more. The Malvins, however, were to lose Arthur who had finally been declared fit for duty.

"It was no fun being laid up for so long," he said to Hugo and Lallie when he came to make his farewells, "but at least I saw you safely wed, old fellow."

"Go thou and do likewise," Hugo retorted. He managed to speak amiably although he had to force a smile.

"Not as long as I'm in the military," Arthur replied seriously, "perhaps in a year or so if the peace holds."

"Would you sell out then?" Lallie asked.

"Yes. I would never ask my wife to follow the drum." He kissed Lallie's cheek. "Goodbye, my dear. You're far too good for him, but that is often the case."

"Goodbye and good fortune, Arthur. I hope it won't be too long before we meet again."

He shrugged. "It depends on where they send us next." He set the black stovepipe shako on his head and clapped his uncle on the shoulder. "Good luck, old man."

"I'll walk to the door with you."

"What has you so in the dumps?" Arthur asked once they were out of earshot of the parlour.

Hugo made a face. "Lallie found out about the duel."

Arthur whistled. "Was she very cut up?"

"I don't know. She just asked me was it true and then declined to say anything further. She has never referred to it again but it's there between us. I don't know what to do, Arthur. An apology would be worse than useless."

"You'll have to play it by ear; take your cue from her. She's not the sort you can appease with a diamond necklace."

Hugo laughed shortly. "No, thank God, although it would make matters a lot easier."

"You'll come about," Arthur said reassuringly and took his leave.

But would they, Hugo wondered, as he headed back towards the small drawing-room. She had been very quiet today. She came towards him as he walked down the corridor. So she had not expected—or wished—him to return to her.

"I'm going to lie down, Hugo," she said. "I fear I am indisposed today."

This was how she always let him know that her menses had begun. "My poor dear," he said sympathetically, "Let Nancy look after you."

Was this an olive branch, he wondered as he watched her climb the stairs. Uncertain of his reception, he had not gone to her bed since the night of Clarissa's ball, but in letting him know of her indisposition, surely she was making clear that he was not generally unwelcome? He would know for sure when she advised him of her recovery.

"Lady Holton's ball is always such a crush, but this year seems worse than ever," Mrs Dunford sighed, fanning herself. "Come and talk to Mrs Rembleton with me, Mrs Tamrisk. I understand her nursery governess is leaving and I wonder would she do for us, but I find Mrs Rembleton quite daunting."

"I thought so at first, but in fact she is very kind." Lallie replied. "You will see."

Mrs Rembleton listened graciously to Mrs Dunford's request and agreed to enquire whether the departing governess would be interested in accompanying a military family to Brussels or Paris.

"I miss my younger sisters," Lallie sighed. How long would it be before she could join the ranks of the mothers?

"How old are they?" Mrs Rembleton enquired.

"Eleanor is eleven and Beatrice six."

Mrs Rembleton smiled. "If you wish to forego the pleasures of Hyde Park for bat and ball in Grosvenor Square, you would be very welcome, Mrs Tamrisk. The Duchess and I take the children there most afternoons and we can always use another pair of hands."

"May I?" she asked eagerly. "I should like it above all things."

Damn it, if he had wished for a society bride, he could have married one long since and spared himself his father's bad-tempered preaching on his duty to posterity, Hugo thought sourly. What was wrong with him, that he was always shut out, kept away from the warmth? It wasn't only that cursed duel—Lallie had kept her distance even before then. Take your cue from her, Arthur had said. She had not rejected him last night when he went to her bed, but the ease that had developed between them was gone. He had finished quickly and she had not even given her little sigh.

He was hanged if he was going to beg his wife for the affection that was his due. He hadn't begged his sisters and he wouldn't beg her. Her annoyance over the duel had been more about Sabina than about him. She didn't care about him. Surely even the angriest wife would have enquired whether he had suffered any injury.

Pride, however, required Mr Tamrisk to display his newly acquired proficiency at waltzing. He stalked across the room to where Lallie stood with Mrs Rembleton and another lady and held out a commanding hand. "My dance, I believe."

He doesn't ask me to stand up with him, Lallie thought resentfully as she walked onto the dance floor, but simply commands me, regardless of any other commitments I might have made. Inwardly she braced herself for his touch. While other partners had no effect on her, when she danced with Hugo she was inevitably reminded of their more intimate comings together. And now to waltz with him! She tensed as his arm came around her shoulders and lifted her own arm to mirror his action. Yesterday she had plucked up her courage to tell him that she had recovered from her indisposition, but when he came to her, Lady Albright's alluring features had seemed to hover between them and she had not found it difficult to lie still, the passive receptacle of his seed. That was all he wanted from her and that was all she owed him.

Hugo tightened his hold, clasping his wife in a closer embrace than would have been approved by his dancing instructor. Here at least she had no choice but to follow his lead. But she still contrived to hold herself at a distance from him, resilient rather than pliant.

"Would you like some champagne?" he said abruptly when the music stopped.

"Why not? There's Henrietta. Let's join her."

They were soon caught up in an animated discussion of Mr Kean's appearances at Drury Lane and before he noticed it, his wife had slipped away to join another group.

"Come and play, Mamma," seven-year old Lady Tabitha Staunton demanded, pulling her mother to her feet, "and you, Mrs Tamrisk."

"If you please," the Duchess of Gracechurch reminded her daughter.

"If you please. It's bat and ball and we have three ladies and five children, so that gives us four each side."

Lallie threw herself into the game, transported back to happier days playing with her sisters and their friends. She ran, bowled and fielded, triumphant to make a catch or to reach 'home' safely and was sorry when the carefree game ended and it was time to be Mrs Tamrisk again.

Made uneasy by the sight of Lallie's father in close conversation with Frederick Malvin as they exited the *Huntley Coffee House,* Hugo had come home at once to reinforce his instructions that Mr Grey was never to be admitted to Mrs Tamrisk's presence without her prior consent and that he was to be informed immediately should Mr Grey call. As usual, his wife was not at home. It was after half-past six. Where the hell was she and with whom? Now that he thought about it, Arabella had mentioned that Lallie didn't join them as often for the afternoon promenade in the park.

He went to the library door when he heard her voice in the hall and watched unobserved as she hurriedly gave her instructions. She was glowing and looked dishevelled, almost as if she had dressed too quickly. She didn't notice him, of course.

"I'll need the carriage again in an hour," she said and disappeared upstairs.

So she was going out again. Where? When he finally yielded to temptation and went to her bedchamber, Nancy had just helped her into a ball-gown. She tied the last little bow and disappeared into the dressing-room.

"Good evening, Hugo. I thought you were dining out," Lallie said.

"I am, but later. Where do you dine tonight?"

"With Clarissa. I'm going on with her and Arabella to Almack's. Would you fasten these for me, please?"

He gently laid the pearls around her neck, admiring the delicate nape bent before him. He could not resist pressing a soft kiss to it. She shivered and raised her head with an odd little smile. It was not for him—she still stood with her back to him—but he could see it reflected in the mirror. A response, by God! But then he remembered her ruffled appearance earlier. Was she still caught in the aftermath of some earlier indulgence?

He stepped back and said coolly, "I won't delay you. Enjoy yourself, my dear."

"Thank you, Hugo." Her voice was as crisp as his. She went to the dressing table, tilted a little perfume bottle, removed the stopper and touched it behind her ears, and at the base of her throat.

It was a new scent, heady and floral, reminiscent of secret trysts in lush conservatories. It wreathed about his charmed senses, making him want to strip her and touch the little piece of glass to all her secret places then seek them out again, languorously sniffing and trailing his mouth from one to the other. It made him want to dampen a cloth and rub all traces of it from her, forbidding her to wear it outside her bedroom. It made him turn on his heel and leave her without saying another word.

Mr Grey sauntered in to the library at Tamarisk House as if he were the owner and his son-in-law the guest.

"I'm glad to have caught you at home, Tamrisk," he said languidly. "I have a rather delicate matter to put to you."

"Indeed?" Hugo said dryly, indicating a seat facing his desk.

"It is only my concern for Lallie that brings me here."

Hugo raised an eyebrow. "You appear to have forgotten that my wife is no longer your concern," he said forbiddingly.

"Nothing of the sort," Mr Grey protested. "She is still my daughter."

"Is she?"

Mr Grey ignored this interjection. He set his hat on the floor and folded his hands on the top of his cane. "I regret to have to tell you, Tamrisk, that I was very much mistaken in my friend Malvin. Only consider; he talks of bringing an action against Lallie for breach of promise of marriage."

Hugo laughed. "What foolishness! I doubt very much if he would get any solicitor to assist him or any jury to find in his favour. He has forgotten the small matter of the lady's consent, sir."

His father-in-law favoured him with a patronising smile. "I am persuaded you would not wish her to be dragged through the courts or indeed to have the whole business made public which it will be if he sues me for breach of contract. That, he says, is his other option." He sighed. "It will come to one or the other and, reluctant as I am to say it, for Lallie's sake it would be better to settle with him. Regrettably, it is beyond my means to do so at present and that is why I have come to you."

Hugo raised an eyebrow. "Indeed? To put it bluntly, Grey, you are suggesting that I buy him off."

"You are the one who benefited most from the whole affair," Mr Grey pointed out. "Be reasonable, sir. I am sure he would accept ten thousand pounds. What is that to you? Your wife's dignity and reputation are surely worth as much and more."

Hugo prowled around the desk to stand in front of his father-in-law. Arms folded, he stared down at the other man for a long minute. "What sort of a fool do you take me for?" he asked finally. "Frederick Malvin would not dare risk the derision of the *ton* by taking either action. This is a nice sort of plot you have hatched between you, but I'm neither a gull nor a chub and I refuse to allow you to use my wife as a bargaining tool. You will do well to remember that I will do whatever is necessary to protect her from scoundrels like you and him."

Mr Grey shrank back as Hugo gripped the arms of his chair, caging him in.

"You have battened on Lallie long enough, sir. Take this as your only warning. If it becomes necessary I'll drop the word in certain circles that sadly I have discovered things about you that compel me to forbid her any association with you. You get my meaning, I am sure. I need not elaborate; no one would dream of asking me for details, although of course there would be speculation. Your good name is all you have. If it's tarnished will you still be so welcome at the tables, so well-received at the best addresses? Words have wings, Grey, and you know how quickly they take flight."

Mr Grey was chalk-white. "You wouldn't do it, Tamrisk. Destroy me and you destroy Lallie."

"Nonsense. Very few people associate her with you. I would prefer not to have to do it, of course, and if you leave her in peace there will be no need for me to undertake anything. Have we an understanding?"

His father-in-law nodded.

"I beg your pardon—I didn't hear you, sir."

Mr Grey swallowed. "Yes, I agree."

"Excellent. I rely on you to convey my response to Mr Malvin. I need not remind you that Lord Malvin is my brother-in-law," Hugo added with a shark's smile. "Come, let me see you out."


"What did he want?" Lallie asked as soon as the front door closed.

She leaned over the bannister at the top of the stairs, her hands clenched on the polished wood of the rail. There was a strained look in her eyes that reminded him of the morning he had found her at the *Belle Sauvage*.

"Hugo?"

'Nobody tells me anything but it doesn't stop them talking', she had said the night she had confronted him about the duel. Was it right to keep things from her, even for her own good? It would be better if she were forewarned.

He hurried up to her. "Come into my mother's parlour."

"You had Phipps take me in here that first day," she remarked inconsequentially, sitting on the chaise longue.

"It was her favourite room."

"I prefer the one below it; I like being able to step directly into the garden, but this is comfortable too."

"You may refurbish it if you wish."

"Oh no," she cried, "or at least only in so far as it is necessary to keep it in good order. It is the same with your grandmother's rooms at Tamm. I like the idea that the various mistresses leave something of themselves in the house."

"What will you leave?" he asked with a smile.

"It is far too soon to think of that," she protested. "I have not been mistress for even a year. I'm still finding my way."

I forget that, he thought guiltily.

"What did my father want?" she asked again.

He sat beside her and took her hand in a comforting clasp. "I'm afraid he has been up to his old tricks again."

"Do you think you stopped them?" Lallie asked, when Hugo came to an end.

"I'm sure it was all a bluff," he reassured her. "Malvin would destroy himself if he proceeds. I'll ask Tony to remind him of it. He values the connection and would hate to find himself ostracised by the family."

Her hand tightened on his. "I'm sorry you should have to deal with it."

"Frankly, I enjoyed it. I think they both got off too lightly the last time."

She smiled gratefully at him and rested her head on his shoulder.

Hugo released his hand very carefully and slid his arm around her, holding her to him.

"Leave it to me, Hugo," Tony Malvin said. "He has very few relatives, you know. Apart from us, there is just an old aunt of his mother's, a Mrs Horne. He is her heir, or so he says, and I doubt if she would be pleased to read of him in the scandal sheets. He'll hold his tongue."

# Chapter Twenty

*The Mountains of Hatred are lofty, and extremely rocky and barren; according to tradition, people of gigantic stature have been known to inhabit them. The celebrated Giants Gorge and Revenge were, after a hard battle, defeated; many lost their lives in this engagement.*

"Thank you, my dear Mrs Tamrisk," the dowager Lady Needham said. "It was good of you to think of an old woman."

"I thought immediately of this salve when the countess mentioned that you suffered badly with rheumatism of the hands. My grandfather swore by it."

"You must give me the recipe, Mrs Tamrisk," the Countess of Needham said. "I am always interested in new salves and potions."

"The Marchioness of Martinborough; the dowager Marchioness of Martinborough, my lady," the butler intoned.

A cold weight settled on Lallie's heart.

After a babble of greetings, the countess drew Lallie forward. "My ladies, may I present Mrs Tamrisk."

Lallie curtseyed stiffly. So this old woman who stared at her so rudely was the mother who had ignored Grandmamma's desperate appeal.

"Mrs Tamrisk." The dowager Marchioness extended her hand. She clutched at Lallie's fingers when they touched hers and subsided onto a sofa, drawing Lallie down beside her. "Forgive me, Mrs Tamrisk, but may I ask what your name was before you were married?"

"Grey, my lady. Lalage Louisa Grey."

"Who were your parents?"

"Louisa Staines and Robert Grey."

"And your mother's parents?"

Lallie regarded her inquisitor with faint disdain. Her voice was cool as she answered, "You are correct, ma'am, in assuming that I am the granddaughter of Lady Anna Martyn and William Staines."

She ignored the gasps from the company and sat erect, maintaining as much of a distance as she could from the old lady who had retrieved a lace handkerchief from her reticule and was weeping quietly into it.

Lady Martinborough put out a trembling hand. "Don't condemn me, my dear, I beg you. I swear I didn't know she had written. My husband was so furious when Anna eloped with her brother's tutor that he cut her off completely and permitted no one to have anything more to do with her." She turned imploringly to her daughter-in-law. "Maud, tell her how Martinborough found Anna's letters only two years ago, the year after his father's death. He had kept them hidden, unopened, all these years."

"It's true, Mrs Tamrisk," the elegant woman whom Lallie supposed must be her great-aunt by marriage, confirmed. "We were all very shocked and my mother-in-law was distraught. Martinborough went immediately to the address your grandmother had given, only to discover she had left there following her husband's death and was now dead herself. No one could tell him where you might be. Your father had come for you, they said, but nobody could quite remember his name; White or Black, they thought."

"No one said Miss Grey." Lallie agreed quietly, "It was always Lallie or Miss Lallie."

"Poor Anna wrote only three times," the dowager Marchioness said through her tears. "Once to beg our forgiveness, a year later to inform us of the birth of your mother, whom she had named Louisa after me, and the last one was a dreadful, tear-blotched note telling me of Louisa's death and your birth and begging me, if I had ever felt a mother's love for her, to come to her now. But she was so distressed that she never mentioned her son-in-law's name. And to think that to the day she died she thought I wouldn't forgive her and had refused to come to comfort her."

All the ladies were crying now. Lallie's heart softened and she put her arms around the frail shoulders of her great-grandmother, gently drawing her to her as she murmured, "She knows the truth now."

"It's a miracle," the Marchioness whispered to the two countesses. "Martinborough will be overjoyed. We were sure she was lost for ever. I can understand why my mother-in-law was so stunned. She has a little miniature of Lady Anna—if it were not for the old-fashioned costume, it might be of Mrs Tamrisk. Poor girl, it must have been a shock to her, too."

"From the moment you were announced," the elder Lady Needham replied drily. "I have rarely seen a stiffer, more perfectly gauged curtsey."

"You think she knew who we were?" The Marchioness sounded surprised.

"I am sure of it. You must realise that she was lost only to you. Why should her grandmother not have told her the whole story, even if only to explain why there was no connection with her own family? And it would take but a glance in Debrett's Peerage to tell her the Dowager was still alive."

"And Lady Anna's name expunged from the record," the Marchioness added ruefully.

"It is restored in the new edition just published," her mother-in-law declared, sitting up but clinging to the hand of her newly-discovered great-granddaughter. "My son insisted on it."

Lallie, who had been touched by the way Lady Needham immediately sprang to her defence, now felt the tears well up again. "He reinstated her? She would have been so pleased. Did he recognise her marriage as well?"

"Yes. He had been quite attached to Mr Staines, you know. He felt his loss most severely."

"You must come and dine, Lalage," the elder Marchioness said firmly. "Martinborough will wish to meet you and your husband too, of course. It's a pity you are married already. With our recognition you might have looked much higher than a barony, even that of Tamm."

"I am very fortunate in my marriage, ma'am," Lallie replied equally firmly. To criticise Hugo like that was the height of effrontery.

"Well done, Mrs Tamrisk," the dowager Lady Needham said to her when the ladies had departed. "They'll take you over if you are not careful."

"They may try, ma'am. Once I married Tamrisk and began to move in society, I realised that I was likely to come across some of Grandmamma's family, but I did not think they would realise who I was or acknowledge the connection."

"Did you never consider making yourself known to them?"

"Never. Grandmamma accepted there would be no reconciliation when after twenty years her parents would not relent, not even when she was in such dreadful straits. And for all that the ladies today blamed the old Marquis, I cannot but feel that it would have been possible for her mother to find my grandmother if she had made the slightest effort. Her husband may have remained obdurate to his dying day, but could her ladyship not quietly have requested her son to make some enquiries once he was of age?"

"Old Martinborough was a despot," Lady Needham said dispassionately, "and he kept his wife very much under his thumb. I don't think she would have set herself up against him. And George—the present Marquis—was only a young boy then, so I suppose by the time he had grown up he had almost forgotten his sister."

No, Lallie thought, as the carriage took her home, she would not give up her new-found independence. Her new relatives might accept her as she was or not at all.

Hugo received the news of her reception into the Martyn family with equanimity. "It's all one to me. I married you, not your forebears. I've more than enough of them myself."

"I should like to meet the others, especially Grandmamma's brother." She paused for a moment and then said rather hesitantly, "But you will come to dine with them, won't you, Hugo?"

He shrugged. "If you wish."

Lallie was stung by his careless reply but then swallowed her pride and confessed, "I should welcome your support."

He smiled more warmly at her. "Then of course I'll come."

"So you are my great-granddaughter's husband," Lady Martinborough announced two days later.

"I have that honour, my lady," Hugo replied with an abbreviated bow as she raised her mother-of-pearl and silver lorgnette.

Erect though leaning on a silver-topped ebony cane and dressed in silver, grey and black from her lace cap to her silken hems, her old-fashioned round gown draped majestically from the quilted bodice and falling into a graceful train from the pleated back, she reminded him of the malevolent fairy at Sleeping Beauty's christening in his sisters' book of fairy tales. However he seemed to have passed her initial scrutiny.

"Hmm. You'll have to do, I suppose, though she could have done much better for herself if she had had a proper come-out, especially with my support."

Had Lallie already been favoured with similar comments? He felt her step closer and place her hand on his arm. Heartened, he covered it with his own while he looked the old lady in the eye. "I'm sure of it, ma'am, with or without your help."

"See that you deserve her," the old Marchioness commanded and released them to her younger daughter, Lady Benton, an attractive woman some ten years older than Hugo.

"I never knew my sister Anna," Lady Benton said, "but I always found her story so romantic. Indeed, I named my own daughter after her."

Lallie was touched by this tribute. "She would have been so pleased to know she had not been completely forgotten."

Her smile faded when her father was announced and she had to watch him pass down the ranks of the Martinboroughs, contriving to suggest the bereaved widower while modestly accepting his elevation as new-found grandson and nephew by marriage of one of England's noblest families. When he reached his daughter, he kissed her cheek. "It is sad that Lady Anna and my poor Louisa could not experience such a reunion but they would surely rejoice to know you restored to the bosom of their family."

"Indeed, sir," was all Lallie could reply to this effusion.

"Poor Anna, I thought she was dead," the Marquis said sadly. "That is what my father told me. 'She has gone with Staines and she is dead to us, dead, dead, do you hear?' I was just ten and didn't understand the difference between 'dead' and 'dead to us', so I accepted that she was gone and never thought to look for her. Was she, were they happy?"

"Apart from the loss of my mother, I think they were. They were comfortable with one another; she would stroke his hair back from his forehead as he sat bent over his sermon and he would put his arm around her waist and catch her to him. And they did little things for each other—she ordered his favourite buttered crab even though it didn't agree with her and he searched the banks and hedgerows so that he could bring her little posies of wild flowers. They were greatly loved in the parish as well."

"Let us pass Malvin House," Lallie suggested as they drove away from the Martinboroughs. "I know it is late, but if there is light to be seen, I should like to go in. The dowager has taken it into her head to present me at one of the two drawing-rooms in June. I told her Clarissa has offered to do so, but she is determined to call on her and explain."

"She's like a juggernaut, isn't she?" Hugo commented.

Lallie laughed. "Old people are inclined to be that way. Just look at your father. Perhaps it's because they feel they don't have much time left."

"Tamm was always like that," Hugo said with a grin.

Clarissa was not put out by Lady Martinborough's proposal. "In fact, if you don't mind, Lallie, it will suit me very well. Arthur writes that his company is to go to Holland to support Graham and we thought we might move to Brussels for the summer. I had quite given up hope of a drawing-room this year and was more than surprised to read the Lord Chamberlain's announcement. Also, it will be much more pleasant for you if Lady Martinborough has the entrée. She may use the private entrance and you will be admitted before everyone else."

Having lost the Malvins, he had gained the Martyns, Hugo thought dejectedly. Between Lallie's preparations for the drawing-room and a series of important debates in Parliament, he saw even less of his wife than usual. The romantic story of Lady Anna swept the *ton* and Lallie, as its embodiment, was the heroine of the hour. Worse, word of Lady Anna's fortune had somehow made the rounds and he found himself the recipient of congratulations on having made such an astute match.

"You sly dog, you stole a march on all of us," one gentleman had said jovially to him.

Hugo had looked him up and down before deflating him with a cold, "You flatter yourself, sir."

He could not dismiss the Marquis so easily when he called to make arrangements for the transfer of Lady Anna's portion to her granddaughter's husband.

"My father refused to disburse it but he couldn't touch it," Lallie's great-uncle explained. "It's been sitting in the funds for forty-five years. It's Lallie's now or, more properly, yours."

He would have to discuss it with her, Hugo decided after Lord Martinborough had left. She was easier to talk to now, still reserved, but no longer seemed to buttress her defences when he approached. He rose when he heard her voice in the hall. It was a sad reflection on their marriage that he left the library door ajar in order to be aware of her comings and goings. She must be ready for court, he thought, and stood spellbound when she appeared in the doorway.

Beautifully gowned in rose-pink taffeta, with an over-skirt of filmy lace, she looked as if she had stepped out of one of Perrault's tales. *Cendrillon* ready for the ball, he thought sentimentally. The modiste had cleverly selected a hoop that did not distort her petite form; on the contrary, the artificially wide hips drew attention to her neat torso and the pretty breasts that were framed by the wide, low neckline. The dark curls piled high on her head were adorned with white feathers and lace lappets that almost brushed her bare shoulders. Diamonds circled her brow and glittered at her throat. She had carefully looped her train over her left arm and carried a fan in her right hand.

Hugo cleared his throat and said gruffly, "You look exquisite."

"I feel a fool," she confessed. "You have no idea how difficult it is to manage. I thought I would come in here until my great-grandmother's carriage arrives. I don't want to keep her waiting." She touched the delicate necklace. "She insisted on giving me these diamonds. She'll never wear them again, she said; they are more suitable for a young woman and she would like Anna's granddaughter to have them. I couldn't refuse."

She perched on the edge of a chair and sighed. "Thank heavens it's just the once. I'll never have to do it again."

He shook his head. "I'm afraid that when I come to my title, you will have to be presented again. I will too," he added consolingly, "but I need only go to Prinnie's levée. It's tedious, but not as tortuous as the drawing-rooms."

"Perhaps by then they will have agreed to do away with the hoops," she said hopefully.

She's nervous, he realised, she does not usually chatter like this. "We must hope that His Majesty dies before Tamm," he remarked in a wicked attempt to distract her. "Then we will be spared having to attend Prinnie's coronation."

She smiled sweetly. "I fear I shall be unwell that day, Hugo."

He shook his head again. "Oh no, Lallie. We're in it together. If I must suffer, you must too. I shall have no choice but to attend. Baron Tamm is the premier baron and must do homage while the other barons swear their fealty."

"Wearing your robes?" she demanded.

"Yes."

"And kneeling, I presume?"

She laughed at his rueful nod. "The thought of watching you cope with skirts makes me feel better already, Hugo," she teased.

"Minx," he said softly and leaned down to kiss her.

"The Marchioness's carriage has drawn up, madam."

Hugo formally offered his hand. Lallie placed hers on it and let him lead her out. Nancy came forward to place a shawl around her shoulders while Mrs Phipps stood together with the maids at the back of the hall. It's an occasion for them too, he realised, as the butler bowed deeply as she passed. Liveried footmen waited either side of the door and at the bottom of the shallow steps.

Her fingers tightened on his as she stepped up into the carriage. When she had arranged her hoop and train and taken her seat, she gave him a small, closed-lipped smile.

"You will do splendidly," he assured her before he closed the door, "I am convinced of it. Until this evening."

Now that they had reached the ante-room to the Presence-Chamber, Lallie felt calmer. Her train had been spread behind her, as had those of the other ladies. We're like so many peacocks avoiding each other's finery, she thought, amused. An official had advised them of the order in which they would approach the throne and the ladies who were to be presented removed their right gloves. She was just wondering why the delay when the door opened again to admit a richly clad, stocky young lady with prominent eyes and ornately arranged golden-brown curls beneath her elaborate headdress. She was accompanied by an elegant, dark-haired woman who was not much older than Lallie.

"Your Royal Highness."

Lallie followed Lady Martinborough's example and curtsied deeply. This must be the Princess Charlotte, 'the Daughter of England', only legitimate child of Prince Regent and heiress apparent to the throne. She had turned eighteen in January and apparently was to make her formal come-out today. As soon as the trains of the Princess and her companion had been arranged, the doors to the Presence-Chamber were thrown open and the little procession commenced.

"Who is the lady who will present the Princess?" Lallie whispered to her great-grandmother as they waited.

"The Tsar's sister, the Duchess of Oldenburgh."

They entered a long, brightly lit room whose tall windows were draped in the same red velvet that covered a canopy at the far end. The wall behind the canopy was also hung with red velvet on which the royal arms were worked in gold. When the lady in front of her curtseyed, Lallie could see an upright old lady sitting on a gilt throne. The Prince Regent stood on her right—presumably he had come to witness his daughter's presentation—and with him stood two of his sisters.

"Only two and the Prince? That's not too bad," Lady Martinborough whispered.

The lady at the throne rose from her curtsey and moved aside, the next lady stepped forward and the Marchioness nodded to Lallie. As she proceeded down the Presence-Chamber, fortified by the rustle of silk and the faint drag of her train along the thick pile of the carpet, she seemed to step out of herself, watching little Lallie Grey walk towards the Queen. *Pussy-cat, pussy-cat!* She bit hard on the thin skin behind her lower lip to stifle the giggle that threatened to well-up and disgrace her.

"The Marchioness Dowager of Martinborough presents her great-granddaughter Mrs Tamrisk of Tamm."

Lallie sank into the elaborate court curtsey, her left knee almost touching the floor and extended her bare right hand in an elegant curve, palm inwards. Head bent, she waited for the recognition of the royal touch.

"Your great-granddaughter, Lady Martinborough?" she heard Queen Charlotte say. "I had not thought Martinborough to be a grandfather."

"No, your Majesty. Mrs Tamrisk is the granddaughter of my daughter Lady Anna."

"Lady Anna?" the Queen asked sharply. "You have found her?"

"Too late, ma'am. I regret she and her daughter have departed this life. We are overjoyed to have Mrs Tamrisk restored to us."

As the two old ladies talked over her head, Lallie wondered how long she could maintain her awkward position. Was the Queen about to reject her, have her unceremoniously ejected from court? It would be the scandal to end all scandals. Then she felt Her Majesty's hand rest lightly on hers and she bent lower to kiss it.

"You are welcome, child," the Queen said. "We know how sadly the Marchioness grieved for her daughter."

"Thank you, your Majesty." Lallie managed to rise gracefully and step sideways to curtsey in turn to the Prince and Princesses before backing to the door that opened into a long gallery. An equerry helped her gather her train and loop it over her arm.

"Excellently done, my dear," her great-grandmother said to her. "How kind of Her Majesty to remember Anna; we often talked of her when I was Lady of the Bedchamber. Now, if you would give me your arm, we shall stroll together before we enquire about the carriage. We must remain at least as long as Princess Charlotte and the Duchess do."

# Chapter Twenty-One

*The River of Esteem disembogues into the picturesque and delightful Lake of Affection.*

The nine Muses stood ready to make their entrance at Burlington House. Identically gowned in white Grecian robes, their hair and faces obscured by matching white wigs and masks, and their bare arms, necks and shoulders shimmering with a white maquillage in the style of the last century, they lined up in their agreed order, musicians at their head.

It had been the Duchess of Gracechurch who suggested attending the masquerade in honour of the peace between England and France and the nine ladies had quickly agreed to go as a group. Lallie had not discussed the idea with Hugo. It had been mooted while he was at Ascot and he, after all, had not invited her to accompany him there although the Queen and the Princesses had attended with the visiting allied sovereigns. But now, as she jiggled with nervous excitement, she couldn't help wondering how he would react to her presence. Very likely he would just shrug and say, 'well met, my dear'.

Even if he were here, he could not recognise her. Her wig and heeled sandals gave her additional height and her only identifying feature was the emblem of her Muse painted on her mask—scrolls listing Wellington's famous battles and denoting Clio, Muse of History.

Anthea Lovell, the mistress of ceremonies, clapped her hands. "Is everyone ready? The footmen will clear the way for us and escort us so that no-one may approach too near. Remember, don't rush. Spread your arms as far apart as you comfortably can while retaining hold of your neighbours' hands. Heads up! We are goddesses favouring the mortals with our presence. And from the moment we leave this room, we are on stage," she commanded. "No giggling or slacking. We can't know who might be prowling around the corridors and it will add to the sense of mystery if we remain in character even when we might not be seen. Musicians, please!"

A masked flautist opened the door at her commanding gesture. He waited with his flute to his lips until two tambourine players fell in behind him, then commenced a haunting melody and led the way into the corridor. Anthea followed, one hand extended gracefully before her, the other reaching behind her to the next Muse. This position caused her to turn her body a little sideways, an effect that was heightened by having each Muse face in the opposite direction to her predecessor, as if on a Grecian vase.

Head erect and arms spread, Lallie joined the slow procession, taking up the rhythm of their stately dance. People who came towards them flattened themselves against the wall to allow them pass and then followed. As they neared the ballroom, the press of those accompanying them grew greater but the footmen had no difficulty in making them keep their distance; it was as if they did so of their own accord. A passage was cleared for the dancers through the throng that crowded at the door and when they entered the large room they were greeted by a ripple of applause and a hectic murmur that died down once they reached the centre of the floor and formed a circle.

The music quickened. Initially Lallie concentrated on her steps, on maintaining her distance from her neighbours as well as the graceful posture Anthea had drilled into them, but she became more and more exhilarated as they revolved now to the right, now to the left. The clasp of her partners' hands, the swirl of draperies, the trickle of perspiration between her breasts all heightened her elation. She breathed faster, the motion wafting the floral spice of the perfume that had been created just for this occasion to her nose. Beneath the high-pitched notes of the flute the insistent tambourines beat a rhythm that pulsed through her.

"Now!" Anthea called. They released their hands and Lallie spun with the others who faced outwards so that all now looked to the centre of the circle. As the tempo increased, they closed ranks, raising their hands in invocation. Suddenly the music peaked and stopped abruptly to a hushed silence that continued for a long moment until it was broken by rapturous applause. The dancers smiled beneath their masks, their bosoms lifting as they fought for breath.

"Well done, ladies," Anthea said quietly as the clapping and cheering began. "Ready?" She raised her voice slightly. "Right about—turn!"

As one, they released hands, whirled to face outwards and linked hands again.

Lallie looked about her. The company appeared to be quite mixed; the pick of the *beau monde* as approved by the members of Watier's and the pick of the *demi-monde,* similarly selected. She noticed Lady Westland, tastelessly attired as the late Queen of France with a scarlet ribbon fastened around her neck and wondered uncharitably into which category she fell. It was surprising how many guests had not thought to disguise a distinctive feature, whether it was a mole on her breast as in the case of her ladyship or the cleft in the chin of her own husband who stood masked and clad in a black domino at the edge of the crowd, alone and not part of it.

The gentlemen present quickly lost any reverence they might have had for the goddesses in their midst and inundated them with forthright invitations to dance and dalliance. Lallie grew more and more uneasy. Foolishly, perhaps, she had not thought beyond their performance. She was to take the early carriage at midnight and had assumed that there would be no problem in getting through the intervening hour. But this gathering was a lot more louche than the normal *ton* entertainments, even *bals masqués*. Some of the costumes were more suited to opera dancers and she could already see liberties being taken that would have had the culprits expelled forthwith from any respectable assembly.

"Each Muse will select a partner for the next waltz," a self-styled Apollo announced.

She hastily inspected the surrounding gentlemen. There was Luke Fitzmaurice, dressed as Hamlet with a skull-mask on a stick—poor Yorick, she assumed. He would be a good choice, but before she could gather her courage and beckon him to her, a sister Muse called imperiously, "Prince Hamlet," and he immediately obeyed the summons.

Others had also chosen their partners and, panicking a little, Lallie sought Hugo's eye. She did not know whether to be pleased or annoyed when a coquettish glance paired with a seductive curve of her finger brought him to her side.

"Clio," he bowed. "I am honoured."

It was different dancing with him when she didn't have to conceal her reactions. The Grecian gown permitted only the lightest of stays and she shivered when his hands clasped her waist and she had to mirror the position for the jetées of the valse sauteuse. She felt his every movement beneath her fingers and had to resist the temptation to pull him closer to her. To her relief the music slowed and they could move again into more open attitudes, revolving about one another in seductive harmony.

Who was she? Although the fast waltz did not permit much conversation, her voice was tantalisingly familiar but Hugo could not match it to any woman of that height. She danced very lightly and followed his lead so exquisitely that he conjectured she had come from the ballet. If only he could waltz like this with Lallie. Then he felt guilty for thinking of his wife with another woman in his arms. He didn't know what impulse had made him obey the unspoken invitation. Perhaps it was because the Muses' entrance had provided a welcome distraction from his cheerless thoughts. He was sick of London, sick and tired of the Season, but dreading the return to Tamm. How would he and Lallie fare once back in its cold halls? If it were not for that cursed duel, he might have had some hope, but she still held herself aloof. He had never thought he would miss that little sigh of hers.

"Ah, Clio," he said as they took a turn about the room afterwards, "how fortunate we would be if you only recorded our victories, but sadly our defeats and lack of judgement must also be noted in your scrolls."

"If I were to remember only his victories, man would look continuously to the past, seeking to repeat it. But he may learn from his mistakes, sir, and perhaps even earn forgiveness or, at least, a second chance."

"To err is human?" he asked seriously.

"Indeed, sir and are we not all called upon to forgive? But see, my sister comes for me." As she spoke, another Muse took her hand and pulled her from him to disappear into the crowd.

"The carriage is outside if you still wish to leave early," Thalia whispered.

"I do. And you?"

"I think I'll stay awhile."

Nancy had a bath waiting so that Lallie could remove the white maquillage that covered her exposed skin. It was a relief to be free of the heat of the mask and the wig, to have the tight braids unravelled and her hair brushed out. Finally she was in bed, undisturbed and able to recall the events of the evening. She closed her eyes, recalling the pleasure of her husband's touch, the joy of matching his movements almost instinctively, of feeling the brush of his leg against hers as they turned. It had been exciting to know who he was while concealing her identity from him. How would he have responded if she had revealed herself? Amused or disappointed? At least he had behaved correctly. She could not have borne it if he had taken liberties or suggested they withdraw to a more private place.

What had made her talk to him like that? Perhaps it was time she let go of her resentment. Did she really want to harden her heart against him, remain bitter and unforgiving for the rest of her life?

Hugo remained only half an hour longer at Burlington House. He could find no more enjoyment here tonight. He walked home deep in thought. What had driven him to speak so freely to his unknown partner? Was there really such a thing as a second chance? Would Lallie forgive him for that cursed duel? Could they make a fresh start?

He dismissed his valet and looked at the door that connected his bedroom to his wife's. It would be very inconsiderate to disturb her but, unable to stop himself, he slipped into the room and went quietly over to her bed. He wouldn't wake her, but at least he could lie beside her.

The mattress dipped beneath his weight and he felt Lallie stir, then her searching fingers reached him. "Hugo?" she murmured drowsily.

"Yes," He resigned himself to apologising and leaving her, but to his amazement she turned towards him, her hand sliding up his chest to his shoulder.

"Sweetheart," he whispered.

"Mmmmm," she sighed with a sleepy, irresistible chuckle and he drew her into his arms.

Half asleep, Lallie did not try to suppress her instinctive response to her husband's caresses, which tonight seemed more prolonged and demanding than usual. She moved with him, mirroring his touches and daringly returned his kisses. This did not appear to repel him, but rather encouraged him to greater efforts. When he came into her, she put her hands on his buttocks, pulling him deep inside her and he groaned before commencing an insistent rhythm that drove her up and up until she was overcome by a wave of strange pleasure as he reached his climax. He collapsed beside her, his head on her breast and she gently smoothed his hair before falling back into sleep. She woke briefly at dawn and was amazed to find him still beside her, but when she next opened her eyes she was alone.

Had it just been another dream? It wouldn't have been the first time she had dreamt Hugo had come to her, but always before she had woken with a strange, empty ache in her lower abdomen. Now she felt relaxed and satisfied. She had slept restlessly in recent weeks, but this morning she was tucked beneath the bedclothes as if a caring hand had smoothed them over her shoulders. Another pillow had been pulled down to lie beside hers and it still bore the impression of a head. She felt sticky between her legs, but it couldn't be her courses.

He must have come to her in the night. She blushed as the details of her dream came back to her. Had she really behaved like that? But he hadn't seemed to mind.

"Good morning, Miss Lallie." Nancy drew back the curtains and came to stand beside the bed. "It's as I thought; we must wash your hair—there's some of that white paint in it. I'll send for hot water and we'll do it now. If you sit here in the sun while you have your breakfast, it'll be dry in no time."

Lallie was about to protest. What would Hugo think if she didn't join him for breakfast? She caught sight of herself in the mirror and realised, aghast, that the combination of tight plaiting and perspiration caused by the wig had left her hair pasted to her head in narrow waves. Thank goodness her room had been dark last night! Surely even he would have noticed?

"We must be quick," she urged. "I can't have anyone see me—they would wonder what I had been doing to get it like this."

Hugo whistled an intricate aria as he returned from an early morning bout with the foils at Angelo's. Lallie's sweet reaction last night had given him new hope. Perhaps all was not lost. Surely she was not completely indifferent to him. He had never had to woo her, he thought suddenly. Was that where he had erred? He stopped a passing flower-seller to buy a posy of cream rose-buds whose petals were just beginning to unfurl.

"Has Mrs Tamrisk come down?"

"I understand madam is breakfasting in her bedchamber this morning, sir,"

His spirits dampened, Hugo glanced down at the flowers, tempted to have them sent up to her. No, he thought, you resolved to try.

She sat at a table pulled up to a window, her loose hair rippling over her shoulders like a silk shawl. Seeing him, she put down the cup of chocolate she had been sipping with obvious relish.

"Good morning, Hugo," she said cheerfully. "I thought to take advantage of the morning sun to dry my hair."

She ran her hands through the long tresses to loosen them and then shook her head so that they flew about her in a gleaming swirl of raven black and midnight blue before falling softly back into place on the pale gold of her dressing-gown.

"Good morning, my sweet. I saw these and they reminded me of you."

"Oh, Hugo, thank you! What beautiful roses! But how could they remind you of me when I am as dark as night?" she asked with an impish grin

"Only your hair," he corrected, tasting chocolate when he kissed her. "Your skin is like cream and as soft as these petals."

He ran a gentle finger down the side of her neck as she stared up at him. There was something to be said for wooing your wife; you need not worry about chaperons and were permitted much more freedom.

Now his wife looked deliciously flustered, a faint blush staining her cheeks. She took the flowers and raised them, inhaling deeply.

"What a lovely scent! Please ring for Nancy; she'll fetch a vase for them."

"Would you like to drive out to Richmond Park later?"

Her smile deepened. "That would be delightful, Hugo."

"May I try my hand at the ribbons?" Lallie asked impulsively. "I've never driven a pair."

Hugo stopped his team. His horses were well-trained and the drive from town had shaken the fidgets out of them. He could safely entrust them to her here in the park. He slid nearer and put the reins in her hands, showing her how to hold them and the whip.

"Take them gently—they're very responsive," he admonished as she signalled the horses to walk on.

"Rum prads, I know."

He raised an eyebrow. "Who has been teaching you cant?"

"My brother James. Once he went to school, his vocabulary expanded considerably." She shot him a saucy smile but then concentrated on her task and soon had the bays trotting nicely along the avenue.

Hugo sat contentedly beside her, ready to intervene at any moment, but Lallie seemed to be a born whip, coping easily when a riding party comprised mainly of frivolous young men and girls cantered carelessly towards them, spreading across the avenue and calling loudly to one another as they came.

"Well done," he murmured once the group was safely past, and then suggested, "There are some fine old oaks over there, just the spot for our pick-nick."

We'll soon leave town, I suppose, Lallie thought as they headed back towards the heat and smells of London. His lordship will no doubt expect me to be with child when we return. I hope he keeps his tongue between his teeth. He probably will with me, but I wonder what he will say to Hugo when they are alone.

Her husband glanced down at her inadvertent sigh. "Had enough?"

She shook her head. "No. It's is wonderful to get away from London. Could we stop at the gate for another look at the Pagoda at Kew?"

"Should you like to drive up to it? I don't think any of the royal family is in residence."

"It's a peculiarly narrow construction for its height, isn't it?" Lallie said as she admired the tall, tiered building with its over-hanging tiled roofs ornamented with gold dragons. "And so fantastical. It must be wonderful to see such structures in their own landscapes. It's so different to our styles——just imagine how out of place a Norman castle would look in China."

"So you won't be seeking to erect a Chinese tower at Tamm?" Hugo teased.

"No, though it would be lovely to have a little summerhouse like the rotunda at Larchwood, where one may sit and admire a pleasant view."

He nodded. "We must look into that—and, in general, what changes you would like to make at the manor."

"Would you like to go abroad for a few months?" Hugo enquired, helping himself to another raspberry tartlet. Lallie's comments at the pagoda had reminded him how envious she had been of his travels. Perhaps a trip to the continent would deepen the growing understanding between them. Look how successful today's outing had been. She had even expressed her own wishes without being asked. The ice has thinned noticeably, he thought with satisfaction.

Now she turned a glowing face to him. "Could we? Must you not return to Tamm?"

"I would have to go for a few days, just to satisfy myself that all is as it should be, but I've been getting comprehensive reports from Jenkinson and he seems to have everything in hand."

"Where could we go?"

"Not Paris, I think. I would prefer not to take you to the capital of an enemy so recently defeated—one cannot rule out unpleasantnesses. Brussels, perhaps, to start—we could see how Arthur goes on—and then I thought to travel to Cologne or Bonn. From there we could take a boat up the Rhine, if you wish."

Lallie's eyes were like stars. "If I wish? Oh, Hugo, it would be above all things marvellous."

"If we move on at the end of September, beginning of October, we would be there during the wine harvest. It is astounding how the peasants clamber up and down the steep hillsides and there are many quaint festivals I think you would enjoy."

"Please may we do it, Hugo? What shall I need? When can we leave? We must close up this house. Oh, I don't know whether I'm on my head or my heels." Lallie was stammering with excitement and he smiled indulgently.

"Let's adjourn to your parlour and start to make plans."

"Do you have maps or guidebooks?" she asked as she ruthlessly cleared the table in front of the sofa and went to fetch pen and paper. "Come, sit down," she patted the seat beside her.

"Not here, they're at Tamm. I'll dig them out when I'm there—there can be nothing more up to date because the war prevented any travel since I bought them. But I can sketch an outline map for you now."

# Chapter Twenty-Two

*The Rocks of Jealousy are a dangerous group on which ships have frequently been dashed to pieces. The Shoals of Perplexity lie near.*

Once settled at the *Hôtel de Flandre*, and too soon for Hugo's liking, the Tamrisks were discovered by the English visitors to Brussels, most of whom seemed determined to recreate the London Season with all its fads and follies; the so-called Ladies in the Park resolving to call only upon those with whom they were on calling terms at home.

"We must maintain our standards," Hugo overheard one matron decree, "or who knows whom we'll be obliged to recognise once we're home."

Lallie's forehead wrinkled in disgust when he told her this. "They are like snails, taking their houses with them and establishing little colonies as soon as they are able. Only imagine being fortunate enough to travel abroad and then condemning 'foreignization', as they call it."

"Many have come to escape their creditors at home," he pointed out. "They are more than happy to create their own little enclave here. But we do not have to join them. Where would you like to go tomorrow? Should we ride, drive or boat?"

Travelling with Lallie was so enjoyable. She delighted in exploring the churches and public buildings such as those of the magnificent *Grand Place* as well as the small shops in the narrow streets behind it. Everything interested her; the peasants in the fields and at the market stalls, quaint inns in the pretty little towns and villages, a blacksmith at his forge or a lace-maker sitting in her doorway with her pillow to catch the light. She loved to take a trip in a canal boat, to glide through the countryside to the strains of a small orchestra and dine with the other passengers.

Best of all, she continued to soften towards him, or so he felt, and he was hopeful the picturesque Rhine journey, where they would be able to enjoy the privacy and seclusion of their own barge, would finally mend matters between them. Already she was more … receptive, he supposed was the best way of describing it, in bed. Even if she did not return his caresses as she had that memorable night after the masquerade, he no longer felt she had to steel herself to accept them. She even gave her little sigh again at the end.

They could not completely avoid their compatriots, of course. The Duke of Wellington, on his way to Paris to take up his appointment as British Ambassador to the court of Louis XVIII, detoured to visit the new United Kingdom of the Netherlands and received an ecstatic welcome. To compound Hugo's disgust, there were also lavish celebrations of the birthdays of both the Prince Regent and his brother the Duke of York and he once again had the dubious pleasure of watching his wife waltz with Luke Fitzmaurice. When she was later invited to dance by no less a personage than the young Prince of Orange, Hugo's only consolation was that she had not caught Wellington's roving fancy.

Lallie had never been so happy. While Hugo had not asked her in so many words to make a fresh start, his actions suggested that this was his desire. He was more the man she had met last year and, as the summer wore on, she felt a renewed confidence that he cared for her. She would never again be the girl giddy with new love who had blithely accepted his proposal of marriage, but she hoped that they would find their way to a new understanding. Just look at the way they sat quietly together this evening, he reading and she writing her journal, each looking up from time to time to exchange a few words.

She wondered whether he realised that she had twice missed her courses. The first time had been the week he went to Tamm, so perhaps not. She felt a little unwell in the mornings and had had to forego her morning chocolate and rolls in favour of tea and toast but everything was so different here that even if Hugo had noticed, he had not considered it worthy of comment. He looked up from his book and smiled at her, as if her thoughts had broken his concentration, but before he could say anything, there was a tap at their sitting-room door.

"Captain Malvin."

"Arthur!" Lallie jumped up in delight. "We had not expected to see you today."

"I rode in with despatches that Wellington must have before he leaves for Paris," he explained as he kissed her cheek. "I looked in on my parents but Mamma is giving some cursed dinner. Higgins said you weren't invited so I decided to make my way here." He accepted a glass of wine from Hugo and raised it to Lallie. "Your very good health, my dear. I need not ask how you do—I see that you are blooming. Belgium obviously agrees with you."

"I love it here—it is so different. And Germany will be different again, I am sure."

"When do you leave for the Rhine?"

"On the nineteenth of September."

"Splendid!" He turned to his uncle. "Hugo, a few of the chaps are getting up a hunting party in the Ardennes—the forests there teem with stag and boar, apparently. There's even talk of wolves. What do you say to joining us? We'll be staying at a little hunting-lodge that belongs to the father of a major in the Dutch-Belgians."

"It sounds very tempting."

"I should say it does. We'll be back on the seventeenth, so it fits perfectly with your plans," Arthur said persuasively.

"When do you leave?"

"On the third."

Hugo shook his head. "Leave Lallie alone in a foreign city for a fortnight? It's out of the question, Arthur."

"Would you like to go, Hugo?" Lallie intervened.

"Of course he would," Arthur answered for him. "You don't get such an opportunity every day, I may tell you."

"Then he should avail himself of it," she stated calmly. "No, Hugo," she put up her hand to stop him interrupting, "you need not be concerned about me; I'm quite sure Clarissa would put me up—as it is, she can't understand why we chose to go to a hotel and not to her."

"What did you tell her?" Hugo enquired.

"That this is in some sort our wedding journey. I couldn't think what else to say—I could hardly admit you had refused to entertain the idea."

Arthur frowned but made no comment while her husband smiled and raised his glass to her.

She took advantage of the short pause to press her case. "I shall be perfectly comfortable with her, I assure you. I can remove from here the morning you leave. I'm sure she will be agreeable to your trunks being sent to her as well and we may set out from there on the Monday."

"Leave it to me," Arthur made haste to strike the bargain. "I'll talk to Mamma tonight—I'll warrant she'll be more than happy to have you stay."

By the beginning of September, Lallie was almost certain she was with child. She would have to tell Hugo when he returned from the Ardennes. Would he still come to her bed once he knew? Did she want him to? If he stopped, it would prove that she was no more to him than a vessel to carry his heir. And she enjoyed the closeness, especially when he laid his head on her breast at the end, but it was becoming more and more difficult to conceal her instinctive response to his touch.

But he didn't seem to mind that night after the masquerade, she thought suddenly. I'm no longer a virgin or a bride. Perhaps I have been refining too much on what Grandmother said. When Hugo came to her later, she smiled up at him and tenderly brushed a wayward lock back from his forehead. He didn't recoil from this caress but caught her hand and kissed it. Later, when he entered her, she put her arms around him and held him close. He paused for a moment, then kissed her deeply before proceeding with increased vigour and did not resist when she tilted her hips to take him deeper. The pleasant, rocking motion was somehow not enough and she was fighting the urge to meet and return his thrusts when he finished. Next time I'll be more daring, she thought, gently stroking his head where it lay on her breast.

Hugo watched Lallie dart about their rooms, busy with last minute preparations and wondering how quickly he might lure her to bed. He was to be without her for a fortnight. And after last night! Her tentative caresses had inflamed him. Tonight he would try and last longer.

She flitted back in from her bedchamber. "We have it all sorted out now. What each of us will need for the next two weeks, what we'll need while travelling to Cologne and the rest is in trunks for the Rhine journey."

She spread out her arms and spun in a quick circle and he caught and twirled her again, elated to see her so happy.

She leaned back in his arms, smiling up at him. "Oh, I'm so looking forward to it, Hugo. I hear the scenery is wonderfully romantic. And it will be most agreeable to be away from society. Brussels has become too hectic, too like London, I think. It will be much more restful on the boat."

"I hope you won't find it too boring, my sweet, with only your husband for company."

"Fishing for compliments, sir?"

"Not I! Are you sure you have everything?"

"Everything except the contents of that table. I was just about to empty the drawer but you may do it for me, if you wish."

"I'm at your service, my dear," he announced, stooping to his task. "What's this?" He held up something wrapped in tissue paper.

She took it from him, a curious little smile playing about her lips, and opened the packet to display a white and gold mask.

He glanced fleetingly at it. "Pretty."

She nodded. "It's part of a masquerade costume. I was wondering where we had put it—the rest is packed already."

"The rest?" he asked.

"A white wig, gown and sandals, all in the Grecian style."

"Not representing one of the Muses, I trust?" Hugo asked lightly.

"Yes. It is most becoming."

"That I know," he replied drily, "but it's not for you. It's too distinctive and could give rise to the worst scandal-mongering."

"I don't understand."

"You must trust me in this, Lallie," he declared. "From whom do you have it? She can't be a fit person for you to know."

"What do you mean? I don't have it from anyone. It's mine. It was made for me."

"It was made for you? When? Where have you worn it? I don't recall you going to any masquerades."

"And of course you always knew where I went," she retorted with a glinting smile, "just as you always told me where you were going. But you have seen it before," she added playfully "and others like it too."

Aghast, Hugo stared at his wife. In his mind, he was suddenly back at Burlington House. Through a half-open door, he could see one of the Muses bent over a desk, her white skirts flipped up to bare her bottom and legs while a man in the distinctive blue domino worn that evening by all members of Watier's took her vigorously from behind.

"You were one of the Muses at Watier's masquerade?" he asked incredulously.

Her smile faded. "Yes." Turning her back on him, she strolled to the window.

She was putting him at a distance again. His temper sparked.

"I had not thought you so shameless! How can you stand there and calmly admit you not only participated in but performed at one of the most notorious events of the Season?"

Lallie swivelled and faced his contemptuous scrutiny, her head held high. Her eyes flashed green fire.

"Don't be hypocritical, Tamrisk. You were there yourself, after all."

"The rules of society are different for men," he snapped. "Besides, I didn't create a spectacle such as the Muses did on their entrance. Not to speak of how they comported themselves afterwards!"

"But as a man you may disport yourself with whom you please?" Her voice was a rapier of sugared steel. "So Tamrisk might dance with Clio, but not Clio with Tamrisk?"

It was a thrust to the heart. "You were Clio?"

She held the mask to her face, displaying the scrolls listing Wellington's battles. Her lips curved beneath it. "As I recall, sir, we discussed victory and defeat."

And the chance to learn from one's mistakes, he thought grimly as he gazed at the expressionless features that concealed hers. What a fool he was, to have been inspired by his own wife in disguise. She had clearly recognised him. Had she secretly laughed at him while they danced—and later?

"I confess I never expected to find my wife amongst the incognitas," he countered disdainfully.

"You need not sound so scornful, sir. You came quickly enough when I crooked a finger."

The derisive reminder flayed him. "Of course you are well used to crooking your finger," he retorted savagely. "You have admirers enough to summons at your whim; Fitzmaurice for a start. Are they not enough to satisfy your vanity, madam, or do you require a husband in your train too? In a suitably lowly position, of course." He laughed bitterly. "You have made it clear enough where I stand in your affections."

"You have no idea of the state of my affections! Luke Fitzmaurice was there when I badly needed support. And what of Lady Albright?" Her voice went from fire to ice. "But I forget; a wife must not concern herself with a mistress."

"That, at least, is true." His tone was as frigid as hers. After her endorsement of her *cicisbeo*, he had no intention of discussing Sabina with her.

"And you dare accuse me, when all the world knew from the beginning that your marriage vows meant nothing to you? But sauce for the gander is also sauce for the goose, sir."

Her words whipped him to a jealous fury. Oh, God! Had he slaked a fire that night that had been stoked by another man? Fitzmaurice perhaps? He had heard him twitted about capturing one of the Muses.

"You little hussy!"

He closed his eyes briefly to blot out the excruciating image. She remained silent and when he looked at her again, she had retreated behind that icy veil, a mocking smile on her lips.

"Shame on you, sir, to refer so to your wife."

"My wife! And who else's woman? My fault lies in not having curbed you before now. But all that will change on my return. And do not think to take advantage of my absence. You will conduct yourself with propriety or live to regret it."

"Hugo!" She drew herself up to her full height as the tirade tumbled from him.

"There is no need to play the innocent! You know full well what games you have been playing with your admirers. I suppose I must rejoice that you're not increasing, for I should always wonder who the father of your brat was. Mark my words, madam; you will not foist another man's bastard on me."

It was if he stood outside himself, observing this ranting Hugo from some strange vantage point, hearing his denunciation as if uttered by another man and unable to stop it. It seemed to turn his wife to stone and when at last he paused, they stared at one another for long moments in shocked, bewildered silence.

Finally Lallie took a long, shuddering breath. "I think you've run mad. Hugo, you can't mean that. Do you indeed think so poorly of me?" Her small voice broke on a sob. "This is just a stupid quarrel about nothing, isn't it? I won't wear the costume again if you don't wish me to. Hugo, please?"

Rooted to the spot and horror-struck at what he had said, he watched his wife turn pale, paler. Her hands fluttered down to her abdomen before one rose and was extended beseechingly towards him.

"Only listen to me, Hugo, trust me." She took faltering steps towards him, her eyes fixed on his. "Hugo?"

But he was in another place and could not respond, could only watch numbly when she finally turned and walked away, one hand pressed to her mouth. Her bedroom door shut behind her and the click of the key turning in the lock broke the heavy silence.

# Chapter Twenty-Three

*Cat and Dog Harbour on this coast is the principle port for trade
to the Divorce Island. The sea lying between the main land and
this Island is dangerous on account of the sand banks continually
drifting about, and the rough winds that blow from the east.*

From her vantage point at the side of the large window
Lallie watched the riders assemble in the *Place Royale*, calling cheerfully to one another over the clatter of hooves and the
jingle of harness. Another horseman emerged from the archway
that led to the stable yard of the *Hôtel de Flandre*. Without a backwards or upwards glance, he wheeled his mount to join the carefree group and disappeared with them across the *Place Royale* and
down towards the Namur gate.

"He's gone." Her composed voice broke the tense silence.
"What about Willis and Hobbs?"

"They're to follow within the hour, Miss Lallie. A baggage waggon is to call for Willis. Hobbs will go with the other
grooms. 'Tis all very well arranged, I must say. Now you just sit
down while I ring for your breakfast."

"Please place that table here at the window, Nancy. He—he
might turn back and I should like to be prepared."

Lallie sank into her chair. Behind her closed eyes she saw again
Hugo's incensed features. His hurled insults and accusations rang

in her ears. Had he not regretted them once he had calmed down, realised how unjust he had been in his rage? She had crept from her bed before dawn to unlock the door she had slammed against him the previous night. But he had not come to apologise or even say goodbye. Perhaps he had left a note? She rushed into the sitting room that separated their bedrooms. Her quick, hopeful scrutiny was followed by a more thorough examination of the apartment but this, too, was fruitless. Downcast, she returned to her post where she obediently sipped her tea and toyed with her toast.

A tap on the door to the corridor roused her from her apathy.

"Sit down, Miss Lallie," Nancy said firmly. "I'll go." She hurried to unlock the door but only opened it a little.

A man's voice; Lallie strained to hear what he said. Her heart was beating so loudly that it was moments before she realised it wasn't Hugo but his valet. Perhaps Hugo had entrusted a letter for her to him.

"I'm about to leave. Miss Anderson. The master's trunks are ready in his room. Is there anything I can do for the mistress or you before I go?"

"Nothing, thank you, Mr Willis." Nancy stepped back and shut the door.

A wave of despair engulfed Lallie. He wasn't coming back and there would be no gesture of reconciliation.

"What time is it, Nancy?"

"A quarter to nine, Miss Lallie."

"Over two hours since they left." She pushed herself wearily to her feet. "I want you to take a note to Lady Needham's rooms as soon as is permissible. Would nine o'clock be too early, do you think?"

"Her woman will be up. I'll give it to her."

Half past nine saw Mrs Tamrisk ushered into the bedchamber where Lady Needham reclined against lace-trimmed pillows, sipping a cup of chocolate.

"Now what's to-do? A young wife like you should not be calling on an old lady at this hour. She should have finer fish to fry!"

Lallie smiled wanly in response to this remark.

"Holmes, set a chair for Mrs Tamrisk and then leave us. Wait, fetch her some chocolate, first."

"Nothing for me, I thank you, ma'am."

"If you are sure. Now, come here, child and tell me what I may do for you."

Lallie sat silently, her head bent, her hands clasped in her lap. It had seemed such an easy thing to ask, but once embarked on this journey, there could be no turning back. However, she knew Lady Needham to be discreet. In the end, she just said simply, "You return to England today, do you not, ma'am?"

"We depart at mid-day."

"I was wondering, that is would it be too much of an imposition if I were to accompany you? I must go home—an urgent family matter."

"Where's Tamrisk?"

"He left at dawn for a hunting party in the Ardennes. They expect to be gone for at least a fortnight. I can't wait that long, ma'am."

Lallie's voice trailed away and she pressed a hand to her mouth.

"I see. Can your maid be ready by noon?"

At Lallie's nod, her ladyship said, "Very well. My son has sent his yacht for me, so we shall not attract the attention of the inquisitive."

"Thank you." Lallie was trembling so much she could hardly speak.

Lady Needham summoned her maid. "Go and fetch Mrs Tamrisk's maid. She has had sad news and is not well." She turned back to her visitor. "You are to lie down for an hour.

Come back ready to travel at a quarter to mid-day and leave everything else to me. I presume you wish to retain the rooms here against Tamrisk's return."

"No. I was to stay with his sister, Lady Malvin during his absence and we were to leave Brussels afterwards. Tamrisk's trunks may go to the Malvins' house to await him there."

To her surprise Lallie slept so soundly that Nancy had to rouse her at a quarter past eleven. She even managed to eat a baked egg custard before taking her seat in the carriage which soon rumbled out of the Place Royale. They made difficult progress through the maze of narrow, partly cobbled streets, and the unsteady jolting of the carriage, its windows closed against the dust and malodorous town air, tried her resilience and will-power to the utmost.

Nancy kept a watchful eye on her and seeing her press her handkerchief to her lips, quietly replaced it with another one on which she had sprinkled a few drops of liquid with an aromatic yet astringent scent. Lallie inhaled gratefully and felt the nausea and the lightness in her head recede.

Nancy checked that the door was locked and settled into the little truckle bed. She blew out her candle.

"Good night, Miss Lallie."

"Good night, Nancy."

Lallie wearily turned onto her side. Soon little snuffling snores confirmed that her maid slept but, tired though she was, Lallie couldn't follow her example. Just as she felt she was easing past the barrier to slumber, the events of the previous evening passed again before her inward eye, arousing a sort of sick disgust, partly at Hugo's behaviour and partly at herself for having begun to place her trust in him again.

Finally she slipped into a deeper sleep. But now she walked along a wintry woodland path, hurrying to get home before dark. When she came to a junction, she made as if to turn right to take the path back to Tamm Manor, but her husband stood there barring the way, his legs braced apart and his arms folded.

He glared scornfully at her. "There is nothing here for you, madam."

His voice was harsh, his tone pitiless.

"Hugo, please, if you would but listen to me," she implored, her hands held out to him, but he turned his back to her.

"Miss Lallie, Miss Lallie, wake up! You're dreaming, my dear. 'Tis only a dream."

"Nancy!" Lallie gasped with relief. "What time is it?"

"Four in the morning. Try and get some more sleep. Or should I see if they will make tea or heat a glass of milk?"

"No, thank you. A glass of water will do." She gulped it thirstily and lay down again. "I'm sorry for disturbing you."

But sleep continued to elude her. The best she could achieve was a sort of doze, sometimes light, sometimes heavier, that was beset by half-dreams in which she seemed to relive her marriage. The dream Lallie lifted her face to meet her husband's kiss only for the touch of his lips to dissipate in a burst of morning light.

Nancy ruthlessly drew back the curtains. "Eight o'clock, Miss Lallie. I have your tea and toast here. Now, don't try to get up before you've had it."

Lallie gazed blindly at the bright landscape that glided past the open windows of the canal-boat. This time last year she had been staying with the Halworths in Berkshire. She had just met Hugo. Tears filled her eyes as she looked back on those halcyon days. And then he had appeared like an angel at the *Bull and Mouth*. She had been so overjoyed to see him then, so incredulously happy when he proposed. How could she have guessed he would turn on her like that?

*Nothing! All for nothing! Worse than nothing!* The hooves of the barge-horses plodding along the tow-path beat out the dismal refrain.

If only she had not gone to Burlington House! But it wasn't just her participation at the masquerade that had so infuriated Hugo. He had sounded so—jealous of her 'admirers', as he called them. What nonsense. And so unfair. To accuse her of what he had very likely done himself! Had she been right to leave Brussels? Should she have gone to Clarissa and waited—for what? She couldn't look forward, couldn't see past that awful scene.

What was she to do, where was she to go? The picture rose in her mind of a welcoming house in a shallow valley through which a little stream purled down to the sea. The gentle slope of the land on either side formed cradling arms that shielded the long, low building from the winter storms. There, summer yielded late to autumn; defiant roses lingered against old brick walls and bright fuchsias spoke long of warm days.

Larkhaven—she would go to Larkhaven.

"The captain tells me we should arrive about ten o'clock tomorrow morning. Would you like to accompany me to the Dower House at Needham or should you prefer to hire a post-chaise immediately?"

"Ma'am?"

The older woman smiled and patted Lallie's hand. "You have quarrelled with Tamrisk, I take it?"

Lallie sighed and nodded. "How did you know, ma'am?"

"If your presence had truly been suddenly required in England for family reasons, his departure was recent enough that a messenger could have summoned him to return without undue delay. He would not have refused such a request so he must have been the cause of your decision. In general I am not in favour of abandoning the battlefield, but there are times when a strategic retreat is advisable. You may tell me all about it and then we shall put our heads together."

Lady Needham listened attentively to Lallie's tale, interrupting from time-to-time to pose an incisive question. She was not content to learn only of the quarrel that had set Lallie into flight, but demanded to hear the whole story of their marriage.

"And what now, child?" she asked at the end. "What had you thought to do?"

"I shall go to Larkhaven, my old home in Cornwall," Lallie said slowly. "It was let but is now vacant. Tamrisk is master at Tamm and Tamarisk House. It's the baby, you see. If I only had to think of myself, well I'm not so fainthearted that I would meekly submit to whatever he might decree on his return, and it is possible that he now regrets his words. But I can't risk it. What if he should indeed repudiate our child? I don't think I could bear it. Perhaps he might even try and make me give it up—I know of one woman whose husband did so—and compel me to remain at Tamm until I have given him an heir he is prepared to recognise."

Lady Needham shook her head. "I think you are unfair to your husband, Lallie. He is not Devonshire, nor are you the late Duchess. But I agree that your babe must be your first concern. I also think that it is time that you and Tamrisk engaged in a frank discussion face to face. You are wise not to involve his sisters—I never had the impression that they were overly partial to him. It is very likely they would support you against him, but this would not aid your cause. You need to meet on neutral ground, settle your differences fairly."

"A sort of Congress of Vienna?" Lallie asked with a hint of a smile

"That's it. Don't make it too easy for him, either. Let him work for a reconciliation—he will value it more."

"If he wants one. He may be glad to be rid of me."

Lady Needham smiled knowingly. "My dear girl, no gentleman who forgets himself with a lady to the extent that Tamrisk did with you is indifferent to her. Remember you cannot change what is past. You can only hope to ensure that the future will be different."

"I won't share him," Lallie said stubbornly. "If he wishes to keep a mistress or put his former mistress ahead of me, as he did with the duel, then all he may hope for is the minimum of duty."

"Hmph! Be that as it may, you will do yourself no favours if you spend the next weeks clinging to your resentment. You must give him the benefit of the doubt until you meet again and not harden your heart against him. That can only lead to disaster."

# Chapter Twenty-Four

*The Valley of Regret lies near the Gulf of Despair and is famous for a delicate plant called the Narcissus.*

A glowing log collapsed with a soft hush, sending aloft a flurry of sparks followed by a sudden flame that jolted Hugo from his musings. He rubbed his hand over his jaw, feeling the rasp of an evening's stubble. Dinner over, he had withdrawn from the raucous group of military and civilian gentlemen who made up this party in the Ardennes and once again sought refuge in this small, wood-panelled room. At this late hour he had stripped off his coat and lay sprawled in his chair. A half-empty decanter of cognac was at his elbow and a glass threatened to slip from the lax grasp of his long fingers. He had loosened his cravat and the style of his dishevelled hair owed more to the raking of those fingers than to its fashionable cut.

Arthur stumbled into the room, two other gentlemen hot on his heels and all three out of breath.

"Chauncy insisted on a leap-frog steeplechase around the hall," Captain Malvin gasped, "we three are the last men standing."

He took the glass from his uncle's hand and drained it, then collapsed into the arm-chair opposite him.

"You're playing least in sight again? I swear you are become a staid married man."

"That can happen when you get caught in parson's mouse-trap," one of the gentlemen said jovially, collecting more glasses from the sideboard, "but I hadn't expected it of you, Tamrisk. Surely you haven't married such a shrew that you may no longer divert yourself?"

Mr Tamrisk's head came up at this and he fixed the speaker with a basilisk stare while the captain barked, "Hawthorne! You forget yourself!"

At the same time the third man sniggered, "Many a man has thought to wed a timid country mouse only for her to turn into a flighty shrew, eh Tamrisk?"

The words had barely passed his lips when he found himself pinned by the throat against the wall, held some six inches over the floor to that his dangling feet scrabbled uselessly for purchase while his fingers plucked harmlessly at the strong hands that held him.

"Hugo! You can't strangle him in another man's house! Damned bad form in a guest, you know."

The captain's admonition together with sharp tugs on his wrists finally penetrated Hugo's rage enough that he released his grip, causing his victim to drop to the floor where he gasped for breath while his friend helpfully loosened his neckcloth and put a glass of cognac into his hands.

These duties done, Lieutenant Hawthorne stood up to face Mr Tamrisk. "I beg your pardon, sir," he said formally, "I regret that ill-chosen words of mine gave rise to such an insult. I assure you that I spoke only in jest and stand ready to make any amends you may require of me."

Hugo waved this handsome offer aside, "I accept your apology, sir, but this cur deserves a thrashing." He held out his hand, which his opponent clasped solemnly.

"I apologise unreservedly," came in strained tones from the floor. "'Twas only a jest, I assure you. I've the highest regard for Mrs Tamrisk, nothing personal intended."

Hugo took two quick steps to crouch by the speaker's side and lifted his head by the hair to glare into his eyes. "You dare to mention my wife's name?"

"Not at all. Can't think what came over me."

Hugo let go and the head thudded to the floor. He brushed his hands together as if dusting something distasteful from them, picked up his coat and turned on his heel.

"Arthur?"

The Captain obediently fell in beside him. "He's badly foxed" he remarked as they headed for their bedrooms. "I'm sure he'll be appalled when he realises what he said. I'm surprised, though. I thought all that country mouse business had died down months ago; no one dared revive it after Lallie gave young Norris such a set-down and Lady Needham scolded him as if he were a scrubby schoolboy." He opened his door. "Well, good night, old man."

Hugo put a restraining hand on his arm. "What country mouse business? What the devil do you mean by Lallie, Norris and Lady Needham?"

"You mean you don't know?" Arthur asked disbelievingly and yawned hugely. "I'm half-seas over—too disguised to explain now. We'll talk tomorrow," he said firmly and shut the door on his uncle.

Once in his own room, Hugo lit the candles on the mantelpiece and stirred the glowing logs into flame before settling into an armchair where he sank back into the melancholy brooding that the revellers had disturbed. He shook his head, full of self-reproach. He had attacked a man who made a tasteless, drunken innuendo about his wife, but of what had he accused her—and to her face? He should never had left Brussels without attempting to make up with her, should have cried off from the hunting-party and sought her out the next morning. But what could he have said? Would she even have listened to him? After all, he had refused to listen to her.

When he closed his eyes, he could see her distressed face as she regarded him in painful hope, so profoundly pale that a sprinkling of tiny freckles stood out across her nose and cheeks. Normally he would have been charmed by their appearance, but then he had remained silent and her hand fell, she had turned away from him and, shoulders drooping in defeat, left the room.

When his valet woke him before dawn to prepare for his journey, he had half-wanted to go to her, but the fear of rejection, a feeling of deep shame and a residual sense of hurt and betrayal held him hostage. Apathetic, he had allowed Willis to dress him, mounted his horse as if in a dream and had ridden some thirty miles before the full realisation of what he had done hit him.

Even then I might have turned back. What awaits me in Brussels? If I get my just deserts! He shuddered at the thought. How was he to mend this? Any progress he had made with Lallie in the past two months must be utterly destroyed now.

Captain Malvin came into his uncle's room just as Hugo was about to go down to breakfast. "Frost desires to offer you his most abject apologies and satisfaction in any form you wish."

"What do you think, Arthur?"

"It is as I said. He is genuinely remorseful, horrified at himself, croaks like a frog—it is fortunate that neckcloths are worn high enough to conceal the bruises on his throat—and he has a two-fold headache, one from having over imbibed—I have rarely seen anyone so crapulent and still standing—and the other from the lump you caused by dropping his head on to the floor. He is the sort of young fool who'll delope as well," Arthur added, ignoring the fact that the gentleman in question was as old as himself.

Hugo had to laugh at this catalogue of disaster. "Maybe I owe him the opportunity to put a bullet through me," he said ruefully, "but I'm done with duels. Lallie once said to me we can learn from our mistakes and perhaps earn forgiveness or at least a second chance. I'll accept his apology. Let it be done now, before breakfast. Have Frost and Hawthorne meet me in the little parlour where I was last night."

A pasty-faced, repentant Mr Frost duly came to the parlour. Though obviously very much under the weather, he manfully met Mr Tamrisk's eyes and painfully stuttered his profound apologies and regrets in a voice akin to that of a raven. Hugo accepted them solemnly and offered his hand, which Mr Frost gratefully shook.

"Let's get some coffee," Captain Malvin urged prosaically and the four gentlemen repaired to the breakfast room. The rest of the party had already left for a last day with the guns. Once they had fortified themselves with a substantial meal, Messrs Frost and Hawthorne decided to try for some trout and Mr Tamrisk decreed that he and his nephew would take a look at the stables and also visit the kennels.

"I'm in negotiations for a pretty little bitch," he explained. "She has a strong strain of the old St Hubert's hounds and I wonder how it would be to cross it with my St John's."

"A match made in heaven, I have no doubt," Arthur replied with a grin.

"Now, Arthur," Hugo said, having become the proud owner of a three-month old puppy and made arrangements for its transport the following day, "what was that you said last night about Lallie, young Norris and Lady Needham?"

"Do you really mean you heard none of it?"

"None of what? It was hardly all over society," Hugo retorted impatiently.

Arthur gaped at him. "Well, of course it was. But I suppose you would be the last one they would twit about it. Poor

Lallie had to bear the brunt of it, and with great dignity too, my mother said. Never let on she knew what they were talking about, although she was well aware of what they meant."

"Arthur, if you do not at once tell me what you are talking about, there will be another frog croaking in duet with Frost tonight."

"Why, that country mouse quip of yours."

"What quip?" Hugo growled. "Enough roundaboutation, just give me the facts."

Captain Malvin spoke carefully, as if addressing an idiot. "Hugo, you do remember saying one night at Brooks's last year that if you ever married your bride would be a quiet country mouse with nary a squeak to her, who would know her place and leave you to yours?"

"Did I? I can't say I recall it," Hugo replied carelessly, "but what has that to do with Lallie this year? I never saw anyone less like a country mouse!"

"Fact is, at the beginning of the Season some wags remembered the story and they fell into the habit of quizzing her—nothing direct, of course—you know how that sort of thing is done—remarks in her hearing about mice, and squeak, squeak, and country maidens, glancing at one another as if to say you are too stupid to know we are making game of you and tittering behind their hands and their damn fans. She bore it very well, never showed that it made her uncomfortable, for the worst thing you can do is let them feel they have scored a hit, and we all supported her by ignoring the would-be wits and conversing as if nothing was untoward."

"She never said anything," Hugo said, shocked. "When I asked how she was getting on in society, she always said 'very well, sir', as cool as a cucumber. But why the devil didn't Clarissa or Henrietta tell me?"

Arthur shifted uneasily. "I can't say. Maybe they thought you knew and didn't care."

"Not care!"

"Well you weren't much given to squiring Lallie to parties, my mother said. Seemed quite happy for her and Henrietta to take her up. Of course Mamma was going to all the dos in any event," he added fairly.

Hugo stared at his nephew, remembering how Clarissa had swooped down and gathered up his wife so that once again he was outside the family group as he had been so often in his childhood; excluded from the mysterious female world, to which for some reason Clarissa admitted her sons. As a child he had always felt she disliked him; certainly there were for him none of the warm embraces and caresses she had lavished on his nephews, as she had insisted on referring to them.

"You still haven't told me about Norris."

"Oh, he went too far and Lallie gave him such a set-down that it was a case of the biter bit! He had to rusticate for weeks afterwards; in fact I don't think he has dared to show his face in town since."

"Someone mentioned he was in Paris." Hugo said absently. "Do you know how she came to be acquainted with Luke Fitzmaurice?"

"Haven't a clue. Perhaps through old Lady Needham—I think she's a connection of his and you frequently see Lallie in her company."

Hugo nodded. "I have been a poor husband, I fear. Is there anything else you think I should have known? Has she had any other difficulties?"

"Apart from your calling Norris *père* out for insulting your mistress?" Arthur asked dryly. "I think once she made her own friends it was easier for her."

"Flora and her fillies," Hugo said disdainfully.

"Don't know whether you've noticed it, Hugo—it was Henrietta who pointed it out to me—but the Duchess tends to befriend young wives whose husbands are, well, distant, shall we say? They're safe in that circle, or as safe as they wish to be," he amended. "The older women keep an eye out for the younger ones, warn them of the worst rakes, that sort of thing; keep them out of harm's way, Henrietta says."

Hugo had a sudden memory of one of the other Muses drawing Lallie away from him. 'My sister comes for me,' she had said.

It had been just before midnight and she must have left soon after, for she was sound asleep when he came in at one o'clock and it would have taken her some time to remove the white paint they were all covered in. Now that he thought of it, as Clio she had used a distinctive perfume and there had been no trace of that either. A huge wave of relief rolled through him as he realised she definitely could not have been the Muse he had spied *in flagrante delicto*, to be followed by an equal surge of shame that he had ever suspected her of such a thing. And he had not only thought it, he had as good as accused her of it.

How had Arthur described Flora's fillies? 'Young wives whose husbands are distant.' Neglectful was what he meant. Had he retired from the lists too soon, leaving his wife at the mercy of society? She had said that his marriage vows meant nothing to him. He had been faithful, it was true, but there were other promises in the marriage ceremony. He must ask himself how had he honoured them, had he comforted and cherished her, or had he appeared indifferent, distant, as Arthur had put it? His sisters had thought he would not care if his wife were teased or tormented by the *ton*. And clearly Lallie had not felt she could or should come to him for help.

"Welcome home Captain Malvin, Mr Tamrisk," the butler bowed as the two men entered the vestibule of her Ladyship's house near the Park. "I trust you enjoyed good sport?"

"Indeed we did, Higgins. Where's my mother?"

"Her ladyship is attending a '*déjeuner à la fourchette*', Captain." The butler enunciated the name of this modish entertainment with relish. A 'fork breakfast' taken in the early afternoon was all the crack among the Brussels ladies.

"Did Mrs Tamrisk accompany her?" Hugo asked, unsure whether to hope Lallie was out enjoying herself or somewhere in the house where he might immediately seek her out and commence his apologies.

The butler remained unperturbed. "I understand sir that Mrs Tamrisk was recalled to England unexpectedly and was therefore unable to join us here. Your trunks are in the blue bedchamber, as is a missive from Mrs Tamrisk."

Hugo turned dumbly towards the stairs.

"The blue bedchamber, Higgins? I'll take him up." Arthur grasped his uncle's elbow and steered him up to the second floor and along a passage to a pleasant room overlooking the Park.

Hugo paid no attention to the aspect or to the trunks lined up against the wall, but went directly to the small pile of correspondence on the writing table. He quickly flicked through it and extracted the letter addressed in his wife's hand to the *Honble. Hugo Tamrisk*. Breaking the seal, he scanned the few short lines. His knees gave way and he collapsed into a chair, shook his head vigorously as if to clear it and read the brief note again in the desperate hope that it might not say what he thought it had. He found no comfort.

> *Hôtel de Flandre, Bruxelles*
> *3 September 1814*

> *To the Honble. Hugo Tamrisk*
>    *Sir,*
>    *I find myself unwilling to remain in Brussels and accordingly return to England today in the company of Lady Needham, who*

*kindly permits me to avail myself of her arrangements for the journey.*

*I remain, Sir, yours etc.*

L. *Tamrisk.*

*Postscriptum. I have written to Lady Malvin advising her that pressing family matters require my immediate return home and have reassured her that these arise in my family, not in hers. L. T.*

"Is it bad news, old man? Hugo?" Arthur's voice broke through Hugo's stupor.

"She's left me," he said tonelessly. "I knew it would be hard to face her, but it never occurred to me that she might not be here."

"You'd quarrelled, I take it?" Suddenly enlightened as to the cause of his uncle's distraction over the past two weeks, Arthur went to the decanters and splashed cognac into two glasses.

Hugo accepted one mechanically. "I was at fault. I should have never come with you but stayed to apologise."

"When the time came, didn't she want you to join the hunting party? A young wife might complain at being left on her own in a foreign city, I suppose."

"No; it was something else entirely. I lost my temper, said unforgivable things."

Hugo continued to stare at the letter as if he could alter it by will alone.

A sharp rap on the door heralded Clarissa, who swept into the room in a rustle of skirts. She went first to embrace her son and then offered a cool cheek to her brother.

"What caused your wife to turn tail the minute you had left Brussels? If it were not for the fact that she is travelling with Lady Needham, I would have thought she had left you for another man."

Hugo did not react to this crass remark but he saw Arthur wince.

"It must have been very sudden indeed," his sister continued. "I went around to the hotel as soon as I received the letter to see if I could be of assistance but I was away from home when it arrived and they had left some five hours previously. Is that her letter?"

Without asking permission, she twitched it out of Hugo's hand and had read it before he had recovered enough to protest.

"My letter, if you please, Clarissa."

"Oh, very well," she snapped as she handed it back, "but I collect I am half right and she has left you. Well it was to be expected, I suppose. No woman could wish to remain married to a Tamrisk. I'm sure it's entirely your fault, Hugo. Poor child. If only she had come to me. I know what it is to live with a Tamrisk man. She should never have married you, of course. But it was too late for me to warn her! We shall have to see what we can do for her."

"You will do nothing," Hugo snapped. "I leave for England at first light."

"To force her to return to you? You're just like Tamm," Clarissa cried. "It does not matter how much your wife suffers as long as you have your heir."

Hugo tried to rein in his temper. "It may surprise you to know, Clarissa, that Lallie is my chief concern, not the siring of the next but one Lord Tamm."

She stared at him. "You will not have me believe that you care for her. You are a Tamrisk, after all."

It was too much! Hugo turned on his sister, not in a flare of passionate jealousy as he had with Lallie, but in the cold resentment forged by the accumulated slights of a lifetime.

"I wish you will tell me, Clarissa, what have I ever done to you to make you hate me so? My earliest memories are of your cold disdainful words, your lack of any natural, sisterly affection, your complete repudiation of me. You did not start to use my name until after you had met Anthony—until then I was 'the boy' or 'boy', said in the same way you addressed Mamma's dog. 'Here's the boy, Mamma', you used to say when I was admitted to her withdrawing-room or 'it is time for you to go back to the nursery, boy'. The first time I recall my name on your lips was when Anthony came for your marriage. 'And this is Hugo, the heir', you said. The other children were presented as 'my sister' or 'my son' or 'my daughter'. I was just 'the heir'. And, of course, after Arthur was born, 'your uncle'."

"You're raving, Hugo!" his sister declared disdainfully. She moved to a high-backed chair and took her seat deliberately, as if sitting in judgement.

"I'm not, I assure you, sister." He looked at Arthur. "You remember, don't you? Was there ever anything more ludicrous than a two-year-old nephew attempting a formal bow to his six-year-old uncle? I was old enough to feel ridiculous, but not so old that I could recognise that my sister, who was almost twenty years older, a married woman, was making game of me."

Arthur looked uncomfortable at this appeal. "I haven't thought about it for years, but it always felt wrong, not like when we bowed to Amabel or even Henrietta," he admitted. "They were girls and Henrietta was ten by then."

"But I was marked with the mark of Cain. Wasn't that right, Clarissa?" Hugo asked scornfully. "Later, when I saw how loving you were to your own sons, I felt that I must be very wicked or have done something dreadful, although I could not think what, that you could not love me. After Mamma died, you took Henrietta and Amabel married Bynge and they moved to be near his parents. So I was left alone with a half-mad old man who cared only for his ancestry and his noble line."

For a shocking moment Hugo felt his voice quiver. He steeled himself to continue.

"You know what my crime was, don't you?" He flung the question at his sister who sat rigidly upright, her face impassive. "I was male, as if I had any more choice in being born male than you and the others had in being female."

She frowned at this but he swept on. "For that sin I was to be punished, ostracised and excluded. And it didn't take you long to draw my wife into your cosy, feminine world. What poison have you been dripping in her ear, I wonder?"

"Hugo, you forget yourself. How dare you accuse me so? It was not like that."

"Was it not? When the *ton* was making a sport of twitting my wife about some careless words I am supposed to have uttered long before I met her, did you encourage her to seek my support? Did you come and tell me? No. From the day you arrived in town, you made a point of arranging parties and outings from which I was excluded. Do you know how often Lallie said to me, 'I'm going or have been to such a place with Clarissa'? And do you know how often you invited my wife and me together this past Season? Once only, to your ball, to which you invited half the *ton*."

"You must have got that wrong, Hugo," Arthur protested. "Why, Lallie always seemed to be at Malvin House."

"By herself," Hugo agreed. "I was not included and only learnt about these excursions just before or, more likely, after the event."

Arthur looked horrified. "Tell me that you didn't deliberately plan it so," he begged his mother.

She had seemed startled, but now she retorted, "Of course not. It is all in Hugo's head. Someone had to look after poor Lallie, for he would not."

"How can you possibly say that?" Hugo demanded, advancing on her.

"Wait!" Arthur gripped his uncle's arm. "I remember, early on Lallie said something about Hugo escorting you to the British Museum, Mamma, or accompanying you to the opera. You pooh-poohed it, said she could suggest it to him if she wished, of course but gentlemen led their own lives; it wasn't the thing for couples to live in one another's pockets and if they were seen to go about together, it would be said that he was living under the cat's paw. She seemed disappointed, but accepted it.

"And then there were your usual diatribes about Tamrisk men. I no longer pay any heed to them, for it is quite clear that Hugo is cut from a different cloth than my grandfather, and Matthew and I are half Tamrisk and don't consider ourselves monsters,"—his mother looked up at this—"but I can see that for Lallie it may have been different, more serious. After all, why would a sister talk so about her only brother if it weren't true?"

"Why indeed?" Hugo interjected.

"I'm sorry, Hugo," Arthur said, "I should have paid more attention."

Hugo nodded, a little comforted by this apology. His point proven, he turned away to tug the bell-pull. "I'm wasting time. I must make plans for my departure as well as cancelling our other arrangements."

"Leave all that to me," Arthur said. "I'll tell Higgins you require your carriage at first light and he should send on ahead to hire a boat. Someone can set out tonight."

"It must be able to take the carriages and our riding horses— my two and Lallie's mare." There was a tap on the door. "Ah, there's Willis."

Having sent his valet off to arrange for a bath, Hugo said politely if coldly to his sister, "Clarissa, I should like to see Lallie's letter to you, if you please."

When she opened her mouth to protest, Arthur intervened. "Come, Mamma, I'll go along with you to your boudoir and fetch it."

She took his proffered arm and, unusually subdued, departed without saying anything more.

Hugo tugged off his boots and began to undress. When Arthur returned, he stretched out his hand and Arthur wordlessly placed the letter in it.

*To the Viscountess Malvin*

*My dear Clarissa,*

*I regret to inform you that an urgent family matter requires my immediate return to England and so I will be unable to come to you today as we had agreed. There is no need to be alarmed; to the best of my knowledge nothing untoward has happened at Tamm—the matter is one that concerns my family only. Tamrisk is departed these many hours and I have taken the liberty of sending his trunks to you as already arranged. I also enclose a note for him explaining the circumstances of my departure.*

*The Dowager Countess of Needham has kindly agreed to take me up in her carriage and also permits me to avail myself of the other arrangements made for her journey. Nancy travels with me, of course, so I shall be well looked after. I have asked Miller to take my little mare to you too. No doubt Tamrisk will make arrangements for them on his return.*

*With renewed thanks for your kind offer of hospitality, I remain, my dear Clarissa,*

*Your affect. sister-in-law*
*Lallie Tamrisk*

After some minutes Arthur said, "Mamma said she had heard that Needham was sending his private yacht to collect his mother and she thinks it very likely they will have sailed directly to Ipswich, which is the nearest harbour to Needham. What route shall you take?"

"To Dover, I think. It's shortest. I'll call at Alwood Hall on the way to London, although it is unlikely she went there. If there is no word of her at Tamarisk House, I'll try Needham House and if necessary from there go on to Needham. At the least Lady Needham should be able to tell me which direction she took."

"You don't think she went to Tamm?"

"I very much doubt it." Hugo sighed. "Well—I need not explain your grandfather to you."

# Chapter Twenty-Five

*The chief building of Divorce Island is the Fort of Repentance, but this being situated in the Vale of Tears, is scarcely ever inhabited, unless it be by those who wish to return to the continent.*

The sound of tiny paws scrabbling on leather had Hugo reach down and lift the puppy away from his highly polished boots. "Willis will not be pleased if you scratch them," he said severely, but could not resist gently stroking the silky, chestnut head and outsize ears. "Well, *Mam'selle 'Ubertine*, how do you like your new country?"

He had not been pleased when his groom had suggested that the new puppy accompany him in the carriage, 'for I can't manage her as well as the horses, sir—she came here with the baggage waggon, but of course we won't have one now,' but in fact he had found the little bitch a welcome companion on his lonely journey. The first night he had taken her to his cabin for want of an alternative. At Willis' suggestion they had made her a bed out of a coat that had suffered during the hunt and now she took this arrangement as her right.

"How am I to explain that to Horace and Virgil?" he asked her now. "A lady's privilege, I suppose. And what will your mistress say?" His smile faded. Would there be a mistress?

He had learnt on his arrival in London that Lallie had spent one night at Tamarisk House, and had ordered a carriage for early the next morning. She was going home, she had told Phipps. But where did she call home? Not her stepmother's house and, much as he would have liked it, he didn't think she meant Tamm. Would she go to her grandparents again? He hoped so. He didn't look forward to explaining himself to Sir Howard, but at least she would be safe there.

The sharp rat-tat of the door knocker made him jump.

"Is Mr Tamrisk at home?"

Henrietta hurried into the library holding out her arms. "My poor Hugo," she said as she hugged him, adding at his puzzled look, "I had a note from Arthur; he sent a packet with a fellow-officer who was bringing despatches. My letter was quite brief, but this is for you. I came round immediately, hoping you would be here."

Hugo took the thick packet of papers. "Have you heard from Lallie?"

"No," she said regretfully, "I wish she had felt she could come to me. Sit down, Hugo, before you collapse. You look as if you have neither eaten nor slept properly for a se'nnight and more."

"I don't think I have," he confessed.

"You will be no help to Lallie if you make yourself ill," Henrietta said severely and went out to the hall footman. "Have Cook send up coffee and something substantial for Mr Tamrisk and some tea for me."

"Now Hugo," she said on her return, "Sit here with a glass of madeira and read your letters."

Hugo broke the seal on the packet from his nephew. To his surprise, it held two letters.

*Dear Hugo*

*Mamma was very distressed following your conversation with her yesterday evening and after a long talk with my father—I*

*suspect she was weeping, which I have never known her to do—*
*determined that she must write to you immediately, especially as*
*she had not seen you prior to your departure this morning. I will*
*arrange for this to go with tomorrow's courier to London and hope*
*it catches you.*

*In case you are afraid Mamma is sending you a philippic and*
*are not inclined to read her letter, my father assures me this is not*
*the case and begs that you will reply to her as soon as may be and*
*in a generous spirit. He sends his compliments and best wishes for*
*a successful conclusion to your present enterprise and hopes you*
*will call on him if he can be of assistance in any way. He said*
*too to remind you that Julian and Millicent are at the Abbey and*
*that Lallie's uncle, Sir Jeremiah Halworth, is not too far removed*
*from them.*

*Best of luck, old chap, and don't forget to let me know how*
*you go on.*

*Yours,*
*Arthur*

Having read this astonishing missive twice, Hugo slowly
reached for his sister's letter.

*Dear Brother,*

*Your harsh words yesterday distressed me greatly. I confess*
*that at first I felt unfairly accused by you, but the obvious sincer-*
*ity of your speech did not permit me to dismiss your comments*
*as I would have wished. Indeed, they would not leave me and*
*having contemplated them throughout the night and reviewed my*
*treatment of you over the years, I cannot but conclude that I*
*have wronged you greatly, having failed in my duty of care and*
*affection towards you, which was considerable, especially as I am*
*your eldest sister and dear Mamma's health was so poor. With*
*a difference in our ages of seventeen years, it would have been*

natural to expect me to assume her maternal obligations towards you, especially once her health failed completely.

I will not weary you with explanations of the circumstances which led to my excluding you from my affections. Sadly, we cannot turn back the clock or return to the past to make right what we have done wrong. And so I can only offer you my deepest, most earnest apology for the hurt I have caused you.

Whatever excuses I might plead for the young girl I was then, there are none to make for the woman I have become. I deeply regret that my heart remained hardened against you even as we both grew into adulthood, I a lot sooner than you. I must recognise that I have remained mired in the past, refusing to see the error of my ways or to accept you as the man you are now. For this, too, I am deeply sorry.

Hugo, please believe me that it was never my intention to foster an estrangement between you and your wife. I am sorry that you felt unwelcome in my home—and I fervently hope that you will afford me the possibility of showing you that this is no longer the case. I do not know how to make amends for the damage I have done, but beg you to extend a fraternal hand to me, that I may try to do so.

If there is any way I can help you to come to a better understanding with Lallie, please do not hesitate to call on me. If you think it would be of benefit for you to show her this letter, pray do so. Although I do not know what has caused the present rift, I must recognise that my actions and omissions may well have contributed to this breach between the two of you.

Dear brother, I sincerely beg your pardon for the wrongs I have done you. I dare to hope that you will find it in your heart to forgive me, although conscious that in requesting this I ask you to be more generous to me than I have ever been to you.

I remain,
Your affectionate and truly contrite sister,
Clarissa Malvin

Hugo perused this frank confession with increasing astonishment and, ultimately, admiration for his eldest sister. She was a proud woman and he could guess what it had cost her to write it. He laid it aside when Henrietta called him to the table, where a large platter of beef steak flanked by sausages, kidneys and mutton chops awaited him. A ragoo of mushrooms and a dish of potatoes, sliced and fried with onions, completed this repast.

"Coffee, sir?"

"No. A glass of Burgundy," he replied, feeling the first stirrings of appetite since the morning he had ridden away from Lallie.

"Clarissa wrote to me as well," Henrietta said to Hugo once they were alone. "Lallie must be your first concern, of course, but Clarissa is awfully upset—horrified at herself and at what she may have caused."

"I realise that," he replied, thinking of his brother-in-law's request that he reply to his sister 'in a generous spirit'. "I'll scribble a short note now and promise a proper reply later."

"I don't want to excuse her but, being so much younger, we can have no idea of what she went through with Mamma, especially before you were born. She talked about it one evening when we were at Tamm for your wedding. Lallie had already retired—it was the night before she was so poorly, perhaps she already felt unwell—and we sisters gathered in my drawing room. Clarissa described very bitterly how Tamm used to rant at the uselessness of girls and how he permitted Mamma only four weeks to recover each time—apart from those buried with her, there were other babes that did not come to term—before resuming his tri-weekly demands on her, as Clarissa put it. She couldn't have a come-out of any sort because Mamma was so unwell after your birth. Instead, she had to help look after her, later as well when she miscarried again."

Shocked, he looked up, trying to imagine his niece Arabella in similar circumstances.

"That was why they went to Bath, where she met Malvin. Tom Bynge recommended that Mamma take the waters as she was very weak. I'm sure that if dear Tom had not convinced Tamm that the children of ladies who were at the end of their child-bearing years were sometimes weak and even feeble-minded, he would never have given her peace. Her remaining years were her happiest, because he ignored her, more or less."

"Henry, do you think it's possible that Lallie might have overheard you three talking?" Hugo asked urgently. "I never knew what caused her malaise the next day but she was different afterwards, less open. And another time, after we had returned from our wedding journey, when Tamm had the impertinence to instruct her maid to inform him each month when Lallie's menses came—"

"What?" his sister squawked. "You cannot be serious, Hugo. Even he would not have such a lack of delicacy."

"Believe me, he did. Apparently Mamma's maid was used to report to him. I soon put a stop to any such notions but you may imagine how furious Lallie was. She made some remark about the family having no sense of decency or propriety. I thought she referred only to that episode, but maybe there was more."

"It's possible, I suppose. Even if we had heard someone in the saloon, we wouldn't have heeded it, thought it a servant seeing to the candles or the fire." Her hand went to her mouth. "Hugo, I must tell you, we didn't talk only about Tamm, we also spoke about you."

"Me?"

She nodded unhappily. "Clarissa said she was sorry for Lallie and hoped she would soon present you with an heir so that she would not have to suffer as Mamma did. And we talked about your remark about wedding a country mouse and—I am very sorry Hugo, but I mentioned Lady Albright and Clarissa said how intimate you and she had seemed at Lady Nugent's."

He dropped his head into his hands, remembering how he had sat with Sabina while she told him of her pregnancy.

"Lallie was at Lady Nugent's too. She must have seen us. That would explain her reserve."

"Hugo, I don't mean to pry, but if you wish to talk about what went wrong?"

"I don't know, Henry," he said despairingly. "She became reserved and remote and I grew resentful and jealous, I suppose, but I don't know why. I don't even remember making that damned country mouse remark that everyone talked about. And then there was the cursed—" he stopped short.

"Duel? Did you really think we would not hear of it? Lallie did too, I suppose. I am sure she was charmed to hear that you were prepared to make her a widow and for such a reason."

He reddened at her acerbic tone. "It wasn't like that."

"Was it not? Even the scandal sheets called you a *preux chevalier* protecting his *Dulcinea's* good name."

"What!"

"Anonymously, of course, but it was quite easy to work out to whom they were referring. Lallie never said anything about it, but she must have found it most humiliating."

"I called Norris out because he said I was dallying with Lady Albright while I was wooing Lallie. Lallie was the one who mattered. It was both untrue and insulting to her." He shook his head. "Now that I come to think of it, he referred to her as a country mouse but I didn't think he meant anything more than that she had not had a Season before we were married."

"Did you never try to talk to Lallie, ask her what was wrong? I mean before that?"

He sighed. "It was so intangible—what should I say to her? You don't love me the way I want you to?"

"Did you love her?"

"From the beginning, but then we married so quickly and I didn't want to rush my fences, wanted to give her some time. And indeed these past two months, we have become closer again, or so I thought. But that last night in Brussels I exploded," he confessed sadly. "What I said to her—I am too ashamed to repeat it even to you, Henry. Suffice it to say that I resembled the old man at his worse. I don't know if she'll ever forgive me."

"We all have something of him in us," Henrietta said ruefully, "but you and Clarissa the most, because you were most exposed to him. I sometimes think that verse about the sins of the father being visited upon the children is not a threat or even a punishment, but a solemn warning not to repeat their mistakes."

"And we must learn from our own mistakes. I must think about where I went wrong with Lallie."

Henrietta regarded him compassionately. "Don't despair, dear Hugo. You've been married less than a year. It is not infrequent for couples to experience some difficulties in their first year. I'm sure that if you open your heart to Lallie, she'll listen."

"Give me a second chance, you mean?" he asked bitterly. "When she wouldn't give me a first one?"

"Why do you say that?"

"She apparently believed the worst of me with no evidence apart from what others said about me. I had never been unkind to her or given her occasion to believe I wished us to lead separate lives."

"You seem to have resented it, perhaps even blamed her for it, but you never objected, did you?"

"It was what she wanted!"

"Are you sure? Did she refuse you when you suggested you might do something together? London was so new to her—did you offer to show her the sights or to take her to the theatre or the opera, for example? Or take her driving?"

"Once you and Clarissa came, she had no time for me." He sounded petulant, even to himself.

"Did you just think that or did you put it to the test, Hugo?" Henrietta pressed him.

"I assumed it, I suppose," he agreed, defeated.

"Don't you see, if you, in turn, cooled towards her, this would support her perception that you wanted a more distant type of marriage? If you ask me, each of you laboured under the illusion that you knew what the other wanted and were too proud to complain when it didn't suit you. It would have been better if one or both of you had been a little more humble and deigned to explain what you were looking for in a spouse. I know it's easier said than done," she added with a rueful smile. "To ask for love is to expose our most personal feelings and risk rebuff and even ridicule."

Hugo was struck by this. Had he been too proud or too cowardly to confront Lallie about her rejection of him? Had it been easier to blame her?

"Don't forget that Lallie had very little notion of the ways of society," Henrietta continued. "And frequently, you know, mothers warn their daughters not to become too attached, for girls often have their heads full of dreams of love and romance and many gentlemen do not wish for it in their wives. They look for different qualities in them than they do in a mistress."

"Deuced interfering of the mothers," he grunted.

"They only wish to save their daughters from hurt, Hugo. Can you honestly say that you know no gentlemen who have retained their old way of life after their marriage?"

"I know quite a few," he conceded.

"It's not the fashion for husbands to be uxorious. Sadly, there is no way of knowing beforehand how a man will behave after the nuptials. And frequently the Mammas do not care so long as it is a good enough match." Henrietta smiled wickedly. "Did you never wonder why so many meek, timid girls were brought to your attention last year? Mice, every one of them." At the look on his face, she broke into laughter. "To think you did not even realise the reason for it."

"I was too busy avoiding yet another girl who was 'the sweetest, most biddable creature you can imagine, Mr Tamrisk'," he retorted.

"And yet their parents would have handed them over to you without a blink, even though you had made clear, or so they thought, that you wanted an obedient bride who would not protest if she were neglected. Marriage is dangerous for women, Hugo. Sir William Blackstone writes that, *'the very being or legal existence of the woman is suspended during marriage'*."

"Why, Henry, you have become a regular blue-stocking," Hugo interjected.

"It's no laughing matter," she rebuked him. "A wife is at her husband's mercy. She has no separate existence, her husband may deal with her person, her children and her property as he pleases and she has no recourse to the law, no matter how badly his treatment of her might be. Only think how Tamm more or less incarcerated Mamma and ruined her health in his obsession with having a son. And she couldn't refuse him. The law does not accept there can be rape within marriage."

Hugo reddened at this frank speaking. "I hadn't thought about it like that," he admitted.

"I wonder who explained to Lallie about marital congress." Henrietta said and then blushed vividly. "What a very singular conversation to be having with one's brother!"

"Don't stop, Henry," Hugo urged her. "I feel I've been both ignorant and careless."

She took a deep breath. "Her grandmother, I imagine. I've never met Lady Grey but she must be very old. There are women who find the whole business distasteful and would consider it unladylike to respond to their husbands. It is referred to as one's marital duty, after all, and they instruct their daughters to lie still and let their husbands do as they wish." She smiled impishly. "I know of one lady who uses the time profitably, as she puts it, by planning her menus and her parties."

"No wonder some husbands retain their mistresses," Hugo said drily. "Is this what ladies talk about among themselves?"

"The married ones, at least. Unfortunately there is still the convention that girls are to remain ignorant of such things. But there is, I suppose you could call it, a confederacy of enlightened women who look out for young wives who appear to be at a loss or in need of support or advice."

"Did you know Lallie was at Watier's masquerade?" he asked abruptly.

"At Burlington House? Did you go with her?"

"Of course not! Did you hear about the Muses?"

"Was she one of them? How famous! Their costumes were so becoming and ingenious; you couldn't tell one from the other, they were so well disguised. We were all wondering who they were. Their entrance was superb."

"You speak as if you had seen them."

"Of course I did. Charles took me. I take it you didn't ask Lallie to accompany you."

He shook his head.

"Well, if you neglect your wife, you needn't be surprised if she seeks her own amusement. How did you discover it?"

"I found the mask in a drawer in our sitting-room in Brussels. She had brought the costume, thinking to wear it if we went to a masquerade there."

"That might have been a little indiscreet," Henrietta conceded, "but it shows how innocent, even naive she is that she would even think of it. Is that why you quarrelled?"

Hugo nodded. "I danced with her that night," he confessed miserably.

"And didn't recognise her? I can see how that might make you feel foolish and even angry, especially if it was clear that she knew you."

"And so I struck out at her."

"Hugo!"

"Oh, not physically," he hastened to reassure his shocked sister, "but verbally."

"Words can hurt just as much as blows. All Father's children should know that."

"I do know it, and I must and will beg her pardon. But what if it comes out about the masquerade? Would it cause a great scandal? Not all the Muses went home as early as Lallie or indeed behaved as well as she did. I saw one in a very compromising situation."

"All you have to do is say you knew about it, danced with her and she went home early. Then it will appear as if you indulged her, but kept an eye on her. How did you come to ask her to dance?"

"I didn't. After their performance, they were besieged by a crowd of men and some fool announced each would select a partner. I was on the edge of the group, more observing than participating, and she caught my eye, beckoned to me."

"There you are! She obviously had recognised you. That is very promising, Hugo, for she wouldn't have chosen you if she had an aversion to you. It's clear that she felt safe with you."

"That never occurred to me." He smiled at her. "Thank you, Henry. It has been an odd conversation, hasn't it? Unlike any we've had before."

"Yes." She came and put her hand on his arm. "I too must apologise, Hugo, for keeping you at arm's length, as it were. I am so very sorry. If we had been truly sisterly towards you as well as

Lallie, we might have been able to help avoid your estrangement. You don't easily reveal your feelings, of course."

"There was never anyone who was interested in them," he replied simply.

"That will change now. We'll all be so concerned for you that you will soon wish us to the devil."

An hour later Hugo sat back against the comfortable squabs of his carriage, one hand idly caressing *Mam'selle 'Ubertine*, who had taken it for granted that she would travel in comfort with her master and now lay curled up beside him on the seat. He felt somehow set free. He had reached a new understanding with his sisters and was more hopeful that Lallie would at least listen to him when, no, if he found her.

"There are times when a woman wants to be wooed, pursued even," Henrietta had said. "Lallie may need to be reassured that you are willing to make an effort to find her. It's like a game of chess. She has made the opening move, but you now determine the pattern of the game."

"That's beyond the scope of my masculine mind," he had replied with a grin.

The puppy snuffled in her sleep. "You may well be my best hope," Hugo said to her. "I think Lallie will find you irresistible." He yawned hugely, closed his eyes and fell into his first sound sleep in more than two weeks.

# Chapter Twenty-Six

*On the coast of the Barbarian Desert, near the Gulf of Self-Love, stands a large castle called Bachelor's Fort. The inhabitants are very domesticated, and distinguished for their peculiarities. They live upon the produce of their own country, never being able to establish trade with any other. This is partly attributed to the unfavourable Harbour of Self-Love.*

Mrs Frederica Horne addressed her great-nephew with fond severity.

"It's high time you married, Freddie. You are now more than forty. If you would only settle down with a suitable girl, I would make you a handsome present, 'pon my soul, I would, and another when your first child was born. After all you are my heir and there is no need for you to wait until I am gone to have the benefit of my money."

Frederick Malvin could not but agree with this last sentiment although he greatly resented the conditions his aunt attached to her magnanimity. That it should have come to this! A particularly black settling day at Tattersall's had caused him to seek the shelter of the old lady's handsome estate in Cornwall. She had a fondness for him and in the past had been more than willing to help him out of a 'scrape' as she had termed his temporary embarrassments, tolerantly ascribing them to youthful high jinks. And now it seemed she was preparing to tighten the purse-strings. If it hadn't been for that Grey chit none of this would have been necessary. He frowned as he recalled the humiliation of her rejection but then saw how he might turn it to his advantage.

"You are right, Aunt," he replied meekly, "and if all had gone my way—" He sighed heavily. "Sadly, ma'am, unlucky at cards does not always mean lucky in love. Had all gone as I hoped, my bride would be with me on this visit. But she chose to marry for a title and position!" He broke off, biting his lip.

"My poor boy! If I had known you had suffered a disappointment, I should not have said a word. Who is she? I'm sure she didn't deserve you, Freddie."

He shook his head mournfully. "Let us not speak of her, Aunt. She is married to another and lost to me." He assumed a brave smile. "Are we not to have a hand or two of piquet? You owe me my revenge for last night."

"Capot!" Mrs Horne triumphantly claimed the last trick.

"That's me lurched," Mr Malvin said ruefully and began to tot up the score.

"It is time for me to retire. Good night, my dear boy."

He rose to escort her to the foot of the stairs. "Good night, Aunt."

"You will accompany me to church tomorrow morning, will you not?" she asked as they parted.

"It will be my pleasure, Aunt," he declared before retreating to the library and the solace of the brandy decanter. His aunt had no head for cards and it took some skill to lose convincingly to her. That last miserable hand had helped. Perhaps he had better win tomorrow night—it wouldn't do for her to question her run of luck.

"My namesake, you know," Mrs Horne confided for what seemed to be the hundredth time while her great-nephew gritted his teeth and endured the interminable after church chit-chat.

"Have you heard that the Larkhaven tenants have left and Mrs Staines's granddaughter has returned?"

"Lady Anna's, you mean," his aunt sniffed. "I'm sure I know what is due to a Marquis's daughter, even if she chose not to claim her rank. I knew her mother," she continued proudly. "Lady Louisa Frome and I made our first appearances at the same Birth Night Ball. Lady Louisa was near to fainting and I gave her my vinaigrette. I often thought afterwards I might have acted as an intermediary between her and Lady Anna, but did not like to presume. But according to *The Ladies' Universal Register*, the breach has now been healed and she has acknowledged her great-granddaughter."

And Robert Grey basks in reflected glory, Mr Malvin thought sourly. He's decided to play safe. It's time he settled down, he says. He has no intention of losing this fine new connection!

The current dear friend gestured discreetly. "Look, there she comes from the churchyard. She must have visited her grandparents' grave. Her mother is buried there as well."

Mr Malvin looked over to where three ladies were escorted down the path by a provincial worthy. The two elder ones he dismissed at once as dowds, but his eyes narrowed at the sight of the youngest who revealed shapely ankles and tempting curves as she gathered her skirts to climb into a waiting carriage.

"Her husband hasn't come with her, or so I hear. That is Mr Lambe, the solicitor." Mrs Horne remarked. "I suppose he's her man of business too."

"Her husband's, you mean," the dear friend tittered. "It is he who has the disposal of her fortune now. But no, he is not with her. I believe she wishes to decide whether she will let the house again or keep it for her own use. It is a very pretty estate."

That should have been mine, Mr Malvin thought savagely. It was beyond everything to be so confronted with his loss. At least

I was able to make her pay a little. It's marvellous how quickly a little scandal-buzz spreads, especially when an adept fuels the flames. I wish she knew who was behind those little paragraphs in the gossip columns too. That duel was an additional stroke of luck. It was easy enough to keep Norris's indignation at a simmer. But the cursed chit and her husband seem to weather everything.

Now his aunt was in transports of delight as she related how the Queen had particularly welcomed Mrs Tamrisk at the recent drawing-room.

"Come, ma'am," he said solicitously as soon as she drew breath, "you'll catch cold standing in this wind."

He managed to escape, but not before his aunt had accepted for both of them an invitation to a card party the following evening.


"How kind of you to call, Mr Tamrisk. Is Lalage not with you?"

"Not this time, Lady Grey. I did not wish simply to pass your door, but I must not keep the horses standing too long."

Twenty minutes later a dejected Hugo was on his way again. At least her ladyship had given him his answer before he had had to embarrass himself by asking if she harboured his wife. Where might Lallie have gone? Circumspect enquiries at the posting inns had revealed that she had indeed travelled this way two weeks previously. He still couldn't believe that she would go to Tamm but they continued to receive confirmation of her passing.

"We'll put up here for the night," he decided when they reached Exeter.

An hour later his groom knocked on his door. "They changed horses at the *Half Moon Hotel*, sir. The next stage was Crockernwell, the post-boys said."

"Crockernwell?" Hugo snapped his fingers. "She's going to her old home near Truro. Larkhaven, it's called. We'll leave at half-past six."

Lallie sat at the table in the back parlour at Larkhaven. This had been her schoolroom; in addition she had spent many hours here with her grandmother, learning how to manage a household. Mr Lambe had sent over the most recent account books and the old ones had been restored to their shelves. Bit by bit, the house was becoming hers again. I wish I could simply remain here, she said to herself, but it would be impossible. People will talk, especially once they notice I am with child. What if Hugo heard of it or, worse, Lord Tamm?

I must think of the baby. Will Hugo believe it's his? If he doesn't, I'll come back here, she resolved. Her thoughts drifted back to her husband. Perhaps I should write to him. But where to? What could I say? That his unjust accusations broke my heart? Would he care?

The distant peal of the doorbell shattered these jumbled reflections. Was that a man's voice in the hall? Lallie's heart fluttered in her throat and she rubbed suddenly damp palms on her skirts. Could it be him? Her heart beat even faster. She both longed to run to his arms and dreaded his renewed rejection. Her throat swelled and her eyes blurred with tears. She jumped up, the abrupt motion causing her head to swim.

A dark masculine shape loomed against the low afternoon sun in the angle formed by the opening door. Her heart stopped and then started again. That wasn't Hugo! Disappointed, she turned away.

"Your mistress has no further need of you. Go!"

She started forward at the stranger's words, "How dare you, sir! Mary!"

The heavy door was slammed shut and the key turned in the lock.

"Open the door at once, whoever you are! You have no business here!"

Frederic Malvin turned and with a sardonic smile skimmed his hat onto a table. "Why, Mrs Tamrisk, is that the way to greet your husband?"

"You are not my husband," she snarled as she darted to the bell-pull.

"But I should have been and your servant was quite willing to believe I am." He had clearly ridden here, and ridden hard. His boots and breeches were mud-spattered and he reeked of the stables.

"You're deranged!" she spat, skirting around him to run to the door. The lock was stiff and as she struggled with it, his heavy hand grabbed her wrist.

"No, you don't!"

She screamed and banged on the door with her free hand. As he yanked her away, the door knob rattled as if someone tried it desperately from the other side.

Lallie raised her chin defiantly as she tried to pull her hand free. "What are you doing here?"

"Collecting what is owed to me!" His breath stank of strong spirits and there was an ugly gleam in his eyes.

"There is nothing owed to you here."

"Nothing!" His face darkened. "You little bitch! You deprived me of forty-five thousand pounds! 'Twas all agreed with your father; it was mine if I took you off his hands. But hoity-toity madam refused to obey. Now it's all up with me. But first I'll make you pay—and Tamrisk too for spoiling sport." He ran his eyes over her. "You're a cosy enough armful now that you're no longer such a scrawny little mouse."

"You're disgusting!"

With a violent tug, she wrenched her wrist free and dashed to the door but he pounced and dragged her away, swinging her around to face him. When he pulled her towards him, she cracked her hand sharply across his face. "Let me go!"

"Like to fight, do you?" he grunted, seizing by her shoulders. "It will be all the sweeter to tame you!"

"Take your hands off me!" She kicked out ineffectually, her satin slippers sliding off his top boots.

He laughed then and kissed her brutally, bruising her lips as he forced his foul tongue between them. She instinctively bit down hard and he retreated. His grasp eased and she reached up to rake her nails down his face.

"Release me, you cur!"

"Now, now, there is no need to be unpleasant, my pet." He widened his stance, displaying the obscene bulge of his breeches, and licked his lips. "I see you must be taught to behave," he said, pulling her to him.

A lesson Mrs Rembleton had insisted on teaching her flashed through Lallie's frantic mind. She stopped resisting and, once close enough, drove her raised knee hard into his crotch. He howled and lurched away, bending forward to cup himself. She ran for the door.

The casement window crashed open and a burly footman sprang down into the room.

"Get away, ma'am! Leave this scurvy wart to me," he ordered, advancing on his victim who was curled like a shrimp on the floor.

Her hand trembled so violently that she could scarcely grip the key. At last she succeeded in opening the door and stumbled into the hall where she looked wildly at the little group gathered there.

"My poor Miss Lallie!"

Nancy came forward, arms outstretched, but another, larger figure was also moving towards her.

"Lallie! My God! Lallie!"

Hugo's sudden appearance and appalled exclamation were the last straw. Her vision dimmed and she felt herself crumple and fall.

Hugo lunged to catch his wife before she hit the floor. He swung her up into his arms where she lay limp, her arms trailing and her eyes closed. Her lips were bruised and swollen against the deathly pallor of her face. What the devil had happened? Behind her, in the room from which she had escaped, a man cowered on the floor while another loomed menacingly over him. He would deal with them later.

Nancy plucked at his sleeve. "This way, sir."

He followed her upstairs, ordering over his shoulder, "No-one is to leave that room. Put a watch on the door and window until I return."

"Yes, sir."

Nancy beckoned him into an airy bedroom. "Put her down here, sir."

Hugo obeyed, shocked to the core by the livid finger-marks emerging on Lallie's slender wrists. There were muddy streaks on her light gown. He lifted one hand carefully. Her beautiful nails were broken and blood-stained and he shuddered at the idea of her being forced to use them to defend herself. He carried her hand to his lips. He should never have left her! If he had not gone on that cursed hunting trip, they could have thrashed everything out the next day. She would not have been left on her own.

"I'll look after her now, sir." Nancy's tone was uncompromising. "The last thing she'll need is to find you here when she comes to herself."

He opened his mouth to damn her eyes but she forestalled him by adding, "Best if you go and deal with that dratted scoundrel downstairs. From what Miss Mary said he's gentry and Ebenezer won't be able to hold him for long."

"Who is he?"

"We don't know, sir."

"Then how the deuce did he get in?" Hugo demanded wrathfully. His arrival at the climax of the disturbance had not permitted any explanations before now.

"It seems Miss Mary thought he was you, sir. He asked where his wife was and followed her to the parlour, then pushed past her, said she wasn't needed and locked her out," the maid answered concisely without taking her eyes from her mistress. "She's trying to open her eyes. Please go, sir; we don't want her to swoon again."

He cast a despairing glance at his wife and departed, somewhat heartened by the prospect of venting his distress and rage on the one responsible for her state.

"Ebenezer, isn't it?"

The man turned away from the armchair he was guarding. Its back was to the door and Hugo could not see the occupant.

"Sir?"

"I'm Mr Tamrisk. I have to thank you for coming to the aid of my wife."

"'Twas nothing, sir. I only had to make sure he didn't go after her. Not that he could," he added reflectively, "I reckon she gave him a good one in the ballocks."

Hugo was torn between admiration of Lallie's resourcefulness and anguish at the necessity for it. "You may leave him to me, but wait in the hall."

As soon as the door closed, he rounded the chair to find Frederick Malvin sitting hunched in on himself. One cheek was reddened as if from a blow and bore the marks of Lallie's nails.

"'Pon my soul, Tamrisk, a queer notion of hospitality your wife has," Malvin drawled nasally.

Hugo grabbed him by the cravat, lifted him to his feet and ploughed his fist into his jaw. Malvin recoiled but came back at him, arms flailing. Hugo stepped neatly to one side and floored him.

"Get up," he growled.

Malvin scrambled to his feet and raised his fists defensively. He managed to land a couple of hits but was clearly outclassed and it wasn't long before Hugo dropped him to the floor again. This time he let him stay down.

"If you dare approach my wife again, or speak of her or disturb her in any way, it won't be my fists you'll feel but my whip."

Malvin did not reply but occupied himself in mopping up the blood streaming from his nose and a cut eyebrow.

"How did you get here?" Hugo demanded.

"Rode."

Hugo considered him. "You're in no state to ride back and I want you out of my wife's house. I'll have you taken to Truro but see that you leave these parts by tomorrow at latest."

The other laughed harshly, pressing a hand against his ribs. "I'm taking a bolt to the Continent. It's either that or be taken up for debt!" He hesitated. "I don't know what came over me, Tamrisk. For what it's worth, I apologise, also to your lady."

Hugo's brief nod signified acknowledgement rather than acceptance. He had no desire to offer his hand and Mr Malvin clearly did not dare to venture his.

Fifteen minutes later, Hugo watched with grim satisfaction as Frederick Malvin hobbled painfully out of the house and gingerly climbed into the gig. Once the equipage was moving, he returned to the house and took the stairs two at a time. He must see Lallie at once; satisfy himself that she had taken no lasting hurt.

# Chapter Twenty-Seven

*The River of Benevolence is supposed to derive its source from the mountainous parts of Gratitude and after passing the delightful Valley of Content separates into the two branches Respect and Esteem already noted.*

Aromatic compresses cooled her brow and wrists and someone was gently dabbing a soothing lotion on her lips. Lallie opened her eyes. She was in her bed in Larkhaven and Nancy was tending to her.

"What happened?" she asked when she was able, then, "I remember—Mr Malvin and—was Hugo here?"

"Yes. I sent him down to deal with that mangy cur." Nancy's voice shook. "Did he, did he hurt you, Miss Lallie? Apart from what we can see, I mean."

"No." Lallie smiled weakly. "Who sent Ebenezer?"

"I did. Miss Mary came to me. She said the master was three sheets to the wind. He had pushed her out and locked the door, which didn't seem like Mr Tamrisk, I admit. When we heard you scream, I told Ebenezer to break the window if he had to."

"Thank goodness you did. Had Hugo already arrived?"

Nancy shook her head. "He drove up just before we heard the window break."

Lallie groaned. "What a scene for him to walk in upon! What must he think of me? And Frederick Malvin of all people!" She struggled to sit up. "Help me get up, Nancy. Can you make me more presentable?"

"Let me tend to your wrists first. If you wear your dark green dressing gown, the frills will hide the bandages."

Lallie rested in the big armchair beside the fire, swathed in the vibrant reds and golds of an Indian shawl. She had refused to stay in bed—she wanted to meet Hugo on as equal a footing as possible. She hadn't thought to see him so soon. He must have left Brussels the minute he received her letter. What lucky or unlucky chance had led him here so quickly?

He came in silently and walked over to stand before her. He had lost weight, she noticed; his face was haggard, the dark eyes sunk deeper in their sockets and the cheek-bones more prominent.

"Lallie!"

Despite the heat of his touch, she had to repress a shiver when he lightly tilted her chin and tipped her face towards the light. He regarded her without speaking for a long moment. A small sigh escaped him and he dropped to his knees and gently took her hands.

"Before I say anything else, Lallie, I most sincerely beg your pardon for my behaviour that last night in Brussels. It was inexcusable. I'll never forgive myself for it. I'm so sorry. I was in such a jealous rage—I even knew I had lost control, but couldn't stop—it was like watching a horse bolt, but I swear I didn't mean what I said."

Lallie considered him silently. This was supposed to excuse everything? Was all to be forgiven and forgotten? Yes, she was relieved at his apparent change of heart, but could she be sure it was genuine? Perhaps he merely sought to make the best of things.

"Then why did you disappear the next morning without a word of farewell or any attempt at reconciliation?" She fought to suppress a sob. "You could have apologised then—explained that you had not meant what you said. I waited and waited, Hugo. I watched you leave and afterwards searched everywhere in case you had left a note. I even sat at the window for hours in case you returned. What else could I do but assume that you had meant everything and that the contempt in your eyes was real?"

A sick despair welled up in Hugo. She had been willing to listen to him. Notwithstanding his shameful accusations and his refusal to hear her pleas that last night, she had hoped he would seek her out before he left Brussels, try and make amends. He could picture her watching in vain, imagine how her painful hope faded and died. Henrietta's reproachful 'you did not object, did you?' echoed mournfully in the depths of his mind. Inaction was also action; he understood that now. Had he already thrown away his second chance?

"I'm so sorry," he said again. "I remained trapped in the nightmare long after we left. When finally I came to myself, recognised what I had done, I was so ashamed. I should have turned back then, I know, but I was too mortified to explain to Arthur why it was necessary." He shook his head. "I still hadn't learnt my lesson, had I? But believe me, Lallie, all I wanted to do was apologise to you, try to make things right between us. And when I realised you had left me—I know it was no more than I deserved, but my only thought was to follow you and win you back."

He remained kneeling beside her chair, his gaze fixed on her. Her own gaze had turned inward. What was she thinking? Would she believe him?

"Lallie?"

She stirred at his soft prompt.

"I still don't understand what happened," she said despairingly. "I don't think it was the masquerade that had you so incensed, it was the rest—that nonsense about Luke Fitzmaurice and where you stood in my affections and how I had been playing games with my admirers. It was ridiculous and so unfair." She glared at him. "The news-sheets weren't full of my *affaires* or speculation about the father of my child. I was just the country mouse that everyone could make game of because she was too stupid to be up to snuff!" Her voice rose. "And then to say that about me, about our baby! How could you, Hugo!"

She broke off suddenly, her hand covering her mouth.

Their baby? She couldn't mean—please let him not have been that cruel.

"Our baby," he repeated in an agony of apprehension. "Do you mean in the future or—or now? Lallie? Tell me, please," he begged. "Are you increasing?"

"Yes," she confirmed with great dignity. "I am over three months with child."

"Three months—so you knew that night, when I said—that?"

"I strongly suspected it but I've spoken to the midwife here and now am sure."

No wonder she ran from me, he thought bleakly. I am worse than Tamm ever was.

"Have you no more to say, Mr Tamrisk?"

Her complexion was chalk-white and she sat rigidly as if steeling herself for judgement. His judgement, he recognised and felt even more ashamed.

"Say? Only that I am the most despicable cur that ever lived. I should be flogged!"

She began to shake and her eyes brimmed with tears.

"Oh, my sweet, don't cry!" He caught her in his arms. "Ssh, now. Oh God, Lallie, I'm so sorry. Can you ever forgive me?"

He crooned an incoherent litany of apologies and endearments interspersed with meaningless words and phrases. He stood, lifting her with him so that he could take her onto his lap where she curled into him as if she could no longer hold herself upright. At last the storm subsided and she pushed away to sit up and blot her tears. She tried to stand, but he wouldn't let her, holding her firmly to him. Her hand cradled her stomach and he laid his over it, noticing with a surge of tenderness the new, firm curve.

"I was so afraid," she whispered.

"Of me?"

"Of what you might say or do when I told you, or you found out."

"About our baby?"

"If you wouldn't accept it."

"And cast it or you or both out to starve?"

"Now you're angry with me."

"Not with you, or perhaps a little that you would think that of me," he added candidly, "but furious with myself that I gave you cause to do so." He put a finger under her chin and gently lifted her head so that he could look into her eyes. "Lallie, my dearest Lallie, I am very sorry I hurt you so and ashamed that I put you into such a position, exposed you to such fears, especially when you have this precious burden to carry. From now on I will be by your side. I swear it."

She sniffed, blew her nose again and collapsed against him with a long sigh.

"What a poor husband I've been to you! But I'll do better, I promise."

She smiled weakly then fought to conceal a yawn. "Pray excuse me."

"You're worn-out," he said remorsefully, "and no wonder. Will you lie down on your bed for a little?"

He felt rather than saw her shake her head.

"You will stay here tonight, won't you?" she asked drowsily, her voice fading.

"Of course, sweetheart." He dropped a kiss on the top of her head. Her body relaxed against him, her head pressed heavier on his shoulder, her eyes fluttered closed and she slept.

Hugo couldn't see the time but night had fallen some time ago. He stretched over and tugged the embroidered bell-pull that hung by the fire-place.

"I don't want to wake her," he murmured to Nancy when she quietly opened the door, "but she should be in bed."

"I'll fetch a warming-pan, sir."

"Now, sir," the maid said five minutes later, "If you help me remove her dressing-gown, I'll manage the rest." She unfastened Lallie's gown and carefully eased the sleeves down her arms. "Lift her a little, sir," she instructed and deftly whisked the gown away before kneeling to remove her mistress's stockings.

Hugo gently laid his wife on the warmed sheet and pulled the bed-clothes up around her, kissing her tenderly before he turned away.

"What will you do for breakfast, Miss Lallie? Mary has had it set up in the dining-parlour, but would you prefer to have it here as usual?"

"Has Mr Tamrisk gone down?"

"Willis just fetched his shaving water. He spent the night in here—said you had asked him to stay and he was afraid that villain's assault might give you bad dreams. He wouldn't disturb you but pulled the chair over here and I gave him a blanket. He was snoozing when I came in at half-past six and I told him to seek his own bed for a few hours."

Lallie was touched by this evidence of Hugo's concern. His remorse had been genuine too, his self-loathing evident. Lady Needham's admonition rang in her ear: 'Remember you cannot change the past. You can only hope to ensure that the future will be different.'

"I'll come down for breakfast," she said.

"Hugo?"

He put down his cup and smiled at her. "Yes, my dear?"

"You didn't call Mr Malvin out, did you?"

He shook his head. "His behaviour yesterday put him beyond the pale. I thrashed him and told him if he came near you again he would feel my whip."

"Hugo!" She was terrified. If Mr Malvin had been resentful of her before, what would his attitude be now?

Her husband must have seen something of this in her face, for he said, "Don't worry, Lallie. He apologised before he left."

She shook her head. "I shall never understand the male sex."

After the agony of the past weeks and yesterday's fraught confrontations, it was strange to sit together peacefully over breakfast. She felt almost shy; she stole a glance at her husband who was looking around the cosy dining-parlour.

"I like your home," he said. "Will you show me around later?"

"Of course, but it's rather bare now. If I don't let it again, I'll bring back some of the things that went to Tamm. There are some larger pieces in the attic here as well that can be brought down."

He put down his fork. "If you don't let it again," he repeated impassively. "What else might you do?"

"I haven't yet decided." She could hardly admit she had considered retreating here with her child. "We don't have to spend all our time at Tamm, do we? Larkhaven is so beautiful, even in winter."

He smiled delightedly. "Come here on our own, just us and the children, you mean? Have a holiday from the world. I'd like that, Lallie."

She longed to smile back. This was the Hugo she had fallen in love with. But what would happen when they left Larkhaven? She couldn't bear to have her hopes raised, only for him to dash them again when they returned to their everyday life. Thanks to her premature revelation of her condition, they had never discussed his accusations or, indeed, his expectations.

This might be her last chance to speak frankly before it was all glossed over. She must do it now, before leaving the room. Without pausing to devise a more subtle way of putting her question she demanded, "Hugo, where do we go from here?"

"Wherever you wish," he replied with a rueful smile. "I acknowledge I am in no position to demand anything of you."

"What sort of an answer is that? I never know where I am with you!"

"What do you mean?"

She ignored the reproof implied in his cool tone. "When you proposed, you asked me to bear your children and be mistress of Tamm. Later I learnt you wanted a wife who knew her place and would leave you to yours—a country mouse with nary a squeak to her—and indeed you are less distant when we are not in town."

"That cursed remark," he interrupted, groaning. "I have no recollection of having made it—it's the sort of stupid quip men make late at night when they're in their cups. I never thought of it again."

She stared at him. "But it was on everyone's lips earlier in the year."

"Believe me, I only heard about it last week when a drunken pup made a foolish jest. Arthur had to pull me off him before I throttled him, but fortunately no serious harm was done. Later

Arthur said something about how he thought all that country mouse business had died down. I had to ask what he meant—he was just as staggered as you by my ignorance."

Lallie shrugged. "It's over and done with now."

"Arthur told me you dealt with it splendidly. But is it really over for you, Lallie—did it—does it not affect your opinion of me?"

She shrugged again and began to pleat the napkin on her lap. "It did, I suppose, but it wasn't only that. There is no denying that I was a provincial nobody, Hugo. And then there was Lady Albright. I had heard about your connection even before the duel and I saw you with her at Lady Nugent's."

"Henrietta thought you might have heard her and the others talking at Tamm about the country mouse and Lady Albright."

"I did. I didn't mean to listen, but I was transfixed with shock. And then, when Stiles had me kneel to you at the chapel door—"

"I was as surprised by that as you were," he confessed. "I was just about to tell them to take away that damn cushion when down you went."

"Be that as it may, I didn't find it an—encouraging start to our marriage."

"I suppose not."

"Then, after Christmas, when your father requested me to write to Lady Albright after her husband died, you bade me ask him to frank the letter. Remember? If there had been nothing between you, you would have done it yourself without a thought. Later, people wondered whether you regretted marrying me so quickly now that she was free."

"Lallie, I swear to you I didn't," he said urgently. "Yes, she was my mistress last year, but it was over before I met you."

She ignored this interjection. "My grandparents were gratified that you had done the right thing and made me an offer without prompting. They considered I had been compromised by visiting your house and travelling with you in your carriage. It had not occurred to me but—you proposed so quickly—was it because you had felt compelled to offer for me?"

Hugo took her hand and kissed it. "You're putting the cart before the horse. I wouldn't have intervened at the *Belle Sauvage* or offered to take you to Hampshire if I hadn't already considered you as my bride but, yes, I was conscious of the implications in doing so." He cocked a teasing eyebrow. "They were not repugnant to me. I had already indicated my interest, if you remember?"

He was rewarded with a little smile.

"That's what I told myself. In the end, I decided I would just have to wait and see what my new life would be like. I was ignorant of the ways of the *beau monde* and had to take my lead from you, and Clarissa and Henrietta of course. Once we were in London, you seemed happy for us more or less to go our separate ways. You had your own commitments and never complained when I went out without you or protested we did too little together or issued any invitations to me, at least not until the day we went to Richmond. You never hinted you were dissatisfied with the way we lived or jealous of other men.

"And then, that night in Brussels—" she paused, "I don't want to throw it all in your face again, Hugo, you've made your apologies and I've accepted them—but I don't think we can put it all behind us until we know why it happened."

He jumped up from his chair, drawing her with him. "Lallie, sweetheart, there is so much I want to say to you but first tell me you forgive me. I long to hear the words."

She put her hands on his chest and looked up at him, a wealth of tenderness in her gaze. "I forgive you, Hugo."

He bent his head and rested his brow against hers. "You'll never regret it, I promise you," he whispered. "Will you seal it with a kiss?"

Hugo first stood motionless, the better to savour the sweet pressure of her lips, then tightened his arms about his wife to hold her fiercely to him. This was where she belonged, where they belonged. Listening to her earlier explanations, he hadn't known whether to laugh or cry. He had been fifty times a fool; that much was clear. Now he must disentangle this confounded coil. But not over the remains of breakfast.

"Where can we talk undisturbed?"

She led him to a small sitting room that was painted in a soft, pale green with wall panels decorated with sprays of spring blossom. He looked round appreciatively. It was simply furnished with two old-fashioned upholstered wing chairs either side of the cheerful fire and a table and two chairs at the casement window. A cunning round mahogany table fitted with three columnar tiers of shelves held books he recognised as those Lallie had brought to Brussels. Two magnificently caparisoned Delft horses pranced on the mantelpiece, their splendour reflected in the over-mantel mirror. Hugo smiled to see them. She had discovered them in a little shop in Ghent and he had insisted on buying them for her. Her needlework lay on the table where she would have the best light, beside her travelling writing box. She had the knack of putting her stamp on a place, he thought, delighting in the subtle aromas of the potpourri that scented all her rooms.

"So this is your nest?"

She smiled. "I suppose it is. Grandmamma had it decorated for me when I was sixteen. She wanted to buy more fashionable chairs but I insisted on having these. They had been in Grandpapa's library and I often curled up in one and read while he was writing his sermon. He liked me to keep him company, he said."

She'd lost her home twice, he realised, no, three times when he considered the way Grey had as good as cast her out. She clearly felt diffident, unsure of her place in his life. It was no wonder, he supposed.

"I love you, Lallie," he said simply. "I fell in love with you last year in Berkshire. I should have told you much sooner but from the day we married you seemed to retreat from me."

"Because I didn't know what you wanted from me! I can't read your mind, you know, Hugo," she said seriously. "You say you love me, but what does that really mean? It's not so long since you fought a duel over another woman."

He shook his head. "That wasn't why. It was because he dragged you into it."

"Me?" She was dumbfounded.

"You," he confirmed. "Norris said I was courting you while I was cuckolding his cousin. It wasn't true—that affair had finished with the Season. The mere suggestion was so insulting to you—I couldn't let it stand. But my rakish days are behind me, Lallie and have been since the day we met. Since then I have wanted no-one else but you."

She paid no heed to this declaration but sprang up and advanced on him until she was standing between his legs, her own touching the seat of his chair. She seized his shoulders and shook him as hard as she could. Sitting solidly in the big chair, he barely felt the force of her attack which, in truth, he welcomed. If only she had behaved like this the night she confronted him about the duel.

"How dare you play ducks and drakes with your life like that? I suppose you think I should be grateful to you for defending my honour! What cold comfort that would have been if you'd been killed or injured."

He tried to suppress an appreciative smile at the sight of her, flushed from her efforts, her curls tossed with every movement and her breasts rising and falling with her quickened breath.

"You blockheaded, thoughtless oaf! How would you feel if someone came to the door to tell you I was dead because of some foolish start and they would be arriving at any moment bearing my corpse?"

This snuffed his delight. "Don't say it even in jest, Lallie."

"But it wasn't a jest with you. It could have been very real."

He slid forward on the chair and drew her closer. "I know. I've never called someone out before. I didn't do it lightly, Lallie, I swear it, but it seemed the only right thing to do. There's a limit to what a gentleman can permit, especially where his wife is concerned."

"And you thought I would prefer the humiliation of it being said that you had risked your life in defence of your mistress?" she retorted incredulously. "There's a limit to what a lady can permit, especially where her husband is concerned."

"I'm a fool," he offered, a rueful twinkle in his eye.

"You are," she agreed, an answering smile lurking in hers. "But why did you tell me it was about—her?"

"I suppose I was too proud to say anything else," he admitted. "You put your questions so calmly, as if you simply wished to verify your information. You didn't even ask if I had been wounded. So I wasn't going to confess that you mattered that much to me."

Lallie freed herself from the circle of his arms and stepped away. "Was it I that mattered or your notion of gentlemanly honour?" she asked coolly.

Hugo surged from his chair and caught her shoulders, turning her to face him. "Don't freeze on me, Lallie, please. Argue with me, scold me, fight with me, but don't hide from me. When you turn away, retreat behind that icy veil, I don't know what to do. I can't reach you."

She bit her lip. "That night—first I was distraught and then so angry with you, Hugo, but by the time you came home I had—subdued it."

"Because of Lady Albright?"

She scowled at him. "She did exacerbate things. Of all the reasons to be widowed!"

"I'm sorry, sweetheart," he said. "I know it won't undo it, but I am sorry."

"Would you do it again, Hugo?"

"Now that I have truly considered the burden it might have placed on you, I would do everything in my power to avoid it but," he added honestly, "there could be an occasion where honour would not permit an alternative."

She raised her eyes to heaven in an appeal for patience. "Will you at least promise to tell me in advance should such an occasion occur?"

"You could not have thought of a more powerful deterrent, but I promise," he answered with a wry grimace and then grinned at her complacent smile. He sat and pulled her onto his knee. "Sweetheart," he said again and kissed her. "You matter to me," he muttered, framing her face with his hands and looking deeply into her eyes. "Without you, my life is empty; with you, it has been either heaven or hell. But I'd prefer that hell to the void when you were gone. Now you must promise me you'll never leave me again."

"I promise," she said solemnly, "I'll stay and fight it out with you."

There was a tap on the door and she scrambled off his lap. "Yes?"

The housekeeper came in. "I'm that sorry to bother you, Mrs Tamrisk, but Martha wants to know about the dinner, especially with the master here and all."

Hugo held his breath. Would Lallie take umbrage at this description of him in her home? But she just smiled and said, "Assemble all the servants so that they can be presented to Mr Tamrisk. I'll speak to Martha once that is done."

"I hope you don't mind," she said apologetically after the door had closed again. "It won't take long and we can stroll in the gardens afterwards."

"Yes. I must also make known to you the companion I brought from Belgium. I think you will like her."

# Chapter Twenty-Eight

*The Fort of Felicity stands on an eminence and is a majestic building, commanding a fine view of the Gulf of Sincerity which lies between the Cape of Good Hope and the Bay of Delights.*

The servants were waiting in the hall when Hugo and Lallie came down. Just as they arrived, Hobbs came through the door from the garden, followed by an excited bundle of ears, tail, snout and paws that greeted Hugo as if they had been parted for six weeks and not less than a day.

"Quiet!" he commanded. "Do you wish to disgrace us altogether?" He firmly removed the front paws from his pantaloons. "Down! If you destroy another pair, Willis will disown us both."

"Oh, isn't he sweet?" Lallie dropped to her knees beside the little dog. "What a lugubrious little face!"

"She," Hugo corrected her as he knelt beside her. "May I present *Mam'selle 'Ubertine*, hound of St. Hubert and late of the Ardennes? Should you object to a companion on our walk?"

"Of course not." She stroked the silky head. "She's beautiful, but first you must meet my household."

Yesterday Hugo had been too concerned about the imminent meeting with his wife to appreciate Larkhaven's beauty but now he looked appreciatively at the bounteous orchards and smooth lawns dotted with rare trees and bordered by pretty flower beds that in turn were separated from a stream by a gently curving path. The other side of the stream was apparently left to nature, but Hugo quickly realised that considerable effort was required to contain that force in such an unobtrusive fashion. The puppy at their heels, Lallie and Hugo crossed a rustic bridge and strolled along a winding path until they came to a little clearing where they could sit and look down the valley to the glimmering sea beyond.

Lallie sat with a little sigh. "This was Grandmamma's favourite spot."

"It's beautiful. We have nothing like this at Tamm."

"But you could have; not the same, of course, but with a little thought and interest much could be done to make it less dreary."

"We'll think about it over the winter," he promised. "But"—he took Clarissa's letter from his pocket—"I'd like you to read this. Clarissa said I could show it to you. It will help me explain something to you."

After a first, astonished glance at him, she read steadily to the end of the page. "Hugo, what can you possibly have said to Clarissa to elicit such a reply?"

"I lost my temper," he admitted. "She snatched your letter from me and immediately decreed that it was my own fault that you had left me, which it was of course, but it was the way she said it. I don't know, Lallie, like with you that night, something gave way in me. But this time it was not a fiery volcano, but more like a dam that had been holding back icy torrents. She was never kind or loving to me, you know, not even when I was a child, and I cast at her head all the slights I had endured at her hands. And then I said that she had seduced you away from me; always arranging for you to do things with her, but without me. She protested, but Arthur supported me—he remembered how she had dismissed your suggestions that I escort you on various occasions."

"She said you wouldn't be interested and I accepted it. Oh Hugo, you must have felt I had betrayed you—gone over to the enemy."

"Something like that," he admitted.

"Why did you never say anything?" she continued reproachfully.

"I suppose I was too proud to complain, Lallie, I see that now. I wasn't going to beg for your affections."

"A gentle hint would not have gone amiss," she pointed out with a wry smile.

"You don't understand, sweetheart. All my life I have been excluded from any warm family life, always seemed to be outside, observing families but not belonging to one in any meaningful way. In you I thought I had found the woman who would welcome me, make a place for me at her fireside, love me even." He paused for a moment, afraid his voice would break shamefully.

"Oh Hugo!" Tears clung to her lashes, "And I thought you didn't want me to hang on your sleeve!"

"So I found myself relegated to the periphery of your life, from where I might watch you enjoy the social round, see you flirt and dance with a host of gentlemen or bow to you across a theatre."

"And how odious you were when we met at a rout or a ball," she said, jumping to her feet and sketching a cool bow. "Well met, my dear. My dance, I think."

"I beg your pardon?"

"Hugo! If I may not freeze, as you put it, you may not poker up in that horrid way you do." She climbed onto the wooden bench so that she could look down her nose at him and raised an eyebrow. "I beg your pardon?" she repeated disdainfully. "It's really a polite way of saying 'go to the devil', isn't it?"

He had to smile at the sight of his wife on her perch. She looked like an offended cat staring down a yapping puppy, sublimely aware of its superiority to such an animal. But then his smile faded. Was that how he seemed to her? It was second nature to him to repel boarders, as one might put it, with what, if pressed, he might have described as a proper reserve, but now had to admit others might well call arrogance. Apparently he had treated Lallie in a similar fashion. If he asked her to change her behaviour towards him, must he not be willing to do the same for her?

"You're right," he conceded ruefully, taking her by the waist and lifting her down. "Very well, madam. No ice for you and no pokers for me!"

She looked up at him, her hands on his shoulders. "I'm sorry, Hugo. If I had had the courage or the, the *nous* to challenge you sooner we could have come to a better understanding much earlier. I did, do love you so, how could I not?"

"Lallie! Sweetheart!"

His lips teased hers until they opened to his tongue. He felt her hands clasp behind his neck and moved his own down to shape her sweet behind before drawing her flush against him and lazily plundering her mouth, relishing her familiar taste. At last he lifted his head. "That's how I see you in my dreams, your lips plump and red from my kisses, your curls tousled and your eyes soft and smiling," he murmured, gently tugging a stray lock and releasing it to spring back into place. "Lallie, I'm not imagining this, am I? You do want it, want me?"

"No, you're not imagining it." She lifted her hand to caress his cheek and he turned his head to kiss her palm.

"Come back to the house. I must love you now!"

Arrived in her bedchamber, he drew her down onto the daybed and began to trace the line of her throat, first with his hands and then his lips. Tenderly he explored the new fullness of her breasts. "I must see you," he whispered, "see the changes our baby has made." Suddenly he stiffened. "When you spoke to the midwife, did she say anything about this?"

"I didn't ask, but she told me." Lallie straightened and assumed a prim face and a prosy voice. "'For now, your husband may continue to take his pleasure, madam, but he should refrain from exercising his rights for the last week or two before the babe is due and for four weeks after the birth.'"

The dry recital shrank his ardour. "Good God! Lallie, promise me that you will never again admit me to your bed because it is your duty or my right. Let us come together out of love, for our mutual pleasure and comfort, or not at all."

"I promise," she said solemnly and then blushed deliciously. "But—I don't know what to do, Hugo. Grandmother just said I must permit you any liberties you wished."

"There is only one rule, sweetheart." He kissed her throat and pushed down the lace at her bosom. "We only do what we like, what pleases us. And I will like anything you do—any way you wish to touch me or kiss me or caress me."

"Me—you?" she squeaked as his searching fingers found her nipple.

"You—me," he confirmed, "but only if you wish to." His lips followed his hand. A shudder went through him when she stroked the nape of his neck.

"Hugo?" It was a whisper.

"Mmmmm?"

"What about moving?"

His head shot up. "Moving?"

She nodded, flags of embarrassment flying in her cheeks. "I've often thought when you, when we," her voice faded and grew stronger, "are together, it should be like a dance, where you lead and I follow, but Grandmother said I shouldn't be too ardent and you said I shouldn't move."

He gaped at her. "I said what?"

"After the dinner Clarissa gave for us. You undressed me and laid me on the bed and said 'don't move'. You said it twice."

He groaned. "Because you were so beautiful and I wanted to worship you that night. But sweetheart, no time is quite the same as the one before. It is indeed like a dance, the most intimate, perfect dance with so many different figures, and sometimes you will take the lead."

"Just not approved at Almack's," she said with a seductive little giggle.

"But that night after Watier's masquerade was different wasn't it, Clio? You moved so enticingly then and afterwards I felt more welcome in your bed."

"You took me by surprise that night, when I was almost asleep," she scolded him sweetly. "And earlier, when we danced, you didn't know who I was and so I didn't have to be on guard so that I wouldn't reveal my reaction when you touched me."

Hugo was suddenly enlightened. "Is that why you were always so stiff when we waltzed together?"

"Yes," she confessed sheepishly.

"Silly Lallie." The murmured words were a caress. "Did you know me from the beginning?"

"Mmmm. Your ears, your mouth, your hands," she touched each briefly as she spoke, "your voice, your stance, your ring, the way you hold your hand when you bow, even that little extra not quite skip you give at the beginning of the *pas de bourée*."

"I see I have no secrets, Clio," he said, amused and flattered by this evidence of how closely she had observed him. "But you were too clever for me, concealing this sweet little mole," he pressed a kiss on the top of her breast, "and shading this seductive lip," he gave it a tiny nip, "and your pretty ears," he ran his tongue around the rim of one and she shivered, "were hidden by your wig."

"We spent hours in front of our looking-glasses, discovering which feature or distinctive mark might give one of us away and designed our costumes to conceal them all."

"You were taller that night."

"I had heels on my sandals," she told him with a smug little smile.

"So that is how you cheated me! But, enough of Clio! Now I want my sweet Lalage. And enough of talk and theory; there's a school of thought that says we learn best by experience and, as your governess no doubt told you, practice makes perfect."

He soon coaxed her out of her embarrassment at finding herself naked in broad daylight and faced with an equally naked, aroused husband who reverently shaped her breasts and caressed the sweet new roundness below her navel before kissing it.

"Lallie, I just want you and the child to be well," he said. "I refuse to ruin our lives and spoil our marriage because of an obsession with having an heir."

He kissed her again, lingering over each caress in a way that was new to both of them. This time she did not conceal her response and her sighs and gasps seemed to spur him on to greater efforts.

"Stop," she whispered, "I want to see you."

She pushed him onto his back and rose on her elbow to look down into his face, brushing his hair out of his face and tracing the outline of his lips with her fingers. He snapped his teeth playfully at her and she frowned in mock reproof before leaning down to kiss him deeply.

He lay motionless as she explored him with her gaze and her hands, learning the textures of silk-covered steel, stroking him to a frenzy that had him suddenly snatch her to him. He wrapped her in his arms and rolled them both until he was above her, between her legs. When he joined with her, her arms came round him to hold him close and he stilled, resting his head over her heart.

"In your arms like this, I feel I've come home," he whispered later, much later, when they lay in a blissful satiety that was beyond any girlish, romantic imaginings.

He came to her again that night and, to her joyful amazement, was still in her bed the next morning, taking up more than his fair share of space and covers, it was true, but more than making up for this, first by his sweet smile when he opened his eyes to spy her beside him and then by acquainting her with the pleasures of morning love.

# Finale

*To the south of the Lake of Affection stands a building called Baby Fort which has always been much visited, on account of its being situated near Caudle Bay and Cradle Point.*

"It's such a relief to be able to escape the house at last. That must have been the dullest, dreariest, wettest winter ever," Lallie complained to her husband as they strolled through the walled garden. "I thought it would never end."

They reached the stone bench beside the central pond and he stripped off his coat and folded into a cushion for her.

She sat gratefully, a hand on her protruding belly.

Hugo took his place beside her and put his hand over hers.

She rested her head on his shoulder. "This is a part of marriage no one tells you about," she said softly, "Just being together."

"One of the quieter joys," he returned, smiling tenderly down at her. A quiet joy, indeed. It wouldn't be long now until the babe came.

"Do you remember when we first strolled here?"

"The day before our wedding?"

"Yes. Do you ever wonder what it would have been like if I hadn't gone down for my reticule that evening? Would we still have finished so at odds with one another?"

"It's hard to say, but I think it is likely," he answered slowly. "You would still have been twitted about the country mouse remark. Clarissa wouldn't have behaved any differently and I would have resented her in the same way. And Lord Albright would still have died."

"You may be right," she said slowly. "But if one of us had been brave enough to say we were uncertain or unhappy—"

"Or wanted something more," he finished for her. "It would have changed everything. Lallie, let us promise each other that in future we will say what is in our hearts no matter how difficult it is."

"And that we will listen to each other too. I promise, Hugo."

"I promise," he repeated solemnly and sealed the vow with a kiss. As he deepened it, they heard the gate open and then quick, almost running footsteps on the gravel.

"Sir, Madam! Mr Carey's compliments and would you please come at once. It's his lordship!"

"What has happened?" Hugo asked sharply, as he unfolded his coat and shrugged into it.

"I don't know precisely, sir, just that he's been took bad, I think."

"He has suffered another apoplexy," Dr Fennell said an hour later. "I'll be blunt with you, sir, it is much worse than any of the previous ones and his situation is very grave. I do not hold out much hope of recovery. You may wish to inform your sisters."

"How long does he have?"

"We'll know better tomorrow," was all the doctor would say.

"We'd better send for the others," Lallie said when appealed to for advice. "I know they have never had a close relationship with him, but they may still wish to say goodbye. If you quickly pen the notes, a groom can take them immediately to the receiving office."

Hugo complied, grateful to have a straightforward task to complete. It's the suddenness, he thought. Even though we knew his condition was deteriorating, we didn't expect it to happen so quickly.

When an urgently whispering Nancy woke him in the early hours of the morning, Hugo refrained from disturbing Lallie. He sat at his father's bedside as Lord Tamm relinquished his tenuous hold on life and remained there alone for some time afterwards, subject to a peculiar mixture of numbness, sadness, relief and guilt at the end of what was in many respects a wasted life.

He expressed some of this the day after the funeral when the bustle caused by death had given way to that strange hiatus which intervenes before the threads of life may decently be picked up and a new pattern begun.

"I hope he and Mamma are at peace now," Amabel said softly.

"As do I," said Clarissa, with a sigh.

"We should not overly dwell on the past," Tom Bynge asserted. "You have all of you had to struggle with it these last months in one way or another. Now it is time to let it go and look forward."

"But to what?" Clarissa's lips trembled. "Arthur planned to sell-out this year. He said he would wait for twelve months after Bonaparte's abdication to ensure that it was an enduring peace. Now we see what came of it. Oh dear, what a tempestuous year this is proving to be and we are only just at the end of March."

"It's a bad state of affairs," Charles Forbes commented dryly. "I never understood why they sent him to Elba in the first place. When all is said and done, it's only a hop, skip and jump to France. Now 'tis all to be done again."

"Wellington has outsmarted Bonaparte before, he'll do so again," Hugo declared.

Lord Malvin agreed. "They can't wait for him to arrive in Brussels, Arthur says. To be under the command of a young cub like Slender Billy, as they call the Prince of Orange, is not at all to their liking."

"I can well imagine."

"But what of you, my lord and my lady?" Tom asked. "You have much to think about. You will have to take your seat, Hugo."

"Time enough for that," he said firmly. "Lallie and the baby are my chief concerns now."

Lallie smiled down the long table at him. "I want to look around when someone says 'my lady'. It took me long enough to get used to 'Mrs Tamrisk' and now I must change my name again."

"Before long it will be 'Mamma' as well," Henrietta said, "but you won't find that strange at all."

Lallie stirred restlessly, disturbed by the pressure on her bladder. "Hugo?" she whispered apologetically. He had made her promise she would wake him if she had to get up during the night.

He was awake instantly. "Let me light the candles."

Once the bedroom and dressing-room were illuminated, he helped her down from the high bed and into the dressing-room, where she withdrew behind the screen that hid the close-stool. He retreated to the door, waiting to assist her back to bed.

When she crossed the floor a few minutes later, she was brought to a halt by a most peculiar sensation, as if an internal soap bubble had been pricked. This was followed by a gush of warm liquid between her legs.

"Oh!"

Hugo was beside her in two strides. "What's wrong?"

"It's the baby. The midwife said this might happen."

"The baby?" he repeated stupidly.

"Yes. It's on the way." She picked up a little bell and shook it, calling, "Nancy!"

Nancy bustled in from her little chamber next door, her night-cap askew and a shawl hastily caught around her shoulders. "What is it, Miss Lallie?"

"The waters have broken."

"So I see," Nancy said dryly. "Now, sir, if you'll leave me with Miss Lallie for a few moments, I'll make her comfortable."

"I'll go and get Bynge," Hugo announced, relieved that his brother-in-law was still at the manor.

"Tell him to come to the blue bed-chamber," Lallie called after him. "It has been made ready for the birth."

Twelve hours later Hugo was ready to storm the blue bed-chamber He had known he loved Lallie, but had not understood how much. To know she was suffering and be forbidden to go to her was a hell worse than anything he had experienced in Brussels. Then he could resolve to win her back. But now he was helpless, at the mercy of a higher, more awful power, one that could take her from him, as her mother had been taken from her.

Charles poured him a stiff cognac. "Only one, mind," he warned. "You don't wish to go to her reeking of spirits. Better eat another sandwich."

"You'd be wise to," Tom said when Hugo shook his head. "I've had more trouble with husbands who get into their cups while their wives are lying in than with anything else. You don't want to stagger into Lallie's room when you are called and collapse on her bed as one idiot did. He is still doing penance, I believe."

Hugo grinned reluctantly. "Ring for more coffee, will you, Tony?" He resolutely ate the sandwich and took another but dropped it back on the plate as quick steps were heard on the stairs. He rushed to open the door.

"All is well. You're to come with me," Clarissa said with an exhausted smile.

"Is the babe there?"

"Yes. Come. Lallie wishes to present it to you herself."

He caught her in a quick embrace before heading for the stairs and taking them two at a time. Henrietta was waiting in the boudoir.

"Go in, Papa," she whispered, kissing him.

He stumbled into Lallie's bedroom, eyes only for his wife who lay against her pillows, a little bundle cradled in her arms. She was very white, but still able to smile at him from some remote state of exhausted bliss. She held out her hand as Amabel, who had remained with her, slipped out of the room.

"Come and meet your son."

As Lallie spoke, she folded back the soft shawl that swathed the baby and he looked down at a little creature whose eyes were squeezed closed against the strangeness of this new world. A tiny hand waved aimlessly and Hugo gently laid a finger in the palm.

"He's so perfect," he murmured, awed. "Look at his little fingernails." The minute hand closed around his finger and he felt tears prick his eyes. This was his child, his son. He was a father; he had helped create this whole new person who was less than one hour old. He bent and pressed tender kisses first on his wife's lips and then on his son's forehead.

"Welcome, Geoffrey Anthony," he whispered. The little head turned.

"Can he hear me?"

"I'm sure he can," she answered tenderly.

"My poor love, was it very bad?"

She smiled weakly. "I can't say it was pleasant, but when I see him—it was worth it all and more."

Hugo sat cautiously on the bed and carefully put his arm around her.

"Lallie, you know I would love you and the babe just as much if you had given me a daughter?" he asked anxiously.

She laid her head on his shoulder. "I do, Hugo, truly I do."

"The only important thing is that you are both well." He felt her nod. There was no need to say anything more and they rested together, propping each other up after the ordeal of the last hours.

There was a tap on the door and Clarissa came in accompanied by the housekeeper who carried a tray of tea and toast.

She set it down and curtsied. "Congratulations, my lord, my lady."

"Thank you, Mrs Morton."

"Would you like to see him," Lallie asked softly.

The housekeeper tiptoed over and looked down, a gentle smile on her lips. "A fine boy. What will he be called, if I may ask, my lady?"

"Geoffrey Anthony," Lallie replied.

"Master Geoffrey," Mrs Morton nodded. "A new heir—it is a wonderful day for Tamm."

"Thank you, Mrs Morton," Hugo said curtly.

It was a dismissal and the housekeeper curtsied again and left the room.

Hugo released his wife and helped her sit up so that she could take the cup.

"Here, you take him," She smiled at the panicked expression on his face. "You must get used to it, you know," she chid while showing him how to cradle the infant in the angle formed by his elbow with the head securely supported against his upper arm.

"Stand there for a moment," she whispered.

He obeyed but looked questioningly at her.

"It suits you, Papa!" Her smile was glorious. "All has changed again. Now we are a family, the three of us."

"Come and eat, Hugo, before you collapse."

Hugo obediently followed Amabel. When the first toast to his new son was drunk, he experienced an unusual surge of affection for his family.

"I have to thank you all for being here, for your support of Lallie and me today. I never knew time could pass so slowly," he added wryly.

"Are you pleased you have a son, Hugo?" Amabel asked.

"Immensely, but not because he is a boy or 'the heir'. I would have been just as pleased with a daughter and Lallie knows that. The important thing is that she and the baby came through it well and that we have our child." He looked around the table and flicked a glance at Morton who stood proudly at his elbow. "Let us drink to new beginnings at Tamm, to a new family where all children are welcomed and loved; where the present and the future are more important than the past."

His toast rang out like a proclamation.

His sisters and their husbands rose to drink with him. Clarissa had tears in her eyes.

"To you, dear brother and to Lallie, founders and guardians of a new tradition," she said softly. "Tamm will be a different place now."

# Historical and Background Notes

This is a work of fiction, but set in a real place and time. While it would be impossible to list all the sources consulted, I wish to mention the following:

- The chapter headings are taken from the *Matrimonial Map* published by lithographers Callaghan Bros., Cork in the early nineteenth century and are quoted courtesy of the National Library of Ireland, Dublin. To view this map, please visit my website www.catherinekullmann.com
- Hugo's recollections of hearing the *Miserere* sung in Rome are based on *'An Irish Peer on the Continent (1801–1803) as related by Catherine Wilmot'* and edited by Thomas A Sadleir.
- Beau Brummell's final break with the Prince Regent was indeed caused by his 'fat friend' remark.
- The Princess of Wales's habit of making, roasting and causing to melt at the fire a wax effigy of her estranged husband the Prince Regent is described by Lady Charlotte Campbell in her *Memoirs of a Lady-in-Waiting*. She mentions it in January 1814, but as she quotes *Lady*——as saying *'the Princess indulges in this amusement whenever there are no strangers at the table,'* I

have taken the liberty of presuming it to have begun at least six months earlier.

- The formalities of the duel between Hugo and Mr Norris Snr are based on *The Code of Honor or Rules for the Government of Principals and Seconds in Duelling by John Lyde Wilson,* first published in 1838 and the report from *The Guardian* of 28 March 1829 of the duel between the Duke of Wellington and the Earl of Winchilsea.

- Princess Charlotte was formally presented to her grandmother Queen Charlotte by the Duchess of Oldenburg and not by her mother, the Princess of Wales because, perhaps unsurprisingly, the Prince Regent forbade his mother to admit his wife to the Drawing-Room.

- Watier's masquerade at Burlington House was a real event but the participation of my Muses is, of course, fictional.

- How rich was Lallie in today's terms? In 2016, the relative worth of £65,000 from 1813 was approximately £4,186,000. Invested at 5%, this would give an annual income of £209,300. *Source: inflation.stephenmorley.org.*

- Lord Tamm is a fictional character who for the purposes of this novel I have made Premier Baron of England.

# About the Author

Catherine Kullmann was born and educated in Dublin. Following a three-year courtship conducted mostly by letter, she moved to Germany where she lived for twenty-five years before returning to Ireland. She has worked in the Irish and New Zealand public services and in the private sector.

She has a keen sense of history and of connection with the past which so often determines the present. She is fascinated by people. She loves a good story, especially when characters come to life in a book. But then come the 'whys' and 'what ifs'. She is particularly interested in what happens after the first happy end—how life goes on around the protagonists and sometimes catches up with them.

Her novels are set in the late Georgian/early Regency era of the nineteenth century—one of the most significant periods of European and American history. The Act of Union between Great Britain and Ireland of 1800, the Anglo-American war of 1812 and more than a decade of war that ended in the final defeat of Napoleon at Waterloo in 1815 are all events that continue to shape our modern world. At the same time, the aristocracy-led society that drove these events was under attack from those who demanded social and political reform, while the industrial revolution saw the beginning of the transfer of wealth and ultimately power to those who knew how to exploit the new technologies.

Catherine has always enjoyed writing. She loves the fall of words, the shaping of an expressive phrase, the satisfaction when a sentence conveys her meaning exactly. She enjoys plotting and revels in the challenge of evoking a historic era for characters who behave authentically in their period while making their actions and decisions plausible and sympathetic to a modern reader. But rewarding as all this craft is, she says there is nothing to match the moment when a book takes flight, when the characters suddenly determine the route of their journey.

To learn more about Catherine and her books, you can read on to discover *The Murmur of Masks*, now available worldwide on Amazon and *A Whisper of Scandal*, coming in November 2017, visit her website www.catherinekullmann.com or check out her Facebook page fb.me/catherinekullmannauthor

# The Murmur of Masks

It is 1803. The Treaty of Amiens has collapsed and England is again at war with France. Eighteen-year-old Olivia must say goodbye to her father and brother, both of whom are recalled to active service in the navy. Not long afterwards, her mother, who has been her anchor all her life, dies suddenly. As a result, she loses her home. Adrift and vulnerable, she accepts the offer of a marriage of convenience from Jack Rembleton, an older man whose brother, Lord Rembleton, is pressuring him to marry and sire the heir to the title Rembleton has failed to provide. Olivia hopes that love will grow between them, but Jack's secrets will prevent this and Olivia must learn that she has thrown away her youth and the chance of love.

When Luke Fitzmaurice, a young man prevented by ill-health from joining the army, meets Olivia at a ball, he is instantly smitten but she must tell him she is already married. Ten years pass, during which each faces up to life's challenges but then fate throws them together again. Olivia is finally free, but before they can explore what might be between them, Napoleon escapes from Elba and Luke, who is determined this time not to be found wanting, joins Wellington's army in Brussels. But even after Waterloo, there is a final challenge—can he win Olivia's hand and heart?

*A* Five Star *novel now available as e-book and Paperback from Amazon.*

They say: "*I read it very quickly as the story was very compelling and the characters really came to life and engaged me.*" "*Depicts both the harsh reality of the battlefield and the pleasures and challenges of society life in England.*" "*I was hooked from start to finish.*" Winner of a **Chill with a Book Award**.

# A Whisper of Scandal

*If only he could find a lady who was tall enough to meet his eyes, intelligent enough not to bore him and had that certain something that meant he could imagine spending the rest of his life with her.*

It is high time Sir Julian Loring married, but he certainly does not expect to discover 'that lady' in his half-sister Chloe's governess. After all, when he first met Rosa Fancourt, the orphaned daughter of a naval officer, she was a gawky girl fresh from a Bath Academy. But when he returns to his father's home for a house-party, somehow she sparks his interest. Then, just as he begins to get to know her better, she disappears—in very dubious circumstances. Julian cannot bring himself to believe the worst of Rosa, but if she is innocent, the real truth is even more shocking. Despite this, he is determined to find her and to ensure justice for her.

But this has repercussions for his own family, not least for his sister, Chloe. And how is he to pursue his courtship of Rosa when she has taken refuge with her cousins? Driven by her concern for Chloe, Rosa accepts an invitation to spend some weeks at Castle Swanmere, the home of Julian's maternal grandfather, whose heir he is. But his cousin, the widowed Meg Overton, has also been invited and she is determined not to let such an eligible match as Julian slip through her fingers again. When a ghost from Rosa's past rises to haunt her and Mrs Overton discredits Rosa publicly, Julian must decide where his loyalties lie.

*Coming November 2017*